BEDTIME STORIES FOR GROWN-UP GIRLS

A NOVEL BY
E.B. LANDE

LEAPYEAR
PRESS

For D.

CONTENTS

Cast of Characters:

LILLIAN COOPERSMITH

Marc CooperSmith – Lillian's husband

David, Jonny, Adam – their sons.

Samuel Cooper – Lillian's father

Sir Geoffrey Kuper – Lillian's grandfather

Lady Alice Kuper – Lillian's grandmother

Isabelle Chanteclair – Sir Geoffrey's second wife

CYDNEY MALLONE

Kevin Mallone – Cydney's father

Bianca Chanteclair Mallone – Cydney's mother

Carmen, Mel (Camelia), Risa (Clarisa) – Cydney's sisters

Pauline Chanteclair – Cydney's grandmother

ROBERT BRETTON

Claire Bretton – Robert's mother

Marjorie Wallace Bretton – Robert's wife

Herbert Wallace – Marjorie's father

"Why, sometimes I've believed as many as six impossible things before breakfast."
Alice in Wonderland

"So Scheherazade began."
Anonymous, *The Arabian Nights*

PROLOGUE

LILLIAN HAD NOT EXPECTED the day to go this badly. Mistake #1 was attending the funeral of her old nemesis Marjorie Bretton in the middle of nowhere out in the Berkshires. How likely was it that her former business partner, Cydney Mallone, would show up? Very. She hadn't seen Cydney in fifteen years (for very good reasons) and within an hour she was reminded of every single one of them.

Mistake #2 was driving Cydney to the cemetery to mingle with the crowd of mourners, chief among them the bereaved widower, Robert Bretton, Republican senator for Massachusetts. For years Lillian had been dragged into the triangle of Robert and Cydney and the hateful Marjorie, and God damn it—here she was again.

Mistake #3 was agreeing to Robert's invitation to return with the mourners to his country house without writing down the precise directions because she assumed that Cydney knew the way. But, as the skies darkened and it started to snow and she took one wrong turn after another, it became clear that what Cydney did and did not know would dictate the rest of the day and maybe even the rest of Lillian's life.

And mistake #4 was the fucking moose.

Sunday, Nov. 5, 2006, 11:30 PM.

"WHO ARE YOU?" CYDNEY raised the gun. "Where's Lillian? What did you do with her?"

Lillian looked around to be sure she wasn't dreaming. "Cydney, it's me."

"You're lying." Cydney's eyes had gone dead cold.

"This is no time to joke; they're almost here." Lillian knew that she had to stay calm; rescue was on the way.

"*What* did you do with her?" Cydney's voice rose to an unfamiliar pitch.

Lillian put her hands up in surrender like in the movies. "Cydney! This is me. *Obviously.*"

"Prove it."

"I've been telling you stories about us for hours!" Lillian was close to tears but forced herself to think through the symptoms of Lewy Body Dementia that she could remember – paranoia, delusions, hallucinations, Imposter Syndrome. *Imposter Syndrome?* She wore a coin around her neck with the names and birthdates of her three sons. Cydney had been with her in 1987 when she went to Lenny the jeweler to have it made. She pulled it out. "Remember this?"

Cydney peered at it. "Take it off so I can see it better."

Lillian did, numb.

"Yeah, it looks like it. But you stole it from her," Cydney pronounced, dropping the coin.

"Wow. Cydney, listen up! This is me. I remember what you were wearing when I met you twenty-five years ago. Who else would know that?"

"Yeah? Prove it. What was I wearing?"

"Pink. Pink leather. And a polka-dot ribbon in your hair," Lillian answered confidently.

Cydney thought about this. "Probably. But so what? You could've seen a picture."

Lillian clasped her head in her hands. *Think!* "What about…Bud and Storm and the other one…Lutz! And the bloody beef. Remember? I just told you that story. *Or*…what about T.Rex Toys and Marvin and…the breast pump?"

"Impressive," said Cydney, staring at her hard. "They did a good job training you. They have a secret headquarters, huh?"

"Who? T.Rex Toys? You know their headquarters – that dump in New Jersey!"

"Everyone knows that. Who are you, really?" Cydney lowered her voice but kept the gun raised. "Tell me the truth. I won't tell him."

"Who?" Lillian had no idea where this was going.

"Robert. He's the head of the CIA. Uh-oh. I shouldn't have said that." Cydney inhaled deeply and shook her head. "Uh-oh. Too dangerous."

Oh my God. Lillian could hear the chain saws getting closer. *Hurry up hurry up hurry up!*

"Ok – ok. How about this?" Lillian swallowed hard and tried a new tactic. "You know how much I hate being stuck in a car with windows that will not open. You know that better than anyone! I was terrified that I would fly off a bridge and not be able to get out of the car because I couldn't open the windows! Remember? The Tobin Bridge? Cyd, please – I just went over this with you."

"Interesting. I do remember. That's how Celeste died."

"Celeste! That's right! See, your memory is fine. So do I pass?" – *maybe if I make it sound like a joke?*

"Not yet. You haven't proved anything that they couldn't have trained you with."

"I know!" Lillian had an inch-long scar on her shoulder from falling off the stage when she was a dancer on the ship. Cydney had suggested turning it into a tattoo, saying that she had always wanted to be a tattoo artist and maybe Lillian could be her guinea pig…

"Here," said Lillian, struggling out of her coat sleeve and pulling her sweater down over her shoulder. "The scar, remember?"

Cydney put her face very close to Lillian's shoulder, dark eyebrows knit together. She stared for a long time. "Excellent reconstruction," she pronounced, very serious. "But where are the track marks?" She examined the length of Lillian's arm.

"What track marks?"

"The drugs they pumped you with so you could pull this off," Cydney said, dropping Lillian's arm. "Now it all makes sense: They sent you to the funeral, you picked me up, got us lost, they released the moose—just like them to sacrifice a helpless animal—and now I'm a sitting duck. Robert will come to get us and put me away. I'm sure he has his orders. Yeah, that's it. Not so crazy, huh? Screw those doctors at Mass General—I figured it out."

"Wow. About the only person who could come up with something that paranoid is me!" Lillian said, starting to laugh, a hysterical edge to her voice. *Wrong.* She stopped immediately at the look on Cydney's face.

"Funny, huh?" Cydney said, her voice dropping, her grip on the gun tightening. "What did they do with the real Lillian? Did Robert buy her off? If he told her she'd get the jewelry back, forget it. It's history."

I

THE FUNERAL

12 hours earlier.

Sunday, Nov. 5, 2006. Late Morning.

LILLIAN HATED THE WEEK AFTER the clocks were turned back. The light leaked out of the afternoon by the time the school buses finished their routes, just when there should have been enough light to contemplate the last of the autumn foliage. But, really, who wants to contemplate falling leaves? The whole thing reminded her of a lid on a slowly closing coffin, bit by bit, year after year.

But here she was at Marjorie Bretton's funeral, so coffin imagery wasn't inappropriate. Except that Marjorie's coffin was firmly closed and not about to open any time soon. Lillian thought what she always thought at funerals: *Who is really in that box and are they really dead?* She could see Robert Bretton standing next to the casket up at the front of the church, the Republican Senator from Massachusetts – in the middle of...what... his fourth term? Strange that Marjorie should be buried out here in the Berkshires, far from the hilltop family estate in Lawrell, a gentrified old mill town north of Boston. But there were many things that Lillian did not know about Marjorie Bretton, although there was a time when she would have paid good money to find out.

The church was crowded, as you would expect when the wealthy socialite wife of a US Senator dies suddenly in the company of a much younger martial arts instructor at an exclusive retreat, but maybe Lillian was just being her usual cynical self. Maybe the church was crowded because the people of Massachusetts genuinely liked their up-from-his-bootstraps, gee-whiz Senator Bobbie B., and were sorry – and a little bit curious – that his gorgeous meal ticket was dramatically dead.

Lillian hadn't seen Bobbie up close since…well, probably since the last time she had seen her former business partner, Cydney Mallone, maybe fifteen years ago, and that was reason enough for the detour en route back to Boston after visiting her son, Jonathan, at Cornell. It was a short hop off the Mass Pike to drop by the Lenox Church of the Holy Cross, and Marc, her husband, told her to take her time and spend the rest of the day in the Berkshires.

"Don't rush back. What's the point? Besides, maybe you'll run into Cydney," Marc had said over the phone as she was getting ready to leave Cornell. Lillian hadn't seen the Boston papers and Marc took great pleasure in reciting some of the little known details about Marjorie's demise:

"Foul play is not ruled out. Marjorie Taylord Bretton was fifty-eight years old…"

"No way. That bitch had to be older than that." Lillian felt compelled to respond out loud to news reports whether in print or on TV.

Marc ignored her and continued, *"…and had been married to Senator Robert Bretton, her childhood sweetheart, since 1968, when he assumed control of Taylord Mills and turned it into the most successful textile venture on the East Coast."*

"Childhood sweetheart, huh?" Lillian said. "Gee, it's nice to have your own PR staff. Cydney will go nuts when she reads this. So will her mother, if she's still alive." Lillian had a sudden pang that she didn't know if Bianca was alive or dead. But surely Cydney would have called if Bianca had finally – as she threatened to do for many years – let her heart give out.

"Hey, listen to this," Marc continued. *"Her personal fortune is esti- mated at over twenty million in stock alone...*Wow! Twenty million dol- lars? No wonder he stayed married to her...*from the sale of Taylord Mills to General Electric two years ago. She died unexpectedly of a freak accident while surveying the construction site of her exclusive Berkshires resort, La Brettonia, which is scheduled to open next spring."*

"What was the accident?" Lillian asked.

"Doesn't say. Just while walking unsupervised on the construction site. Although it does mention the presence of one of her partners, a personal trainer. There's a picture; he can't be more than in his thirties. Very buff. Looks gay to me."

"Marc, everyone under two hundred pounds looks gay to you. Walking unsupervised? What does that mean? She tripped? A beam fell on her head? She screwed every guy on the construction site and died of exhaustion...what?"

Lillian could hear Marc stifle a sigh, or maybe a yawn. "Hey, it's wa- ter under the bridge, doll. None of us is remembered in her will, that's for sure. Lil, go check it out—maybe Cydney will be there; it's about time the two of you got together."

"Yeah, but I don't know, Marc. Would that be a good thing or not?"

It was all so long ago—Cydney, Robert, Marjorie, the Baby Grand Company—but in some ways Lillian felt as though she were still recov- ering. Even though the company had long since been successfully sold and she was able to pay off her substantial debts; even though Robert was safely in Washington and not hiding out in the back room of her factory; even though Marjorie was apparently dead; and even though Cydney was a stage designer of some renown—you just never knew when the past might sneak up your spine and grab you by the back of the neck.

Even so, Lillian decided to bend her rule about funerals—she hated them—and go. Besides, maybe—just maybe—the coffin would be open and Marjorie would be all decked out in the Art Nouveau necklace.

Fat chance, thought Lillian. *Wherever that necklace is, it won't be going in the ground.*

LILLIAN SAT IN THE BACK of the Church of the Holy Cross and waited until the service began. The front pews were jammed with mourners standing in line to pass the casket—not open, she noticed—and offer their condolences to Senator Bretton. White lilies were piled on the coffin and banked in front of the altar, which was ablaze with white and gold candles. Looks like a wedding, Lillian thought, yawning. Very dramatic...totally Marjorie's style. There was a steady murmur of hushed voices and a shuffle of feet down the center aisle, but Lillian did not recognize anyone in the pews around her.

From a distance, Bobbie Bretton was as handsome as ever, black hair almost silver, dark skin still tanned and tight, although dark glasses covered his heart-throb blue eyes. He looked slightly stooped and had put on some weight, but the trademark Italian silk suit still fit impeccably and he still moved like a cat. He stood next to the coffin for over twenty minutes, accepting the condolences of perfect strangers with a disarming, slightly crooked smile, as Lillian watched, incognito she hoped, from a distance of several rows. His quiet equanimity was infectious; Lillian found herself thinking that despite what must have been a marriage from hell, Marjorie was, after all, his partner. Maybe Cydney should have bowed out of the picture long ago and left their marriage alone.

It was hard to imagine a more unlikely long-term affair than Robert and Cydney's. Robert was the calmest man she had ever met and Cydney was a force of nature. 'Portrait of the Artist as a Gathering Tornado' as Lillian used to describe Cydney in the years when they had somehow managed to run a business together. To be fair, Marjorie was no shy and retiring character herself. Maybe calm guys need hellions to keep their blood pressure up. Who knows? Lillian scanned the crowd for the second time for Cydney, and although she hadn't set eyes on her in years, how could she not recognize someone who had once been closer to her than her own husband?

The line at the front of the church was beginning to thin out, as people took their seats. The priest, dressed in white, tiptoed around the altar and the sacristy, preparing the accouterments of the funeral mass.

Purple light and haze streamed in from the stained glass windows arched around the alcove behind the altar. Lillian settled down in the hard wood pew, wrapping the lining of her raincoat around her legs, and realized that she hadn't stepped foot in a church in years. Did she miss it?

WHILE JEWISH, LILLIAN WAS RAISED (or as she often said – benignly neglected) by her eccentric grandparents in the very Catholic province of Quebec, while her own parents were busy divorcing and remarrying each other. By the time she was ten, and her parents finally collected her and settled down in the boring world of Vermont, she was attached to her grandmother's devout French-Canadian maid, Isabelle, and furious that she hadn't been able to receive first holy communion along with the rest of her class at the convent school she was attending. No amount of dedicated Bat Mitzvah preparation could completely extinguish the Catholic infusion of her childhood.

Her former business partner, the missing Cydney Mallone, lapsed French-Canadian and Irish Catholic to the bone, refused to allow the occasional hapless nun who wandered into their former factory in an old East Cambridge brewery to leave religious literature behind, although it would have taken some amount of misguided missionary zeal to enter the rundown artists complex in the first place. Lillian couldn't help it; her heart leapt at the sight of nuns in full habit. It must have been some weird holdover from childhood, and she would gladly accept the offered literature, dropping everything to ask about the Holy Blood of Lost Lambs and the mysteries of stigmata, while forgetting all about payroll and eighteen-wheelers rolling up to the loading dock.

But, Lillian reasoned, this was about the only time she ever slacked off. And how could you compare that to the chaos of Cydney, who could go out to buy a cup of coffee, find herself in the middle of a bank robbery, chase down the culprit in high heels and deliver him to the police. When she showed up half an hour late for a business meeting, instead of using a lame excuse like, "sorry, I forgot my wallet," or "the car wouldn't start" – she would just tell the truth. The truth – though unbelievable – often involved the police, a narrow brush with cheerful death, or a rare animal that had escaped from the zoo and was now residing in her living room. It turned out to be a great way to charm men—which Lillian did not need—but a nonstarter if you wanted them to invest in your business, which she did.

Lillian's reverie was broken by Robert Bretton standing down from the side of the coffin and seating himself in the front pew.

The priest put on his glasses, cleared his throat and began: "Dear friends. We have come on this sad day to commit to eternal rest our dear sister, Marjorie Miranda Taylord Wallace Bretton, whose life has been taken from us so tragically..."

"Miranda, huh?" said a throaty voice behind Lillian. "Sounds like a goddamn law firm if you ask me."

"Hey, Cyd," said Lillian without looking around. "I knew you wouldn't miss this for the world."

25 Years earlier. 1981. Spring.

LILLIAN SAT BY THE EDGE of the chipped claw-footed tub in her partially renovated bathroom, with 16-month-old Jonny in the bath and three-year-old David jumping up and down, demanding to join him, a trail of Cheerios in his wake. Just eight years earlier she was touring the world as a dancer on a cruise line while Marc volunteered with the Peace Corps. She was going to be an actress; he was going to save the world. Now they had between them—in addition to two fine sons sixteen months apart—a law degree, a business degree, an old Victorian house in the Boston suburb of Newton that had asbestos in the basement, bats in the attic and a leaking roof; two mortgages, two car loans, two IRAs, no furniture, and fine lines in their recently smooth brows. Plus, Lillian's phobias were getting worse; she could barely cross a bridge, much less be on open water, without a panic attack.

MARC APPEARED IN THE BATHROOM doorway wearing his tennis whites and holding two cups of coffee, one of which he gave to Lillian, who was deep in thought. What was she waiting for? It was time to get back to Cydney and get their business off the ground. She made a snap decision.

"I'm going to Cydney's loft today and stealing a shopping cart. It's early, the stores won't open 'til noon, and I'll find a broken cart and haul it into the station wagon. Want to help?"

"As an officer of the court? If you get caught, don't call me." He looked at her. "Are you ok?"

"I'm looking forward to it actually. It's time I broke some rules."

"By the way," he added, "we have no money to start a business, in case you hadn't noticed. I'm not sure we have enough money to pay next month's daycare bill."

"We'll see. There's always Alice's jewelry. She promised it to me." Lillian's grandmother – Lady Alice Kuper, wife of a British baronet who had immigrated to Canada after WWI and founded the country's largest department store, *Chez Kuper* – had left her a rare matching set of Art Nouveau necklace, earrings, and bracelet composed of jeweled hummingbirds that had graced the cover of Vanity Fair in 1933. As a child, Lillian had spent hours in her grandparents' large, echoing house in Montreal, transfixed as Lady Alice demonstrated the tiny moving wings of the ruby-throated birds that hovered above flower petals encrusted in tiny pearls. It was as close to a living fairy tale as she could get. Before Lady Alice had died the previous winter, she reminded Lillian that the hummingbirds were hers, pressing the key to the bank vault into her hand.

"I ADMIRE YOUR OPTIMISM, DOLL," said Marc. "You must get it from your grandmother. Along with the jewelry, I hope."

"I can't do much about the jewelry while Sir Geoffrey is still alive." Lillian pulled Jonny out of the tub and wrapped him in a towel. Everyone referred to Lillian's grandfather as Sir Geoffrey – even his own children.

"Still on a yacht in the Bahamas?"

"Yeah. No one can reach him. My father keeps trying. They need to settle Alice's estate because she left a ton of debts," Lillian said, letting the water out of the tub. "But that jewelry is going to help me get this business started, I have no doubt."

LILLIAN COOPERSMITH MET CYDNEY MALLONE a few weeks earlier when Lillian took an afternoon off work at BYO Advertising and followed the directions to East Cambridge that she had scribbled on the back of her lunch napkin. The area where Cydney lived spread out beyond the rusting span of elevated MBTA tracks and access ramps to McGrath Highway into a low flat grid of abandoned industrial buildings seeking new life. Old textile mills, shoe manufacturing plants, factories, warehouses lining the north side of the Charles River just before it joins the Mystic and heads into Boston Harbor, were turning into urban shopping malls, brick and butcher-block restaurants, hi-tech start-ups, New Age Galleries and funky design firms. Rents quadrupled and suburbanites bought. Longtime residents – Portuguese, Italian and French-Canadian – moved out and on the periphery new ethnics moved in – Vietnamese, Cambodian – wearing coats too thin in winter and letting their tiny children play soccer in the middle of the street.

But three or four blocks in from the river the scenery hadn't changed in generations. Row houses, some brick, some wood, intermingled with small factories, tool supply shops and plumbing equipment warehouses – their windows plastered with aging campaign slogans for city councilors long since departed. Somewhere in this less gentrified maze of squat buildings, Lillian was looking for what had once been The Old Steamboat Brewery that took up half a city block and was surrounded by a moat – or at least a very large ditch.

Lillian carried her trench coat over her briefcase, which held her high heels, as she trudged up and down Archibald Street in her cracked Etonic running shoes and sweat socks. Because she was tall and somewhat lanky, she could get away with wearing a business suit and sneakers, and because she was always rushing – to pick up or drop off two toddlers on her way to and from work, the day care center, the supermarket and home – the four points on the compass of her ever-shrinking life – she didn't care how she looked. In fact, she was still nursing Jonny, who was sixteen months old and not yet walking – *what was wrong with that kid?* – and had never lost the ten pounds she had gained from her first pregnancy with David, who, unlike his younger brother, never stopped running. Lillian put down her briefcase and examined the hieroglyphics on the crumpled napkin.

"Follow 2nd Street off Archibald to Bridge," she read out loud. "Ok, there is no Bridge Street here, so what is she talking about? Maybe it's a real bridge?" Facing her was a short chunk of street that spanned what could have been a large gutter or a small moat. It led into an arched gateway and beyond that into a courtyard. Embedded in a recently sandblasted limestone arch, a greened copper plate bore the proud curli-cued numbers '1880' entwined with leaves and vines, and under it, 'Old Steamboat'.

Eureka, she muttered, stuffing the napkin in her jacket pocket. This was about the only bridge that Lillian was able to cross these days, hav-ing become – she hated to admit – increasingly phobic about being over or on open bodies of water. The part of her brain that didn't threaten to explode as she approached a bridge told her that this was nuts for some-one who had spent a year and a half working on a cruise ship as part of a dance company. But that was the part of her brain that spent each anxi-ety attack hunkered down and under cover. She crossed the street and peered into a waterless trench about six feet deep that was littered with junk food wrappers. No water. She was safe.

Inside the courtyard, which must have been built for horse-drawn carts, Lillian scanned the doorways fitted into the old brick and granite cornices for signs of Cydney Mallone. She found her on a dumpster spray-painted, *Touch this and you're dead, Mallone.* Hard to tell if this was a warning to Cydney or from Cydney, and Lillian was not sure that she wanted to find out.

The dumpster was stuffed to bursting with pieces of fabric, arms of sweaters, rolls of zippers – rusted and dripping – hanging out from under the top lid, which was held down with chains wrapped around it like a birthday bow. Lillian dug out the napkin and squinted at it away from the sun.

'Ok,' Lillian said out loud, 'next to the dumpster behind the banner…' She picked up a limp piece of pink nylon which, when stretched out, read *Cydney Mallone Cut & Sew*. Someone had inserted an 'n' between the 'u' and the 't' and crossed out 'Sew' altogether. *Cydney Mallone Cu-n-t*. She let the banner fall back, lifeless, over a discarded wood stove next to a door that she assumed was Cydney's.

'Do I want to go on,' Lillian asked herself, 'or have I seen enough?' She looked at her watch. It was 3:00. She had to pick Jonny up at 4:30 and David had an ear infection check-up at 5:00, which meant not getting home until after 6:00. Another late dinner with cranky kids. Marc would be home early tonight for the first time all week. Early for him was being home for the slapshot chaos of dinner – chaos that he could not understand now that she was only working part-time. Lillian, who had been Director of Market Research at BYO Advertising, was phasing herself out of advertising so she could start a juvenile products company, tentatively called Baby Grand, intending to make a pile of money selling fun and creative infant products to Woodstock yuppies and never having to work for anyone but herself ever again.

ACCORDING TO MICKEY KLEIN, PERSONAL secretary to BYO's President, Lillian needed the right fabric and textile designer to help her create the baby product that Lillian kept yapping about when she should have been paying more attention to her clients' market share. And Mickey knew just the one: a woman named Cydney Mallone, who had recently come up with the brilliant trade show display for Purity Enterprises, one of BYO's largest clients.

Purity was introducing a new laxative at a food and drug convention and needed an eye-catching show stopper. Apparently Cydney produced a series of larger-than-life constipated worms in neon colors with bulging eyes and bulging humps, giving them a dromedary effect. The eyes rolled by means of some hidden mechanism and an internal tape deck pumped out strategic groans.

"Sounds gross," Lillian told Mickey. "How come I didn't know anything about this?"

"You were out on maternity leave," Mickey said. "It was a sensation. The only thing we couldn't figure out was why the worms were not allowed to come into contact with water. Turns out she had stuffed them with dried kidney beans. One accidentally got wet and boy, constipation was not a problem, I can tell you. That thing blew to Kingdom Come."

"Sounds like a ringing endorsement, Mick. Thanks."

"Suit yourself, but I got her name from The New England Opera Company where she designs sets and props. She's hot stuff; I think she's the one you want."

So Lillian called Cydney and tried to explain over the phone what she had in mind. But Cydney sounded like she was half asleep – her voice husky, almost moldy. She appeared to be stifling a yawn when she said, "Yeaahh, sure I've done consumer stuff, lots of it. Come see my portfolio, it's hard to explain."

But Lillian kept right on trying to explain about a seat that should fit into the top part of a shopping cart to hold an infant, and then convert to an upright seat for a toddler. "Believe it or not, there is nothing like it on the market," she added at the end of her speech.

"Oh, you wouldn't believe the things I believe, so take down the directions and come anytime. I'm always here. I live here, I work here, I have a studio and a factory with little dwarfs sewing away; they even cook for me, so I'm always here, ok?" She hung up before Lillian could respond.

LILLIAN BENT DOWN TO TIE a shoelace that threatened to actually touch the muck surrounding the dumpster, when the door behind her swung open, almost knocking her down.

"*Hey!* Watch it!" she yelled to a girl in tight jeans carrying a load of pillows in a clear plastic sack over her shoulder, a sack that hung almost to the ground and threatened to engulf her. She kept right on walking, which Lillian noticed she managed in remarkably high heels – slingbacks actually, the kind of shiny purple pumps that come with Barbie Dolls – straight to the dumpster marked for death to or by Cydney Mallone.

As she dropped the bag and spun around, Lillian saw that this was no girl, but a petite woman, probably her own age – maybe younger – with hair unleashed by the removal of the bag that shook itself out in waist length waves. She started working on the locks in the chain around the dumpster, with something that looked like a pick, bracing her glass-slippered foot against its rusted side.

"Sorry," she called out to Lillian, not looking up, "but that door is unpredictable."

The lock came loose and the chains clanked to the pavement. She stood on an orange crate next to the dumpster and threw the lid back as though it was made of cardboard and not steel. Lillian had tendonitis in both wrists from lifting her kids and could barely hold a milk carton.

"I'm Cydney," she continued, "you must be Lillian. Don't tell anyone I'm dumping this stuff. People are so fussy around here, you wouldn't believe it." She grabbed hold of the bottom of the sack, shook out the contents of ripped pillows whose insides looked like milkweed pods gone to seed, gave the lid a tug, and watched it fall back down with a crash that shook the dumpster and the fillings in Lillian's teeth.

Over the phone Cydney had a throaty voice that suggested a large woman, backed up by her industrial address adjacent to several auto body shops, which Lillian could now see through a gateway leading into a second courtyard. She would not have been surprised if Cydney had weighed two hundred pounds and been part of a motorcycle gang. Instead, she probably weighed half that, and stood several inches shorter than herself, even in the purple pumps.

"Is there some place we can go and talk?" Lillian suggested, because she was here on business, after all.

"Of course," said Cydney briskly, aging ten years, and striding with surprisingly large steps over to the door next to the pink banner. "Hope you don't mind dogs," she called out over her shoulder as she took out an enormous ring of keys. Lillian was just about to ask what kind of dog when the door flung open and out raced a husky larger than Cydney, who leapt up to embrace her with its paws on her shoulders.

"He's pretty gentle if he knows you," Cydney said, grabbing the dog by the collar as it lunged at Lillian. "*Down*, Boris, down, boy; that's a good boy." Cydney looked back at Lillian, who was cowering in the doorway, "Don't worry, he won't hurt you. Not used to dogs, huh? Around here a girl needs some protection. That's why I have a wolf. Well, actually part-wolf."

"A wolf? You're kidding…is that even, I don't know…legal?" Lillian was beginning to think that maybe Cydney was the girl that people needed protection from, but just then they entered the inner courtyard that was the decaying heart of the old brewery, and Lillian forgot all about the wolf.

"Oh, wow!" Lillian breathed, looking up at the domed skylight in leaded glass panes, several of them blanked out and boarded up, giving it the look of a jack-'o-lantern. Rising up from the center of the concrete floor was a twisted tarantula of a rusted brass tank with tubes and arms stretching out from the top like flexed biceps. Around it wound an inside staircase in black wrought iron, which climbed, open and clattering, up the four inside levels, each of which looked down from its elliptical position, atrium fashion, into the brass tubing below.

"Don't get carried away," said Cydney. "Ever live in a cylinder? It's like living in a nuclear power plant." Boris the wolf, who had gone from furious to friendly in moments, chose Lillian's upward-looking position to dive-bomb her crotch, despite a skirt and slip—articles of clothing with which the dog was evidently unfamiliar. Lillian let out a shriek and was about to hit him on the head when Cydney grabbed her arm.

"Whoa, there! Are you crazy? This is a cross between a husky and a wolf. If we are going to work together, you had better be nice to him."

Lillian stared at her. Work together? Who said anything about working together? No way was she working with someone who looked better taking out the garbage than she could after a day of beauty treatments. (Whatever *that* was—one of those $150 gift items she always saw at silent auctions.) And secondly, no way would she work with someone whose favorite color was pink.

Lillian hated pink; it was a color she could never wear, and here was Cydney draped in it from head to toe. Her jeans were custom dyed, because no denim of that shade existed, as was the jacket, a soft leather that could have come out of Liberace's closet. Even the ribbon in her mass of dark curls— *Were they natural? Who could perm all that hair?*— was a pink and white check, although somewhat ratty at the ends, Lillian noted with satisfaction. An artist—she was sick of them—and a natural beauty, with olive skin and aquiline nose. Somehow this annoyed her deeply.

"How long does it take you to wash your hair?" Lillian wondered aloud, taking herself by surprise. Her own blonde hair was short and straight as a stick, cut in a wedge up from her neck. Suddenly she felt like a shorn sheep and shivered. Whenever she contemplated growing it back to its adolescent Alice-in-Wonderland glory, the prospect of different lengths and hair getting in her mouth stopped the thought cold. And she had looked this way since, well, since she had become a professional real life grown-up. She couldn't even remember when she had first cut it off—probably on the ship. But then she had been dancing every night, or was always in rehearsal, and she had better things to do than wash her hair.

"This hair is a major pain in the ass, let me tell you," Cydney was saying, "and I am far too vain to cut it off. But if I had straight thick hair like yours, with all those blonde colors, I'd blunt cut mine in a minute. It'd make me look taller, I bet. Wouldn't have to walk around in these heels all day long."

Lillian had almost forgotten that Cydney was short. At 5'10", Lillian towered over her and suddenly felt like an awkward giraffe next to delicate Bambi. She jammed her hands in her peanut butter-stained pockets—she just noticed—and stared down at her scuffed sneakers. She hadn't done her nails in months; it was all she could do to remember to shave her legs, and here was Cydney, who worked with her hands (apparently) and managed to have unchipped, one-inch long pale pink nails.

"Yeah, how do you manage to walk in those things?" asked Lillian. "I have mine in my briefcase, but they look like orthopedic shoes next to those."

Cydney broke into a smile, showing off dimples and very white teeth. Her eyes were an intense shade of sea blue rimmed by thick black lashes that Lillian couldn't have managed with several layers of mascara. "Aren't these shoes a riot? I got them at the toy store for my niece who's eleven. But I have small feet and I just started wearing them and voilà! I figure I'll get her something else. You know, I've been thinking about what you said over the phone," she added, grabbing the dog's collar and motioning for Lillian to follow, "about the baby thing. I've got it. A cantaloupe cut in half. It's perfect."

"Excuse me?"

"Really, I think it will work," Cydney said, her voice suddenly rising as Boris started to run frantically in place at the sight of a dark-haired man in an expensive suit who was just coming down the stairs. He did not look as though he either lived or worked in the building. In fact, he looked like one of Marc's law partners. Boris wagged his tail furiously and leaped up on his hind legs.

"Down, Boris!" both he and Cydney said at the same time. The wolf pawed the air and the man backed away.

"Who says wolves don't shed?" he said from the landing, brushing real or imagined fur from his jacket. "Uh...excuse me, Cyd, but it's getting late and I'm on my way. The material looks good though, better than the last run. I'll talk to you in a couple of days about the next delivery." And he pivoted to go back up the stairs, retreating quickly along an upper corridor.

Lillian was sure that she had seen him somewhere before – mid-thirties, sharp dresser, tanned – moved like a boxer – big creased smile, but she couldn't remember where. She started to say, 'Haven't I met him somewh...' when Cydney grabbed her arm in an amazingly strong grip and started walking in the opposite direction.

Now Lillian really wanted to know who he was. "Is he a client of yours? I'm sure I've seen him before."

Cydney shrugged. "A supplier. One of the only surviving textile mills left in the area, up in Lawrell, where we both grew up. He owns the mill and I own a dumpster. That's the way it goes, huh?"

"What kind of textile business?" Lillian asked. *Had she met him at a party?*

"Nothing sexy," she answered, sounding vague. "Government contracts, defense department stuff, lots of camouflage fabric, much to my chagrin. If I hate the color, watch out. I'm giving you fair warning."

Warning taken, Lillian said to herself, thinking that he must be a local politician and she would have to look him up. "So where were we?" asked Lillian, checking her watch and noting with alarm that she had to be at the day care center in twenty-five minutes. "Something about a melon—sorry, that went right over my head. It's to hold a baby in a shopping cart, you know. Do you have kids by the way?"

"No, it's all I can do to manage my animals and my employees, but I know what you're looking for—I'll do a prototype. Tonight. You don't believe me, do you?"

"Well," she said diplomatically, "I don't believe anything until I see it. Look, I hate to spoil this," she added, "but I gotta go. I have to pick up my kids." Lillian had worked with lots of designers over the years; they were mostly unreliable and full of excuses. Maybe she should end this now. "You know, this has been real interesting but I don't think a melon is going to quite make it. So… uh…thanks, but probably not."

"Look, come back on the weekend," Cydney said, suddenly all business. "And bring a doll, a large doll, or better yet, bring a baby. I'll mock something up and show you how I think it will work. Really."

Lillian sighed. Maybe Cydney was her last chance. She couldn't keep toying with an idea in the back of her mind forever when she knew it was something that could get her out of the corporate rat race and into her own business. "Sure, ok, I guess. I mean it would be nice to see your studio."

"Great. Oh, and bring a shopping cart. We'll put it on the lift."

"Where will I get a shopping cart?"

"Where everybody else does…steal it. I'd do it but you know the city; the carts are disgusting. We've met before, you know," Cydney said casually, popping a large stick of gum into her mouth.

"We have? Where?" No way, thought Lillian. I would remember anyone who looked like this.

"Long time ago, at the Candy Shack–Combat Zone." And Cydney turned abruptly and walked away. "See ya this weekend; don't forget the cart."

Lillian shook her head. Hardly. The Combat Zone was local vernacular for the strip joints that had spread out along Washington Street in downtown Boston. She hadn't been there since college. And besides, people were always telling her that she looked like someone they knew.

LILLIAN COULD HEAR MARC RUMMAGING in the hall closet for his tennis gear. He hadn't said anything to her about the BYO party the night before. He was pretty good about that, although she wasn't sure that was the kind of support she needed. Maybe she should see a different therapist. It was hard to live in a city on the ocean and on a major river and freak out every time you had to cross a bridge or go near the water.

The previous night, BYO had hosted a party for select clients on a boat in Boston Harbor; a good sized boat – maybe eighty feet – with four or five staterooms and a crew of six. For weeks Lillian pretended that this was not going to happen. All the senior BYO staff were excited about it; after all, it was a real luxury to be treated to a dinner cruise with live music on a private boat, but every time Lillian thought about it her scalp started to crawl and her stomach churned. She spent all day Friday debating whether it was better to take valium before she got on the ship or drink after she was on board, or both. Some of each, or a lot of one? Secretly, she hoped that one of the kids would get sick and she would have to stay home; but she had used that excuse a number of times already. Or that the weather would turn awful, bringing early hurricanes and gale force winds, but it was predicted to be a balmy evening with a spectacular sunset.

Lillian called Mickey Klein late Saturday afternoon in a panic. Mickey worked closely with Tom Monahan, BYO's wunderkind president, to whom she was personal secretary and administrative assistant. It was assumed but not confirmed that she was assisting him in other matters during the two-and-a-half hour Friday lunch breaks they each routinely took, leaving the office separately and returning five minutes apart, Tom looking flushed and Mickey gazing off into space for the rest of the day.

"Hey, Mick," Lillian said over the phone, feeling it grow slimy in the cold sweat of her palm. "Are you…um…coming tonight?" Lillian knew this was a stupid question because Mickey had spent the past three weeks organizing this event. "I mean, do you think the weather will hold up?"

"Lillian, where are you? Look outside; it's a clear blue sky."

"Yeah, you're right, I guess. I mean, what should I wear? It's a boat. Should I wear rubber soled shoes?"

"Didn't you get my memo? You can wear anything from casual to very fancy. Just don't embarrass Tommy. Listen, I have to do something with my hair; I'll see you tonight." And Mickey hung up.

LILLIAN HAD LEANED HEAVILY ON Marc. She wore dark glasses so no one could see the panic in her eyes. She stayed in the inside cabin, midship, where she could still keep her eye on the horizon, even though the sea was dead calm. She talked intently with Jack Goldfarb about the confidence levels on his new dog food market study, pointing out that all the statistical analysis in the world would not compensate for the reality that dogs hated the food. She watched Mickey trail Tom whenever Tom's eight-months pregnant wife lumbered to her feet and squeezed herself into the bathroom. She counted the minutes, then the hours, and when she knew she had made it through three-quarters of the evening she felt her grip on herself relax. She dropped the tiny balls of paper napkins torn and shredded and kneaded in the palms of her hands into the nearest ashtray and had a drink. She hated herself.

It was time to get control of her life. The phobias had been strangling her since the previous spring when Lillian had returned to work after her second maternity leave in little more than a year. After five months at home avoiding bridges, she had almost forgotten about her phobia. But not for long.

Three days back in the office and the Transamerica Shipping file landed in her lap.

"They've got a regional office in Chelsea," Tom Monahan said, sitting on the edge of her still clean desk, "and I think you should go see their operation ASAP."

"Chelsea?" Her heart sank. "Come on, Tom, no reputable company has an office in Chelsea."

Chelsea was on the other side of Boston Harbor behind the airport. The most direct route was over the Tobin Bridge, favorite haunt of suicide jumpers, and so heavily circled on her "how to avoid bridges" dashboard map that it looked like the site of a crime scene. It was the fastest way from Boston to Chelsea via Purgatory.

"Chelsea's going to make a comeback. I'm betting on it. Beautiful views. Right on the water. Just get on the Tobin and you'll be there in a jiff..." Tom said, sliding his hip off her desk and signaling that, as far as he was concerned, she was on her way. "Here's their card; let me know how it goes."

Lillian claimed that her car was in the shop on the day of the Chelsea appointment, taking the subway to East Boston, which, because it traveled under and not over water, she could handle, and then a cab from there. The guys at Transamerica thought she was brilliant for avoiding the traffic over the bridge, and she immediately rose several points in their estimation. Not good news; she did not want this client.

IT WAS SOON AFTER THE Transamerica episode that Lillian found herself food-shopping one evening on her way home. Preoccupied with her anxieties (which she knew were getting out of control) she had baby Jonny in a backpack, and 20-month-old David seated in the front of the cart. Lillian was staring at a fistful of green beans when she turned to see David standing up with one foot on the handlebar, arms spread wide, ready to jump. She tackled him with a flying leap and half lay there, draped over the cart, her teeth in the shoulder of David's windbreaker, listening to Jonathan's terrified shrieks as he struggled in the backpack. A voice popped into her head as clear as an early bird song on a still morning.

"You're going to get me out of this," it said, just like that. It was a low, quiet voice, certainly not her own, and hovered somewhere behind her left shoulder, so that she took Jonny out of the pack to look around. The voice filled her with a sense of peace and serenity and purpose, which she had not known in some time. She lifted Jonny on her hip and looked into David's clear brown eyes, a golden brown, the color of a lion's mane. She kissed him gently on the cheek.

"Davey, it's ok. Mummy has it all figured out. You're going to get me out of this." She sounded calm and controlled, without her usual edge of panic; so calm that David looked shocked.

Lillian knew that something had to change.

ONE YEAR LATER THAT CHANGE was about to take place. En route to Cydney's loft with her kids and the stolen cart on board, Lillian checked her dashboard map. "Let's see," she said out loud, "if we take the Mass Pike we can get off at Allston and take the River Street Bridge. I can do that bridge." Her finger landed on a light blue streak on the map with three stars and an exclamation point. "Yup, that's what we'll do, right guys?"

Cydney met her in the courtyard and directed her to the loading dock that led into the freight elevator. She was delighted to have the cart, which she unloaded from the back of the car with considerably less difficulty than Lillian had getting it in.

"I lift weights," she explained, "or at least I did until three months ago when I fell down the elevator shaft and broke half a dozen ribs. But I'm just about ready to go back to the gym." In fact, she was wearing a weightlifter's wide leather belt. Her waist didn't look much bigger than David's head.

"So these are the kids, huh? How old are you, sweetie?" Cydney asked David, who kept his thumb in his mouth and shook his head. "They look like they're almost the same age, Lillian. How exactly did you do that?"

"I've blocked it out—three years of nonstop pregnancy and nursing."

The corridor on which they walked and half carried the cart to Cydney's studio entrance was open grating and looked down through the next two floors to ground level. Lillian suddenly felt a bridge panic coming on. She tightened her grip on David's hand, and hoisted Jonny up higher on her hip. *Don't look down,* she told herself fiercely, *and you'll be fine.*

Cydney glanced behind her and sensed Lillian's discomfort. "Don't worry," she called out. "You'll get used to it, although it's a bitch in high heels. Ooops, sorry. Gotta watch my language, I guess."

They stopped at Cydney's door and stepped into another world. Before them unfolded a length of polished bowling alley floor, perhaps a hundred feet long and forty feet wide, bordered with huge glass windows covered with flimsy bamboo shades in irregular shapes and sizes. The windows—some original with small opaque panes, and some recently replaced, startling in their expanse of clarity—faced south. Through the windows the sun streamed onto the high-gloss floor, bouncing off bolts of fabric, bins of patterned remnants, yards unrolled on cutting tables, rows of unused sewing machines, racks of thread and scattered tools. Several muslin curtains hung in a large archway created in the center of the long work area. Beyond them the space curved off into an 'L' with the windows carrying light from the west, looking out toward the clapboard three-deckers of Somerville.

Through the curtains Lillian could see an unmade bed and open bureau drawers. On a dressing table stood a heavy silver soup tureen, very ornate, tarnished to a smoky blue. It was filled with daffodils just past their prime, and fat, red tulips spilling petals on the coffee-stained lace tablecloth beneath. Boris, the half-wolf, stood next to the curtains – Lillian had forgotten about him – looking horrified at the group of cart-bearers and small children approaching. David took off down the slippery floor toward the dog, who – because he was so used to terrifying newcomers – was momentarily confused and stood rooted to the spot, legs tense, ready to spring.

Cydney called out, "Stay, Boris!...good boy...don't move."

Lillian started to run to David but Cydney grabbed her arm. "Don't run. You'll scare him."

David walked right up under the dog's chin and said, "Hi Doggie! Woof!" Boris wagged his tail slowly without committing himself to a clear course of action until David saw a ragged Donald Duck lying on a low lumpy couch and started for it. Cydney must have anticipated this move because, just as David reached for the doll, Cydney grabbed the dog's collar before he could lunge for the duck now in David's hands.

"Uh-uh, David," Cydney said sweetly, crouching down to his level, "the doll and the couch belong to the doggie and you must never touch them because that's the only time Boris ever really gets upset, understand?"

David nodded his head in time to the rhythm of her voice. He didn't seem the least bit disturbed as Cydney took him by the hand and led him through the curtains and into her living space, talking all the while. Lillian followed, weakly, once she was sure her legs, which had been rooted to the spot, could move.

"Now that's the bird cage," Cydney was saying to David as Lillian trailed behind, balancing Jonathan on her hip. "It's a pretty big cage, huh? Probably as big as your closet at home. Actually, it's called an aviary; can you say that? And yup, there's the cat lying on her mat right next to the cage. She's given up on trying to get those birds; they sort of have a live-and-let-live attitude. I figure it's a pretty good example in case I ever get married and...let's see...oh yeah, there's the fish tank – it's a little dirty, which is why you can't see a whole lot of fish. Why is it so dirty? Because I haven't cleaned it, to tell you the truth. You see, a friend of mine asked me to keep it for her when she went away on vacation two years ago, and she never came back, so I kept it. There could be prehistoric fish in there by now. Actually, she fell in love; that's why she never came back. No, I don't think it's like falling IN something, like a cave or a hole, although maybe it is, let me think about that..."

Cydney rambled on, making David a glass of chocolate milk, as though she were talking to a short person of equal intellectual powers. Lillian could see that David was completely infatuated; gone – hook, line and sinker.

Lillian cleared her throat. "Uh, can I walk past this dog and back to the shopping cart?"

"Oh *suuure*," Cydney answered, "he's harmless."

Lillian walked back to the studio where the cart was now balanced on three wheels, having lost one in the heave-ho into the lift. Cydney followed and plunked a piece of canvas and foam in the front seat. There it was – the size and shape of a watermelon cut in half, just like Cydney had said – nestled in the cart with silver hooks gleaming at either end.

"See," said Cydney, demonstrating, "the baby lies down like it's a cradle, and then when it gets big enough to sit up, Presto!" She picked it up and flipped it over, folding one panel down and another up. "It's a seat and the hooks wrap around and fasten on the front end and at the back to hold the baby in. Let's try it."

They left the canvas in the seat position and Lillian plunked Jonathan in, forcing his reluctant legs through the seat holes. This was a new one for him. Although less active than his brother, he was used to hauling himself up in the cart to stand at chest level with his mother. Suddenly he was buckled front and back. A look of panic crossed his face, and he reached as far forward as he could to shake the handlebar. He looked from his mother to Cydney with his brows knit and his mouth open, screwing up his face for a howl.

"Hey!" Cydney said. "It works! He can't go anywhere."

"You're right." Lillian was not quite as carried away. "He can't stand up and swan dive, that's for sure," she said, walking around the cart.

"You see?" Cydney said to David. "Because of you and your brother, your mother and I are going to get rich."

"Well, we're a long way from that, but I do believe we have a product here, and I've seen enough new gizmos cross my desk to know that this could really work." The thought exploded in her head—this really could work.

"See, guys, you're going to get us out of this!" Cydney was saying to David while the two of them danced around Jonathan.

"Out of what?" Lillian asked. *Where had she heard that before?*

"It'll get you out of a stuffy job and me on the road to financial independence; I can't hang on short-run contracts or the good will of rich men forever."

Jonathan started to clap his hands, resigned to his stuck position. Both kids had fallen in love with Cydney as she danced with one around the other.

"Ha, ha, ha! You're going to get us out of this!" she sang. She helped David climb into the basket of the cart, then turned to Lillian.

"Well, what do you think? I have to thank you: You're going to get me out of this, I can feel it."

Lillian looked at the kids in the shopping cart and was hit by something in Cydney's voice—the same voice that had floated over her shoulder a year ago in the supermarket when David had almost jumped out. The voice that had filled her with some inexplicable hope and calm. That's what it did then; that's what it was doing now.

Cydney smiled at her. "Hey, wake up! Don't blank out on me. Did you hear what I said?"

"Yeah, I did. Probably a lousy reason to start a business…"

"Good as any, I bet."

"I wouldn't know how to get started; it must cost a fortune…"

"You know what? Enjoy the moment. We'll cross that bridge when we come to it."

No question about it; Cydney's voice. Lillian had no choice. She grabbed David and scooped him up. It was meant to be.

Sunday, Nov. 5, 2006. Early Afternoon.

SITTING IN THE CHURCH PEW, Lillian kept looking straight ahead because she wasn't sure what she would do if Cydney had really changed. Cydney had been the most beautiful woman she had ever known, with wild black hair that tumbled in perfect curls down her back. Despite her Irish and French-Canadian heritage, she had the dark skin and exotic slant to her eyes of a Gauguin goddess.

Lillian and Cydney had not seen each other since they sold their business in 1991—even though they only lived twenty-five miles apart in the Boston suburbs. There was no particular reason, mostly the exhaustion of being constantly and interminably intertwined for several intense years. Lil had invited Cyd to various family events, but there was always a reason why she couldn't make it: a broken car, a restraining order that she had just received or was about to send, a big client, Bobbie sneaking back in town—really, it was exhausting to be around Cydney. Lillian did not know how she had ever put up with it.

The eulogies were almost over. Robert Bretton hadn't said a word. He and Marjorie had no children, (*"Don't be ridiculous,"* Cydney once said. *"She would have eaten them,"*) and no sobbing relatives stepped up to the plate. A colleague of Marjorie's on some charity board gave the last eulogy, during which Cydney kept making sounds directly behind Lillian that could not be mistaken for grief. At the mention of 'legendary kindness,' Cydney practically choked and Lillian couldn't avoid it any longer. She turned around and grinned at Cydney.

"Christ, Cyd, you haven't changed at all," Lillian stage whispered, flashing her a big grin. Well, that wasn't quite true. Cydney's hair was still mostly black but streaked with auburn highlights. Her eyes were still a bright aqua blue, set off by her dark skin, but creased in a net of fine lines, and her teeth looked like they had undergone a fairly expensive transformation from white and slightly uneven to super white and perfectly straight. But Lillian would have known her anywhere. She was surprised at how happy she was to see her again in the flesh.

"Neither have you," said Cydney with a straight face and a big smile. Lillian had to believe her because Cydney could not tell a lie.

The casket rolled down the long aisle and Lillian shrank as far into the crowd as she could. When was the last time Cydney had seen Robert? Lillian watched the distance disappear between Cydney and the remains of Marjorie as the entourage approached, but Cydney stood impassively, shoulders squared, hair flying loose. She must have been wearing spike heels—out here in the woods, that would be just like Cyd—because the top of her head came all the way up to Lillian's nose.

Robert walked behind the coffin, flanked by a few aging relatives, his eyes lowered. This was no place for campaigning, and he walked right past them without any sign of recognition.

Cydney folded her arms and rocked back and forth. She turned to Lillian with a big grin. "So, Lil…are we going to the cemetery? Cuz I don't have a car. I was in New York working on a set for a 42nd Street road show, and I read all about Marjorie's death over my morning coffee. So I took the train up and figured I'd know somebody who could get me back to somewhere."

"Well…I wasn't planning on it, frankly. I came mostly because it was on my way back from Cornell…"

"Who goes to Cornell?"

"Jonny. He's in law school."

"*No way.* He's just a munchkin baby face. How could he be out of college? I am not that old. How's…um, Christ I forget his name, isn't that awful?"

"David?" That's weird, thought Lillian. David, Lillian's eldest son, had been Cydney's favorite and had spent his childhood adoring Cydney. He flat-out worshipped her.

"David, yikes." Cydney rolled her eyes. "Stupid me. I just blanked out there. How's my guy? Do you think he's old enough for me yet? Is he married? Just kidding…relax."

They had slipped into the aisle at the end of the procession and were trailing the crowd walking out of the church doors into the gloomy afternoon. Gray rain clouds threatened overhead and umbrellas started to pop open as the crowd assembled at the foot of the church stairs.

"David's working in a high-tech start-up, but I couldn't tell you what he does because I don't understand the first thing about it," Lillian said, noting that her shoes were starting to hurt, and she would never make it if she had to start walking through a cemetery in the rain.

"And the baby?" asked Cydney.

"You mean Adam?" Lillian said, surprised. Adam was born while Lillian and Cydney were in the full-blown midst of their partnership. Cydney was responsible for Lillian's gaining fifty pounds by force-feeding her ice cream and clam chowder. Cydney had practically cut the umbilical cord. What did she mean, the baby?

"Of course...Adam," said Cydney, looking vague.

"What's wrong with you? Are you ok?" Lillian turned around to stare at her. "I know it's been awhile but I haven't forgotten the names of your sisters, for example—and how are they by the way—or your mother? I'm afraid to ask how Bianca is, but you get my drift."

Cydney shrugged and looked past Lillian, her eyes clouded over, as though she had momentarily been sucked into another dimension. Then, just as suddenly, she was back. Her eyes cleared and she gave Lillian a big-dimpled smile. "Mom's great; isn't that amazing? All those years with a heart condition and she's still going strong. And my wonderful sisters; let's see. Carmen is still a bitch; I'm surprised she's not here, frankly—that would shake Robert right up—and Risa is living in Amsterdam doing who knows what—giving tours of the red light district maybe—and Mel is teaching at UCLA—the only one of us who made our mother proud."

Lillian thought that she sounded like the old Cydney, catty and matter-of-fact, with that school-of-hard knocks, tough girl front. But something wasn't right.

"So, are we going to the cemetery or can we go get a drink and catch up?" Cydney asked, standing in the doorway and blinking hard in the light. "And then you can give me a lift to Boston; I have a doctor's appointment tomorrow. Say yes. Come on! I'll tell you all about my fabulous life in stage and screen."

Lillian could see the casket being lifted into the back of the hearse at the bottom of the steps. Cydney had really creeped her out for a minute. Part of her wanted to get to her car as fast as possible and leave. But the rest of her wanted to check up on Cydney and see what was going on. "Only if you tell me what's doing with you. Are you on drugs or something? That was weird, your not remembering my kids' names."

"Hey, just checking," Cydney said, tapping her perfectly manicured pearl nails on Lillian's forehead. "Just making sure you are still the same sharp, obnoxious and critical bitch you always were."

"Look, Cyd," said Lillian, pulling away from Cydney's nails, "don't start with me or there is no way I'm driving you back to town. And where are you living these days?"

"Small studio in Waltham when I'm not in New York. Sold the Brewery ages ago. How about driving to the cemetery then? Maybe they have booze." Cydney rummaged in her large purple leather handbag for a cigarette.

"Don't blow that shit in my face. Purple bag, huh? What happened to pink? Beautiful..." said Lillian, fingering the soft leather.

"Purple? It's fuchsia, dummy – but look who I'm talking to. And I designed it myself, see?" She held the soft leather bag out proudly at arms length, brass zipper opened.

Lillian wasn't sure, but she thought she could see a...gun? Was that possible? The barrel of a gun in the bag?

"Christ, Cydney, what is that?" Lillian said, grabbing the bag to pull it open.

"Relax! It's a fake. Boy, you are still so jumpy. I work in theatre, remember? I work with weird people who are up all night entertaining visits from guys selling them large quantities of illegal substances. Occupational hazard. And I'm not married; I don't have grown sons to protect me like you do, so lighten up already."

Cydney took a drag of her cigarette and blew the smoke away from Lillian in a long thin stream. "Look, are we going to the cemetery or aren't we? The cars are all pulling away. Besides, don't you want to see Robert? Ask him about product liability insurance; wasn't that one of your favorites? Or, how about the price of rubies and their effect on rare Art Nouveau jewelry? C'mon, Lil, let's go," Cydney said, putting her arm through Lillian's and grinding out her cigarette under the pointy toe of her matching fuchsia shoe. "That bitch couldn't have kept it from him all these years."

1981. September.

WITHIN A FEW MONTHS OF their acquaintance, Lillian and Cydney had developed a promising business relationship. Lillian spent two days a week at Cydney's manufacturing space in the brewery, and three days a week at the BYO Agency where she still collected enough of a paycheck to pay for day care. Cydney had turned out to be very knowledgeable about the rag trade, ordering materials and producing enough prototypes to generate appointments with large retailers, any one of whom was able to place orders worth tens of thousands of dollars. Lillian had cajoled one of BYO's best graphic designers to come up with a company logo for Baby Grand, a product logo for their first product, Carta-Babe—which was indeed a melon as Cydney had predicted—and a package design for the prototypes Cydney was hand-stitching. As far as Lillian could see, things were going really well. Except that she needed money, lots of it, and no bank would lend it to her without taking her house as collateral. Lillian decided that she was confident enough to borrow against the jewelry left to her by her grandmother, whose last appraisal had been valued at over one million dollars. Lillian had no intention of parting with the jewels, but surely she could borrow against them.

And so, in conversations with her BYO client, Mel Rickhauser, in the advertising department at T.Rex Toys, largest national chain retailer of toys and infant products, Lillian told Mel that she would kill for an appointment with the T.Rex buyer of infant soft goods. Mel was willing to set it up if her product samples and packaging were far enough along in development. And far enough along, Mel was quick to point out, meant more than two samples and hand-colored cardboard boxes.

"Far enough along, honey," Mel said to her one day in her BYO office, his feet up on her desk, "means you should *look* like a business, you should *smell* like a business, you should prove to me that if I give you an order, and go through the aggravation of setting you up as a vendor, you're gonna deliver the 10,000 pieces."

"But, Mel," Lillian hesitated, rummaging through her desk for the preliminary spread sheets she was doing by hand, "it will cost about $15.00 each to make an initial run of—say—five hundred Carta-Babes. That's $7,500. Plus we have no credit, so I have to shell out $8,000 cash for an initial custom fabric run, and another $5,000 for webbing and hardware and laminating—so now we're up to $20,000 plus. On top of that are the incorporation fees and the patent and trademark search and application, and the cost of both poly bag and cardboard box packaging. Do you know how much the tooling for the die costs to make those damn boxes? $10,000!"

"Listen, honey," said Mel, leaning far back in Lillian's chair and tapping his shoe on her desk, "you are gonna need—no kidding and don't argue with me—at least 100K, and don't choke. When you're ready, call my friend Vinnie at Benjamin Finance because he's the man. Forget these fifteen percent interest rates. He'll do much better. You got something here with this Carta-Babe thingy. All you working dames with kids—what are you gonna do with all that cash? Spend it on the kids, what else? Sales at T.Rex are way up. Why shouldn't you get a part of that?"

And while it was true that commercial lending rates were at fifteen percent or above for novices like Lillian with no credit to speak of, it was also true that Benjamin Finance made the borrowing of $100,000 about as easy as going to the supermarket to buy a gallon of milk. This should have been her first clue that Benjamin Finance, while located in a high rent office suite in the Customs Tower, was not entirely on the up and up, but Lillian was too caught up in the march toward the coveted appointment at

T.Rex Toys to use her peripheral vision. So caught up that she neglected to pay attention to basic math, because a balloon payment of $120,000 in six months worked out to something like forty percent interest.

WITH THE CASH INFUSION SHE was on track. Three months went by with orders and commitments coming in and Lillian's hopes rising with them, until the day she returned home to find two unannounced representatives from Benjamin Finance in her living room. The sight of strangers sitting uninvited around her coffee table almost caused her knees to buckle.

"Here, have a seat," said the small guy with hair so black it looked like it was shoe polished. "Take a load off. Cute kids. How old?"

"Excuse me..." Lillian stared at the men from her entrance hall, backing away toward the still open door. "Who are you? How did you get in here?" She had Jonny on one hip and reached down to hike David up onto the other.

"Hey, take it easy. No harm intended. We're here from Benny Finance. Vinnie sent us to check up on our investment," said the taller one. Thin and balding, he was wearing a white shirt open at the collar, revealing hair curling halfway up his neck. He leaned over and handed her a card that read, Angelo Ferrati – Collections. "Call me Angie, why don't ya. This is my associate Ritchie Donovan." He pointed to the small dark-haired guy with bad false teeth.

Lillian stood in her own doorway with a child in each arm, measuring the number of steps to the kitchen phone, trying to figure out how she could bend down, pick up her purse and car keys, which had spilled out on the floor, and escape. *Fat chance.* The small dark guy named Ritchie had already strolled over and was reaching behind her to close the heavy oak front door.

She jumped backwards to jam her foot in the doorway and said with as much authority as she could muster, "If this is a business call, then I'd appreciate it if we met during business hours. My husband is bringing clients home for dinner any minute now and you'll have to leave." Lillian stood taller than Ritchie in her heels, and stared down at him, hoping this bluff would work. In fact, Marc was preparing for a lengthy trial and was practically in seclusion in a downtown hotel. She had talked to him for a total of twenty minutes in three days.

"Oh yeah? What's for dinner?" Ritchie sniffed the air ostentatiously, wrinkling his nose. He spoke quickly, stumbling over his words.

David started to whimper in her arms. Lillian reached for the handle of the screen door behind her and pushed it open.

"Call my office," she said, backing out, and I'll be happy to meet with you tomorrow."

Fresh air. At least she was on the front porch in plain view of the neighbors. She walked down the front steps with David bouncing heavily on her hip and Jonny in her arms. Together they weighed over sixty pounds, but at that moment were as light as two cats. It was an Indian summer fall evening and not yet dark. Lillian felt much safer as she walked away from the house.

"Forget something?" Ritchie had scooped up her purse and car keys and stepped through the open screen door after her, following her down the path. "You know, Mrs. CooperSmith," he began in a low voice that was probably his version of soothing, "we came here on a civil business call, not trying to cause any trouble, so don't get all jumpy on us. And since you brought it up, we been trying to call you at that advertising agency all week. But you know what? You never come to the phone, or else we get a message about talking to your accountant, or your lawyer, and that's not the way we like to handle our business. We feel like, see, we lend you the money, in person, personally, and that's the way we want to keep it. In person. No lawyers, no accountants. None of that stuff." Ritchie crossed his arms and leaned back on his heels, satisfied that he had delivered a good speech, even if he did sound like a lawn mower mulching words.

Behind him, Lillian could see that the tall guy, Angie, had emerged from the house to join Ritchie on the front walk. Angie lit a cigarette and waved the smoke away after a big exhale. Lillian had to pee desperately. She shifted Jonny, who was sucking his thumb, wide-eyed, against her hip. David scrambled to get down from her other hip, smacked her in the shoulder, and fell to the ground. She lunged for him as he ran to the house, but Ritchie got there first and swooped him up high onto his shoulders.

"Hey there," Ritchie said, "I'm a horsey. Let's go for a ride."

Lillian stood frozen as he took off down the front steps and trotted the fifty feet to the sidewalk with her firstborn clinging to the top of his head.

"Hey! Put him down," she called, trying to sound calm and commanding. "Davey, honey, it's ok, it's just a piggyback ride." The skin on her temples pulled tight, tingling, right up into her scalp. She started down the front walk after Ritchie, stumbled on a loose brick, and threw Jonny off balance. His thumb popped out of his mouth like a yanked cork and without any wind-up he started to howl.

Good, thought Lillian, *that'll get someone's attention.*

Ritchie trotted back up the front walk, dancing just out of Lillian's reach, with David tilting precariously on his shoulders. Lillian moved toward them, sideways, like a crab.

"It's ok, Davie. Mummy's right here. I know you feel seasick. If you have to throw up, it's ok. Just do it."

The words were barely out of her mouth when Ritchie rolled David off his shoulders, glaring at Lillian and setting the child down while holding tightly onto his hand. Without missing a beat, Lillian walked around and grabbed David's other hand. Now she felt slightly more confident. Jonny had stopped screaming and started hiccupping instead, then stuffed his entire fist into his mouth.

"Look, my payments aren't due for another six, seven weeks; what's the problem?" Lillian held her ground, facing Ritchie and Angie, who turned to observe a neighbor pulling into his driveway next door. Lillian waved at him enthusiastically, thrilled to see someone whose name she didn't even know.

Angie nodded imperceptibly in Ritchie's direction. "Just checking things out, like I told you," he said, exhaling a long stream of blue smoke very close to Lillian's face. "But you're right. We'll catch you up tomorrow during business hours to go over your payment plan." He tossed his cigarette butt onto the lawn and rubbed his hands together. "So, I'll be telling Vinnie about your nice house here, nice kids; we just like to have the whole picture so we really get to know our clients."

"But I'm...this is ridiculous," Lillian blurted out. "My business is just getting off the ground! And besides, I...I have an appointment with T.Rex Toys." Lillian wanted to sound tough, but this came out with a whimper.

"And our business is lending money to people with collateral. We were just checking up on the collateral," Angie said as Ritchie finally let go of David's hand, waving at him with a slow, spidery gesture. "Your husband's a lawyer, huh? He must be real proud of you. Hey, I'm sure your business will do great."

The two men strolled over to a dark blue Cadillac parked across the street. "See ya soon," Ritchie called, and he ducked his glossy head into the driver's seat. Angie's head bobbed out of sight. Car doors slammed.

Lillian watched as the Cadillac pulled away and drove slowly up the street. She jiggled Jonny up and down, while David raced around in circles playing helicopter. Lillian stood still for a good five minutes, afraid to go in the house alone in case they came back. Jonny grabbed onto the pearls she was wearing around her neck and gave them a yank. Lillian looked down at him, thumb in his mouth, long eyelashes wet with tears. What was she waiting for? Her grandmother had left her the jewelry; it was time to claim it.

It had been close to seventy degrees that day and she was wearing a jacket, so she couldn't understand why she was suddenly freezing, or why her legs were soaking wet. She stared at her feet, perplexed, her shoes filled with puddles. Christ. She had peed in her pants.

AFTER THE VISIT FROM BENNY Finance's goon squad, Lillian lived in a constant state of fear. She had been vague with Cydney about the financing for Baby Grand and had never told a soul about her relationship to the well-known Canadian retail chain, *Chez Kuper*. Years ago her father had changed the spelling of their name to Cooper, which, combined with Marc's perfectly un-Jewish "Smith," suited her just fine. When they married, Lillian had insisted that they both change their names to CooperSmith and Marc reluctantly agreed as long as Smith was capitalized.

Both Lillian and Cydney needed their venture to succeed and believed that the other had the matching skills to make it happen. Lillian's skills were supposed to include money – finding it, keeping it, and using it wisely. Lillian had to step it up. Summoning all her courage, she called her father, Samuel Cooper, to ask for permission to take her grandmother's jewelry.

"So, Dad, any word from Sir G?" No one, not even close family, referred to her grandfather as anything other than Sir Geoffrey.

"Not that I know of. He's still on a yacht with Isabelle – last known address in Nassau. I got a postcard from Panama about three weeks ago. Why?"

"Well, I told you about my new business idea, right?" Samuel had not approved of Baby Grand and thought she was nuts to leave a perfectly good job at a rising advertising agency.

"Oh, Lillian, I thought you weren't going to pursue that crazy idea."

Lillian decided she would not take the bait. "Well, I am. And I'm also ready to claim the jewels that Lady Alice left me. She always wanted me to have them, right? And…it's been almost a year since she died – so what am I waiting for?"

Samuel had to acknowledge that this was true, but he was reluctant to accompany her to the bank vaults in Montreal where the jewels were stored. "Your grandfather will have a fit when he finds out. Technically, mother left everything to him. When he dies, it passes to you. Please don't tell me that you need them for your business. Your grandmother would roll over in her grave."

"Actually, I think she would sit up and cheer and you know it."

They ended the conversation with Samuel saying he would think about it seriously and get back to her. Lillian hung up feeling thoroughly depressed. How was she going to meet Benny's first payment of $30,000 before Christmas? They were ready to ship orders worth $25,000, but it would take up to ninety days to collect receivables from the small retail shops they were selling to. She thought they might have enough orders to get a factor to float credit on receivables, but that bubble burst after her conversation with Dominique Russo in the factoring department in the Manhattan office of New England Bancorp. Dominique grumbled at her because he got an answering machine, not a receptionist, when he had called earlier that day.

"What kind of business are you running here? You don't even have a person to answer the phone," he demanded as soon as Lillian called him back.

"You're complaining that we haven't shown a profit and you want me to throw away money on someone to answer the phone?"

"Well, it doesn't make me feel good to think I'm gonna give you this credit and what if I can't find you?"

"Did I call you right back?" Lillian asked.

"Yeah, so what?"

Lillian could tell that he loved his job. "So what, huh? Have you ever tried to run a business? Ever try to deal with people like yourself throwing stones in your already rocky path?" Lillian did not add "asshole" out loud, although she mouthed it into the phone.

Cydney was standing on a stepladder on the other side of the shop, where she was trying to rig up a pulley system to send finished goods ninety feet down the hall and into the packing area, but she could read Lillian's lips.

"*Fucking-A for asshole!*" she yelled from the top rung.

"Who's that?" asked Dominique.

"That's the person auditioning for receptionist. Should I hire her?"

"Very funny. So give me your D&B number again."

Lillian rolled her eyes. "Let's see…for a good time call 356-002-4991. How's that?"

Silence.

"I'm making jokes, Dom. Look, I don't have a bottom line—at least not one that doesn't sink like a stone, but I'm really optimistic. This is the American way, right? Gotta start somewhere."

"Yeah, yeah. Look—fax me whatever numbers you got, ok?"

Lillian looked up at Cydney. She mouthed "F-A-X machine" with a hopeless gesture.

"You got a fax machine, right?" Dom asked.

"I'm not sure I know what a fax machine is. Can I just stick this in regular US mail? Look, we need the credit desperately. I've got fabric on order and they won't release the fabric unless we get the credit. And I've got orders. I can send you purchase orders from serious accounts, department stores, big chains."

"Can I ask you something?" He sounded almost pleasant.

"Shoot." Lillian was hopeful.

"What do you know about running a business, honey? Frankly, there's not much I'm gonna be able to do for you because your numbers are just not there. I'll look at them but don't hold your breath." And he hung up.

Cyd peered down from the stepladder. "No go, huh? Men. Fucking men. Maybe I should send him pictures of my bottom line—in the bikini I crocheted myself."

"The one with the big holes?"

"The very one," she said, climbing down.

Lillian collapsed on top of the phone. "Oh God, I am so depressed. We need the credit to get the order and we need the order to get the credit."

"Well, I'm feeling very action-oriented myself," Cydney said cheerfully, "and since operations is my department, I would be happy to resort to low-level violence and let the air out of this guy's tires."

Lillian could barely speak she was so bummed out. How could Cydney be this cheerful? "He lives in Manhattan; he probably doesn't have tires."

But Lillian's gloom proved to be infectious and Cyd caught it, falling back to earth.

"How come everybody in the factoring department has an Italian name?" Cyd asked, staring at the bank's letterhead. "Stan Sabatini, Dominique Russo, Frank Ficocello. Has the bank been taken over by the mob? This is great," Cydney said, throwing down the letterhead and putting on her coat. "I have no ethnic identity anywhere in this business." Her voice floated down the hall as she headed for the door. "Jews run the rag trade and wops launder the money. And I don't even know what laundering money means."

Neither did Lillian, come to think of it. She just knew they couldn't get any.

Sunday, Nov. 5, 2006. Mid-Afternoon.

LILLIAN AND CYDNEY MINGLED WITH the last of the crowd pushing toward the limousines and hearse lined up at the curb. Lillian recognized two lawyers from Marc's firm, and her old boss, Tom Monahan, from BYO Advertising. Lillian wore her dark glasses, not that it was particularly sunny in threatening rain, but it was easier to stay in the background and not have to look anyone in the eye. She still hadn't seen Robert up close, and she noticed that Cydney made no move toward him. Cydney, despite her own dark glasses and wide black and purple scarf wrapped around her hair and shoulders, was still unmistakably herself. Two guys in dark suits stood ramrod straight next to Robert, evidently assigned to security, never taking their eyes off her.

"Check this out," Cydney said, turning to Lillian and almost twisting her ankle on the last step of the church. "See the G-men over here hanging on the car, like it had running boards or something? What do they think this is – JFK's assassination? They have not stopped looking at me. If I reach my hand into my purse real slow and draw it out carefully like I've got a gun – which we know I do, even though it's fake," she said, doing exactly that, "I wonder how fast they would pounce."

"Cydney, are you nuts?" Lillian tried to grab her wrist but Cydney had already removed her hand, without gun – real or imaginary, to rub the tip of her nose. The procession of long black cars was pulling away, headlights on, little blue flags waving from the antennae.

Lillian had second thoughts about driving Cydney back to Boston. She was exhausted by her already and it had only been an hour. "What kind of game was that? It made sense for those guys to watch you. They probably have a list of all Robert's old friends. Or enemies, for that matter."

"Oh relax, I haven't seen him in years, Lillian. He lives in Washington, he's hardly ever here and when he is, he's surrounded by suck-ups."

"I think it's called his staff."

"Yeah, whatever. I hate them. I hate her too. I'm glad she's dead."

"Could you lower your voice? This is a funeral," Lillian said.

"Well, if it's a funeral, then where's the booze?"

"Isn't that beforehand, like an Irish wake? I think we missed it."

"Look, let's just get in your car and follow them to the cemetery," Cydney said, taking Lillian's arm again. "Somebody will tell us where the festivities are afterwards. And besides, I do want to see Robert. It'll be easier if you're there."

Lillian thought this was like the part in a bad movie where someone suggests going to the locked room in the basement and opening it just for fun. "Gee, Cyd, now there's an idea! Let me stand by while you reconcile with your long-lost lover over the body of his dead wife. I'd rather drive over the Tobin Bridge, not that I have bridge phobias any longer."

"Give me the keys. I'll drive," Cydney said, her hand out.

Lillian looked at her watch. "It'll be dark in two hours and I want to get home before it snows or sleets, or whatever it's supposed to do."

"The forecasts are always wrong, and what could be better than a funeral in the woods in the dark and the rain? Followed by a drink, of course. Well, several drinks..." And before Lillian had a chance to protest further, Cydney moved away from her into the crowd of mourners scrambling toward their cars.

BY THE TIME THEY ARRIVED at the cemetery, ten miles down a two-lane road, following directions that read, "...turn left at the second large oak tree after the stone house. If you think you're lost you're in the right place. Take a right on the dirt road, go straight through the old iron rusted gates..." They had missed the lowering of the coffin and were just in time to see a crowd of hunched black figures throwing lumps of earth into a hole dug halfway down a surprisingly beautiful hill dotted with granite and marble headstones. The view ended in a large pond at the base of the slope with a vista of heathery meadows beyond.

Very English countryside, thought Lillian. *Peaceful. Maybe they own the land?* But Cydney hated the country – too many bugs and unpredictable green leaves carrying poison.

"Where the hell is he burying her? Does she have cholera or something and they're keeping her from contaminating the rest of the stiffs?" asked Cydney, smoking again.

On her way down the hill to the gravesite, Lillian called Marc from her cell phone, her new loafers becoming rapidly soaked from the wet grass. Cydney, in stilettos, sauntered a few steps ahead of her, swinging her large pocketbook and humming, "When the Saints Go Marching In," quite audibly.

"Hi, Honey!" said Lillian over a bad connection. "Guess who I'm hanging out with and guess who's still wearing pink?"

"Where are you, Lil?" Marc's voice crackled, sounding worried. "It's starting to snow."

"It is? You're kidding. It's starting to snow," she reported to Cydney with some alarm.

"Oh relax, Lil," said Cydney, swinging her bag higher. "It's not snowing here, is it?"

"Not yet. Ok, Marc – I'm still here at the cemetery. Why? I'm not sure but take a guess. Because I need a drink, if that makes any sense. Because I'm driving Cyd home. She came up from New York without a car."

"You found her, huh?" Marc's voice was barely audible. "Has she been arrested yet?"

"No, but she's working on it. There appear to be at least two G-men with their eye on her. Look, I don't know how late I'll get back but it could be nine or ten…"

"Well, drive carefully, because this snow is supposed to move west. If it gets bad just get off the road and stay somewhere on the Pike."

Cydney had quickened her pace and was heading toward Robert and his entourage, who were moving away from the gravesite and toward the shelter of a clump of birch trees.

"Uh-oh. I gotta go. She's got Robert in her sights. Look, I'm gonna grab her and head home…" But the connection with Marc disappeared, and Lillian moved quickly to catch up.

Lillian scanned the perimeter of pine trees. In the distance, Cydney and Robert were reaching out to shake hands. Then Cydney was kissing Robert on both cheeks. And then Robert had his arms around Cydney. Then Cydney was kissing Robert (for longer than was really necessary) on the mouth. And then Robert's shoulders kind of collapsed and he was holding onto her.

Lillian felt like throwing her bag on the ground and stamping her foot. *I can't go through this again.*

By mid-afternoon, the sky was slate gray and the rain was turning to pellets of icy snow. *Nothing like the Berkshires in November in a cemetery in the snow,* thought Lillian. *Why don't we just remand ourselves to the custody of Ingmar Bergman? I will never get home.*

Lillian stood at the car shuffling her wet feet and mingling with the last of the funeral attendees. She and Tom Monahan, her former boss, had a brief conversation about the sad state of advertising, in deep recession since the crazed days of the late nineties when Tom and Lillian had often thrust unwanted potential clients at each other. But Tom had pulled away with a wave of his hand, and Lillian was left with long black limos and Robert's security detail.

Cydney and Robert had recovered from their very public meltdown and were walking toward his limo with great reserve, an arm's length apart. Clouds of frozen breath hung between them. Even though the sun was long gone, Cydney was still wearing sunglasses.

Where are the paparazzi when you need 'em? thought Lillian.

Robert walked toward her and extended his hand, a strong dry hand. "Lillian, you look exactly the same, wonderful as always."

He still had those terrific crinkles around his very blue eyes. His and hers eyes. Robert and Cyd—blue, like tropical waters. Weird.

"Oh sure, Robert. So do you. We're not getting older, just seeing less well, that's all. My condolences. It's been a long time, you know, and…I think you've done a great job, by the way, even though you are a Republican, but we won't go there, will we?"

Lillian hadn't spoken to Robert face to face in years and found herself in danger of babbling. To cover up, she punched him lightly on the arm, for old times' sake, and noted that the guy in black with the telephone cord hanging out from behind his ear stiffened and looked ready to spring in her direction.

"Listen," Lillian continued, not sure whether their old familiar but cautious vein was still appropriate, "I hate to rush, but I promised Cydney a lift back home, so I'd like to get going if you don't mind. I don't recall exactly how I got suckered into this, but Cydney has that effect on people, as you well know."

He cleared his throat. "Well, Lillian, in fact I wanted to ask you both to join us at the house, we…" He stopped himself and cleared his throat, shaking his head. "I guess it's no longer we, is it?…I have a country house about twenty miles up Route 62 off the Lake Williams road. It's clearly marked, La Brettonia—that was Marjorie's idea—she was really into this branding thing—I guess she should have talked to you…and anyway it would be a pleasure to have you both stop by."

A pleasure, thought Lillian. *Is he kidding?*

"And, besides," he added, lowering his voice with a cough, "we have some old business to wrap up; it's been on my mind. I have some papers of Marjorie's that you should probably see. So please do come on over. After everyone leaves we can talk." Lillian must have looked skeptical because he added, "And Cydney is on board. It's fine with her, and she'd be willing to stay the night if the weather gets bad."

"Oh, I just bet she would, Robert," Lillian said, looking him straight in the eye. She could do that at five foot ten inches—look guys straight in the eye. She loved it. "Not many people talk to you like that, I bet, eh?"

"Eh? Still a Canuck, *eh*, Lil?" he said, playing along.

"Yeah, well, as I recall, so were you, way back when. Or so the local legend goes. Depending on whether the legend generator is Cydney, ready to stew you alive, or her mother, also, come to think of it, ready to stew you alive. Amazing that Bianca is still going strong with that bad heart; she must be in her eighties."

Robert looked at her and raised his eyebrows in a perfect double take. "What are you talking about?"

"Bianca. Cyd told me she's fine."

"Lillian, Bianca died two years ago."

Lillian stood there with her mouth open. She felt a snowflake land on her tongue and swallowed hard. She could hardly get a word out.

"I was at the funeral," Robert continued, "and was frankly surprised that you weren't there."

Lillian felt like things were moving in slow motion. People were closing in on them from all sides—Cydney, staff, G-men—as Robert leaned in close to Lillian's cheek as if to say a warm good-bye.

"Look, just come to the house; we have things to talk about. It's not good, Lil." Then straightening up, he said much more audibly, "Great, see you back at the house, Mrs. CooperSmith, and thanks for your kind words. Just tell the guard at the gate who you are, and my driver will give you directions." He pointed Lillian toward his limo as he turned to his aides.

1981. October.

CYDNEY MALLONE GOT A CALL from her mother, Bianca, to come home because something really peculiar had happened to her grandmother, Pauline.

"Call a doctor, Mom. Don't call me. I'm forty miles away."

"She's not sick," said Bianca, "but something amazing has happened."

Cydney had enough problems without dropping everything in the middle of a workday in Cambridge to drive up to Lawrell and hold her mother's hand. "Just tell me what it is, Mom, or I'm not going anywhere."

"It's a package from Pauline's sister, Isabelle, who's never sent her a thing in her life. It's full of expensive looking stuff. I'm sure it's fake, but what do I know? Come on up and tell us what you think."

Cydney rolled her eyes. "Fake what...fake fur? Fake flowers...? Tell me or I'm not coming."

"Well, fake jewelry, it looks like. Big diamonds. Pearls."

Cydney perked up. "Is this the sister who worked for the rich old guy for years and then married him a few months ago?"

"Yup. This package is postmarked and insured from the Bahamas. What do you think?" Bianca sounded slightly out of breath.

"I think they're probably hot and you should bury them in the back-yard before the FBI gets there, that's what I think." Cydney considered hanging up; her mother called her a dozen times a week to complain about everything from the price of oranges to the neighbor's dog.

But Bianca had a different edge to her voice. "Will you be serious and just drive up? Your grandmother is really in a tizzy. She keeps saying this is a bad omen. I think she's about to have an asthma attack."

"Alright, alright, I'll be there," Cydney reluctantly agreed.

SHE HUNG UP AND PROMPTLY forgot this conversation, because her long time married lover, Robert Bretton, called five minutes later to cancel dinner for the third time that week. She had kept Robert out of sight during the Baby Grand start-up, so she wouldn't have to explain him to Lillian, and in that short time he had begun to consider a run for political office to fill the empty seat left by the sudden resignation of the doddering Senator Blake.

"Robert, come on! How long am I supposed to put up with this? And since when are you considering a run for senator? As a Republican! Isn't your life crazy enough? What is Marjorie doing to you?"

Robert was apparently in a smoke-filled room with wealthy men on the verge of becoming political supporters and couldn't say much in his own defense.

Cydney took full advantage. "So, when are we going to talk? How are you going to run for the Senate and juggle everything else? I need you right now. Don't expect me to be there when you stumble across the finish line."

Robert managed to whisper, cupped hands over the phone, "Cydney baby, please. This could work out for us. Really. I will never win the primary. Marjorie is totally invested in this and when I lose, it will be so much easier to just get it over with."

"And if you do win? Then you'll be off in Washington and what would happen to...?"

"This is Massachusetts, Cyd. They are not going to elect a Republican."

"Do you really want them digging around in your background for dirt? Me, Carmen...the rest of our crazy families?"

AT THE MENTION OF THEIR families, Cydney remembered that she had promised her mother she'd be there an hour ago.

"Oh shit, I gotta run. Something about Pauline and a box of pearls. I'm serious, Robert. We need to talk. Soon. I am getting too old for this."

Cydney hung up and dashed around her loft, grabbing her jacket and pocketbook from underneath the furry bellies of a litter of kittens and muttering to herself. After years of living a double life, how could Robert let himself be drafted for senator? Not that he wants it, but he's such a successful, local boy-makes-good businessman that he's a shoe-in as a last minute compromise candidate. But wait until they find out about Cydney—who would not make anyone's list as woman of the year—the press will have a field day.

Cydney's long time nemesis, Marjorie, Robert's very wealthy wife, would never stand for it. She hadn't put up with years of being the scorned wife so that she could be blown off now that he had a shot at the big time. Nope. Cydney knew she would be hearing from Marjorie any day now. Maybe she should just pack her bags and leave town.

WHEN CYDNEY ARRIVED AT HER grandmother's house in the old mill town of Lawrell, high on a hill overlooking the Merrimack River, packed in tight next to similar three-deckers, she sat in her parked car and stared up at the front porch. It had been a while since she'd come to Pauline's. The junk pile on the teetering front porch was even higher than she remembered—layers of cardboard boxes filled with old news-papers and empty diaper boxes brimming with rags. It would not sur-prise her if the neighbors had called the Board of Health.

Pauline, her maternal grandmother, had lived in this house for as long as Cydney could remember. She should have sold this wreck years ago, when it was still worth something. Besides, she was too old to be living on her own, although she insisted they would carry her out feet first. By then the neighborhood would have gone down the shit shoot; houses on the next block were abandoned and one of them looked like it could be a Cambodian crack house. Long gone were the Irish and French-Canadian residents of the old industrial Lawrell, and impoverished im-migrants from places Cydney couldn't find on a map had moved in.

Cydney walked past the junk on the porch and rapped at the kitchen window.

"Hey," she yelled, cupping her hands to her mouth, "when are you going to get rid of this shit?" Pauline had this screwy idea that the more stuff she piled up and the uglier her house, the less likely it was that the city would repossess it for nonpayment of taxes. Cydney tried the door to find it unlocked.

"Ok, what's up?" she called, taking off her coat. "You guys dragged me away from a busy workday for a parcel from the Bahamas. What's in it? Shells, I bet. Coconuts. I couldn't trust the two of you to recognize a pearl if you bit into it."

Bianca, her short red hair rolled up in pink spongy curlers, had just given herself a manicure and was waving her fingers delicately in the air. She looked her youngest child squarely in the eye.

"I don't know how I could have made it without you, raising four daughters all by myself, as though your father was ever around. You were a big help, you were. Hell on wheels. Can't trust me…who does she think she is?" Bianca asked, appealing to Pauline.

Pauline rarely sided with Bianca when she and Cydney started in on each other.

"Not again, please. I need some help, not the two of you fighting all the time."

"Alright, alright," said Cydney, reaching into her grandmother's purse and pulling out a cigarette, "I was just checking to make sure you were both alive."

"Well…" Bianca waited, her hands now folded primly on the table.

"Well what?" Cydney rummaged further in the purse until Pauline yanked it away from her.

"Well, *are* we?" Bianca glared at her, arching her right eyebrow, which was painted on.

"Oh, for *chrissake*, will you just show me the box, please?" Without waiting for an answer, Cydney wandered over to the stove with the cigarette dangling from her mouth and lit it from the gas-fired front burner.

"Will you stop doing that? You're going to burn down the house. I hope you never do it at your place."

Pauline shuffled out of the kitchen in her old pink slippers, which had once been fluffy as foxtails, and padded back with a shoebox. It was covered in plain brown paper marked with black ink, green customs slips, and several gaily-colored stamps. She set it on the table and squeezed herself back into an armchair. They all stared at it. Cydney pulled the package toward her and flipped open the lid. She tossed out a wad of tissue paper and an envelope, and then lifted out a red velvet box about the size of a paperback novel. She looked up. Pauline and Bianca were leaning forward.

For a full minute after she snapped the top back, she stared at the contents. Cydney had never seen anything like it. She wasn't sure but her jaw may have dropped to her chest. She lifted out the necklace and dangled it, fire and light flashing from thousands of tiny facets.

Three silvery baroque pearls the size of a man's thumbnail, with luster like the sea reflecting a sunset, formed the bodies of three humming-birds fluttering over honeysuckle. Cydney stared, mouth still open, as light flashed from the birds' ruby throats, feathers shimmering with seed pearls and tiny emeralds, the crests of their heads sparkling in blue-green cloisonné. Stylized honeysuckle blossoms, bursting with diamonds, wound around the birds' delicate movable wings – all nestled in a filigree of emerald petals set in a whorl of platinum.

In the other half of the box nestled matching honeysuckle diamond earrings, a ring with an enormous ruby and tiny hummingbird head, and a bracelet repeating the necklace in miniature.

"Wow..." breathed Cydney, "will you look at this. This came in a shoebox? Your sister must have been out of her mind. I told you it was probably stolen."

"So, you think it's real?" asked Bianca.

"Look at the workmanship. It's gotta be made by some design house." She looked at the inside. "There's a hallmark, looks like 750 – that's 18K gold – and something else. Gram, get me a magnifying glass." Bianca and Pauline waited patiently while Cydney held the necklace upside down and stared at it through the glass.

"Looks like...Cartier. Wow! Cartier. And something like a maker's mark – can't read it, but the numbers are clear. Shouldn't be hard to look that up. Let's call Shreve, Crump & Lowe."

"Who are they? Lawyers?" Pauline wanted to know. "Because I don't want no lawyers here on this."

"Gram," Cydney said as she put the glass down on the table, "Shreve's is the biggest jewelry store in Boston—I'm calling now."

After fifteen minutes on the phone with the appraisal department looking up the mark, the year, 1929, and the marker's numbers that followed, Cydney made a series of noncommittal *'uh-huh's'* and *'hmm's'* that kept Bianca and Pauline in the dark. Then she described the necklace and the matching pieces—bracelet, ring, earrings, all of which she was wearing by now, dragging the phone into the bathroom to stare at herself like a child wearing her mother's best forbidden clothes.

"So what's it worth, do you think?" she asked into the receiver at her collarbone while she preened in the mirror. "Yeah, at auction, probably. That's more money than retail, right?" She nodded for a long time, said thank you, and hung up, nonplussed.

Bianca and Pauline looked crestfallen. "Not that much, huh?" Pauline said.

"Nope, Gram, not that much. Just about...oh...depends on the market...it's an estate piece...collector's item...of course it's worth more as a set...could be...oh, eight or nine *hundred thousand dollars!*" Cydney stood there with her arms flung open, waiting for them to start screaming and jumping up and down like contestants at a game show. They didn't. They sat and stared.

Pauline sighed. "I knew it. They're fake," she said, leaning her head in her hands, "but they sure are pretty. So what? I'll wear them for Christmas."

"*Gram!* Did you hear me? They're worth a fortune!"

They didn't buy a word of it, until Cydney dove through the tissue paper and retrieved the envelope that was still sealed and addressed, simply, to *Pauline, l'aînée,* or the oldest. Which she was—the oldest of twelve siblings, while her sister Isabelle was the youngest. Cydney thought it strange that Isabelle would send a letter to Pauline—who was illiterate and had never learned to read in the frozen Quebec of her childhood. Pauline had been too necessary in a household where her mother kept popping babies every fifteen months. As the eldest, Pauline raised every one from the time she was four. But Isabelle, evidently, did not know this about the big sister she hadn't seen since Pauline left home at twenty to move to the textile mills of New England.

Cydney picked up the letter. Pauline would never admit that she couldn't read.

"I don't have my reading glasses, *ma petite*. You read it for me."

"Sure, Gram," Cydney said, playing along, "whatever you say."

September 15, 1981
Eleuthera, The Bahamas

Ma chère Pauline: I am sending along this set of jewelry that belonged to my husband's first wife. She had no daughters and Geoffrey has given the set to me. I hoped that we would have returned home to Montreal by now, but we are still on the boat. My husband has been very unpredictable lately and I am sending these jewels to you for safekeeping—they are too valuable to keep at sea. I'm sure you don't believe me, but it's been a hard few months—I'm nervous all the time and anxious to go back home.

Aren't the birds beautiful? I've always loved them. They remind me of the honeysuckle climbing the trellis on the front porch, chez maman. Do you remember? So long ago—you left when I was just a baby! Maybe I will come and visit my big sister and collect the jewels in person.

À bientôt, adieu
Isabelle

"WELL," SAID CYDNEY, DROPPING THE sheet of onion skin, and picking up the thick, sealed envelope, "I wasn't far wrong, was I? Stolen."

Pauline looked worried. "What should we do?"

"Sooner or later someone will discover that the jewelry's gone," Cydney said. "By the way, if the old geezer has changed his will to leave this to Isabelle, his kids will have it contested up the wazoo, so don't plan any retirement homes in Florida just yet. I say hang on to the jewels until you know Isabelle is back and then send them on to her."

Pauline shook her head. "There's something wrong here. That letter was too...final. Isabelle knows there's something wrong too."

"Oh, come on, Gram. You said yourself you haven't seen her since she was a baby! The only thing wrong is that you're up here feeling sorry for her, and she's down there having dinner served to her on a private yacht. Wrap these rocks back up and put them someplace safe." Cydney stood up and got ready to leave.

Pauline looked panicked. "I don't have anyplace safe!"

"Well, no one in their right mind would try to rob this house. It looks like it's been condemned." But that would not calm Pauline down, and she insisted that Cydney take the shoebox home with her and put the contents in her safety deposit box.

Cydney looked at her watch. "It's almost 2:00. I'll never get to the bank before it closes. I don't want the responsibility of keeping this stuff."

Bianca intervened. "Your grandmother is very upset. Pretty soon she'll have an asthma attack. Will that make you happy? Just take the box and get to the bank when you can."

Cydney started to argue and gave up, realizing that neither of them had any idea of the kind of neighborhood she lived in, on the top floor of a converted brewery in East Cambridge. If she wanted to get out of there, she had better take the damn box and go. This made her very nervous. What if she left it in her car and forgot to lock the door? What if she hid it so well among the boxes of old running shoes that she forgot where it was? A hundred things could go wrong, and this was the most potential money Cydney had ever seen in one place in her life. She had better write a large note to herself to get this to the bank tomorrow morning. But first she had to remember where she kept the key to the bank vault.

WHEN CYDNEY RETURNED TO HER loft in the brewery she found two messages on her answering machine. One was from Robert saying that he had been scheduled for out-of-town fund-raising trips for the next two weeks and felt as though his life was being taken over by his handlers. The other was from his wife, Marjorie, saying that Cydney should expect a visit from her accountant, and she had better pay attention because she had a few debts to settle.

Cydney unplugged the answering machine and considered throwing it out the window. But it would have made no difference because in her mailbox was a registered letter from Flanagan & Flanagan, Certified Public Accountants, announcing that an audit of Robert and Marjorie Bretton's personal finances had found outstanding loans to one Cydney Mallone made between 1970 and 1981 totaling $925,000, not including interest. Said loans would look embarrassing, to put it mildly, if found on the books of a fiscally responsible Republican candidate for US Senator and had to be cleared up immediately. It would be appreciated if Ms. Mallone would forward by registered mail the principal due, by cashier's check, the interest to be dealt with on a subsequent date.

Cydney could feel the vein in her forehead start to throb. She looked at the clock. Only 4:00. Too early for a drink. She looked back at the letter. Marjorie wasn't kidding. Did Robert know about this? Why had he kept written records of all the money he had given her or loaned her for various small time business ventures, most of which had strategically gone belly up. Except for this building.

She owned this building, didn't she? Robert held the mortgage and she was paying it off. But he had given her the down payment, so this was like robbing Peter to pay Paul. Maybe she could get a second mortgage on the building, but they had just squeaked by on the first, and the brewery had not appreciated much in the last two years. It was filled with artists and musicians who barely paid their rent and never on time. Maybe fifty or sixty thousand is all she could clear, but not after the appraiser realized that the place needed a new roof.

Robert was out-of-town for two whole weeks. That gave Marjorie all the time she needed to make life miserable for Cydney. Marjorie didn't need the money, so what was she trying to pull? Cydney stood up in a daze and tried to remember what it was she had to take care of immediately. The shoebox fell out of her lap and the contents spilled out on the floor. She stared at the necklace, transfixed for several minutes. She didn't like what she was thinking.

"Eight or nine hundred thousand dollars, huh?" She picked up the necklace and let the light catch on the diamonds, bursting into prisms. The hummingbirds dangled, shimmering, their wings, delicate filigree, almost moved. Cydney felt herself calming down. Options. She always worked best if she had options.

"I could give her the necklace as payment on the loans. When he doesn't win the Senate race, I'll take the necklace back. Yeah, sure...how am I gonna do that? Well, I'll tell Robert that it's stolen, which it sort of is. Not sort of – let's face it – it is."

She put the necklace back in the jewelry case and snapped it shut.

"I can't believe I am even considering this! That woman is going to make me nuts. I don't care what time it is. I'm ready for a drink."

The phone rang while Cydney was looking for the tonic water that she was sure was in her kitchen somewhere. With a glass full of gin and ice she scanned the loft looking for the whereabouts of the portable phone Robert had given her last Christmas. Was it under a cushion? She listened to the shrill but muted beeps. Cydney groaned. She was turning into Pauline, with stacks of last month's unread newspapers all over the living room floor. She tripped on a laundry basket and out fell the phone, still ringing. Maybe it was Robert. Sometimes he called her ten times a day to complain about everything from Marjorie barking at him to his secretary's having PMS.

"Hello?" Cydney answered, hoping she didn't sound too out of breath.

"Did you get the letter?"

Marjorie's voice. Cydney hung up.

TWO DAYS LATER, WITH CYDNEY sitting on a shoebox full of priceless jewelry, Robert – now on the campaign trail – still hadn't called. But Marjorie's accountant had – at least six times – politely but forcefully insisting on immediate repayment of principal before Robert's books came under public scrutiny. Cydney, in desperation, took the shoebox and its contents into downtown Boston to the Jewelry Building on Washington Street to see Leonard Mendelsohn, an old friend of her father's, for an appraisal. Leonard was probably not the swiftest gemologist in the city, but at least she could trust him.

"So, little Cydney, will ya check her out! Some looker you turned out to be. Just like your Dad, poor Kevin, may he rest in peace. What...?" Leonard reached across the counter and grabbed Cydney's left hand. "No wedding ring? A good-looking girl like you can't land herself a rich husband? What's the world coming to?" Leonard was an old drinking buddy of Kevin's who had managed to keep his liver intact, as Kevin had not, although he did look a decade older than his fifty-five years.

Cydney took the shoebox out of a Star Market grocery bag and put it on the glass counter. Leonard had a small showroom off the center aisle of the building and at that moment Cydney was his only customer. "Ok, Lenny, lock the doors." She opened the box and lifted out the humming-bird necklace, holding it out on her spread fingers.

He whistled, long and low. "Where the hell did you get that?" he asked, fixing a small lens into his right eye.

"It's a long story. But it's not stolen. Sort of on loan."

He stared at her with his left eye, squinting. "On loan, huh? *Ohhhh Kaaay.* You know, something like this was once on an old cover of Vanity Fair, back in the 1930s. So, what's it doing here, Cydney?"

"Safekeeping. I'm holding it for my grandmother. Her sister is married to the guy who originally bought it for his first wife. What I really need to know is whether or not it's genuine."

Leonard let the jeweler's glass drop out of his eye. He shook his head. "Frankly, I'd say this looks almost too good to be true. The diamonds are flawless. It could be a very expensive fake. That wouldn't be unusual for a signature piece, to have a costume match made. The original must be worth close to a million. If this is the duplicate, and I think it is, then it's still worth a few thousand, say four or five, for the workmanship alone, but I think the diamonds are synthetic. I'd have to send it out to be assayed, to be sure. Take about a week."

Cydney knew that she didn't have a week. Frankly, she was relieved it was a fake. Now she could give the necklace to Marjorie and pretend it was real. That would shut Marjorie up until Cydney could get in touch with Robert. By then Marjorie might have figured out that it wasn't real, but that woman was so vain she would already have worn it to a dozen fundraisers and gotten so many compliments that maybe she wouldn't care. And even if she did, it bought Cydney a little time to come up with the next battle plan. Perfect.

"Thanks, Lenny. You've been great. You told me what I expected to hear. Forget about having it tested. Can't let this baby out of my sight." Cydney wrapped the necklace up in the shoebox, feeling as though a tremendous weight had been lifted from her. "So who're you voting for in the Senate primary?" she asked as she started to leave.

"Hey! No contest. Local boy makes good. Bobbie Bretton, of course. Known that kid since he was in diapers. Didn't he used to go out with your sister before he married that rich bitch and took over her father's mill? Never voted Republican in my whole life, so this is a new one for me."

"Well, Len, do me a favor. If you see a picture of the rich bitch wearing this necklace to some gala fundraising event, don't be surprised."

Cydney winked at Leonard's open mouth and waved herself out the door.

As CYDNEY OPENED THE DOOR to her loft, she could hear Marjorie's low, honeyed voice on the phone answering machine. "This is no joke. Robert's on the road. We've hired a crackerjack campaign manager who's run three senate races before and really wants this. I've given him a list of people who are not allowed through to Robert and guess who's name is at the top of the list?"

Cydney could tell that Marjorie had been drinking. She picked up the phone mid-sentence. "Nice try, Marjorie, but forget it. Robert isn't a dog you can lead around on a leash. He's already called me twice this afternoon. I know exactly how to reach him at any time."

"Look, cut the shit." The honey drained out of Marjorie's voice. "I want that money repaid, and I want it within twenty-four hours."

"Or what?"

"Or I will make your life a living hell. And I'll make sure that you never see Robert again. You've ruined our lives and I'm sick of it. And, by the way, don't think you're the only one. Not exactly fresh meat anymore. Tainted meat maybe..."

Cydney could tell that Marjorie was getting sloppy drunk. Maybe she wouldn't even remember the conversation.

"Why is he still mine? He knows where his bread is buttered – believe me," Marjorie continued with a hiccup, "and you can kiss him goodbye, because we're going for something we both really want – to win this Senate race and get out of this shit-box city and into the limelight where I belong."

While her voice rose, Cydney could hear something crash in the background.

"And you are not going to stop me. Just try selling your story to some tabloid. Who's going to believe an ex-stripper? Besides, Robert would be so pleased to see you strangle his one chance at the big time. Nope, it's curtains for you, sweetie. This is a pay up or die phone call. Pay up and I'll leave you alone..."

Cydney cut her off. "Marjorie, the answering machine is still on, so now that I've taped the call, maybe I can sell that to the tabloids. Go threaten the housekeeping staff. You've picked the wrong girl." Cydney hung up, furious. "Fuck him!" she yelled, throwing a stack of pillows against the wall. "She can have his sorry ass. I never wanted to marry him. If I had he would have left her ages ago." Cydney hated being shoved in a corner with no options.

When she calmed down, getting sloppy drunk herself, emptying the contents of her father's whiskey flask, she realized that Marjorie was right. She had no credibility, and she couldn't blackmail Robert, even to save herself. Was any of this true? He had said that he would hardly be able to call for two weeks, which was unlike him. And she had twenty-four hours until Marjorie hit the warpath. She picked up the shoebox and opened it; these jewels had to be fakes. If she gave them to Marjorie as repayment of the loans, maybe she could buy herself some time.

Sunday, Nov. 5, 2006. Late Afternoon.

AFTER LEAVING THE CEMETERY, LILLIAN and Cydney drove in silence for almost an hour. The trees on either side of the unfamiliar country road shook out the last of their leaves onto the wet pavement, leaves swooping like dying birds and landing splat on the car windshield. Lillian drove in a dark fog, the air misty with the sudden change of seasons from autumn to winter. Robert's driver had given her directions that, had she not been so unnerved by the casual announcement of Bianca's death, she should have been able to follow.

Instead, she must have missed the turn-off to the private Lake Williams Road several miles back and was stuck on a back road with no sign of human or commercial life. The Berkshires had become increasingly built up over the last few years, and it was vaguely unsettling to find herself so far from what should have been a recognizable signpost to somewhere. Her cell phone couldn't get a signal and Cydney didn't have the phone number of Robert's house. And to make matters worse, as Marc had warned her, it was really starting to snow, changing from big dancing snowflakes to long sheets of white drifting down from the skeletal treetops that formed a canopy over the advancing car.

"Well, that was interesting," said Cydney with a straight face, staring out into the changing weather from the passenger seat.

"Which part, exactly?" Lillian had slowed down, looking for anything resembling a road sign through the sleet and blowing leaves. "The part where you stuck your tongue down Robert's throat? Or the part where you looked like you were going to pull a gun on his security guys?"

No answer from Cydney. Unusual.

"Cyd, take off the glasses and look at me. What's with you? Even Robert asked me."

"Asked what?"

"Well, like—why I wasn't at your mother's funeral, for example. How stupid did I feel? Here I am, babbling away about how great it is that Bianca's heart is still going strong, and he's looking at me like I'm nuts."

But Cydney didn't budge. "Do you have any water in the car?" she asked.

"Yeah, right behind you on the back seat."

Lillian watched as Cydney rummaged through her bag and pulled out a large brown prescription bottle from which she took three different colored pills and popped them in her mouth.

"Headache," Cydney said with a shrug.

"Must be some headache." Lillian tried to concentrate on the road, now single lane and deeply rutted with trees leaning in on both sides, blocking out any remaining light. "Then why are we fighting our way through the woods if you have a headache? At this rate we'll have to spend the night there. This is the wrong road for sure…"

"What time is it?" Cydney asked.

"Why? Is there someplace you're supposed to be?"

"I need to remember what time I took those pills."

"Then get a watch, Cydney. What are you? Eight years old?"

"Look, I'm asking you a simple question. What time did I take the pills?"

"It's 5:30; we've been driving for almost an hour. What are the pills for?"

"I told you. For my head."

"Oh, the jokes I could make," Lillian said, gripping the steering wheel and starting to make a u-turn. "Seriously. What are they for?"

"To improve my memory."

"Good idea. Your memory could use improving. How's your mother, by the way?" Lillian knew she might be pushing Cydney with the mention of her mother.

"Dead."

That stopped Lillian short. "Cydney, what is going on? I shouldn't be making jokes about this. I'm sorry." She turned to look at Cydney in the light of the dashboard. "What's going on? Seriously. Are you sick?"

Cydney was silent for a long time, chewing on her lower lip. "Mom died about two years ago; you knew that, Lillian. I sent you a card."

Lillian tightened her grip on the car and stopped mid-turn. "Cydney, you are really creeping me out. I got no such card and you just told me, I swear to God, a few hours ago – I asked you how Bianca was…"

"Oh yeah. You did. I just didn't have the heart to tell you. But now that I've seen Robert I guess I feel differently." Cydney stared into her lap, hands folded. "Look, I have to take my pills again at 7:30, ok? Will you remember that, please? It's an experimental protocol; they have to be right on time."

"Ok, 7:30," said Lillian, distracted by the sleet pinging the windshield and the wind picking up. "Look at the map again and try to figure out where we are."

"I should plug in my phone – it's almost out of juice."

"Shit, I should plug mine in too – it's in my bag," Lillian said, trying to reach behind her.

Cydney grabbed the steering wheel to steady it. "Watch out! You're going to drive us off the road…" Just then she pointed to the right of her window. "What's that?"

From the corner of her eye, Lillian saw a large shape crash out of the woods toward the car. Instinctively she hit the brake and the rear wheels spun out, bucking the car forward in a dizzying spin. It plunged into something massive – so large that the thing blocked out any light from the windshield, crashed onto the hood of the engine and shook the car violently. The engine stopped dead, jerking Lillian and Cydney forward into the inflating air bags, as the creature thrashed on the collapsing hood. Another jerk and something kicked through the windshield on the passenger side, showering glass pellets over Cydney. Lillian heard someone shrieking from a distance, short high-pitched screams, unearthly – *stop it, stop it now* – until she realized that her own mouth was open and the sounds, like gargling splinters of glass, were coming from her.

II

THE BREAKDOWN

6:00 PM. Sunday, Nov. 5, 2006.

LILLIAN AND CYDNEY SAT PARALYZED in the front seat of Lillian's Volvo, protected from the shattered glass by the airbags that threatened to choke Cydney. The thing, whatever it was – a large creature – had collided with the right front fender and collapsed on the engine hood in a heap of flailing hooves and bellowing grunts. Within seconds it slid off the hood and onto the pavement in front of the car, continuing to buck and flail in a death spiral. Blood splattered down from the cracked windshield onto Cydney's legs. Lillian kept screaming. Cydney did not say a word and stared straight ahead.

"I killed it, *oh-my-god I killed it.* I'm afraid to look," Lillian wailed, head in her hands, eyes covered.

"You killed it alright. I think it was a moose. It could have killed us."

"I am a much bigger baby than you, go out and see what's going on." The thing, whatever it was, bellowed in agony and the car shook again.

Cydney struggled with her door, which was dented off its hinges from the impact. "I can't. It won't budge. I'm stuck." The reality of sprayed glass and blood all over her began to sink in. "Christ, I'm covered in shit, get me out of here."

"Ok, Cyd, relax." *Why*, thought Lillian, *would anyone relax?* Her mind raced. "Ok, stay calm."

"I am calm; I'm disgusting and I hate it when animals bleed to death all over me," she said, her voice rising and returning to her no-bullshit self. "What is *wrong* with you, Lillian? Running over a moose? Are you *out* of your *fucking* mind? *You* get out of the car," she ordered. "Your door is the only one that will open."

Lillian gingerly pushed her door open, terrified that more moose, a whole herd of moose, might be out for revenge. She stumbled out onto the slippery road, one shoe on, the other stuck somewhere under the inflated airbag.

It was a moose, glassy eyes staring up at her in reproach from the crooked angle of its contorted head. It breathed snots of steam from its huge nostrils, as it tried to get back on its feet. Lillian felt faint and couldn't control the shaking in her right knee. She leaned against the car for support and threw up on a pile of oak leaves just as Cydney squeezed herself out the driver's side door, gun in hand.

"Christ, it is a moose. We could have been killed. What do we do now?" Cydney was wrapped in her black and purple shawl, both shoes on and intact. She held the gun in both hands at arms length and dug her feet into the ground. "Rule number one of driving is *never* run over a moose. They are the caterpillar tractors of the animal world. We're lucky we're alive." She fired once at the animal's head and absorbed the gun's retort with a roll of her shoulders. She fired again, and the moose fell back to the ground with a thud, one hoof quivering violently, a dark pool spreading under its head. Cydney stood silent in the road and watched. "Poor thing. I hope its mother wasn't around." She turned back to Lillian. "But your car is sure fucked…" she said, as she sidestepped Lillian's crumpled figure hanging on the side of the car and still retching, unable to stop shaking.

"*Oh* my god, you said the gun was a fake…" Lillian could barely process what had just happened.

"I guess not, huh? Good thing. Poor creature. It's just a baby. You can't let them suffer like that." She walked over to the dead moose, its hooves still twitching.

"Are you fucking nuts?" Lillian thought she must be dreaming. "I'm going to faint."

"You've already puked. You're not going to faint because we have to figure out what to do. I doubt that your car will start."

"Thanks for that observation," Lillian said weakly. "That's great. My car is totaled, the gun is loaded, you've lost your mind and I'm stuck in the woods looking for the house of a US senator, so he can tell me the whereabouts of my grandmother's jewels, missing, thanks to you, for twenty-five years."

"Look, I am not listening to you rant. I'm walking to somewhere. Are you staying here or are you coming?"

Lillian straightened up and wiped her face. "Get back in the car, Cydney. It's really coming down, and you can barely see the road. You can't walk in those shoes anyway. Why you would wear spike heels to a funeral is beyond me," said Lillian, reaching in the back seat for her water bottle.

"I could take off these spike heels and use them as a lethal weapon on your head right about now." Cydney paced back and forth in the middle of the road, suddenly furious.

Lillian was focused on the gun that was still in Cydney's right hand. *Medications. What was she taking?* Maybe Lillian had totally misread everything; maybe Cydney was really unstable. "Ok," she said, trying to sound calm. "Ok. A car will probably come by any minute now. Please, let's just get back in the car and stay warm."

Cydney continued pacing in the inch deep snow, the gun dangling loosely from her right hand. She made no move toward the car.

"Come on, Cyd. Give me the gun, Ok? You did the right thing. You can't let an animal suffer. You're right." Lillian hoped she sounded reassuring and not freaked out. No answer. Cydney stopped moving and her shoulders seemed to sag. She shook her head and burst into tears.

In the thousands of hours they had spent together years ago, Lillian had never seen Cydney shed a tear.

1981. November.

BABY GRAND WAS STRUGGLING TO get off the ground. Orders were coming in and Lillian and Cydney produced goods as fast as they could, but their cash was running out. The only way Lillian could meet the December deadline of her first payment to Benny Finance was to collect her grandmother's jewels and use them for collateral for a major loan. So, before Thanksgiving she drove up to her parents' home in Burlington, Vermont, to appeal directly to her father. Shortly after she arrived, word came that the private plane carrying Sir Geoffrey and Isabelle home from the Bahamas had crashed on takeoff. There were no survivors. In shock, she and her father drove up to Montreal to prepare for the funeral.

TWO DAYS LATER, WAKING UP to a late autumn snowfall, Lillian surveyed the state of neglect that had befallen the mansion that her grandfather had won—or so the story went—from a famous railway baron in a grand stakes poker game in 1920. Standing in the entrance hall and staring into the gaping darkness of vast rooms leading off in four directions, Lillian was struck—as she had been many times—by the realization that this was why her grandmother had gone nuts. The living room was cavernous, larger than a basketball court, and filled with heavy antique furniture whose ornately clawed feet poked out from under the protective cover of white sheets. The house had been closed up since Lady Alice's death eleven months earlier, and large sections of it had been unused for many years prior to that.

Lillian stood in the middle of the living room unable to move. Maybe it was the cold, or the sudden turn of events, but she suspected it was fear. How could her timing have been this bad? Why hadn't she claimed the jewelry earlier? As soon as the funeral was over she was heading down to the bank. Her father assured her that no one had access to the bank vaults and they hadn't been touched since her grandmother's death, but still...the whole thing made her uneasy. Sir Geoffrey had always made a big deal about timing; how it was the intangible element in every business success. And now the timing was all wrong. He was dead, and she was in hock to all the wrong people.

With only an hour before the funeral, Lillian forced herself to get moving. She grabbed the corners of the furniture covers and yanked them off the sofas and wing chairs. Dust rose like the dawn. Pulling open the velvet tasseled drapes on the floor-to-ceiling windows, she hoped that the view would be dazzling enough that no one would notice the cobwebs. It was some view: the snow had stopped, leaving a thick layer of white crystals. The sun glistened from every surface all the way down the cantilevered terraces blasted into the side of Montreal's second and smaller mountain – Westmount – down the two thousand foot granite drop past dangling rock gardens, down further to the city curled at its feet, out to the blue winding ribbon of the St. Lawrence and into the foothills of the Adirondacks and White Mountains beyond. It was the precursor to another unyielding winter.

As a child, Lillian had loved this view; it was like growing up as a princess in the tower of a castle and scanning the horizon for just the right battle to fight. She had lived in this huge house with its butterfly staircase and dumbwaiters and grand pianos and Victorian conservatory until she was ten, when her own parents finally remarried eachother and took her with them to what could have been the opposite end of the world – one and a half hours away – to the sturdy barns of Burlington, Vermont.

LILLIAN'S FATHER, SAMUEL ADAM KUPER, was the fifth and last son of British immigrants and department store founders, Sir Geoffrey and Lady Alice Kuper. Samuel's birth in 1929 heralded the onset of some indefinable affliction of Lady Alice's mind that was to cause her to smile vaguely at everything and everyone, and largely excused her from the rules of social etiquette for her remaining years. At the same time, Sir Geoffrey became devoted – in a fashion altogether unseemly for someone in his position – to his wife's sixteen-year-old maid, Isabelle, and the result was that Samuel grew up without much supervision of any kind.

The Kupers had immigrated in the early years of their marriage from post-WWI England to Canada, settling in Montreal in 1919. They brought with them their titles and little else. The titles greatly improved their social standing in their adopted land, given that they had two strikes against them: they were broke and they were Jewish. With the little money he could put together, Sir Geoffrey bought three small furniture stores and amalgamated them under the name, *Chez Kuper*. He knew that in New York his cousins, in the same business, could offer larger selections of merchandise at better prices and turn their inventory faster. Using the same model, *Chez Kuper* was an immediate success and within two years had trebled in size. *Chez Kuper* was especially popular among the French and the Jews, groups that were usually looked down upon by the establishment Anglos. The French frequented the store because the merchandise was cheap, they could pay on credit, and the salesmen spoke their language. The Jews were devotees because Sir Geoffrey was one of their own.

By the time of the birth of their eldest son, Sir Geoffrey and Lady Alice had purchased a grand stone Tudor-style mansion perched at the top of Westmount, the smaller of the two mountains dominating the island of Montreal. The summit mansion was a symbol of Sir Geoffrey's success in a bilingual city with as many social layers as an onion has skins.

Although Sir Geoffrey spent a good deal of time spreading the story that he had won the house in a poker game, it was actually purchased – for a song – from a bankrupt railway baron who had built it out of the side of a cliff at the turn of the century in a marvel of engineering. Westmount at the time was largely uninhabited except at its lower reaches. At its 2,000-foot peak, the mountain was heavily forested and dropped precipitously down its granite southeastern cliff to the city below. Since no roads had been constructed up to the summit, anyone who chose to live there was either an ecclesiastical hermit living in harmony with the elements, or a self-made millionaire attempting to conquer them.

With the birth of their last child, Samuel, came the stock market crash of 1929, and the ruin of several prominent men who owed Geoffrey Kuper a good deal of money that he would never see again. After the crash, *Chez Kuper* – having expanded from furniture to a major department store – suffered greatly. A good deal of the store's merchandise was sold on credit, and that credit was suddenly worthless. Sir Geoffrey's fortunes would have teetered on the edge of disaster if he hadn't been blessed with an unexpected trump card. Throughout 1928 and 1929 he had invested heavily in the stock market, but, in anticipation of expanding *Chez Kuper* beyond Toronto, had been forced by the bank financing the expansion to sell off as much as half his stock market holdings. Even though they were sold at a tremendous profit, Sir Geoffrey was furious at being forced to liquidate in the bull market of August, 1929. Although he couldn't have anticipated it, that act proved to be a godsend. Two months later, when the market crashed and the world economy lurched into the Great Depression, he was sitting on a mountain of cash.

It was out of the question to expand *Chez Kuper* beyond Toronto, and Sir Geoffrey was consumed with rage at not having acted more boldly. Why hadn't he sold off even more of his stock holdings? In fact, he had done far better than many of his contemporaries, who, facing financial ruin, were jumping out of windows. The inadvertent stock market windfall supported the Kupers, albeit in somewhat reduced circumstances, for some time to come.

GEOFFREY AND ALICE WERE SECOND cousins, sharing the same great-grandmother. They did not, however, look at all alike, except in one respect; they were both exceedingly fair, with white-blonde hair and pale skin. Otherwise they were a curious couple, with Alice towering over her husband, smiling into space as though she knew he was somewhere down there but wasn't entirely sure where. It was a good thing that her sons were tall, or she would never have been able to keep track of them. Alice drifted from room to room, humming, almost floating, smiling with equal depth at the dog, a child, or the coffee table. Her hair was often worn loose, draped over her shoulders like the fringe on a shawl, combed out to the texture of linen several times a day.

Alice was considered quite beautiful, in an ethereal, drowned-Ophelia way. She had a perfectly chiseled profile with a long nose and long neck, cocked slightly to the side. Her eyebrows were always raised, as though she was about to ask a question, and her round eyes were a clear luminous green. Perhaps it was the lack of color in the eyelashes and eyebrows that gave her a perpetually staring, quizzical look. Or perhaps it was being surrounded by her growing sons and robust husband, whose lust for life included a series of prominent mistresses, as well as a collection of less socially desirable consorts.

Her health, after Samuel's birth, was a subject of some concern. Alice seemed to float off into another world from which she never completely returned, aided perhaps by the unfamiliar presence of her husband, whose business affairs, which were up in the air, provoked his own crisis of confidence. He stayed at home and brooded and shut out his children, his wife, and his consorts. He no longer dressed in the crispest suits ordered from New York or London. He lost weight, making him appear to be smaller than he already was. His brown eyes lost their elfin twinkle, and his beard and whiskers grew out untrimmed.

LATER THEY ALL AGREED THAT it was Isabelle who saved his spirits, and hence his life, and probably Alice's mind as well. Isabelle was no more than sixteen years old when she came to live in the house on top of the hill. Only one road suitable for cars made it up to the front driveway, and trolleys were unheard of in that part of the city. It could take two hours to reach the house on foot from the city below. Because of this it was very difficult for the Kupers to hire help by the day. In snowstorms no one would show up at all. And so, when they bought the house, Sir Geoffrey insisted that the entire staff should live in. Two months before Samuel's birth, Alice's personal maid suddenly gave notice and left without reason. Alice, a gentle soul who never lost her temper, nevertheless persisted in demanding an explanation.

It appeared that the young lady was leaving with enough money to live comfortably in the bosom of her large French-Canadian family and raise the illegitimate child who was to be born five months hence. Sir Geoffrey, whom Lady Alice assumed was the culprit, had little to say about the matter, but the very next day, Isabelle Chanteclair, the great niece of *Chez Kuper*'s office manager, showed up at the front door to apply for the position. She told Alice in broken English that she was nineteen years old, but Alice knew straight out that she was lying.

She hired her because winter was coming and once snow was on the ground it was difficult to entice anyone to the top of the mountain. And thinking her to be as young as fifteen, Alice hoped that Geoffrey might leave her alone. For several months he did, absorbed in business disasters, five growing sons, a wife who wore nothing but nightgowns and the surprising disappearance of his avid libido. But one early spring day, when Alice refused to get out of bed and the cook and the nanny had the afternoon off, Isabelle ran in frustration to Sir Geoffrey's room to complain that she couldn't possibly do it all. She did not come out for two hours.

The next day, Sir Geoffrey rose, shaved, ordered coffee on the terrace, dressed and had the chauffeur bring the car round so he could drive himself to the office. As soon as Geoffrey was out of the house, Alice got out of bed and life continued much as it had before Samuel's birth. Isabelle lived with them for the rest of their lives, sharing the affections of both, although in rather different ways.

LILLIAN STARED OUT THE BALLROOM window. "Snap out of it," she said to herself. Once she had thought the mansion magical; now it was just creepy and a nightmare to maintain. They really should have rented a hotel to invite people back after the funeral, but everything had been so rushed that no one had thought further than just getting Sir Geoffrey in the ground. Lillian retrieved the morning newspaper, opened to the obituary pages, from where it had been tossed onto the parquet wood floor. Sir Geoffrey merited a half-page obit with a picture from at least twenty years ago, and no mention of his second wife, whom he had married the day of his first wife's funeral, eleven months earlier.

THE WESTERN SLOPE OF MOUNT Royal, an extinct volcano that gave shape and name to the island city of Montreal, had been set aside as a gigantic cemetery. Here, Roman Catholics, Protestants of all varieties and Jews mingled together, and together crumbled to dust—albeit with some haggling over position, the highest terrace, the best view. And it was here, eleven months earlier, in a wild December snowstorm that Lady Alice Miriam Kuper was borne on the shoulders of her five sons to eternal rest. The men struggled with the coffin up the icy hill, while their eighty-six-year-old father, Sir Geoffrey, threatened a temper tantrum.

All of the Kuper progeny got their height from Alice. Geoffrey was shorter, portly as he aged. He had all his hair, worn long and wavy almost to his shoulders, hair so white it looked as though the color had been sucked out. His eyes were chocolate brown, wide and impish, which complemented a misleading dimple in his left cheek. One might think the appearance of the dimple meant a smile was on the way, but it was just the opposite. Often it signaled a rage so intense that blood vessels might shatter across his cheeks and nose. After these attacks, which became more frequent with advancing age, he looked more like an Irish drunk than a Jewish Baronet, although no one would have dared point this out.

Suddenly, in the midst of his bullying during the heave-ho of Alice's coffin up the hill, Geoffrey demanded a snowmobile. His eldest son, Ernest, told him point blank that this was ridiculous. His youngest,

Samuel, Lillian's father, suggested that it might violate the natural peace and quiet of a final resting place. No matter. The man was a self-made retail magnate who was accustomed to getting his way. He plunked himself down on a snow bank, looking like a fur-clad leprechaun with an ivory handled cane, and announced that he would not move until they brought up a snowmobile.

"Then to hell with you," said Samuel, and the group continued on without him.

So it might have been as they were lowering his wife of sixty-five years into the frozen ground without him—while he sat downhill in a snow bank—that Sir Geoffrey plotted his revenge. At the time, Lillian thought she would never forgive her grandfather for choosing that moment to make a scene. She should have known better. This was a man with perfect timing, and he had saved the best for last.

After the family and several dozen mourners had trekked back to the Kuper mansion, Sir Geoffrey announced to those assembled that there would be no traditional eight-day period of mourning. His wife had lived a good long life, dying in her sleep at eighty five, and what was there to mourn? And besides, he was going to marry Isabelle, Lady Alice's longtime maid, at last.

Well, the scraping of winter boots and slapping of fur coats was nowhere to be heard in the Kuper's majestic dining room. Friends and relatives froze over the trays of smoked salmon and whitefish as if they had been zapped with a ray gun. Sir Geoffrey had the chutzpah to produce a judge right there and then, pluck two reluctant witnesses from the astonished crowd, and take Isabelle Chanteclair to be his lawful wedded wife before God and the company of mourners present.

Once they got over the shock of his remarriage, Samuel and his brothers became concerned about their father's will. An estate worth between thirty and forty million dollars was no trivial matter, especially one managed with a tight fist by an aging eccentric. It wasn't just that their father had up and married the maid; it was also his increasingly erratic behavior that worried them. Who was in charge while he headed off to the Bahamas? And as for their new stepmother, well...everyone had known about Sir Geoffrey and Isabelle all those years, including Alice. Secretly, the whole family admired Isabelle for putting up with him.

Now they were both dead, their bodies recovered and returned to Montreal for burial.

LILLIAN COULD HEAR HER FATHER and uncles moving about on the upper floors as she entered the red velvet darkness of the shuttered dining room. Voices drifted down the stairwell as she rummaged through the sideboard looking for a tablecloth to fit the twenty-foot banquet table. Something about *"...getting dressed, the limousines would be here, had anybody called the caterer, had Sir Geoffrey been on speaking terms with the Rabbi...?"*

Lillian wrapped the bathrobe tightly around her, a robe she had borrowed–if that was the right word–from her dead grandmother. What a stupid question. Her grandfather had barely been on speaking terms with anybody, much less the Rabbi, especially after he had up and married Isabelle when his wife was barely in the ground.

But for the moment, she had to concentrate on feeding at least two hundred people who could be counted on to return to the house after the funeral. Since the family was skimpy on women–she was the only female progeny of her grandparents' five sons–and abundant on men–she had two younger brothers and twelve first cousins, all boys–another reason for Lady Alice to have slipped into questionable competence–no one had ordered food. Lillian asked two of her uncles as they stamped the snow off their boots in the entrance hall, but neither of them had called a caterer.

LILLIAN TRIED TO PAY CLOSE attention during the standing-room-only Memorial Service, but three or four hecklers claiming to be Isabelle's family made that difficult by interjecting pleas to acknowledge her death as well. Where was security? Any minute now her grandfather was going to spring to life, jump out of the coffin and start pounding his fist on the lid. He hated being interrupted. Over the years he had cracked four or five coffee tables by banging on them when somebody was rude enough to cut him off.

But the Rabbi had a voice that was accustomed to speaking to multitudes. He turned up the volume. "Founder of a mighty retail chain, famous world-wide, and bearing his name, *Chez Kuper*, of which he was enormously and rightly proud…"

Her father, Samuel, who was sitting beside her, whispered, "…and mad as a hatter."

She wondered if the Rabbi would get to that part. He didn't. He overlooked Sir Geoffrey's brief marriage to Isabelle Chanteclair, and her relatives in the back went nuts.

LILLIAN WAS POSTED AS SENTRY at the carved gates to the cemetery, while the women waited in the limousines below and the men struggled up the hill in the wet snow. She was fairly sure that no interlopers could have followed them here after the chaotic service at Bronstein & Sons, because the tiny Spanish and Portuguese burial ground – the oldest Jewish cemetery in Canada – was not to be found on any map.

Lillian stamped her feet and wiped the fat wet snowflakes from her eyelashes. Her right toes were frozen; she couldn't feel them at all. What was taking so long? She needed to get to the bank and open the safety deposit boxes before everyone returned to the house. She fingered the keys in her pocket. A lifeline.

In the distance, she saw the group of men slipping down the hill toward the limousines behind her. Her sentry role over, she dashed past them to put a bouquet of lilacs – Lady Alice's favorite – on her grave, and then turned back to meet her father, who was waiting for her in his old green Toyota.

"We're going to the bank vaults this minute," he announced, starting the engine as soon as Lillian was in the car. "Evidently," he continued, slightly out of breath, "the house and all the accounts are under control of a temporary Executor until the estate is sorted out, which might take months. It's open season on his assets. Isabelle's relatives and creditors are appearing out of the woodwork. It's a mess." He pointed the car downhill and Lillian gave him no argument.

She had her father's permission. Her fledgling business would get off the ground. She could pay back the $100,000 plus $20,000 interest. Her children would never set eyes on Ritchie and Angie again. And Marc would know nothing about Benjamin Finance. Even though it was open season on Sir Geoffrey's estate, the timing could still work in her favor.

THE FORMER HEAD OFFICE OF The Royal Bank of Canada sat at the bottom of the hill. A rubber ball, dropped from the back terrace of the Kuper house, could have bounced down a vertical drop to the lower levels of Westmount, and kept on rolling until it hit sea level at the banks of the St. Lawrence River. Here the original port and city of Montreal grew up as the disembarkation point for tidewater ships offloading freight for overland bypass of the ferocious Lachine Rapids. Beyond lay the vast interior waterways of the Great Lakes, stretching into the heart of the continent. Banks, the lifeblood of commerce, made their mark on the old port city, and—even though power had shifted westward to Toronto and oil-rich Alberta—the Royal Bank still held some sway. Geoffrey and Alice Kuper, peers of the British Realm, felt very comfortable banking with an institution that was not shy about announcing its regal affiliation, even if in name only.

Alice's jewelry had been quite famous in its day; it was purchased by her husband in 1929 from the Madescu Atelier of Cartier in Paris. Madescu, a Romanian gypsy who had been an apprentice of Salvador Dali, designed a collection of necklaces known for their sinuous nature themes—twisting vines, wilting roses, splitting seedpods. Only a select number of pieces included animal forms, most of which were eventually bought up by the Duchess of Windsor, except for the hummingbird necklace owned by Lady Alice Kuper and bequeathed on her deathbed to her only granddaughter, Lillian.

SAMUEL SHIFTED THE CAR INTO low gear and kept his foot on the brake. Father and daughter instinctively leaned backwards in their seats against the pull of the steep downward grade, as they crunched their way slowly down the twisting roads. Lillian peered out through the condensation on the car windows at the passing houses of brick, granite, and stone, massive and impermeable against the elements. As a child she thought them stern and solid, big blocks of grey, brown and ochre. Now that she was older she was more generous in her interpretation; they had strength – unlike the flimsy clapboard houses of New England where she had spent most of the past fifteen years.

Checking her watch, Lillian knew she couldn't sound too eager to get that necklace. She crossed her fingers and willed the car to go faster.

Lillian and her father ran across Place D'Armes while shielding their faces from the wind whipping in from the St. Lawrence River a few hundred yards away. It was a wind that carried up through picturesque alleys and lanes, past boutiques and restaurants carved out of old warehouses and factories, a wind with its origins thousands of miles to the frigid unadorned north. A horse-drawn caleche clopped by, sleigh bells jangling. Plaid blankets were piled high on the seats of a cart pulled by a horse wearing earmuffs and plastic flowers. Waving his cigar at Lillian, the driver beckoned to the empty bench behind him with a wide, discolored grin. Lillian tried to smile back and shook her head. Depressing that she should be mistaken for a tourist in the city where she was raised.

She followed her father up the wide marble steps of the head office of the Royal Bank, steps that looked like they belonged to a cathedral and not a bank. Now that they were almost inside and the RCMP hadn't jumped out from behind a statue to nab them for grave robbing, she started to relax.

SAMUEL KUPER PUSHED A BUTTON next to an ornate slat of a thick iron grill, and a balding man wearing half-spectacles let them into the secured area. Samuel and Lillian both signed an index card that he carefully compared to a sample signature card on file, and the shiny head of the bald man bobbed up and down in satisfaction. He brandished a ring of dozens of keys that must have weighed five pounds and asked in heavily accented English if they would follow him through the two-foot thick metal doorway and down a flight of stairs to the basement.

After the balding attendant removed three large safety deposit boxes, Samuel and Lillian carried them to a private windowless room and listened while the man's footsteps receded, echoing up the narrow stairs. The door closed slowly behind them. Lillian blinked in the white fluorescent light, light-headed that they had made it this far. Her father, unshaven, looked much too tall for the cubicle.

He shook his head. "I feel like a criminal. I can't believe this is what two lives come down to. Stuff in boxes."

Lillian nudged him; they had to hurry. "Valuable stuff, Dad. You lived your own life. Nobody took anything from him while he was alive. It's ok." This was no time for Samuel to start getting sentimental.

He opened the first box, lifting the lid to reveal the glossy silver and blue trademark jewelry cases from Birks and Tiffany. He picked them out one by one, at least a dozen. Carefully, he snapped them open. Empty. He opened the second and third. Empty. Lillian gasped. She picked up another and slowly opened it. Empty, every one.

Calm down, she told herself. *There are two more boxes. Maybe Alice had moved the jewels into the wall safe at the house?*

They tried the second deposit box. Same thing. Now Lillian was starting to panic. She looked at her father. His hands were trembling; his face had turned white and waxy.

"Dad," she said, her throat dry, "is there anyone else with access to this box?"

"No. Only your grandfather. And he hasn't been here since last year. I brought everything down to the vault myself right after Mother died."

The third and smallest box was the one with the Art Nouveau jewelry suite. Lillian remembered precisely the size and shape and feel of the two purple felt Crown Royal bags with the gold drawstrings that held the necklace, earrings, bracelet, brooch and ring. Her scalp tingled as she lifted the first bag. Weight! It had weight.

"Thank God," she sighed as she pulled it out. It plunked as it landed on the linoleum tabletop. She tugged at the drawstring and pulled out a string of cut glass ornaments. She and Samuel stared at them in the palm of her hand. Ordinary glass. Lillian leaned back against the wall. It was much too hot in that room. Sweat trickled down her spine. Samuel's mouth was open. He looked like a fish gasping for air.

"That bastard. I can't believe he'd do this. Check the last bag."

Lillian lifted it out, feeling through the felt with her fingers. There was something there, heavy, and something rustling. She pulled out another chain of glass baubles, wrapped in paper. She undid the paper and held it open. It read:

Sorry, my dears, but consider this an IOU. No time to buy a proper wedding gift for Isabelle so this will have to do. Don't tell me... counting your chickens before they're hatched...? Haven't I taught you anything?
P.S. Please reattach these crystal pieces to the dining room chandelier. Make sure they're securely fastened.

The handwriting was Sir Geoffrey's. The timing was definitely Sir Geoffrey's. In life he had been a hard man to like, and so far, in death he was holding his own.

6:20 PM. Sunday, Nov. 5, 2006.

CYDNEY STOOD IN THE MIDDLE of the road, shoulders slumped, the gun dangling from her right hand, left hand holding her forehead. Lillian had never seen her cry, and this freaked her out almost as much as hitting the moose. She needed Cydney to be her practical, tough self.

"Hey, it's ok. Come back to the car, Cyd—we need to get out of the cold." Bracing herself against the wind, Lillian stumbled over to Cydney, who was standing in snow-covered leaves, and held out her hand. Cydney took it, swaying slightly in her heels. Lillian managed to grab the gun, still warm, and pull it away. She opened the back door and put the gun on the floor, pushing it out of reach under the driver's seat. Her knees almost gave out with relief. It occurred to her that the only other time she had held a gun was in Cydney's presence.

"Look, I'm sorry about the moose. Obviously, this is not the way I thought the day would go. But I didn't ask to be here, Cyd; I am doing you a favor, remember, by taking you to your boyfriend's house."

Cydney jerked her head up, eyes clearing and icy blue. "What is this, high school? You're not doing me a favor. He asked you to come talk about Marjorie and the goddamn necklace."

How did Cydney know that? Had she and Robert planned this in advance? "Yeah, well…" Lillian knew she was entering dangerous territory but couldn't stop herself. "That necklace saved your ass when Robert didn't want it anymore."

"Fuck you."

"Fuck *you*. You stole it, Cydney."

"You know damn well what happened." Cydney brushed her wet hair out of her eyes. "At least I didn't ransack my dead grandmother's bedroom looking for her fucking art ducko jewels."

"Art Deco," said Lillian emphatically. "Art Nouveau, to be technically correct."

"I knew that." Cydney glared at her, smaller than usual and soaking wet. "I'm an artist, remember?"

"Oh don't start with that shit. Get back in the car. Your legs are covered in blood—I can't tell if it's blood from you or from the moose. Here's a towel. It's the dog's towel, but it's all I've got."

"If I stay out here in the snow it will wash off."

"You can't stay out here. We're not dressed for a storm!" Lillian ducked as a large branch overhead groaned in the wind. "Suit yourself; I'm getting back in." Lillian squeezed past the collapsed airbag to crawl into the driver's seat and tried to start the car. The engine turned over and groaned. *Stutter. Stutter. Out.* It occurred to her that even if she could get it started, there was no way they could get around the moose. And from the looks of the collapsed hood, the engine was totaled.

Well, if they were stuck, and there was no place to walk to for help, at least she could try to clean up. With another towel from the back seat she brushed away the glass and examined the shattered windshield. It had caved in but stayed largely intact, as though a huge spider web was holding back a million shiny baby glass spiders from spilling all over the seat. She hung the towel over the windshield and sat back wondering what the hell to do. Maybe Robert would send someone to look for them.

She could see Cydney, pacing up and down just ahead, smoking and cradling her head in one hand. Her hair had lost its curl and was hanging down the back of her coat like a wet pelt.

"Cydney," she called out the window, "get back in the car. You're going to freeze." Lillian could hear pellets of sleet pinging as they hit the car. The temperature was falling fast.

"Look, there's water," Cydney pointed up ahead. "You can see it through the trees. Hear it, actually, pretty fast-moving. I think it must be a stream, maybe a river. Check the map and look for a river with a road that goes over it."

They must have had the same thought simultaneously, but Cydney came out with it first. "If this had happened a few feet from here, we would have been stuck on a bridge. What do you think of that?"

A shiver shot down Lillian's spine. "I do not have bridge phobias any longer, as you well know." She repeated this to herself.

Somewhere in the car a phone rang. Both women jumped and Cydney ran back to the car.

"Ok, it's my phone but where the hell is it?" It was too dark to see and the glass shards made it impossible to thrust around blindly. Lillian got out to give her more room. The phone rang at least six times and then stopped.

"I'm sure it's Robert and he'll call back. It'll be fine; it's not as bad as you think," Cydney said, hugging herself, teeth chattering.

"Not as bad as I think? Every time I see you some disaster is on the make. Look, Cydney, we have to stay in the car or we're going to freeze.

The trees are starting to ice over. The snow is really starting to come down – shit, I knew it."

Both women climbed into the back seat, waiting for the phone to ring, hoping that the battery hadn't run out. Lillian found a flashlight and a granola bar in the twisted glove compartment, and took a blanket and a bottle of water out of the trunk. They wrapped themselves in the blanket, shivering. Cydney leaned back into the seat, eyes closed, chewing her lip. In the ghostly light, she looked years older.

"What time is it?" she asked. "When did I take my pills?"

"Wait a minute…" Lillian sat up straight, remembering what Cydney had said about the pills. *"It's an experimental protocol. They have to be right on time."*

"What experimental protocol?"

1981. December.

After Lillian and her father left the Royal Bank vault empty-handed, they raced back to the Kuper household, where Lillian avoided the executors and snuck into her late grandmother's bedroom. She flung open the hidden drawers to Lady Alice's mother-of-pearl inlaid dressing table to find a ruby ring and a Rolex watch with diamond numerals. The bedroom safe had been emptied except for eleven gold Krugerands. She stuffed all of these in her purse and, in a last-minute survey of the room, grabbed the two miniature Gainsborough portraits off the wall. These were small enough to fit into her briefcase and together should fetch $50,000 at auction. Last, she picked up the framed St. Germain menu signed by Picasso with a note to Alice dated 1924 with a sketch of a dove. This, she would keep.

Authoritative male voices drifted up from the grand front staircase, and she had just enough time to slip out the back stairs and down to the kitchen when she heard the executor ask that all the bedrooms in the house be sealed. Over the next few days the news went from bad to worse. Dozens of relatives of Isabelle Chanteclair had filed claims to the Kuper estate, and Samuel predicted that it would be tied up for years in court, even if most of these were nuisance suits. Plus it was beginning to look as though Sir Geoffrey had been in far greater debt than anyone realized.

"I'm not surprised he was in debt," fumed Samuel. "He spent the last ten months on a private yacht. God knows what that must have cost."

As soon as Lillian returned from Sir Geoffrey's funeral, Angie from Benny Finance took to calling her twice a day.

"Heeyy! Where ya been, sweet cheeks? Skipping town?"

"It was an emergency, for heaven's sake. A funeral. Or doesn't that mean anything to you?" Lillian thought the fear in her voice probably measured nine on a scale of one to ten.

"It don't mean shit, unless somebody's left you big clams."

"Well, that's the point. I am selling some jewelry and can give you half the first payment ahead of time."

"Half? I'm jumping up and down with excitement."

"Look, it's two weeks early, ok? Can't you just take this as a goodwill gesture."

"Ouch…you really know how to hurt a guy. All right, first payment early – points on that. So what's the rest of the deal?"

"Meaning what?"

"Meaning what's in it for me? Or when do I get it in, if you get my drift." He made a clucking sound as though he was calling a chicken.

"Very funny…" was all she could manage.

"Yeah, I'm dying of laughter over here. Listen up. You got two weeks. *Two*. Next time you gotta leave town, make like I'm your travel agent. You know what I'm saying?"

Lillian started to answer, but all she could do was nod her head, useless over the phone.

"Good girl. Don't call me – I'll call you."

"Heeeeyy," ANGIE SAID WHEN SHE handed him the envelope in a restaurant on Hanover Street in the North End. "Good going. I knew you could do it with a little motivation." He sucked on a toothpick, flicking it in and out, like a serpent's tongue.

"Stay away from my kids or I'll call the cops. You think I don't mean it?" Lillian drew herself up to her full five-foot-ten. She stood a good inch above Angie and wished she were wearing heels.

"You're cute, you know that?" Angie spat the toothpick out. It hit Lillian on the floppy bow she wore at her neck and bounced onto the floor. "I've always had a soft spot for blondes, especially if they're natural, wink, wink." He traced his bitten-down fingernail along her wrist until she jerked her arm away, spinning around to pick up her purse.

"Don't touch me again," she said, swallowing hard, "or I'll...my husband's a lawyer you know..."

"Yeah? Big deal. We buy 'em by the pound. Next payment, thirty big ones, two months from today. Same time; same place." His hand was back on her wrist, stone cold. "And don't dress so fancy. Show some skin. We're pretty casual here." By "here" he was referring to the back room of the Paesano Ristorante where conversation stopped dead when Lillian walked in to see a dozen wizened male faces staring at her through clouds of cigar smoke.

Lillian grabbed her briefcase from the small café table and practically ran out to the light that spilled in from the North End's main drag, Hanover Street, her spirits rising in direct proportion to the growing distance between her and Angie. She had just enough time to put in a few more hours at BYO before their winter gala that evening.

WHEN LILLIAN AND MARC ARRIVED at the recently refurbished Cabot Center for the Performing Arts, the place was packed. The senior partners at BYO Advertising were holding a gala fund-raiser for the major arts organizations in Boston and expected to raise their goal of $2,000,000 before the night was over. It was a 'who's who' of the local arts scene and Lillian noticed that Robert Bretton's wife, Marjorie, was prominently featured on the steering committee. Lillian hadn't seen the candidate at Cydney's since her first visit, and every time she asked about him, Cydney changed the subject. Something was going on between them, but Lillian was too preoccupied to give it much thought.

"WHAT DO YOU CALL SOMEONE who's running for Senator?" she asked Marc, as they settled into their red velvet seats for a special performance by The New England Ballet. The orchestra was tuning up, sounding like an autistic child humming to itself off in the corner. "I don't want to make a faux pas."

"Just wave your boobs at him and gush. Don't shake his hand – he probably has to ice it down every night. Go for the eye contact and call him Senator. He'll love it."

"He may love it, but his wife may not be too thrilled." Lillian was quite proud of herself for fitting into the one long black gown she owned, but it was true that her breasts threatened to burst out of her décolleté.

"Have you seen his wife?" Marc asked. "I hear she's got big bucks and balls of steel. And a knock-out if you like that type. Mid-sixties look with the big hair and too much make-up."

People on either side of them were putting fingers to pursed lips in exaggerated slow motion.

"Are they trying to tell us something?" Lillian whispered.

"Yes, we're the only loud-mouthed Jews in the joint," Marc answered, just loud enough to be overheard.

LATER – AFTER THE PERFORMANCE and before dinner – while cruising the crowds in the elaborate lobby and balconies, Lillian thought this was entirely possible. It looked like WASP mating season – a blonde hair on black velvet stampede. Groups formed around several grand matrons with steel-wool hair and steel-blue eyes calling to each other in crow voices. The daughters of the grand matrons, marriageable women in their twenties who had once been little girls in tutus with fat, dimpled knees, were all dressed up in black taffeta and white diamonds. They were escorted by proper Bostonians in black tie, with a smattering of academic types in patch-elbowed jackets and threadbare corduroy. These sons and daughters of money and local power draped themselves over marble balconies and white linen café tables, plastic champagne glasses held aloft, eyeing one another over slender vases, each with a single dangerous rose, and then waving gaily.

As intermission was ending, Lillian almost tripped over Mickey Klein from BYO who was wearing a white nylon flight suit with about twenty zippers, many of them unzipped. Her hair was moussed and tousled into a pile of what looked like styrofoam on top of her head.

"Have you seen him?" she asked Lillian, grabbing her wrist.

"Seen who?"

"Robert Bretton. He's gorgeous!" Mickey said with a squeal, shuddering visibly.

But Lillian did not hear her because coming down the grand staircase to polite applause was Robert Bretton, beaming, in a navy blue Italian silk suit, which set off his bright blue eyes and very white teeth against his dark skin and just graying black hair. He seemed quite reserved for a politician, even shy, as he nodded gently to well-wishers and raised two fingers in a half salute to recognized faces in the crowd.

"Well, I don't know that he's gorgeous," Lillian began and then almost choked at the sight that followed.

Marjorie Bretton accompanied her husband at a distance of several yards, walking with regal bearing in his wake. Like her consort, Marjorie was in her early and very well preserved forties. They were the same height, which may have been why she walked behind him, so as not to overwhelm with high heels and hair spun up in a golden beehive. Marjorie beamed at the crowd, as though she were the candidate, extending an elbow-length gray kid-gloved hand to various patrons. She had a dazzling smile and large eyes that turned down slightly at the outer edges, giving her a sorrowful—even mystical—look. The look was reinforced by unnaturally dark eyebrows that were, in fact, tattoos.

As she strolled triumphantly through the freshly painted gold-leaf columns to appreciative murmurs, small explosions of light flared up from the cluster of jewels at her long neck, made longer by an off-the-shoulder gray satin sheath with plunging décolleté. From a distance, the Brettons made a handsome couple, which was exactly what people were turning to each other at that moment and saying, until Lillian let forth a shriek.

"My birds!"

As if on cue, everyone looked up to search the ceiling painted with puffy white clouds and trumpeting cherubs against a blue and gold background. No birds.

THE BIRDS IN QUESTION NESTLED at Marjorie Bretton's throat, part of a rare suite of Cartier jewels, including three lifelike ruby and baroque pearl hummingbirds shimmering amongst emerald-encrusted inlaid flowers and cloisonné leaves—a prized possession of Lillian's recently deceased grandmother, from whose safety deposit box the $900,000 necklace with matching earrings, bracelet and ring had mysteriously disappeared.

"How did you get them?" Lillian demanded, pushing her way to the front of the crowd, reaching for the necklace at Marjorie's bejeweled throat. The crowd hushed for half a second and then broke into a low-level babble.

Robert Bretton had circled back to stand between Marjorie and Lillian with a look of growing concern.

In the meantime, Lillian had managed to regain some of her composure. She took a deep breath. "I believe, Mrs. Bretton, that you are wearing a piece of family jewelry of great sentimental and monetary value. Perhaps you are unaware of its origins, but it belongs to me."

Marjorie gestured vaguely to her throat as though waving a chiffon scarf of minimal importance. "Oh, surely there's been some mistake," she oozed in her most seductive voice, looking around with affected helplessness.

"Perhaps we should talk about this privately," Robert interrupted, taking his wife by the elbow and leaning sympathetically toward Lillian.

"I'd be happy to, Mr. Bretton—nice to see you again—because I'm sure we both want to clear this up before Interpol is alerted that my necklace has been found," Lillian said in a subdued voice.

Robert turned around to stare at his wife's neck as though he had never seen it before. "Interpol...? I can't imagine what you mean." He looked back at Lillian with a sudden flash of recognition.

"There's obviously been a mistake," Marjorie said in a voice as chiseled as the diamonds that twinkled at her throat. But beneath the polish, it seemed to Lillian that husband and wife glared at one another with barely concealed rage, broken only when a young man in silver bowtie and blond hair falling in his eyes appeared and whispered in Robert's ear. Evidently, it was time to get to the head table and put this embarrassment behind them.

"Well," Robert bowed slightly to Lillian, "as you can see we are here for the evening and I assure you that we'll settle this matter. Here is my card with my personal number. Let's meet in my office tomorrow, first thing." At that, the bow-tied blonde pulled him away, leaving Marjorie alone with Lillian.

"I don't know how you got hold of that necklace, Mrs. Bretton, but I intend to have it back before the evening is out."

"Yes, well, my husband will straighten this out. The necklace is on loan from one of his clients."

"Really?" Lillian brightened. "Who?"

"Cydney Mallone. I'm sure you can take this up with her. And frankly," she fingered the hummingbirds, catching a nail on an enameled feather, "I think it's overdone and much too heavy to wear. Now if you'll excuse me, there are a great many people here to meet my husband, and I must get back to him." She turned abruptly and sashayed up to the head table where the hummingbirds with their ruby heads and cloisonné wings shimmered in the light of the chandeliers.

The blood drained from Lillian's face as she watched Marjorie and her inheritance disappear. Turning Robert Bretton's card over and over in her sweaty palms, she leaned against a marble column and thought she might faint.

Cydney? Oh my God – what did she do?

6:45 PM. Sunday, Nov. 5, 2006.

LILLIAN PULLED THE BLANKET TIGHTER around her legs. The temperature in the car was dropping fast, and at least an inch of snow had piled up on the shattered windshield. She blew on her hands and clapped them together. "What experimental protocol?" she repeated.

Cydney's voice sounded dreamlike, slow and almost slurred. "They did a bunch of tests at Mass General about a year ago and told me I have impaired functioning. That's code for some kind of dementia. Most likely a rare disease called Lewy Body. I was always such a trend-setter. They think it might have something to do with falling down that damn lift in my loft – remember? And landing on my head."

Lillian stared at her. "Lewy what? Is this a joke?"

"I wish. I have whole pieces of time when I can't remember where I am, what I'm supposed to be doing, or who I'm with. My lighting designer turned me in. Said I was having conversations with people who were not actually present. It's been going on for maybe two years. Finally, I saw a doctor, when I could remember to keep the appointment. Then another. And another. Tests and more tests."

"How is that possible? You're my age. Your mother was sharp as a pin. It doesn't run in your family, does it?..." Lillian tried to piece this together. The headaches. Bianca's death. The way Cydney's hand shook when she lit a cigarette.

"Well, who knows, it might. My father drank himself to death and his birth mother is – or was – somewhere in Fiji, never to be heard from again." Lillian remembered that Cydney's father, Kevin Mallone, was born in American Samoa – the result of an affair between Kevin's seafaring father and a local girl. "Anyway," Cydney continued, "they put me in a clinical trial on a special experimental program to test these drugs, related to Parkinsons…"

"And…"

"And I don't know. Sometimes I'll be working on a set and I can't remember what show it is, or what city I'm in, or what I'm supposed to do next. I've managed to fool enough people to keep my job. And the doctors say they're pleased, if you can trust them."

Lillian remembered that her uncle, Samuel's eldest brother, Ernest Kuper, had been diagnosed with a new form of dementia a few years back—was it Lewy Body? It sounded familiar. At the time she remembered thinking that it would make a great stage name. *What an asshole I am!* Ernest refused to believe that his wife of fifty years was actually his wife. He wouldn't let her cook for him because he was convinced she was going to poison him. Something called Imposter Syndrome. God, he had become so delusional! Cydney couldn't possibly be headed for something so horrible.

Lillian was quiet for a long minute. "Cyd, I don't know what to say. I really don't. What do they think will happen?"

She opened her eyes and looked straight at Lillian. "You mean, how quickly will I end up drooling in an institution?"

"Well, not…I mean…I hope…but you said the doctors were pleased…"

"Yeah, it's ok. That's exactly what it means. Depends on how well the experimental protocol—the clinical trial—works."

"What can I do? Can I do anything?"

"Well, you can keep talking about us in the good old days. Maybe that will help me remember who I used to be."

"I can do that. Easy. I'll be like…Scheherazade…" said Lillian, dragging out the syllables.

"Sounds like a perfume."

"You're thinking of Shalimar. Scheherazade is the Persian princess from the *Thousand And One Nights* who stayed alive by telling the king a different story every night so he wouldn't kill her."

Cydney thought this over. "Bedtime stories, huh? Ok. Deal. But get the gun, Lillian. We may need it."

"We don't need it, Cyd," said Lillian, although she could see her point. "Does Robert know? Is that why he wanted to talk to me?"

"I told you – I haven't seen him in years."

Clearly this was not true. Why would Cydney lie to her? Or was she lying? Maybe in her head she thought it was true.

"Get the gun, Lillian," Cydney said again, punching her in the arm. Her voice had a hard edge; sharp. "Because there are things out there. And we might need to protect ourselves from…" she looked around carefully, eyes narrowing.

"From…what?" Lillian put her hand on Cydney's to steady her. Cydney pushed it away.

"Maybe from Robert. He could send anyone to find us. They could take me away to an institution," she whispered.

"Cydney…are you making jokes?" Lillian lowered her own voice. "Because I can't really tell."

"He could. I'm the only one left who knows."

"Knows what?"

"I'm not talking anymore. Too dangerous. Give me my purse. You didn't go through it, did you? I can't have anyone touching my drugs. They're in a very specific order." Cydney reached for her purse and stopped, an idea forming. "Why did Robert want to talk to you? Interesting that you should mention this. Are you trying to scare me?"

What? "Cydney! I'm the one who hasn't talked to Robert in years. I have no idea what he wanted to talk about."

"Quite a coincidence that you just happened to show up in the middle of nowhere."

"I told you! I was on my way back from Cornell…"

"Yeah, I'm getting it now. Sure you were," Cydney said, leaning back in her seat, eyes cold and brittle. "So what's his plan? What's he going to do now that Marjorie's dead? He can burn all her papers and make it all go away. What are you doing with my purse? Give it to me!"

Lillian was still holding on to it, shocked. *What was happening?* Cydney yanked open her pocketbook and dug out a make-up case filled with prescription bottles. "What time is it?" She tried to open a bottle but her hands wouldn't work. "They're frozen. You do it."

Lillian noticed that Cydney's hands seemed unusually stiff and not just from the cold.

"*Please*, just open this." Cydney thrust the bottle at her.

"Cyd, calm down. Look, I'm opening it. These child-safe locks are ridiculous, but the bottle is...empty," Lillian said, staring into it with a sinking feeling in her gut.

Cydney took it and stared inside for a long moment. She looked up at Lillian, eyes even colder. "Again, interesting. Who did this? Was it you? Why are you trying to set me up?"

What the fuck? Lillian felt a shiver grip the back of her neck and slither down her spine.

1981. December.

The Boston Globe, December 10, 1981. Metro Section B. page 12:

The Cabot Center for the Performing Arts was abuzz last night with the movers and shakers of the local arts scene. Advertising Agency, Brigham, Yanofsky and Oldham (BYO), hosted a gala fundraiser for the New England Ballet and Opera Co. in the spectacularly renovated lobby and galleries of the oldest performing arts venue in town. The glitterati included recent winner of the Republican Senatorial primary, Robert Bretton, and his socialite wife, Marjorie Taylord Bretton, resplendent in an off-the-shoulder grey silk Valentino sheath and sporting a suite of eye-popping Cartier jewels—hummingbirds at her neck, ears and wrist. Rumor has it that this rare set once graced the cover of Vanity Fair in 1933. A minor incident occurred when a bystander insisted that the jewelry was stolen and belonged to her grandparents' estate, causing embarrassment to the political couple. Mr. Bretton defused the situation quickly and all the attendees proceeded to have a stellar evening of performance and food. Over one million dollars was raised.

Cydney looked up from reading the early morning paper and knocked over her coffee. A bystander? Lillian had left the shop early to get dressed for a fundraiser that Cydney suspected Robert would attend. Her biggest fear was that Lillian and Robert would run into each other and get chummy. She had forgotten that Marjorie might wear the jewels in public.

"Jesus, I am a moron," Cydney said out loud. How was she going to get out of this? So, that's what Lillian had been so upset about. Her grandfather had died – but really, everyone's grandparents were dying, nothing new about that. It was the jewels; they must have belonged to him. And that meant that Pauline's sister Isabelle was married to Lillian's grandfather. Pauline had been crying for weeks, which Cydney thought was overkill, as Pauline hadn't seen most of her huge, spread-out family in decades. Fortunately, neither Pauline nor Bianca had asked about the jewels. But Lillian would. Whatever Robert or Marjorie had told her, Lillian would put it together.

"Think fast," Cydney told herself, downing her third cup of coffee, but the phone rang before any thinking – fast or slow – could take place.

"Cydney." Lillian sounded hoarse, as though she had been crying. "You want to tell me what's going on?"

Cydney couldn't formulate words. She felt like crying herself. "I'm so so sorry."

"You're sorry?" No answer. "*You're* sorry?"

"I had no idea they were yours."

"*Where* did you get them?"

Cydney told her the whole improbable story. "I thought they weren't real! The appraiser said they were excellent fakes. So I gave them to Marjorie to pay back loans Robert gave me that looked bad on his background check. I knew that Robert would get them back to me as soon as he could."

"Cydney, you have no idea how much I have riding on that necklace. I borrowed money—$100,000—to get us off the ground. I borrowed it from some not great guys—loan sharks it turns out, and they want their first payment now. I mean now. I mean they showed up at my house and picked up David and wouldn't put him down."

"Wow. You are messed up with loan sharks? Do I know you?"

"*No!* The real question is *do I know you?* If I can't trust you, then how can we be partners? What do you have to do with Bretton and his wife? I'm not following this at all."

"Oh, we grew up together in Lawrell—Robert and I came from rat-poor dysfunctional families. Marjorie was the little lonely rich girl. She wanted him. He wanted me. She got him. He got her father's business. He got me. I'm still trying to figure out what I got—he was all set to divorce her when this senator thing came out of the blue…that's why you cannot go to the press. Is *that* clear?"

"No. Nothing's clear until I have the necklace back. Is that clear?"

"Listen, call Robert now. If you get nowhere, come over and we'll figure something out, ok? Don't panic."

Lillian called but was informed that Mr. Bretton would be in the western part of the state campaigning for several days. Mrs. Bretton was attending to business elsewhere. No way was Lillian going to wait until later to see Cydney. She had to get over there right now.

Right now turned out to be late afternoon, after Lillian realized that Jonny had another ear infection, waited for two hours at the pediatrician and then practically hog-tied him to swallow the thick pink antibiotic.

By the time Lillian arrived at the Steamboat Brewery it was almost dark. She was about to get out of the car when she saw Cydney emerge from an alley carrying a suitcase. She stopped at her '74 white Pinto and pried open the trunk. She could see the outline of Boris-the-wolf sitting in the passenger seat.

Why would Cydney leave without telling her? Lillian followed the tap-tap-tapping of Cydney's heels at a distance, hanging back in the passageway while Cydney got into a large hand-operated lift, closed the accordion-style iron grate, and chugged upward. Lillian watched the lift stop at the top level and gently sway in its suspended perch. Making a beeline for the open staircase, she ran up the three flights two steps at a time. She reached Cydney's doorway and pushed gently, stepping into the chaos of Cydney's personal design space.

Lillian had barely moved from the doorway when Cydney pushed her way through the muslin curtains, carrying another suitcase. She stopped abruptly, dropping the bag and almost tripping over it. "Lillian!" she said with a gasp, "is that you? Christ, you're tall. What are you doing here?"

"I'm early. Or late, depending on how you look at it."

"Well, I waited for you all day. It's late. How about tomorrow?"

"It looks like you won't be here tomorrow."

"What are you talking about?"

"The suitcases. In the car, under your feet. Sort of hard to miss. Generally it means someone is leaving town."

"You mean you've been spying on me?" Cydney's blue eyes narrowed.

"No, I came to see you and couldn't help but notice you carrying suitcases to your car. Is that a crime?"

"Well…well…why the hell didn't you say something instead of just sneaking around?"

"Because I was surprised. Because I didn't know what was going on. Because I don't trust you. How's that?"

"I'm bringing this stuff to my mother. You're not the only one who's upset. Pauline is hysterical that her sister is dead and the jewels she thought would put her on easy street are missing. Thanks to me." Cydney took off her hat and shook out her hair. She sat down on the suitcase, chin cupped in her hands, and stared at Lillian. "So Robert wasn't there, huh?"

Lillian shook her head, her eyes welling up with tears.

"Yeah, I tried him, too. Marjorie has got the entire housekeeping staff behaving like robots. Yes, ma'am, no ma'am. I'm the one who gives them Christmas presents every year and tells them how to get Marjorie to give them a raise. Suddenly, they're calling me Miss Mallone and telling me Mr. Bretton is unavailable. Christ, you can't trust anybody anymore."

"Well," said Lillian, looking around for somewhere to sit, "I'm so glad you know how I feel. So maybe you'd like to tell me what's going on."

Cydney gestured to an old wing chair in need of reupholstering, which appeared to be used as a cat scratching post.

"Watch out for the lift!" she said as Lillian almost stepped backwards into a long, narrow gaping hole in the floor about twelve feet long by five feet wide, retrofitted as a lift to haul up huge bolts of fabric. Cydney jumped up to turn on the overhead lights as Lillian stared down into the hole, which was surrounded by a flimsy cord on which hung a sign: "Fall down the lift and you're fired."

"Fired! How about dead?" Lillian wondered out loud. "When are you going to cover this damn lift? Our workmen's comp rates will go through the roof."

"Our *what?* Get real. Nobody bothers with that stuff. This is a private elevator shaft for moving things directly in and out of this space. It's not for people, just for stuff. I keep meaning to build a more secure barrier but I never get around to it." Cydney reached over and grabbed the control unit, which hung from a cord suspended over a beam in the ceiling and pressed the "up" button. The lift grumbled its way up from the ground floor, stopping with a jolt about eight feet below Cydney's space. For a second Lillian wondered why, and then she realized that the power had cut out, the lights had shut off, and she couldn't see a thing. She stopped moving, knowing that she couldn't be more than a few feet away from the open lift.

"Oh shit," said Cydney, "not again. I am sick and tired of the prima donnas in this building. Bunch of artists who don't pay the rent on time. Watch your step," she said, directing Lillian. "Keep moving to the right...Ok, the lift is behind you now. They probably haven't paid their electric bills in months and Edison is turning off the juice. Where's the damn phone? This is all I need."

In the dark, Lillian could see Cydney moving toward the wall and groping for the phone. But at that moment something came crashing in through a window behind them, sending splinters of glass flying through the air. Both women ducked, rolling themselves into groundhog balls on the floor, heads covered. Lillian tried to scream but made only choking noises.

A full minute passed before Lillian uncovered her eyes. Cydney had crawled along the floor parallel to the windows until she reached the shattered pane and pulled herself up to look out. Lillian could hear a car engine gunning and the squeal of rubber as the car pulled out fast on the street below.

"*Stop! You assholes!*" Cydney shouted through the gaping hole. "*Hey!* Somebody down there, do something!" She turned around to Lillian. "You ok? That was no accident. That was deliberate." Cydney began to collect hurricane lamps and candles, laying them out strategically on tables and shelves. "Christ, I was afraid of this," she said. "That's why I was I thinking of leaving, frankly." Soft pools of light blossomed throughout the cavernous space as she lit the candles, throwing greatly exaggerated shadows against the far walls. Cydney picked up a hurricane lamp and searched the floor. "Here it is!" she said, kicking a rock that was the size of a man's fist. "Come over here and look at this."

Lillian stood up, swaying slightly as the blood drained from her head. She made a mental note of the open elevator shaft behind her, then picked through the glass and walked over to the rock. It looked like an ordinary rock. Cydney was rolling it around with her toe. "This woman is too much." Cydney shook her head, speaking to herself. "And it is time I started taking her seriously. High time. Maybe even too late."

"What woman?" asked Lillian, looking around nervously. "No woman could have thrown that thing all the way up here."

"See this?" Cydney pointed with her toe. "This is a rock from the Boathouse Quarry in Lawrell—very distinctive, these brown veins. Anyone who grew up around there would recognize it. One side is even polished so you can't miss it."

"Yeah, so?" said Lillian.

Cydney looked at Lillian in exasperation. "Yeah, so it's from Marjorie, obviously."

"Robert's wife?"

"Look, if you can't catch on more quickly you should forget about trying to get that necklace back."

"Wait a minute! *You* are responsible for getting my necklace back. I don't hang around with people who throw rocks in my window—how am I supposed to catch on to any of this?"

"Haven't you figured it out yet? Robert and I have been together for years, which his wife knows only too well. Last night somebody jumped out of a fancy dress crowd and embarrassed her at a critical moment. Maybe she thought I hired you for the occasion, who knows? But she has every intention of paying me back." Cydney nudged the rock with her foot. "Exhibit A: I get this rock in my window, a signature piece, from a quarry where, when I was growing up, missing hoods turned up on a regular basis wearing concrete boots—you know what I'm saying?"

Lillian stared at her, mouth open. This was worse than the Benny Finance goon squad.

"You better understand what's at stake here," Cydney continued. "I didn't mean to lead you around, but that woman would be happy to throw me off a bridge. And if she thinks you're in this with me, you're in trouble too. That jewelry could be buried treasure by now, so my advice is to find Robert and see if he can figure out where she stashed it."

"What makes you sure she's stashed it somewhere?"

"This," said Cydney, hoisting up the rock. She pointed to the flat side on which was scratched: 'Come and get it.'

A GUST OF WIND BLEW in from the smashed window and knocked over a candle. It fell into a pile of fabric and sputtered. In the puff of instant darkness, both Cydney and Lillian tripped on each other to leap at the table and grab the fabric. Cydney got there first, grabbed the burning fabric, and flapped it against her legs and the back of a wrought iron chair until all the sparks were gone. Cydney went to get the large flashlight plugged into the wall and ordered Lillian to blow out the candles, because the wind was picking up.

"I hear something," she whispered, "listen."

Lillian froze as she blew out the last candle. She heard the sounds of footsteps on the stairs, squeaking through the iron grate. Cydney moved quickly through the loft, filled now with the white light of the rising moon, toward the door.

"Did you lock it behind you when you came in?" she hissed at Lillian.

Lillian shook her head. She could see the deadbolt still up at 90 degrees, not locked, the door ajar.

Cydney headed straight for the unbolted door, trying to feel her way around the open elevator shaft just as a black-gloved hand appeared on the inside of the door. Cydney picked up a heavy cardboard tube from a bolt of fabric, big as a baseball bat, and waited.

The hand turned into an arm and pulled the door open. Lillian fell flat on the floor and lay there, too terrified to think. *Where is the damn wolf when you need him? In the car with the suitcases. Shit.* The beam of a flashlight swept through the space, bouncing off the polished floor and ceiling, missing Lillian completely.

"There's nobody here," whispered a male voice, and a dark shape stepped into the room. Dressed in black and wearing sneakers, with a baseball cap pulled down low over his forehead, he shone the flashlight into the back of the loft toward the living space where the pile of glass glittered. But by keeping his eye on the beam of light in the middle distance, he did not realize that in five steps he would fall into the gaping hole of the elevator shaft.

Lillian watched from ankle level as he disappeared from sight with a yelp. The thud as he hit the lift came at the same moment that a second figure sprang through the doorway and crouched in a Kung Fu position, brandishing what looked like a handgun. At that moment Cydney jumped out of the shadows, shrieking like a cat, and smashed the gun-wielder's head with the heavy cardboard tube. She kept pounding on his back and shoulders as he sprawled sideways, rolling away from her and into the open hole. He managed to keep from falling in by grabbing onto a metal pole on the edge, as his gun clattered to the floor. Cydney kicked it aside. She thrust the end of the tube against his throat as he clung to the edge and said, "Don't move, asshole."

Without warning, and as if on cue, the lights came back on and the elevator started moving up to floor level.

"Lillian, kill that switch! *Quickly!*"

Lillian was afraid her legs would not work but they did, and she lunged for the off switch that swung three feet ahead of her, just as the lift came into view with the prone body of the first intruder.

"Ok," said Cydney calmly, "dial 911."

"No! Please!" Figure #1 had come to life, his voice groaning up from below. "Cydney! Don't, please."

"Who the hell are you?" said Cydney, still on guard, adding, "Lillian, dial!"

"It's me, Cyd, it's Carlo. What the fuck are you doin' here—settin' booby traps? Jeeez...my back...I can't move."

"Carlo? Carlo who?"

"Carlo. Carlo Mateo from when we were in school together. I was a hood, remember? You was pretty close yourself..."

Lillian reached the wall phone and dialed 911. Her fingers were trembling so badly that she misdialed three times.

"Carlo Mateo, huh?" Cydney had walked over to the lift, still holding the tube to the throat of intruder #2, and peered down into the hole. "Carlo Mateo. You're still a hood, asshole. Who sent you here? Was it that bitch Margie? She's as stupid as you are."

"Could we, uh, do introductions later, Carlo, huh?" the guy with the tube at his throat said... "Cyd, it's me, Jamie, remember? Jamie Doogan. I went with Carmen to her junior prom."

Lillian was having trouble getting through to 911. She decided to fake it, in case these guys did not turn out to be as helpless as they currently looked.

"Officer..." Lillian said, breathlessly, "we've got breakers and enterers here...they're here...they're on the lift...*what am I talking about?* Could you come right away? It's the Steamboat Brewery, East Cambridge, third floor."

Cydney dropped the tube and hit the elevator switch. The lift rumbled upward.

"Hey, Cyd," Jamie said weakly, rubbing his throat.

"Hey, asshole," Cydney answered, looking fairly imposing from their vantage point, despite her petite stature. "So how about you tell me why you're here—not for tea and conversation."

"Please call off the cops, really. I'll tell you the whole thing, I swear," said Carlo. "I got no bail money and my wife will kill me if she hears I've been messed up with Margie."

"Ok," said Cydney, turning to Lillian. "We've got company. Call off the escort."

"Are you serious?" asked Lillian.

"Yeah. It's story time. Pull up a seat." Lillian had no choice but to fake dial her way through another phone call. "Sorry officer…we've had some electrical problems and we were…uh…mistaken…yeah, thanks." As she hung up she was torn between making a dash for the door, calling 911 for real, and just sticking around to see what would happen. For someone whose life might have been in danger, Cydney seemed remarkably in control. Maybe she was more used to this than Lillian had realized.

Cydney had put down the tube and was holding on to it like a walking stick. She used it to fish for the gun, which had been kicked aside, and drew it over to her feet. Without taking her eyes off her captives, she reached down and picked up the gun.

"Ok, guys. Just looking for any other goodies you might be hiding. Strip."

She made both Carlo and Jamie strip down to their underwear and shake out their clothes, one by one, throwing each article to her as they took it off.

"One knife each. That's it. You got 'em both. No shit," Carlo said, as he peeled off his undershirt. "Ok, so you seen that we ain't packing no other piece, so can we uh, have our clothes back, Cyd?…Please?"

"Why, guys? You cold? *Tough*. I didn't throw rocks at the window to let in the cold. Who gets the repair bill? You? Your wife? Marjorie?"

"Hey, Cyd, give me a break, come on," Carlo pleaded.

"Give you a what? You crack me up, buddy." She cocked the gun at him. "I'll give you a break. Take off your underwear. Right now. Both of you."

Lillian wasn't sure she had heard this right. What if Cydney turned out to be crazier than these hoods? Lillian could not help but notice Carlo's sculptured body standing there in his BVD's, and pretty skimpy ones at that. The guy had obviously been working out for years, with tattooed upper arms and rippling back muscles. Lillian had never seen a man up close who actually had back muscles. His shoulders were about twice the width of his hips.

"This is a joke, right?" Carlo's hands were folded in front of his crotch.

"Nope. No joke. Take 'em off, gentlemen, and then we'll talk."

Cydney pulled over a folding chair, sat down, crossed her legs, cocked the trigger and pointed the gun at Carlo's crotch.

"This thing loaded?" She moved the gun in the direction of Carlo's head. He gulped and started to pull his briefs down over his hips. "Guess so, huh?" Cydney smiled.

Lillian found herself wishing that she had the front view, although the back wasn't bad. Hard sculptured buns, very white against skin that looked like it had seen some sun. She watched as Cydney raised her eyebrows in mock appreciation. Lillian leaned forward to see what Jamie was up to. Less articulate than Carlo, he was less to look at as well. His skin was still marked with the pitted remnants of acne, sallow and sunken. Blue veins bulged out on his neck and arms, thin and white in the T-shirted tan marks of someone who works outside. His hair was long and greasy, tied back in an elastic band. Both guys stood buck naked, their underwear bunched at Cydney's feet.

"Ok, guys, I'm waiting," said Cydney. "What exactly were you trying to do?"

"Look," said Carlo, shuffling from foot to foot, "I owed Margie a big favor. I've done odd jobs for her for a few years now—some carpentry around the house, fixed the cars, helped out with heavy work in the yard. My wife is a waitress at those fancy parties they have, like that, you know. And she keeps her eye on me, been coming on to me for years, you know, ever since way back when."

"Oh, I can imagine," said Cydney with a wide grin. Lillian wished he would turn around.

"So," he continued, "I got into some trouble gambling a ways back, when I wasn't supposed to be – against parole regulations – and I was really trying to stay straight, I swear to God, but I borrowed some money from Ciccolo and the boys and, you know, they don't mess around, they want it when they want it, and they don't care who the hell you are, Jonny's nephew or what, it don't mean shit to those guys, you know what I mean?"

Yeah, thought Lillian, *I know exactly what you mean.*

"So that Marjorie, she's got that EST or somethin' cause she calls me late last night and asks me if I could use some money. So I say sure – who couldn't? And she tells me to go over to Cydney's loft and toss this rock through the window. Then, you know…go upstairs and scare the shit out of you."

"Nice. Nice lady, don't you think, Lillian? Nice to have as the wife of a senator. Care to make a statement to the cops to that effect, guys? I can have them over here in two minutes."

"*Geez*, Cyd, don't. I'm on parole, for chrissake."

"Only on one condition."

"Whatever you say."

"You tell Marjorie to give me back the jewelry, all of it, by tomorrow morning or I'm going to the newspapers with your story. In fact, I'll have a great photo for the *Boston Globe*. *Naked guys caught red-handed in rock job.* Lil – get the camera."

And so, Lillian – who was not much of a photographer – did manage to get a front view – quite disappointing – as she took a Polaroid of Carlo and Jamie per Cydney's instructions, with their hands behind their heads and extremely shriveled dicks dangling between their goose-fleshed legs. In fact, she took two pictures, one to keep and one to send back to Marjorie with Cydney's note on the back… "How do you like these rocks?"

LILLIAN ARRIVED AT THE SHOP early the next morning. By the time she had left the previous night, she and Cydney had barely averted their first serious fight, saved by a phone call from Robert promising that he'd come in to help resolve the necklace mystery. Lillian showed up early to focus on their first shipment to East Coast retailer, Tons of Toys, due out later that day with $40,000 riding on it – money she would need in order to make the second payment to Angie.

Sometimes Cydney was at work in the Baby Grand manufacturing space at that hour, but more often she was upstairs in her own design studio, scene of the previous night's break-in. Walking down the hall to the bathroom, Lillian overheard Cyd's muffled but unmistakable voice coming from the photography studio next door, deep in conversation. A man's voice answered. This qualified as eavesdropping and she started to move on but then Marjorie's name came up and she realized the other voice must be Robert's. Was he here already?

She stopped in her tracks, listening, in spite of herself.

Robert: had no choice…what if it got out?

Cydney: don't want her involved.

Robert: well now she is.

Cydney: how expensive?

Robert: checking insurance…prohibitive.

Cydney: can't go through this again.

What the fuck?

WAS THIS PERSONAL OR ABOUT the jewelry? She didn't want them to see her standing there, so she tiptoed down the hall and banged the door to the office to announce her presence. She dropped her bag on the chair and looked around the warehouse corner that functioned as the shipping office of Baby Grand. The place was a mess. What could Robert Bretton possibly have in common with Cydney? Her desk was piled with invoices, a tool case and a manual Smith Corona typewriter half hidden beneath a stack of colored folders. Above it stretched a laundry line displaying products in various stages of development hanging from brightly colored hooks. Flattened boxes, rolls of tape, foam samples and sheets of drawing paper covered the folding tables that lined the side walls. Next to Boris's dog bed, Cydney had built a playhouse out of discarded cardboard boxes that David and Jonny adored. They spent hours happily sitting in it on the concrete floor, possibly sharing dog biscuits with Boris. (If Marc knew, he would call the Department of Social Services.) The ceiling was strung with twinkling electric lights connected by several extension cords plugged into a Lego-lookalike in one of the two existing outlets. Probably a fire hazard, but not highest on her list of things to worry about at that moment.

"Hey," Cyd said, walking into the office, "you're here early."

"Yup. Work to do." Lillian thought it best to keep her mouth shut until she had a better handle on things.

"You'll be happy to know the order is packed and ready. I had the girls stay late last night and we finished it up." This might have been Cydney's idea of atonement after last night.

"Great. Thanks."

"You're welcome."

"I assume Robert will be here at 10:00, like he said?"

"He's here now." Cydney's eyebrows rose in mock surprise to meet Lillian's.

"I thought you guys were like...hush hush."

"We just make it up as we go along."

"Uh-huh. How long, may I ask, have you been making it up?"

"What if I said it's none of your business?"

"Trust me, I don't want it to be my business, but here we all are."

Robert appeared in the doorway behind Cydney, leaning against the doorjamb, wearing jeans, work boots and a flannel shirt, scratching the back of Boris' ears who hung by his side, happily. His just-greying hair, untamed, curled at the neck, and he appeared ten years younger than when he was in straightjacket business attire. He cleared his throat. "Actually, Cyd, she's right. A business partnership is like a marriage – everything is on the table."

"Whose side are you on?" Cyd asked, turning around.

"The side of truth and justice, of course," he said, grinning at her.

"I am so glad to hear that Robert," said Lillian, "because last night your wife sent her low-life friends to throw rocks in the window. I've got the pictures to prove it."

"Yeah, good photos," Robert said. "But looks like my girl here got the better of them." He put his arm around Cydney's shoulder. "So, I see you've met the real Cydney," he said, turning to Lillian. "Good thing, if you ladies are going to make a go of it. Which I can help you with. Under the following conditions."

Robert moved into the shop, shooed Boris into his bed and sat down in the desk chair. Cydney stood protectively behind him. Lillian felt like she was in the musky presence of two teenagers mooning over each other; it made her feel ancient and she didn't know where to look. But Robert was all business.

"My relationship with Cydney is not for public knowledge, certainly not for the press. If my wife contacts you, ignore her. I know nothing about your jewelry or its whereabouts, but I will do my best to find it. If I can't, I'll file an insurance claim and make sure you get the 100K that you have borrowed — ill-advisedly, I might add — from Benjamin Finance. After you repay them, never contact them again. They are about to be investigated by the Attorney General. Since you still need 100K of working capital, I'll lend it to you at zero interest for one year."

Lilllian started to protest, but Robert put his hand up.

"In exchange," he continued, "I'm asking you to sign a confidentiality agreement that this information never leaves the room. Agreed?"

Should she believe him? "If you could have loaned us the money from the get-go, why didn't you?"

"You didn't ask."

"Seriously?"

"Well, Cydney didn't ask. She didn't want to get me involved. It was tricky enough having my financial records opened up. Plus, it's not the best time for me to shell out two hundred grand — I'm funding a senatorial run, textile manufacturing is about to be history in New England,

and I have a number of other…"–he glanced at Cydney–"pressing financial matters."

Lillian stared at him. *Could it be that easy?*

"I'm sorry–really–to put you in this position, but it will work out. We both have every reason to make this happen. Agreed?" He held out his hand. "You'll have a check for 100K tomorrow, and the second 100K after the New Year. I'll let you know about the jewelry as soon as I can."

Do I trust him? No.

Do I have a choice? No.

Lillian reached out and shook his hand.

III

SCHEHERAZADE

7:30 PM. Sunday, Nov. 5, 2006.

LILLIAN WONDERED HOW LONG IT took for hypothermia to set in. She had calmed Cydney down long enough to watch her go through the drugs in her pocketbook and take three enormous pills—the size of bumblebees—with the last of their water. Cydney insisted that Lillian tell her the story of the break-in by Jamie and Carlo, and then she fell into a deep sleep, twitching and making noises like she was suffocating.

Lillian put her head in her hands and tried to stay calm, but fear was taking over fast. How long could they stay stuck in this car without Cydney seriously flipping out? The wind was howling outside, whipping up the falling snow in sudden drifts. Lillian had heard an enormous crack a few minutes earlier and then something crashing to the ground—a tree? It was in the distance but close enough.

Lillian grabbed Cydney's purple pocketbook—the size of a small knapsack—and went through the many hidden compartments, looking for the drugs and descriptions of possible side effects. Besides the usual makeup and wallet, she found an old-fashioned address book, a notebook with set design sketches, two condoms, a mini pad designed for thong underwear, a pair of control top black sheer stockings, size A, a cartridge of bullets for the gun, the silver whiskey flask that Cydney always carried that had belonged to her father, and a large envelope filled with medical files.

Should she open it? *Duh, of course, you idiot—open it.*

Diagnosis: Lewy Body Dementia. Presenting with auditory and visual hallucinations, paranoia, deeply disturbed sleep patterns, Capgras Syndrome.

'Dementia with Lewy Bodies (DLB) symptoms include:

1. Impaired thinking, such as loss of executive function (planning, processing information), memory, or the ability to understand visual information;

2. Fluctuations in cognition, attention or alertness;

3. Problems with movement, including tremors, stiffness, slowness and difficulty walking;

4. Visual hallucinations (seeing things that are not present);

5. Sleep disorders, such as acting out one's dreams while asleep;

6. Behavioral and mood symptoms, including depression, apathy, anxiety, agitation, delusions or paranoia;

7. Neuropsychiatric symptoms can include hallucinations, behavioral problems, and difficulty with complex mental activities, also leading to an initial diagnosis of DLB.

8. *Capgras Syndrome* or *Capgras Delusion* (Imposter Syndrome) is characterized by a delusional belief that a person has been replaced by an imposter. Capgras syndrome can occur at a younger age of onset, co-occurring with paranoid schizophrenia, schizoaffective disorder, and methamphetamine abuse. Possibly related to prior brain trauma. Of those with Capgras syndrome and Lewy body disease, 100% had visual hallucinations.

9. There are some reported cases where Capgras sufferers have exhibited violent behavior resulting in injury and even death. Very little research makes it difficult to reliably predict violence. This is troubling given that great hostility and resentment are typical of how sufferers of Capgras view "imposters."

10. *Drugs:* Clozapine for psychotic symptoms and hallucinations. Cholinesterase inhibitors can include Ritalin, Dopamine, Aricept, Nivalin.

Lillian stared at the papers in her lap and stuffed them back in Cydney's pocketbook, teeth chattering. She could barely process this – it just couldn't be true. Cydney was much too young. Lillian's Uncle Ernest had been almost eighty when he was diagnosed, and that had been bad enough. She remembered her father telling her that Ernest refused to believe that his wife of fifty years was actually his wife. He made her strip every time she came into the room to prove it. She and Marc had made a joke out of it – horny old bastard. But it was no joke. Cydney! Cydney, who had talked her over bridges and out of her phobias – bullying, cajoling, applauding – and into a normal life, was facing a living nightmare. One phrase stuck in her mind... *difficult to predict violent behavior resulting in injury and even death.* Was she in danger? It had been a long while since Lillian had experienced a full-blown anxiety attack, but she recognized that choking heat as it grabbed her guts, squeezing up her esophagus like a snake, ready to strike.

Calm down. Breathe. This is not about you. You'll be fine. She pulled the blanket around them and wrapped Cydney's wet hair in the towel. Cydney mumbled something in her sleep. Lillian leaned in to listen.

Keep talking.

1982. All Night Long.

"If one more person calls me Cindy I'll punch their lights out," Cydney said, voice rising above the staccato of her sewing machine.

"Since I've seen you punch, I will take note. You are the least likely Cindy – which sounds like fairy dust – that I could imagine," Lillian allowed. Despite standing five foot three and about one hundred pounds, Cydney could lift a bicycle in one arm and carry it up three flights of stairs. "And where did the name Cydney come from, by the way?"

"My mother named us all starting with the letter "C." She can't explain it so neither can I." Cydney ticked off the names on her fingers:

"Carmen, Camelia, Clarisa, Celeste, Cydney. Although I was named for a horse, a good luck horse."

"Who's Celeste? I know the others but…"

"Dead. Before I was born. Just a baby. None of the girls remember her. Although I suspect Carmen does; she must have been five at the time. She stuttered and had nightmares for years, which I can attest to because I shared a room with her."

Lillian stopped what she was doing. "Poor Bianca–to lose a baby. What happened?"

Cydney didn't hear her over the sewing machine. "I thought my older sisters had one name between them–'CarmenMel'nRisa' which my mother yelled out every few minutes, and I didn't think I heard about Celeste until . . . Christ, I think Carmen's wedding rehearsal. Robert came to the rehearsal dinner, now that I think of it. He was probably the only guy there. Took off early and broke my twelve-year-old heart."

"First crush, huh? And look at you now! Screwing the senator. Maybe you are a Cindy, after all." Cyd picked up a king-size spool of thread and flung it at Lillian, narrowly missing her head.

"Ooooh. Touchy when it comes to Roberto, eh?" Lillian teased.

"Eh? You sound like my grandmother."

"The one from Quebec?"

"Yeah. We're probably related. Please don't start about the jewelry."

"It's true–all French Canadians are probably related, like all Jews–and maybe even to each other. I guess we have sealed this deal in blood, eh?"

"Right now you have sealed that box in so much packing tape it could walk by itself." Cydney stood up and walked over to where Lillian was sitting surrounded by Carta-Babe packaging. "The guys on the loading dock will take one look at it and roll their eyes thinking, *Dames.*"

"If you call me a dame I will call you Cindy. So, why are you named for a horse?" Lillian patted her stack of sealed boxes and lay down. "I'm taking a break. And what happened to Celeste?"

1950. The Good Luck Horse.

CYDNEY S. MALLONE WAS NAMED for a good luck horse. At the time, her father, Kevin Mallone, needed the luck badly when he put twenty-five dollars down on '*Cydney Slide*' to Win, Place and Show at 80:1 odds. Twenty-five dollars was a lot of money in 1950 when you were out of work, on the wagon, and waiting for manna from heaven.

Cydney Slide came in by a neck and paid $2,973.54 to Win, $1,675.02 to Place, and $906.55 to Show for a grand total of $5,555.11, which Kevin collected right there at the window, where he began whooping and hollering and stuffing one hundred dollar bills into his hat, his socks, his underwear – anywhere safe enough to hug all the way home. Home was thirty miles away, in Lawrell, Massachusetts, and thirty miles was no small distance when you were on foot with over five thousand dollars in cash in your pockets.

Kevin was on foot because his driver's license had been suspended for one year, which is also why he was on the wagon and out of work. But this was too painful to think about, so, instead, he resolved then and there, stepping out onto the dark highway and holding out his thumb, to name the child soon to be born Cydney if a girl or a boy. That was not his favorite name, but a lucky one for sure. His wife, Bianca, had given birth to four daughters by the time she was twenty-seven, and she considered the fifth pregnancy to be a gift. A year ago she wouldn't have, but now she did.

When Kevin came home after his windfall at the racetrack, he surprised Bianca with a shower of one hundred dollar bills, taking them out of his pants by the fistful and throwing them up in the air where they hovered like little helicopters, then fluttered down to the dark green linoleum floor. At first Bianca thought he was drunk, and her heart went cold. Then she thought he had gone crazy and robbed a bank, and she started to cry.

By now the girls had woken up and their faces peered down through the spokes of the banister, as pale and wide-eyed as the dolls they each clutched. Bianca was seven and a half months pregnant and the doctor told her that she couldn't take any more stress, but by the time she understood that Kevin had won this money without losing more in the process, she decided that good stress couldn't hurt.

They agreed that Cydney was the name for the son they would surely have after four girls, all of whose names started with the letter 'C': Carmen, Camille, Clarisa, Celeste—names that sounded to Kevin like tropical flowers. None of the girls looked like tropical flowers, however, being redheads with pale freckles and sandy eyelashes and light brown eyes.

Until recently they had all been gypsies, on the road with Kevin, who ran the giant Ferris wheel at the Festival Traveling Fair, living in a fixed cycle of circular weeks. Sunday was their day off, and if they weren't too far south, where Catholics were run out of town, they went to church. Monday was a traveling day, moving on to the next fairground. Tuesday was arrival and set-up day, which spilled over to Wednesday morning. And by Wednesday at noon, Festival Traveling Fair was ready to open in a blaze of swirling lights and honky-tonk music, staying open the rest of the week, noon through midnight. Saturday night the fair closed down, and the rig operators hammered and echoed through the dark, ready to pull out at dawn.

By Sunday morning the only signs that they had ever been there, in the wide open fields at the edge of town, in the off-season football fields in back of the local high school, in the empty spaces by the railroad tracks, were the garbage cans bursting with empty bottles of cream soda, and cardboard cones sticky with tufts of pink cotton candy.

Kevin and Bianca loved the fair. They started out after the war when Carmen, their eldest, was just a baby and traveled by train from town to town—New England in the summer, heading down to Jersey and Delaware in the fall, the Carolinas and Georgia in the winter and back up the coast in the spring. Kevin loved the fair because he could lounge around in his undershirt all morning on the front steps of his trailer, drinking steaming cups of coffee while other men went to work. He loved watching fathers dole out nickels to their begging kids, and he loved the begging kids who wanted just one more ride without having to wait in line, please, please. Mostly he loved turning night into day, with organ grinder music, and bright lights, and gaily colored rides that spun into a blur.

Bianca loved the fair because it made Kevin happy, and the happier he was, the less he drank, although sometimes it didn't work out that way. Otherwise, she had to admit that she was getting sick of being on the road, especially with four children under the age of six. What she really wanted was what they couldn't afford—a home of her own. But until she began to worry that Carmen should start a proper Catholic school, she loved watching the girls run across green fields and parks while the rides emerged piecemeal from their trailers and sprawled out across the field, turning to glitter and music and spinning lights against the setting sun.

And all of them loved traveling folk, outcasts every one. There were large men with tattooed arms and bare chests and missing teeth. There were pale women with dyed blonde hair and tight stretchy pants and high heels, women with bright red lips and long red nails, chewing gum and wearing metal curlers under their flowered kerchiefs. It was their time to be gypsies, to damn everything but the circus.

ONE LATE MARCH NIGHT IN South Carolina, the scent of dogwood and magnolia was so powerful it even cut through the lingering whiff of fried dough that Bianca swore would be with her until the day she died. Kevin sat by himself on the front steps of the trailer and finished a fifth of Wild Turkey, drinking it in with the warm and yeasty spring air. It was well past closing, and the rides stood silent like empty birdcages against a purple-rimmed sky. The Ferris wheel stood guard over their trailer, its red and yellow gondolas swinging gently in the light breeze.

When Kevin drank he was sweet and funny and extravagant in praise of his wife and daughters, but he was also as horny as a sailor on shore leave and about as careful, which is why he had four children. Kevin got to thinking that he'd like to get Bianca into one of those gondolas and take her up to the top. The thing was, he'd always wanted to get laid at the very top, with the car rocking in its perch, getting ready for the dizzying drop.

He couldn't very well pull this off while working the controls down below, but he could set the drive in the slowest gear and put it on automatic for up to ten minutes. Ten minutes should do it. And if that wasn't enough, he could jump out when he was two or three cars from the ground and restart the timer. Hey, he could keep going that way for half an hour or more. It was worth a try. He walked over to the glass-enclosed cab, started up the motor, shut off the music, and was pleasantly surprised at how quiet and suggestive the sound was, like a hive of bees coming to life.

He roused Bianca out of her first good sleep in weeks, ready with sweet talk. "Come on, pretty baby, please. It's so beautiful outside. Come smell it. It's the south and we are heading north, girl, where it's cold and nasty."

"Kevin, are you crazy? How much did you drink?"

"It don't matter, baby. Nothing matters but you and me, you know that. You know what I want, baby? I want to take you for a ride."

"Oh, God, Kevin. Please, it's right in the middle of my cycle. Celeste is only six months old. You'll never pull out; you always say you will but you don't."

"But we have such beautiful babies…I will, I promise, I'll pull out. Just come outside. No, forget the robe. You don't need it. See? See how beautiful it is? A full moon and the smell of magnolias! Maybe we should have a baby named Magnolia."

And that night, possibly at the very top of the Ferris wheel under a blanket of stars and falling through space, Cydney Mallone became the physical manifestation of the spark in her father's twinkling, but very drunk, eyes.

A FEW WEEKS LATER, KEVIN decided to take the girls fishing. It was Sunday, their day off, smack in the middle of full, glorious, spring. And Kevin wanted to do something nice for Bianca; give her a whole afternoon to herself.

"Baby doll, how 'bout if I take the girls off your hands for the day and you go get your hair done or something?"

"Why, Kevin! That's so sweet! But you couldn't take them all; it's too much work."

"Am I their father? Is it too much work for a father to look after his own kids?"

Actually you would never know that the girls were Kevin's children from looking at them lined up together. Kevin had the thick hair and olive skin of his Polynesian mother, and the blue eyes and cleft chin of his Irish sea-faring father. His daughters inherited none of his South Seas ancestry, to Bianca's great surprise, and instead regressed back to Kevin's otherwise pure Irish heritage of red hair, freckles and pale skin. But Bianca kept on giving her girls exotic names in hopes that their looks would live up to them, even though they kept on looking like Maureens and Colleens instead of Carmens and Camelias.

So Bianca packed a picnic lunch of bologna and cheese sandwiches, and a bottle for the baby with some Zwiebeck crackers. Carmen and Camelia, who were five and almost four, were dressed in shorts and blouses, but two-year-old Clarisa insisted on wearing her Sunday go-to-meeting dress. Bianca put Celeste, who was the easiest baby of the four, into her traveling car bed with a change of diapers, a hat, and an extra blanket in case the weather changed.

"You sure there's enough room for all of you in that car?" Bianca asked Kevin after he borrowed the blue and grey Studebaker with the shiny chrome fins from their neighbor.

"You just watch me now, baby doll," he said, putting his fishing gear in the trunk and the older girls in the back seat. "See, there's the whole front seat for me and Celeste's own little traveling bed here."

And off they went, Kevin's left arm pumping good-bye out the driver's side window, with the faces of the three girls pressed against the glass pane looking out the back.

In the forty-five minutes it took to travel down the single lane road leading to the lake, he and the girls sang "The Tennessee Waltz" and "Oh My Darling Clementine" at the top of their lungs with all the windows open to let in the sun. The baby was fast asleep. It was a pure spring day.

When they got to the lake, Kevin drove onto a spit of sand at the edge of the water. The girls tumbled out of the car, stretching and blinking their eyes, and started to explore. The baby was still asleep, and Kevin left the passenger door open so he could hear her when she woke up. He took out the fishing tackle and the picnic basket and followed the water about a hundred yards until he found a rocky ledge that looked like a good spot for trout. The girls trailed behind, Carmen carrying a blanket and complaining bitterly about why she was the only one who ever had to do anything.

"Because you're the oldest, is why," said Kevin, setting down his gear and taking the blanket from her. He wished he had brought a bottle with him, or more than the thimbleful in the hip flask that he carried everywhere. He had struggled with himself that morning about filling it up with what was left of the Jack Daniels. But he was with his girls, after all. And he knew the edge in Bianca's voice, the fear fluttering under the surface. Nope. He did the right thing, leaving it empty. Or almost empty. He took out the sterling flask—it had been his father's, and took the last swig. He swished it around in his mouth like mouthwash and gargled, making a chugging noise that set the girls laughing. Down the hatch.

"Ok, who's on the worm brigade? Before you know it, we'll have trout on the line and fresh fish for Sunday dinner. How 'bout that?"

For half an hour he busied himself with worms and hooks and weights, rolling his eyes at the girls' squeals of disgusted delight, until each one had her pole ready and her line in the water. By then they were complaining that they were hungry and Celeste had woken up; he could hear her coo-ing from the car. Kevin told Carmen to watch the others and make sure they stayed away from the water, no closer than the blanket. He went to fetch the baby and bring her back, bouncing her on his hip. She hung on, with her little fists wet from being stuffed in her mouth, and gave him a big toothless smile. Celeste sat up all by herself—she hadn't begun to crawl, which Bianca always said was the very best stage—and took her bottle while the rest of them ate their sandwiches in lazy silence, shushing away the occasional bee.

Kevin caught three fish after lunch to the shrieks of the girls, which startled the baby so much that each time she began to howl. Kevin figured three was a respectable number, and they were big enough for a filet or two, so he told his daughters that it was time to gather up their stuff and get ready to leave. Celeste was asleep again, curled up on the blanket with her thumb in her mouth. He lifted her up, boy she was getting heavy, and told the others to follow him back to the car.

Once Celeste was tucked back into her car bed, Kevin leaned down to Carmen. "I'm going back to get the poles and the picnic basket. I want you and your sisters to play over there, away from the water. And not loud, 'cause we don't want to wake your sister. It's no fun driving home with her howling all the way."

He whistled to himself as he walked back, picking up the occasional flat rock and flinging it sideways into the lake to see how many times it could skip. The flask in his pocket made a slapping noise as he walked, and he thought about how much he could use a drink after he got everybody home. When he reached the blanket, he shook off the ants and the crumbs and threw the leftover sandwich crusts into the lake. Dozens of air bubbles popped up on the surface of the water as fish greedily came to forage. He smiled to himself; where were they an hour ago when he had pulled in only three? It took him no more than a few minutes to get back to the car, and when he did, the car was no longer there.

For a second Kevin wondered if he was dreaming, and then he saw two of the girls standing in the bushes off to the side, clutching each other's arms. He dropped everything, tripped on the basket, and ran to them. "Where's the car? Where's Carmen?"

They pointed to the water. Twenty feet into the lake the back fins of the car jutted up from the surface. The rest was submerged. Kevin ran into the water, weighted down by his work boots and flannel shirt. He saw the driver's door open with Carmen's legs sticking out and he half-swam, half-leaped to her, grabbed a leg and pulled her out. He pushed her up to the surface and dragged her toward shore until she could stand, pounding her on the back, listening for the ragged intake of air. She was breathing; she would be all right.

The baby; he had to get the baby.

Down again. He looked into the back seat; thrust his chest over it, arms reaching out, panicked and finding nothing. He pushed himself out and up for air. Back down and this time, as he grabbed the passenger door, saw a glint of metal beyond the car in the shallows. The car bed was on its side with Celeste half out, facing down. Almost out of breath, he caught her by the back of the neck and thrashed up to the surface, gulping water and air, clawing his way onto the roof of the car where he flung her limp body over his shoulder, slapping her on the back while waiting for the cough that would not come.

CARMEN DIDN'T TALK FOR TWO days. When she did, Bianca asked her if Daddy had been drinking. Carmen said that he had his flask with him and made them laugh with those funny noises like when he swallowed. Carmen was scared of the policemen and the questions and she didn't tell them about the lever that went 'pop' and made the car roll.

Kevin told the policemen the truth: He hadn't been drinking and the parking brake must have failed. The officers found his flask with the remains of whiskey. The children were too terrified to talk, and too young to be credible. At the inquest Kevin Mallone was found guilty of negligence and reckless endangerment. His operator's license was suspended and Festival Traveling Fair fired him on the spot. The Mallones had three days to move out of their trailer.

After six years with the fair, Kevin and Bianca took the tiny white casket and a bouquet of yellow roses and came home to Lawrell, where Celeste was laid to rest next to Bianca's father and brother in the Blood of the Lamb cemetery on April 15, 1950. The next day Bianca found out she was pregnant with Cydney.

1982. All Night Long.

LILLIAN LOOKED OVER AT CYDNEY, who was frowning at the pile of laminated foam that she was trying to coax through the binder on her machine. "I don't know what to say. What a terribly sad story. How do you recover from something like that?" Lillian sat perfectly still, thinking of David and Jonny.

Cydney shrugged. "You don't, evidently. My father struggled with alcoholism for the rest of his life. Carmen must have seen more that she remembers, because she's a mess; my sisters mostly resented me; and my mother just soldiered on. But hey, we're all here and in one piece. Except for Dad, whose liver gave out about eight years ago, which reminds me that I need to call Bianca."

LILLIAN AND CYDNEY WERE BURNING the midnight oil in her upstairs studio, hand sewing and packing a series of perfect samples to send to T.Rex Toys. Cydney didn't trust her crew of Vietnamese stitchers with this specific task, workers who were otherwise the most competent, reliable group of employees Lillian could imagine.

"They'll end up making duck soup in the coffee pot while we're out, and cooking chicken feet in oil that smells like rancid furniture polish, and the fabric will pick up every trace," Cydney had said. In fact, the Baby Grand factory had three coffee pots—one of them dedicated to duck soup. The other two rotated between noodles and green tea. "The buyer will open the packaging and pass out."

"Or order out," added Lillian. "We'll be lucky if they even open the bag. At least they'd remember us." Lillian stood up and yawned, stretching up on tiptoe, watching her shadow spread up to the ceiling. She raised her leg in a second arabesque and fluttered.

"Christ, you're tall. Stop doing that; you'll scare the animals. How could you have been a dancer? Were you dancing with basketball players?"

"Exactly. Gay men who might have hoped to be basketball players but realized their feather boas were going to get in their way. I'm exhausted. Tell me another story or I'll fall asleep on this pile of foam rubber."

Cydney looked up from the fabric she was guiding through her sewing machine, like trying to shove a snowsuit through a keyhole. "Ok. How about this: did I ever tell you about Hector?"

Lillian shook her head.

"When I was only fourteen, I had a job at a nursing home. I was underage, so I told them I was sixteen. They would have fired me the first week except that I was the only one who could get this big lug of a patient—Hector—to do anything. He just sat there like a lump and abused all the staff. But he liked me because I sneaked him cigarettes, which was forbidden because he had a heart condition and high blood pressure. Now that I think about it, it's no wonder that the staff hated me—I was too young, didn't listen to anybody, sang in the halls and shortened all my uniforms until they barely covered my ass. But they kept me because no one else could handle Hector—he could be a mean son of a bitch—but whenever he saw me he just beamed."

"I'm sure the short skirts had something to do with it." Lillian put the last strip of sealing tape on another sample box and stood back to admire her handiwork. Cydney was right; the guys on the loading dock would crack up.

"Anyway, one day Hector disappeared—we couldn't find him anywhere. He couldn't leave the building and there were no windows in the bathrooms and no locks on the inside of the bathroom doors. But one bathroom door wouldn't open. Wouldn't budge. So they decided that he had got himself stuck in the bathroom and wouldn't—or couldn't—come out. No matter how much they pounded on the door, there was no answer. So, since I'm small, they asked me to crawl through an air vent that led from the supply closet into the locked bathroom and look down through the vent to see what was going on. I'm young and stupid – what do I know? – so I agreed. Two orderlies hoisted me up on their shoulders so I could take off the grate and crawl in. The vent was about two feet wide by two feet high, full of cobwebs and had not seen the light of day in years."

Lillian had enough phobias trying to keep away from bridges and water without contemplating claustrophobia as well. Would she rather be in an air vent or on a bridge?

"And there was a turn in the vent. That's right! I don't know how I crawled around that corner but I did. And then I was at the bathroom grate looking down at Hector, who was lying on the floor jammed between the toilet and the door. I knew as soon as I looked down that he was dead. He was sort of waxy, almost blue. And staring up at me. It was like looking at a big old house with all the lights out. I'd never seen a dead person before. But I pushed open the grate and dropped down – almost killed myself because part of the grate that I was clinging to came loose. So there I was on the bathroom floor with a three hundred pound dead man jamming the door shut, but I couldn't get out because there was no way to climb back up to the vent opening. And I couldn't budge Hector, who was lying on his side right up against the door."

Lillian stopped what she was doing. "I'm not sure this is what I had in mind for a story…"

But Cydney was too caught up in her memory.

"So, I decided that he wasn't dead and I started talking to him. 'Come on, Hector, you've got to help me out here, you've got to lift your leg.' Then I started trying to lift him, but he was heavy – dead weight is not just a literary term – and I just kept talking to him. I would lift an arm and it would flop back, just like in the movies. I tried to turn him and he got stuck in this awful shape, sort of twisted with his legs bending the wrong way. Then the staff started yelling at me from outside the door.

Is he all right? Is he breathing?

'No, no, he's not breathing,' I said.

What do you mean he's not breathing, Cydney?

"Now I'm kinda losing it here, crying and talking to him, which the staff could hear through the door. 'It'll be all right, really. Come on, Hector, could you help me out here, please?…Just turn around…like this…oh shit!' And then, flop, he was back on the floor. At some point the head nurse—what was her name? What a bitch! Screamed at me to take his vitals and I started to laugh hysterically. No pulse. He's turning blue! So they called the fire department and Kevin, my dad, was working there as an EMT. This was during his sober period after Carmen and Mel had left home—and he didn't know I cut school for this job or that I had forged his signature on the underage work permit application. I was so worried about my dad showing up that I don't remember anything until they chopped down the door and found me sitting on the floor singing to Hector with his head in my lap."

Lillian sat still for several seconds. "Wow." Somehow Cydney had the ability to take all of Lillian's phobias, wrap them up in a really big ball and throw it back at her. How Cydney managed to get through life smiling and singing was a mystery. Lillian had to hand it to her. It was amazing that she didn't have post-traumatic stress syndrome.

"And that's the story of Hector," Cydney said, standing up and switching off her machine. "Want some coffee?" She didn't wait for Lillian to answer. "We really did meet long ago, you know. And it was the Candy Shack—I just figured it out. You must have applied to be a go-go dancer. I ran past you in the hall on my way to tell Gerry I was quitting, and he got so pissed that he threw a chair at me and then tried to stop me from leaving. There you were, blocking my path, and I pulled you down the stairs with me and out into the street."

Lillian stared at her. The Candy Shack. After her freshman year at New England School of Performing Arts. Holy Shit. As usual, Cydney was right.

"Jeez. You're right. That was me. Flat broke and looking for a job as a go-go dancer."

"You mean hooker."

"Hardly. I was so naïve. I can't believe you remember that!"

"Very memorable. I was quitting to drive across country with my sisters, taking Mel to UCLA. And to escape the lure of Mr. Bretton, recently married and not about to take no for an answer. So…what are you waiting for? It's your turn; tell me a story."

IN THE FALL OF 1968, when Lillian arrived in Boston to study acting at the prestigious New England School of Performing Arts, everyone she met wanted to be Che Guevara. Nobody in her hometown of Burlington, Vermont had ever heard of him, but in Boston he didn't even have a last name – just Che. Sort of like a famous actor, she thought, staring at his picture on the front page of the alternative newspaper, *Boston Underground*, looking for "roommates wanted" while standing in line at a Cambridge post office to buy stamps.

It was a long line and the smell of marijuana wafted in every time someone opened the door. *Right there on federal property!* Two guys wearing dirty T-shirts that were once white, in ripped bellbottom jeans with red bandanas around their necks, stood around barefoot handing out pamphlets that mentioned 'revolution' nineteen times in the first two paragraphs. Lillian tried to balance the pamphlet and the newspaper over her Peruvian saddlebag that served as a pocketbook. Behind her a guy with hair halfway down his back shuffled in sandals thin as paper and droned, "Hey! Hey! LBJ – how many kids did ya kill today?" while shaking his fist at the portrait of Lyndon Johnson smiling out from a perch above the clerks' windows.

A cluster of people behind her were arguing about the conspiracy that led from Bobby Kennedy's assassination to the Chicago convention – Mayor Daley did it, or maybe Hubert Humphrey – and Lillian found herself paying close attention when the short red-headed guy in front of her suddenly spun around and shouted over her head, "Shut the fuck up, you asshole!"

Lillian jumped back, bumping into the conspiracy group behind her and setting off a chain reaction all the way down the line. The guy had a voice like Orson Wells. She turned around to make sure that Orson himself was not in the post office.

"Sorry," the short guy said – definitely not Orson Wells – as he reached out to steady her. "I just couldn't stand it any longer. This jerk is here every day yelling that they should take down Johnson's portrait. Taking down the portrait won't take down the man. You ok?" he asked, peering at her closely. "Hey! I've seen you at auditions."

HANK LESTER, WHO INSISTED THAT he be called Les, "just Les," with no last name because he was working on his future stage name, was the first person whom Lillian had talked to for more than ten minutes since she stepped off the bus from Vermont. Les was a senior at New England Arts, and an acting student with a magnificently authoritative voice who had every intention of making it big. He also just happened to need a place to live because his roommate and best friend, Marcus Smith, had decided at the last minute to go to France to study radical philosophy with Jean-Paul Sartre.

Within two days Lillian and Les had found an apartment on the third floor of a three-decker walk-up in the industrial section of Somerville. Although she would never admit it, Lillian was mildly freaked out about living on her own and about living with a man. The apartment was disgusting, which she ignored in the initial thrill of finding something she could afford. The place was, technically, occupied by a group of girls who were actually living with their boyfriends elsewhere, unbeknownst to their unsuspecting but generous parents. In 1968, young women who lived with their boyfriends were at risk of causing fathers to drop dead of heart attacks and mothers to never show their faces in public again, so preserving parents from the knowledge that their daughters were damaged goods was the holy grail of every living situation.

Lillian struck a deal with the girls: They needed someone who sounded like a real roommate to answer the early morning and late night phone calls from their parents with a standard stopgap response:

"Janet? Oh, Janet's in the shower, and she takes really long show-ers—well, you probably know that, so she'll call you right back, or as soon as she can get to the phone. You know what it's like with five of us girls and just one phone line, hint hint hint! And how are you, Mr. Snyder?"...or..."Susie? (Fake off-stage call...*Soooozeee???* silence...*Soooz are you there?*) Gee, Mrs. Mendelson you must have just missed her. I think she ran out to the store to buy milk or maybe it was yogurt."

Then Lillian would call the girl in question at the apartment of the boy she was currently seeing, and the girl would then return her parent's call—just as though she had stepped out of the shower or returned from the store. Lillian created a large display board with everyone's names and relevant phone numbers highlighted in yellow and put it up on the wall over the phone.

Lillian figured that since she was an actress, she could handle this. And in exchange she and Les got free rent and a second phone line. However, because nobody actually lived there, the apartment had no furnishings whatsoever. Les hauled in an old sofa that he had found on the street on garbage night, and they slept on an almost new mattress on the floor. Other than that, there were some orange crates from the grocery store that served as a bureau, and a concrete block and board bookshelf left by a previous tenant. Lillian pointed out to her phantom roommates that their parents might get suspicious if they came to visit an unfurnished apartment—one in which most of the rooms had, for some reason, been painted black—and maybe they should get their asses over there soon and clean the place up. Gradually a stuffed chair, a kitch-en table, a few large pillows, some Indian print all-purpose bedspreads and Toulouse-Lautrec posters made their appearance.

Lillian thought it was particularly ironic that she was in on this scam, when her own parents appeared to show absolutely no interest in the an-nouncement that not only did she have a boyfriend, but that they were living together after knowing each other for less than a week.

No one referred to these arrangements as "affairs" anymore, which struck notes of illicit thrill that Lillian had yet to experience, but as "rela-tionships," which sounded as cold and gutted as a dead fish. So maybe it was poetic justice that her affair with Les lasted only a few weeks, while their relationship lasted for years.

In fact, Lillian started sleeping with Les mostly because it was awkward not to. He had a great sense of humor and kept her giggling, but Les was not the man of Lillian's dreams. For one thing, he was a good few inches shorter than she, and reminded her of her father's joke about the tall woman and the short man, which went something like...*When they're toe to toe his nose is in it, and when they're nose to nose his toes are in it, and when they're all squared away there's no one to talk to!*...followed by big guffaws that Lillian didn't get until recently.

Les was also a few notches above legally blind and had to hold a script about five inches from his face. He refused to wear either glasses or contacts, convinced that he would land fewer parts. Once when he was on stage in an experimental play in the round, he wandered so far forward that he fell into the lap of a large bouffon-haired woman in the first row of the unsuspecting audience. *(Harry! Is this supposed be happening?)* No, Les' main attraction was something intangible – his voice. Deep, mellifluous, honeyed, and hypnotic, it was a voice that could make women swoon. All Les had to do was turn out the lights and talk, and he could have any woman he wanted, including Lillian. But only until Lillian met Marc, Les' best friend and former roommate, who dropped by for a weekend on his way to France.

Les and Marc had a fierce but friendly rivalry when it came to women: Les brought them home and Marc stole them away. This was not hard to do as Marc exuded confidence and innocence simultaneously – an unbeatable combination. He looked a bit like an Irish setter, with dark auburn hair that hung lanky and straight into his very grey and slightly almond eyes. He was always moving, tapping his foot, humming off-key, drumming his long fingers on the arm of a chair, so that you wanted to reach out and steady him.

So, when Marc appeared on Les and Lillian's Somerville doorstep in early October with two huge suitcases tied down with straps, only to find Lillian but no Les, he unleashed the charm assault reserved for Les' girlfriends.

"Umm, hi! I'm looking for Les, but maybe his place is one flight down."

"Nope. One flight down is the lesbian commune. They won't let Les in the door. You must be Marcus," Lillian said, staring into clear eyes that were a few inches above hers.

"How did you know?"

"Because he never stops talking about you," she said, turning from the door and beckoning him into the room. "Sorry it's so dark in here, but the previous tenants were really into the Stones and painted it black. So it's still painted kinda black. More like one coat of beige over black, which as you can see is really disgusting. We haven't had time to fix it up. Les is always at rehearsal. That's where he is now, I'm sure." *Why am I babbling?*

"So, you're Les' roommate then?" Marc stared at her with a slow smile and raised eyebrows. He wore an old leather jacket with a turned up collar and had sculpted lips like Rudolph Nureyev, the dance partner of her dreams. Lillian thought about this. *Am I his roommate or his lover? This guy Marc is gorgeous. And he's going to Paris to hang out in cafés with Sartre. Am I fickle or what?*

"That's right," she said "I'm his roommate." And from that moment on, she was.

During her first year of college, Lillian and Les made a pretty good living by renting out the top floor of the three-decker at 35 Weymouth Street. The apartment was a standard three-bedroom with parlor, combined kitchen/dining, one bath, and sagging back porch – replicated up and down the street. Except that all three units of the house were rented to students, alien creatures in this part of Somerville and not entirely welcomed by the rest of the blue collar hard-working neighborhood. The ground floor unit was inhabited by three guys in a not-very-good rock band, who slept all day and practiced all night. The middle unit was occupied by a radical, feminist lesbian theatre commune that had started out as a commune, and gradually became radical, then lesbian, then theatrical, in that order. The devotion to theatre was questionable, consisting largely of poetry readings and speeches—inadequate according to Lillian, who was attending a real theatre school.

BY MID-MAY 1969 LILLIAN HOPED that she could convince the current crop of fake roommates to keep up their arrangement through the summer so she wouldn't have to find a real job and could audition for summer theatre. But first she'd had to confront all five sets of fake roommates' parents who had descended on Mother's Day weekend with virtually no notice and sowed panic among their daughters and, by extension, on Lillian.

THE RED PHONE HAD RUNG early that Tuesday morning. Lillian staggered over to it; she had been out late at rehearsal the night before and was cursing the anticipated voice of Mrs. Whosis looking for what's-her-name.

"Yeah, morning," said Lillian, clearing her throat.

"Lillian, oh my god, this is bad, really bad. They're coming!" said Cheryl, fictitious roommate number three, in a frantic voice.

"Who?"

"This weekend. On Friday. I couldn't stop them. They're driving up from the city and they wanted directions to the apartment."

Lillian was wide awake, staring at the wall chart where she kept the bios of all five roommates and their families. *Cheryl, let's see…*

Home = Queens, New York

Parents = Richard and Nancy Macklehenney

Family = sisters: Susanna (fifteen) and Joanne (twelve)

Pets = Dog (shitsu) named Koko

Boyfriend = Mitchell Cohen, Tufts, pre-Med, Jewish. (Cheryl was Catholic so that was a non-starter.)

Dorm phone = 617-728-4395

"Ok, well…um, I guess you better get over here and bring some towels or…a stuffed animal, something they'll recognize as yours," Lillian said, looking around the apartment that was devoid of any feminine touch—no curtains, no rugs, walls painted a cruddy brown decorated with faded posters advertising *Henry V* and *Waiting for Godot*.

And then it happened again. Marcia called in a panic, then Lisa. They both went to Radcliffe, and Mother's Day weekend was something they thought they could avoid. Finally, Janet and Anne, whom Lillian hardly knew, announced that their parents would be showing up some-time Saturday. Within hours all five women descended with boxes of books, cosmetics and angora sweaters.

By Thursday night she didn't recognize her own apartment. Books on art history and Chinese literature lined the walls in newly painted orange crates. Indian print bedspreads covered mattresses that had been hauled over from an empty MIT dorm room. The Roommate/Parent Organization chart was off the wall and replaced by a big poster of flow-ers in a purple peace sign. A lamp with a fringed shade stood next to the sunken couch, its worn fabric hidden under a Navajo weaving. The kitchen was relatively clean, but sparse, and no one cared because they were all going out for lunch.

But then it got hot—over ninety degrees for five days in a row—which made it an official heat wave. The end of Weymouth Street in Somerville backed up to an industrial area next to the train tracks where the sprawl-ing Happy Chick packing plant acted as a dead end block to the street, keeping it traffic-free and relatively quiet. However, the early heat wave did something to the refrigeration system in the poultry plant so that hundreds of unhappy chicks did not live to see the slaughtering facil-ity. Instead their rotting feathered carcasses sat outside in the heat in containers awaiting incineration. The smell was overwhelming, like vats of rancid cat food left in the sun. Even the early flowering of prodigious peonies and lilacs in the neat front yards up and down Weymouth Street could not mask the stench.

Lillian reasoned that all she had to do was pray for the temperature to drop, show up on Saturday, be pleasant to everyone's parents and leave. She just needed to pull the rent scam off for about three more months;

143

by September she could get a whole new crop of fake renters in place. Maybe even raise the rent to $55 each month. Not bad!

SO, ON SATURDAY MORNING, IN more seasonal temperatures, a gaggle of bell-bottomed long-haired young women and their parents dressed in their South Hampton whites and Gucci loafers strolled up Weymouth Street, past the Portuguese grandmothers in shapeless black, smiling toothlessly and awaiting compliments on their spring gardens. Up the street they came, into the smell of rotting chicken, short round fathers slightly out of breath, and tall mothers fresh from the hairdresser, in matching accessories – shoes, bags, scarves – with not a gray hair in sight.

What they saw as they approached was a wobbling three-decker painted pea green about ten years earlier and now badly weather-beaten. The three back porches, one for each level, looked like they were about to slide right off the building and tumble into the lane below. Half the fire escape had disappeared.

What they heard was the guys who lived on the ground floor tuning up their instruments for a rare daytime rehearsal. Usually they rehearsed after midnight, stopping only when Lillian smashed pots and pans out the window. Lately, however, they had started incorporating pots and pans into their act. The adults in the group were already immersed in head-shaking conversation about where and how these girls lived – *Wouldn't they be better off in a dorm?* – before they had stepped foot into the building.

Lillian could tell that the chicken smell was about to get worse as the day wore on, so the noise might be a welcome relief. As they rounded the first hallway, the band boys' door stood open, revealing an empty room except for a mattress littered with discarded bags of *Screaming Yellow Zonkers* popcorn and empty pizza cartons piled in a corner. A roll of sticky flypaper dangled six feet from a broken chandelier and a large tomcat batted at it rhythmically. Lillian shut the door, but not before the smell of marijuana drifted out, blessedly masking the chicken odor for a few minutes.

She looked back at the parent group as she hurried up to the second floor. She could see that *'Where the hell are you living?'* was rapidly turning to *'Let's get the hell out of here!'* She walked faster, right into the radical feminist lesbian communards from Unit #2 who were changing the hallway light bulb that had hitherto gone unchanged since the onset of daylight savings time.

Lillian almost turned back to the group with a desperate, *'Hey, how many dykes does it take to change a light bulb?'* But the answer was, unfortunately, all of them. All five lesbian communards plus a few visitors were out in the hallway, complaining about the smell and climbing on step stools where they stood, wearing red bandanas and revealing a generous amount of armpit hair, as they reached for the ceiling. Dead chickens and rock groups were one thing, but unshaven armpits could be the final straw as far as Lillian could see.

Lillian stopped the proceeding long enough to ask the communards to please – she raised her eyes in her best Joan of Arc gesture – step off the stools long enough for visiting parents to pass; hoping that they wouldn't start with chauvinist pig dialectics. But the encounter on the landing seemed only to propel the parental group faster so that they reached the third floor landing without further distraction, and by the time Lillian opened the door, the apartment looked like a relative haven of good taste and decency.

BY NOW, HOWEVER, SOME OF the parents had begun to suspect that something was not right. For one thing, these girls did not seem to know each other very well. For example, they had trouble with each other's last names, which quickly became obvious in addressing the other's parents.

"Mr. Goldblum...ahhh Mr. Goldberg, I mean..."

"No, it's Greenberg, obviously. I'm Marcia Greenberg's father, so why would it be Goldberg?"

The mothers exchanged looks and placed protective hands on their husbands' arms.

"Now, dear, they're just confused; there are so many of us," said Mrs. Greenberg.

"Confused?" said Mr. Greenberg. "She goes to Harvard, for chrissake! What am I paying for?"

Lillian, having memorized the wall chart, knew names would be their Achilles heel and was about to offer a preemptive tour when the phone rang. It rang five times before anyone moved, during which Lillian realized that no one knew where the phone was. In fact, Lillian wasn't sure which phone it was, so she sprang into action – real audition material.

"Hey, Marcia! Where did you put that phone?" she called, moving into the front room where both red and black phones stood side by side on an old suitcase. It was the black phone, hers, and she picked it up with a cheerful *Hello!* It was Les wanting to know if he could come over to retrieve a script he had forgotten. She ignored his request and launched into a fake speech:

"Hey, no trouble at all. I was just hanging out with Marcia and... and...her parents!" Lillian had a brainstorm that if someone had actually called Marcia in this location, perhaps her parents would believe that she really lived here. "We're all here, it's parents weekend or something, there's a brunch but she's right here and I'll just put her on. Marcia...?" she called convincingly. But Lillian had overplayed her hand, because Marcia was not headed for an acting career and was stunned that anyone would call her at this unknown number. Her first thought was that something must be wrong with Tyler, MIT experimental rat-boy whom her parents detested. Breaking up with him had been a condition of her returning to school in Cambridge. By the time Marcia reached the phone, Lillian could see that she was shaking, ready to hyperventilate, and Lillian tried to grab the receiver back, but Marcia had already blurted out, "Tyler!..."

Dead silence. Panic in the eyes of the other girls. Lillian tried to recover, her back to the parents and her face inches from Marcia's.

"No silly, it's Les!" said Lillian much too loudly. "I don't think Tyler will be bothering you anymore, not with Les around."

Lillian turned to see that Marcia's mother was clenching her fists so hard she thought the nails would draw blood. Marcia stayed on the phone as long as she could, finally playing along and even flirting lamely with Les.

"What the hell is going on here?" Marcia's father exploded as soon as his daughter hung up the phone. For some reason they all turned to look at Lillian.

"Well, I know you've been planning quite a brunch, so I'll get out of your way," she said confidently as she strode past them into the kitchen where she headed for the fridge. "Just left my yoghurt culture in here and I'll be heading off to...uh...you know, rehearsal. Where else do I ever go?" But the fridge contained nothing but a jar of mustard and some moldy cream cheese and she slammed it immediately, standing there with her back to the group, afraid to turn around. *How do I get out of here?* she wondered.

"I know that voice," Marcia's father said slowly. "You're the only one who ever answers when we call. *Oh, Marcia's not here, sir, she's in the library, she's downstairs visiting the other girls*—oh yeah I just bet she is, taking lessons in personal grooming—*she's out buying milk, she's in the shower...*"

At the mention of the shower they all looked over at the bathroom door. Marcia's mother peered inside, gasping. The bathroom was so tiny that Les often joked that he could sit on the can and take a leak in the sink at the same time. *Did he?* Lillian wondered. Lillian showered at the gym. The other mothers gathered behind her, clucking with sharp intakes of breath. They all turned to face Marcia, who had backed up to the wall, eyes wide, both eyebrows a perfect arch.

"So, is that it?" her father continued, shouting now. "I'm some kinda patsy paying for this dump—I don't know whether to be relieved you don't really live here because I should call the health department—or tell you to go support yourself because you wanna throw your life away screwing your scrawny little rat boy." His voice was getting louder and a vein in his forehead had begun to throb, standing out like a mountain chain on a topographical map.

147

"Now Phil…" his wife said, pleading, wrapping her arms around his like a snake. "Phil, honey, don't get yourself all worked up over this; I'm sure Marcia will straighten it out." But not only could Marcia not straighten it out, Marcia couldn't speak. In fact, she started to faint, falling in slow motion to the floor, where her mother ran to catch her and, in the process, tripped over the red phone cord, falling herself and twisting her ankle in the process.

On the plus side, this gave everyone something to do. The doctors in the group could examine the ankle, the girls could call an ambulance, someone had to go get the car, someone else called the restaurant to cancel the reservation, and Lillian disappeared down the stairs and out to Cambridge Street, where she realized she better find another source of income – fast!

WHERE COULD SHE FIND RENT and two hundred dollars a month that also gave her time to go to auditions and rehearsals? And what skills did she have that people might be willing to pay real money for? A few months earlier she had made a list of all the things she was pretty good at. At the top of the list was, first, Dancing (subdivided into – Ballet, Modern, Jazz, Musical Theatre). Next came Acting – Shakespeare, Shaw, Existential Drama. That was the list.

Then she made a list of all the jobs she had ever had: babysitting, waitress, camp counselor, language tutor, ski instructor, doctor's office receptionist, costume department low-level designer and stitcher-upper. She tried to cross-reference skills with past jobs, and came up with dancing waitress, voice-over receptionist, child-care ski instructor, but it didn't look promising.

Sitting on a park bench, she pulled a newspaper out of a trash can and went through *Help Wanted Professional*, which was full of ads for legal secretaries and computer programmers – whatever that was – and *Help Wanted General*, which needed people to clean up after the secretaries and programmers. And then her eye fell on *Help Wanted Specialty:*
DANCERS; $300/week, Flex hours, Call after 3:00.

Three hundred a week? Wow, that was more than she made in a month. She glanced at her watch; it was 2:45. Within twenty minutes she had an appointment for the next day at The Candy Shack, lower Washington Street. The only thing the guy on the phone wanted to know was her age (too young) and her height (too tall). She lied on both counts.

The next day Lillian put on her short leopard print wraparound dress and her white retro go-go girl boots, and took the T from the rusted Lechmere subway stop into downtown Boston, getting off at Filene's Basement and pushing though the crowd of brides-to-be stampeding, like the bulls at Pamplona, toward the annual bridal gown sale.

Lillian turned left on Washington Street at Jordan Marsh and continued walking past boarded-up theatres and movie houses, once elegant, the gold and gilt carvings still visible from the street, now too far gone even for strippers. She hardly knew this part of Boston on the edge of Chinatown—seedy, with decrepit buildings and small parking lots guarded by pot-bellied guys chewing toothpicks.

There it was—225 Washington Street; The Candy Shack. *Big Breath.* She hadn't told anyone she was going there—not even Les. He was furious at her for the parent weekend debacle as it was and would have told her this entire thing was a plot to snatch her into white slavery. Les had a thing about this. He was always clipping articles about people disappearing. "White slavery," he would say with a knowing nod. "Nixon is behind it." According to Les, Nixon was behind everything, so Lillian paid no attention.

But Nixon was definitely not behind The Candy Shack. This she could report with some authority to Les. Above the door was a big neon winking sign with a pair of huge crimson lips opening and closing suggestively. The windows were blacked out and Christmas lights twinkled in their crimson frames.

White slavery…well that remains to be seen, she thought, as she squared her shoulders and marched across the street toward the bright red door.

UP ON THE SECOND FLOOR she walked into a large seating area with a semi-circular bar on one side and a linoleum dance floor on the other. The place smelled of stale smoke, which clung to the red carpet and tablecloths. A couple of men sat at the mirrored bar. They were leaning over a stack of papers, while a guy in a ripped T-shirt and sandals set up an amplifier and speakers on the stage behind the dance floor. Nobody looked at her.

Lillian cleared her throat. "Uh, hi…I'm looking for Gerry? I have an appointment." The larger of the two men at the bar glanced up and put down his pen.

"Yeah? Who's looking for him?"

"Well, I am. We talked about the dancing job on the phone…are you Gerry? Hi, I'm…"

"Forget it, honey, too tall. I asked you. You told me five foot seven. I put you up on that pedestal over there," he said, pointing to a gold cage in the corner that was three feet off the ground, "and your head's gonna be up in the strobe lights." He went back to his papers.

Lillian had already figured out that she could save enough on $300 week, even if she only worked for two months, to pay for all of next year's room and board.

"But, don't you have dancers who dance on the floor?" she asked, walking over to the section of the linoleum with the highest head clearance.

"Look, I told you, forget it. My girls wear spike heels. Looks to me like you're gonna be well over six feet in spikes." As far as he was concerned the conversation was over. Lillian sighed and headed back toward the dark stairwell, almost bumping into a young woman dashing up the stairs two at a time.

That's what they want, she said to herself, looking over her shoulder at the girl in purple bellbottom jeans with a long ponytail. *Petite. The story of my life. I'd be a great dancer if I didn't look like a fucking football player.* She stopped in the stairwell, noticing for the first time that the walls were decorated with black and white framed photos of dancers who suddenly looked more like strippers, covered only in spangles and fishnet and feather boas. Some of them wore plumed hats that must have been a foot tall. "Well, he's probably right," thought Lillian, "even if I had the guts to do this, I'd probably burn my head off…"

A chair crashed to the floor up above and a man's voice yelled, "I'll get you for this, you bitch! Get back here." This was followed by another crash and footsteps coming fast, right behind Lillian.

"Quick!" the girl in bellbottoms ordered. "Down the stairs!"

Lillian obeyed instantly, running the rest of the way, throwing herself at the front door and into the wide arc of sudden light. She kept running, the other girl right behind her, for another two blocks, until she felt someone grab her elbow.

"Stop, it's ok, you can stop…now…boy, am I out…of…shape." The girl stood there panting, shielding her eyes in the noonday sun. "Thank you. I don't know what you were doing there, but don't even think about going back. Gerry's a lunatic. He treats his girls like shit. Find someone else."

"I beg your pardon?" Lillian was surprised at herself for sounding so formal, just like her grandmother, in fact.

"He's a pimp. Obviously." The young woman looked at Lillian with eyes so blue they were almost turquoise. "Or didn't you know? You didn't answer one of those $300 a week ads, did you?"

Lillian nodded, thinking they were probably the same age, so what made her so smart.

"Ohh, I get it," she continued, "you're one of those college girls looking for a summer job. Gerry can usually spot 'em a mile away. What did he tell you? Too young?"

"Too tall."

"Ha! He told me I was too short."

"But didn't you…uh…work for him anyway?"

"Well, I was a waitress until this morning. Better tips. But he's been trying to…let's say…promote me for months now, since he found out I lied about my age. Frankly, I'd consider it if his customers weren't so gross. Anyway, thanks for being there. He probably would have chased me down the street if you hadn't come along. Well, good luck. I'm Cydney, by the way. Take it from me. Go find something else," she said, walking backwards. "Gotta go. See ya." And she disappeared into an alleyway.

"Cydney?" Lillian muttered to herself. "Isn't that a man's name? Didn't she mean Cindy?"

1982. All Night Long.

"HA! CINDY. IT'S ALL COMING back to me," said Lillian, stretching out on Cydney's floor.

"Yes, I saved you from a life of white slavery," said Cydney, still hunched over her machine. "Although that's what some people would call being a housewife in Newton Center."

"Well, if I were a housewife, I'd be home. In my house. But I'm here in the middle of the night with you trying to figure out how to make it to the big time."

"Yeah, yeah. So what did you do with your go-go girl act? Wish I could have seen it." Cydney shut off her machine and whistled for Boris. "Want some coffee?"

"I joined the circus."

"Really? You have just gone up several notches in my estimation!"

"Next best thing. I joined a cruise ship," Lillian said. "And then I became a housewife. Cydney, that dog will get fur all over the place. Get him out of here."

IN 1971 LILLIAN SIGNED A one-year contract to join the entertainment crew of the Norwegian cruise ship, *Sea Breeze II*. Marc had joined the Peace Corps, which kept him out of Vietnam, and Les, who had failed his army physical, had moved to London.

By the time Lillian appeared in the port of Miami, after a six-week intensive dance workshop, minus twenty pounds, hair shorn and highlighted, skin tanned and enthusiasm at full tilt, she realized that she knew absolutely nothing about the sea. First of all, it moved. Constantly. Second, it could go from calm, green blue, gulls calling, soft wind to dark grey foamy-capped ferocity in the time it took to change costumes. Remarkably, she discovered that she was almost–but not complete-ly–immune to seasickness. Even seasickness could not have dampened her enthusiasm. She was being paid to be on stage! A small stage, it was true, but one with a captive and appreciative audience, and an instant theatre family.

Fortunately, all the men in the troupe were gay–immediate best bud-dies–which every dancing girl needed to stay sane. No one to grope her or lie about the size of her ass, or whether her makeup worked or whether something looked like shit.

"Honey," Brett, her dance partner, would say, "that looks like shit. Get it off you right now." And off it would go. Lillian could stand in front of Brett and his boyfriend, Billy, stark naked, and they would look at her through their ostrich feather boas as though she were a statue.

"Lily, babes, who wouldn't kill for those tits!" They were the only men who got away with calling her Lily.

One night, during a performance, she raced out of the dressing room to the bathroom to run headlong into Ignacio Memling, chief stew-ard, blocking the very narrow hall. Memling was definitely not gay. The first time Lillian had met him, she thought her jaw had gone slack and her eyes might have popped out of her head. He moved with an acute awareness of how his body filled space–magnificent and hands-off–like a tiger in a cage.

Memling made it clear that he did not permit any fraternizing be-tween members of his crew, and that included himself, even though he spent eight months on the ship and the rest at home in Argentina with his wife and teenage daughters.

As usual, Lillian was scantily clad as she raced to the toilet between costume changes, when she found herself facing Memling in his very white uniform and epaulettes. They were the same height in her bare feet and did that 'you move this way, I move that way shuffle' ending up stuck together with her almost naked body pressed very tightly against his—wow—really built body. Suddenly Lillian felt weak in the knees as she realized how terribly she missed Marc and hadn't touched a man since—Christ—when?

Billy yelled for her from the dressing room. "We're on! Where *are* you?" And Memling slid away with a Mona Lisa smile.

She wondered if she was losing it. Was that a come hither or a get away? Memling had a reputation of being a total professional. Friendly, distant, charming, attentive, efficient, he had never been more than pleasant and casual with Lillian. No one had heard even a rumor of his fooling around. And since every gay guy she knew had a crush on Memling, she pumped them for information.

"Totally straight, sadly," said Brett.

"And, honey, I have batted my eyes six ways to Sunday," added Billy. "I have paraded my very tightest crack-ass jeans up and down that dining room until my balls are in a knot. Straight as a ruler."

"No girlfriends?" asked Lillian—not sure if she should be hopeful or terrified.

"*No*, girlfriend! No one that I've ever seen. Go get him, honey. We'll all take bets." It was Billy's third winter on the ship and he was the source of all wisdom and most hijinks. The ship was the safest place he had ever worked; no one gave a crap if he was a raging queen in his private life.

THEY SAILED OUT OF MIAMI and through the Panama Canal up the coast of Mexico en route to Los Angeles. Somewhere around the Baja Peninsula a storm blew up without warning; Lillian kept hearing about these storms but had yet to experience one. It was a short performance night, and the dance team was doing backup for a big-name singer they had picked up in Acapulco for a two-night gig. They had just finished when the captain announced that they expected some swells—batten down. Someone had told Lillian that the best way to take on motion was to drink champagne, and even though she didn't like champagne, she downed a glass.

Look at me! I'm walking the plank, she thought as she veered from side to side on the lower deck crew level. Memling rounded the corner and saw her teetering as though she were on a balance beam. Suddenly the boat shifted and bile rose to her throat; the world tilted and her stomach flopped. She put her hand to her mouth and looked around in terror for a sink or a bucket. Memling produced one like a rabbit out of hat and swooped her out of the way and into an alcove where she heaved into the bucket. She was too woozy to think straight, because if she had she would have bemoaned her chances for seduction, which were now – evidently – nil.

"Did you fall for the champagne trick?" he asked in a lilting accent. She nodded and he handed her a wet towel. "First time, eh? Come with me."

She followed him out on deck where the waves sloshed on board and the chairs had been tied down. His voice rose above the roar of the wind. "Look out there – between the waves. The horizon is always flat. Just keep looking. Big breaths." He opened a hatch and grabbed a blanket, wrapping it around her. She was shivering so hard she practically vibrated. Gradually the nausea disappeared as she stood mesmerized by the unchanging horizon despite the thrashing seas. When she turned to thank him, Memling was gone.

She was never seasick again.

BY THE TIME THEY HAD moved up the west coast and into the inside passage for summer tours to Alaska, Lillian was in love with the intimacy of a theatre cabal in which everyone was best friend, worst enemy, frat brother, sorority sister and cell mate all rolled into one. It felt like nothing had ever existed before and might not exist after. Life on the ship in this here and now was it. Marc disappeared. She could barely remember what he looked like. Les wrote that he was understudying Iago, and she could hardly remember the plot of Othello. She lived in a hormonal haze of physical work, rich food, late nights, midnight sun, and the high cheekbones of Memling's face. Not that he noticed hers, but she was in high crush territory.

THE STEAM ROOM WAS ON a schedule of odd days for women and even days for men. Not that anyone could keep track of the days, but they were posted on the door. Lillian wrenched her knee doing a lift with Billy – stupid, she was just too tall for him but he had insisted – and needed to get into the whirlpool and steam. It was late at night and still reserved for men, but Billy snuck her in.

"Coast is clear. I'll stand guard."

The steam room was almost impenetrable. At first she thought it was too hot, but she limped to the tile bench and stretched out on her towel. Her foot touched flesh and she jumped up. "Bill? Are you in here?"

"Not Bill..." came a voice. Memling.

"Oh shit, oh shit, I'm sorry – I'm gone..." She wrapped herself in the towel, now damp, and stumbled toward what she thought was the door. But Memling had also jumped up, and they collided mid-steam, her towel falling, chest to dripping chest. Lillian caught a quick look on his face, both amused and darkly intense, and threw herself at the door.

Billy was nowhere around.

Memling followed her out, towel around his waist.

"What are you doing here? Following me?"

"No, God, no...I hurt my knee and...Billy said..."

"Let's see..." He took her by the hand and led her to the massage table.

"But – anyone could come in; I shouldn't be here."

"Not likely; it's late. Hop up..."

Lillian squirmed up on the table, leg dangling, towel barely around her. And then he kissed her knee.

"I think I may faint."

"You are a mess, aren't you? Throwing up. Fainting. Your knee is fine by the way, moving freely. Ice, not heat." He pulled her to her feet. They stood nose to nose, not touching, and she dropped her towel.

THE NEXT FEW MONTHS WERE the happiest of Lillian's life, albeit the most removed from the real world. There was no one to shake her – get a grip, you fool! No girlfriends to point out that the man was married. And fifteen years older. And had teenage children. Wake up!

No Les to remind her that she was supposed to be auditioning for Shakespearean dramas.

No Marc to suggest creating a grown-up life plan – jobs, graduate school, marriage, kids.

No family to ask why was she still in love with performing and how could she possibly make a living at that?

So she just drifted, in an out of Memling's bed or anything that could be used as a bed; in and out of costume, in and out of rehearsal; in and out of the midnight buffet, in and out of small towns and large cities on their coastal stops. But then a year was over and her contract was up for renewal. Memling was going back to his family for shore leave. She was going to the Philippines to see Marc. Something like reality was bound to creep back in.

AFTER WEEKS IN THE PHILIPPINES on an outer island where Marc's Peace Corps schoolchildren lived in desperate poverty next to a gorgeous beach, it was as though Lillian and Marc had never been apart. Memling disappeared, out there on the horizon – a beautiful dream, the prince at the ball just before midnight. Maybe she should stay off the ship and not be tempted by him again. Marc told her he was applying to law school and hoped to start in a year. And what were her plans?

Keep moving, she thought. Moving where? Toward what? Les was working hard in London; his reports sounded grim. Auditions, rejections, more auditions, parts in small touring companies in grey English backwaters. Lillian knew that she didn't have the stomach for it. Besides, after a year of show tunes, she had to admit that she just wasn't that good. It irked her that Marc seemed awfully friendly with a perky co-worker from Alabama.

"She's cute, Marc. Didn't know you were into the cheerleader type. Should I be jealous?"

"I'm the one who should be jealous. You're practically stripping in front of strangers every night."

"If I were stripping I'd be making more money. And every hunky guy is gay."

"Not all of them. What about the guy in the white uniform with the epaulettes? I bet guys with epaulettes have small dicks."

Umm, no, thought Lillian, but she was grinning from ear to ear. "Marc, we agreed *not* to talk about this."

"*You* brought it up," said Marc. "I'm just saying that I'm thinking about my future; grown-up time. And whether you're part of it."

They stared at each other.

"Well, do you want me to be part of it?" asked Lillian, not sure of her own answer. Yes, she did, eventually. But not right this minute–not while she was as free as a bird.

They agreed to table this discussion for another six months.

"But not for too much longer," said Marc. "If we're going to be together, we have to start making some commitments."

Commitments–jeez. A concept that could make Lillian turn tail and run in the opposite direction.

BACK ON THE SHIP AND heading down to the Panama Canal, Billy noticed straight-out that Lillian had gained weight. They were rehearsing as backup to several big-name performers for Caribbean cruise high season–Marie Osmond, John Denver, Neil Sedaka–and everyone was feeling the tension. "Stakes are up, up, up, honeylamb," said Billy. "What's with the boobs? They are eye-popping! And a little tummy action as well."

Memling was meeting the ship in Panama City in two weeks. She had just received a postcard from him with a heads up that his eldest daughter was joining the crew as an intern. If their affair were to continue, those stakes would be going up as well. "Yeah, I have gained a few pounds. Probably the food in the islands – disgusting – fried pig ears and rice."

"And that's why you're eating ice cream at ten in the morning? Put that down. I am not lifting you if you gain weight." He took the bowl of ice cream out of her hands. "What birth control are you using?"

Lillian stared at him. She had been so preoccupied with burning the candle at both ends that she felt as though she had been sucker-punched. "No way. I...don't...not possible."

LILLIAN WENT TO THE SHIP doctor who wanted a blood test to confirm but thought that yes, she was maybe seven to eight weeks pregnant. She left his office, reeling. Memling? Marc? She always used her diaphragm unless...

"Y'all are white as a Ku Klux Klan grand wizard," said Billy, in his best southern accent. "Listen, we will be in Acapulco in two days. You are going to a private clinic I know. We're docked overnight."

Lillian was too stunned to react.

"I have the word of a friend in LA. This doctor runs a high-end hush-hush clinic that all of Hollywood goes to. Cash only. Not cheap. How much have you saved?"

Billy went with her when the ship docked. The clinic was behind a large gate walled off from the dirt road with its sleeping dogs and pecking chickens. But once inside they entered a restored mansion built around a courtyard with a bubbling fountain and chirping birds in cages – patrolled by staff dressed in crisp white uniforms. *It's a sanitarium,* she thought. *Perhaps I have lost my mind and I'm being committed.* The doctor confirmed that she was close to ten weeks pregnant, which meant that the baby was definitely not Marc's. She would have to stay overnight, even though the clinic used a new technique of vacuum curettage that was much safer and less intrusive. Was this really happening? Lillian started to cry. The doctor, who spoke excellent English and had done his residency in St. Louis, patted her hand.

"I do as many as twenty of these a day. Never had a problem. I assume that you do not want to have a baby."

"I can't. It wouldn't be mine. I mean...the man is married and has children. It's not fair to him."

"What about you? Is it fair to you?"

"No! I don't want a baby. Not now." Maybe not ever, she thought. The idea of something growing inside her was terrifying. Get it out.

After her overnight in Acapulco, which cost the entire $2,000 of her savings from a year on the ship, she took a taxi down to the harbor fifteen minutes before the boat was scheduled to leave. She stood out of sight, watching Billy pace back and forth, hands shielding his eyes, scanning the dock and checking his watch. That ship left on time right down to the minute, and she had to get on board. She stood rooted to the spot, the world swirling around her – dizzy and weak. *I need a moment. Just a moment.* Gangplanks going up. Day trippers on deck waving. Everything was moving too fast. Bret appeared by Billy's side, conferring. She saw him shake his head and Billy's shoulders sag. I'm right here, she wanted to shout, still unable to move. *What is wrong with me? What if Billy thinks I'm sick, or dead?*

Engines on. Exhaust spouting from the main smoke stacks. Finally she found the strength to scramble through the crowd down to the dock. Too late. The boat pulled back, its three decks blending into one whole, elegant lines folding into themselves, a postcard on the horizon.

She sent three telegrams: One to Billy apologizing. One to Memling telling him she was moving on. One to Marc with the answer that she was ready to be a grown-up.

1982. All Night Long.

"ARE YOU ASLEEP?" LILLIAN STOOD over Cydney, who had her eyes closed as she lay curled up next to Boris on the hardwood floor. "Jeez, I have never told anyone that story and it's so boring that it put you to sleep, huh? Great. If I didn't think the dog would rip my leg off I would kick it. And you."

"Don't you dare. I heard you. Just thinking is all. Pretty intense. But it worked out. You and Marc. What happened to Memling?" She sat up and pulled a tangle of green thread out of her hair.

"A few postcards. Sweet nothings. Saw him for a few hours once in Miami and couldn't imagine what I had been thinking. Still gorgeous, but we had nothing to say to each other."

"That is the definition of great sex. Just keep your mouth shut, except where you should keep it open," said Cydney, standing up and rubbing her back. "So, no regrets, huh?"

"None."

"Clinic in Mexico. Only ten years ago—how times have changed, thank God."

"No...no regrets. I have my kids. I guess if I couldn't have kids...don't know. It does make me crazy that I have spent my entire adult life either trying not to get pregnant or trying to get pregnant. You? Robert and Marjorie don't have kids, do they?"

"Nope."

"Might be a game-changer if you got pregnant."

"Not happening. He's had a vasectomy."

"Really?" Lillian thought that was odd. *He's young and wants to be a politician? Families are great assets.* "That's pretty definitive. You won't even let your dog get fixed."

"Yeah, well Robert is not my dog, and his penis is not my property. He has other uses for it, believe me. And the last thing I want is a baby. Unless it's to help sell our carriers so we can make money and I can stop depending on Robert's penis. Christ," she said, looking at the industrial clock on the wall, "three more hours and the truck will be here. Back to work!"

"Only if you talk me through it. Your turn for the next story," said Lillian as she picked up her tape gun.

IN THE SPRING OF 1968, when Cydney, a high school senior, was champing at the bit to get out of her parents' house in Lawrell, her oldest sister, Carmen, who was recently widowed, moved back to town. Right out of school she had married Private First Class Marlon Whittaker, 2nd Battalion, 5th Marines, just long enough to have two children before he was killed in Quang Nam province. A widow at twenty-four, Carmen had returned home from Camp Pendleton with her toddler daughters and started drinking heavily, following in her father's footsteps. Bianca had spent the past twenty years living in fear of her children picking up their father's alcoholism and she wasn't sure she could handle any more heartache.

Carmen moped around the house and ignored her kids, which drove Cydney crazy. Since Carmen had married Marlon on the rebound after breaking up with Bobbie Bretton, Cydney wasn't sure if Carmen's grief was for the loss of Marlon or for the loss of Camp Pendleton in sunny California. After two months of sympathy, Bianca told her to get off her ass and find a job. One day, after interviewing for file clerk at Taylord Mills, Carmen rushed home to report that Bobbie Bretton had moved back to Lawrell from his hot shot job in New York to take over as Director of R&D at Taylord Mills.

Carmen appeared in the front hallway, her face flushed. "Guess what?"

Cydney sat on the living room floor, cutting out a dress pattern. She was trying not to be resentful of babysitting Carmen's kids, but she was not succeeding. "What? You out of beer or something?"

"Why are you such a brat? This is big news. Bobbie is back in town."

Bianca had appeared in the doorway, wiping her hands on her apron. "Bobbie Bretton?" she asked.

"Great, huh? I invited him for dinner tomorrow night."

Cydney looked up from her scissors. "Why would anyone in their right mind come back to this dump after Harvard?" Bobbie – wow – she had had a major crush when he was going out with Carmen in high school. Frankly, she had no idea what he saw in Carmen then, when Bobbie was Mr. Perfect – handsome, smart, polite, and friendly – and Carmen, in her opinion, looked like a rabbit with runny eyes. As a child, Carmen had stuttered badly, and while Cydney tried to be patient about it, the involuted staccato of her speech drove her up a wall. So it was an event of some note when Carmen started going out with Bobbie Bretton, the most popular guy in school. But maybe Carmen had qualities that Cydney had just never picked up on, she reasoned, or maybe Bobbie was just sick and tired of going out with all the blonde cheerleaders and homecoming queens with perfect teeth and just the right amount of lip gloss.

ROBERT BRETTON'S MOTHER, CLAIRE BRETTON, and Bianca Mallone had been close friends growing up in the old, unheated row houses down by the Merrimack River next to the factories, where generations of mill-working immigrant families had lived all crammed together when they weren't working fourteen-hour shifts. Over the years, Claire Bretton and Bianca had stayed close, but while Bianca had to raise four wild girls, Claire's son, Bobbie, was an only child. Her husband, Henri Bretton, had died from the result of a mill accident when Bobbie was only a few months old. Claire never remarried and devoted her life to her son, and it showed.

Maybe good fortune skips a generation or two and Bobbie was blessed with the luck his parents never had. He won a hockey scholarship to Harvard and at the same time managed to hang on to his teeth so that he could continue to charm everyone, male and female, with his patient, mischievous smile. He never made an enemy in his life, and he was always elected to some prestigious office – student council president, team captain, – or pushed into accepting some honor. He was a straight

A Dean's List student at Harvard, graduated Phi Beta Kappa, summa cum laude, and went on to Harvard Business School where he finished third in his class.

Robert Bretton had returned to Lawrell to take a job as Vice President of R&D at the largest employer in town, Taylord Mills. His mother, Claire, was horrified. She had spent her life getting her son out of a dead end industrial mill town and into the hallowed halls of old moneyed wealth and prestige, only to have him come back to work for the place that had killed his father. She was not mollified by his title or his substantial salary because Taylord Mills had been in nosedive decline for twenty years.

In fact, Bobbie was hired because the President of Taylord Mills, Herbert Wallace, was nearly desperate. Taylord Mills had been in the Taylord-Wallace family for six generations, and Herb Wallace had no sons to whom he could leave the business. He had only a daughter, Marjorie, who had attended three finishing schools in five years, and two very expensive girls' colleges in three years, none of which granted her anything like a proper degree, until Herb donated a section of the dining room at the last school to be henceforth known as the Herbert and Betsy Wallace Student Lounge.

Bobbie accepted Herb's offer, perhaps out of some lofty notion of lifting his dead mill-working father's memory onto a shrine higher than the one in his mother's dark bedroom, or perhaps because it was a greater challenge than being a production manager on the line at General Foods. Maybe it was the dinner at Herb's hilltop mansion, with a view over the winding Merrimack River, which did not smell like rotting fish or look as slimy pea green from this vantage point as it had when he was a boy living thirty yards from its polluted banks. Or maybe it was the view up Marjorie's dress as she sat opposite him on one of the three living room couches, with her legs crossed loosely, wearing red crotchless panties and gently bouncing her braceleted ankle on her knee, black strapless sandals dangling from her manicured toes.

At any rate, within two weeks Bobbie had accepted Herb's offer and moved to Lawrell, where he stayed temporarily with his mother while starting to perform miracles at Taylord Mills.

Ever since Robert returned, his mother had been on his case that he should run Taylord out of business and then go back to corporate America. There was no point in telling her that he did not want to work on Wall Street and be gobbled up by a multi-national bank, because he would never run the bank. But if he played his cards right he might end up owning Taylord Mills, and that would be something. A manufacturing turnaround, grab the reins and run that horse...he'd make the cover of every business magazine in the country. Textiles were finished in the US, certainly north of the Carolinas; everything was coming in from the Far East. But he could do it, and do it right, and treat his employees fairly in the bargain. So Robert put his energies in one place and that was work.

It had been years since he left Lawrell, and he knew hardly anyone. Most of his friends had ended up as hoods in motorcycle gangs, or in the jungles of Viet Nam, or doing time for petty theft, or on hockey farm teams. His old girlfriend, Bianca's eldest daughter, Carmen Mallone, had married, had two babies and was a war widow at the age of twenty-four. She called to invite him over for dinner, and, having no reason to decline, he accepted.

WHATEVER THE REASON, THERE HE was again—six, seven years later, having brought Carmen a Joni Mitchell album and Bianca a bouquet of tulips, sitting casually at their dinner table with its mismatched chairs and broken china, looking like a man, and not like the dimpled, curly-haired boy the Mallone women remembered.

Over dinner, Bobbie Bretton picked up where he left off, as though he had never been out there in the world of sports cars, fraternities, prep school ties, and summers at the beach. He was funny and self-deprecating, and told knock-knock jokes for Carmen's toddler girls, and arranged the flowers for Bianca, and never took his eyes off Cydney, now in her last semester of high school.

Cydney, in turn, thought Bobbie was much more handsome than she remembered, even though his hair was cut short and sort of nerdy, while everyone she hung with wore theirs long and scruffy. He seemed so much older than she, she who was counting the hours until the end of school, and yet not as old as Carmen. This was odd because they were the same age, and sad because it said something final and desperate about Carmen, back at home with two kids, no job and an old boyfriend who might as well have moved to another planet.

Something about the way Robert had scooped her up in a big hug when Cydney answered the door brought back a rush of forgotten memories—a sharp spicy smell that wasn't cheap perfume or bourbon, the excitement in the undercurrent of female voices asking, *"Is that Bobbie?"* and everyone rushing to be the first to talk to him.

Kevin was on his best behavior at dinner, sitting at the head of the table and keeping everyone's glass filled, while leaving his empty. He chewed thoughtfully, laughed at all Bobbie's jokes, asked questions about why kids became student radicals when they were lucky enough to go to the best schools like Harvard, remembered some of Bobbie's highlight hockey games, and asked about Herb Wallace and Taylord Mills.

"Heard his daughter Marjorie is back from whatever fancy school he sent her to in Switzerland. That girl is some looker, and she is going to inherit a pile of dough some day. Have you met her Bobbie, m'boy?"

"Well, I've met her often enough," answered Carmen, suddenly very animated. "She used to come to school dances, remember, Bobbie, just to see what she could pick up. Kids used to say that she would hit on some guy and then take him to the back seat of the Cadillac while the chauffeur waited or watched in the front."

"Carmen!" Bianca said, sounding shocked, not that she was.

"Well, Carmen," Robert said, chewing the meatloaf a little longer than necessary, "that was a long time ago and she must have been pretty lonely—poor little rich girl and all. Besides, I heard the guys talk. When guys exaggerate like that, believe me, nothing happens."

"Exaggerate like what?" Cydney asked, ignoring her frowning mother. "Did she ever hit on you?"

"She wouldn't have dared," Carmen answered with her mouth full, before Bobbie could consider the question. "He was with me. Weren't you?" she asked, putting her hand through the circle of his arm as he lifted his fork.

But Robert Bretton was not listening; he was astonished at the change in Cydney. The last time he had seen her she was a child dancing around the house in her sisters' old figure skating outfits, and now she was a woman who could turn heads. Including his.

"So, Cydney...what are your plans after you graduate?" he asked, politely ignoring Carmen.

"Making money. I'm sick of not having any. And getting out of here."

"College?"

"Nope. I'll work for a while until I get my own place and then go to art school. "

"Really? To do what?"

"To get rich."

Robert couldn't help it; he burst out laughing. "No one gets rich by being an artist."

Cydney put down her fork. "Oh yeah? Ever hear of Andy Warhol? His work is a joke and people lap it up. I'll be a fabric artist and work for opera companies. Not only do they have money, they have elephants on stage. It's true. At the Met, in *Aida*, for example."

"Have you seen *Aida*? At the Met? On stage?"

"No, smarty pants. I haven't. Because opera tickets cost a fortune. I'll need a sugar daddy for that."

"Cydney!" Both Carmen and Bianca said at once.

"Any sugar daddies on the horizon?" he asked, casually.

Cydney stared at him and broke into a grin. "How about you?"

Carmen, sitting beside her, pinched her arm, hard.

Robert almost choked and Carmen had to pound him on the back until he could get his breath. "Don't I have to be old and rich? Striking out on both counts here..."

Robert spent a few minutes mentally dressing Cydney up in a strapless black gown with her hair done up in a French twist and elbow length gloves, and then another few minutes taking them off. He gave her a big smile and a wink that he hoped didn't look either clumsy or leering, and prayed that he wouldn't have to stand up until his erection subsided.

This is ridiculous, he thought, *I've known her since she was a child!*

IN THE SUMMER OF 1968, Cydney had recently finished school and could think no further than getting out of the house. Carmen was driving her crazy, sulking in her room, ignoring her children, sleeping until mid-morning and expecting Bianca to pick up after her. Kevin had taken to disappearing again without explanation for days on end, and her mother had picked up a second shift. Cydney got a job working full-time as an aide in a nursing home and intended to save every cent until she could move to Boston in the fall and find a place of her own.

The Elmira B. Planter Nursing Home was located at the top of one of the hills that Robert Bretton was spending his summer lunch hours turning into a racecourse. He had bought himself a brand new, bright red Corvette. It was his first new car and he was in love. Two or three times a week he would leave the Mill at lunchtime and sneak out for a drive. Lawrell was full of hills whose roads abruptly swerved into sharp right-angled turns, offering sweeping panoramas of the twisting Merrimack River below and the foothills of New Hampshire beyond. Robert raced up and down these hills as though he were in a high school drag race, feeling the pulse pound in his temples, heart rising to his throat. He hoped no one would recognize him.

CYDNEY HAD A GOOD MIND to call the cops on the show-off who raced up and down scaring the old folks, until she went out on the wide rickety veranda one hot afternoon and stood watching the red corvette with one hand shielding her eyes. *Why, that's Bobbie!* she thought to herself, annoyance fast-forwarding to excitement.

She walked down the front steps and out to the street, where there were no sidewalks – a constant source of complaint by the residents – and stood by the side of the road, arms waving like a semaphore. Robert roared his way back up the hill while wondering what that structure was that looked like a rambling Victorian house, when he saw a girl in a white uniform with a short skirt and great legs jumping up and down by the side of the road. He was going too fast to catch her face, but he screeched to a stop several feet ahead and idled the car, looking in the rearview mirror, while the woman – who might have been in distress – ran up to the car. As she reached the passenger side and leaned into the car, black hair spilling out of its tied-back knot, he saw that it was Cydney.

"Hey, kiddo, haven't seen you around. How was graduation? What are you up to?"

"Nice wheels, Bretton. Moving up in the world, huh?"

"What's with the uniform, may I ask, and how about coming for a ride?"

Cydney explained that she was working, but ran back quickly, while he waited, to announce that she was taking lunch. They drove to Manny's Take-out Burgers and sat in the car while they ate. Cydney talked non-stop about the car. She was very impressed. "Wow, is this real leather or what?"

"Hey, watch the grease on the fingers. This is a virgin car and I just broke my most solemn rule – no eating in the car. See what you've done to me?" He gave her his widest smile, the one that usually hooked them right away. Cydney looked at him solemnly for a moment, and then turned to stare out the window.

He tapped her gently on the shoulder. "Uh-oh. What's the matter, kiddo? Did I say something wrong?"

"No, no…I just wish…" Her voice trailed off.

"Wish what?…Come on! Tell me. This is Bobbie you're talking to here…"

Cydney flopped back in her seat, dropped the remains of the meal in her lap, licked the catsup off her fingers, and reached over to kiss him. It was a short kiss, a peck, really, but it was one of those moments when all the years of their common past shifted slightly, like the plates in an earthquake, and suddenly they were standing on new and unpredictable ground. They stared at one another.

"Um, well, I don't know what to say." Robert cleared his throat. "Sorta stupid, huh?"

Cydney thought she would try out a line from the movies. "Well, you could say nothing and kiss me, you fool." She'd added 'you fool' just like that. They both giggled. And then Robert leaned over to kiss her, tasting like French fries, not knowing quite where to put his greasy hands. He smelled like cloves, a smell she remembered from his visits to the house when she was a child.

"A real kiss," she said, in a low voice.

Robert held his hands up in the air and leaned into her neck, lips on her ear. "Cydney, you're like my sister."

"Then why are you nuzzling my ear? Kiss me for real…" She held her hands up to his, locking fingers.

"How old are you?"

"Eighteen – you're twenty-five – big deal. You know I've always had a crush on you, ever since I was ten years old."

"You were never ten years old. You were always a wise old woman watching me with those slinky eyes. So, do you still have a crush on me?"

She put her arms around his neck and nodded.

"That's too bad," he said, "because crushes don't last, you know. They could be over in…oh…five or six years."

"By then, I'll be way too sophisticated for you and you'll be ready to settle down and have a wife and kids and I'll never be anyone's wife and I'll certainly never have kids…"

"Whoa, you're getting a little ahead of the game plan."

"Yeah? What's the plan?"

"The plan? I can't stop staring at you. Do you know how beautiful you are? But you get that from all the guys, I'm sure. I'm sorry – I really am at a loss for words." She was young – what was he doing? He took her hands from behind his neck and kissed them, gently. He had been so focused on making a name for himself at work that he had put everything else on hold, cutting all ties with former girlfriends so he wouldn't be tempted to cut out of Lawrell and run back to New York. And here was Cydney – one bright spot from his past who looked like she could make it and get out of this dump. Really, he just wanted to take her back to his new air-conditioned apartment on the top floor of the fanciest high-rise in town, and peel her uniform off on the plush area rug he had bought with the advice of the interior decorator that he was embarrassed to admit he had hired. *Don't do it. Let her go. Make her go.*

"Cydney, I am too old for you. Or too serious, or…something." Again, sounding stupid.

"Are you seeing someone?"

"No – far from it – too involved with work. I'm here for a reason."

"What could that possibly be? You got out. Why come back?"

"Personal. Revenge, maybe?"

"Hmm. Sexy. You really know how to treat a girl."

Robert burst out laughing. "Touché. As I said, wise beyond your years. And you? Boyfriends?"

"Around here? They're headed for jail or Vietnam. Nothing will keep me here."

"Cydney, I don't want to take advantage of you – I mean, I've been a saint – living like a monk. And you're like…water to a man dying of thirst…"

"A monk? A saint? Wow, those guys heading to 'Nam are starting to look good."

"See, I'm totally out of practice."

They stared at each other and Robert leaned in for a kiss – both their eyes open. A gentle kiss. Non-committal. He pulled back. She smiled. "More." Longer, softer, liquid.

"What's next?" Cydney asked in a low voice, trying to keep from trembling.

Robert took a breath and smacked himself playfully on the cheek. "Let's elope before I do something I'll regret."

"I'm not the marrying kind."

"Ok—how about the first date kind—like going out for dinner? But, you know, I'd rather not show up at the house and see Carmen—no point in rubbing this in her face, so let's meet at the Italian place on Fourth."

"Gee, I'd love to rub it in Carmen's face, especially the car, but I see what you mean. So when?"

They agreed on dinner that night at 7:30. Robert drove her back to the nursing home and promised not to terrorize the old folks with his car anymore. They held hands for another minute, not speaking.

"See you tonight, Bretton. I'll get so dressed up you won't recognize me."

"Well, what would be the point of that?"

As she jumped out of the car, Robert remembered that he had a meeting that evening at the Taylord mansion with Herb Wallace, his boss, and called after her that he might be a few minutes late getting to the restaurant, but she better wait for him.

Cydney turned and waved at the sound of his voice. She couldn't hear a word over the idling of the car. She was grinning from ear to ear.

THAT EVENING ROBERT ARRIVED AT the Taylord Memorial Mansion, as he called it, at 6:00 PM sharp.

Herb had invited him over to the house several times, trying to be as magnanimous and helpful as possible. Sometimes the invitations were for working sessions in the dark paneled library with the ten-foot ceilings and marble fireplace, and sometimes they were social occasions with Herb's cigar-smoking banker friends imported from Beacon Hill and Concord. His daughter, Marjorie, the same age as Bobbie, was always there; immaculately dressed with something strategically missing or undone—a silk blouse in a tailored navy suit unbuttoned down to her navel, a red and white demure linen dress with a high collar and a slit up to her panty line, a filmy chiffon party dress that swung and bounced as she walked, just enough to suggest that underwear was not part of her evening attire.

Herb's wife and Marjorie's mother, Betsy Wallace, had been wheel-chair bound and in an oxygen tent for years. She was acutely allergic to practically everything and suffered asthma attacks that prevented her from leaving her room. No one ever saw her; she was the presence up-stairs. Herb or Marjorie or a uniformed maid would descend the wind-ing central staircase to the parquet entrance hall and announce, "Betsy says this," or "Mother would like that," or "Mrs. Wallace asks if..."

So Marjorie filled in as social director of the Wallace household, and as far as Robert could see, she was remarkably competent – sharp, clear, precise, a little crisp, what other women would probably call bitchy. It didn't jive at all with her reputation of being an airhead who hardly knew her own name. In fact, Robert thought she seemed quite calcu-lating, although he had no idea how calculating, because what she was setting her sights on was him.

THAT EVENING, THE BUTLER OPENED the door and ushered him into Herb's study off the drawing room. Robert was not sure why it was called a drawing room and how that was different from a living room or a parlor. He was in the midst of thinking how far he had come, having grown up with a front room that was living, dining, play and every-thing else room including spare bedroom, when he heard the door close and turned around to see Marjorie.

Marjorie had spent the better part of the afternoon getting ready for this evening. Her father had called home from the airport at 2:00 and asked her to let Robert know that he had to cancel their evening meeting.

"Now you be sure to call the Mill and let him know, honey, because he's got better things to do than trek up to the house only to find out that I'm not there," Herb said to her over the phone in his thin reedy voice. She could hear flights being announced in the background.

"Of course, Daddy. No problem. How late will you be?"

"I'll be in New York until the morning. Be back around lunch. Love to Mother." And he was gone. Marjorie was fairly sure that he had a mistress in New York, as he seemed to be there on business a great deal during non-business hours.

So by the time Robert turned to see Marjorie closing the door behind her, she looked like a French movie star. Her shoulder-length honey colored hair was done up in a perfect flip, and her large gray eyes were emphasized by false eyelashes. Marjorie had a large mouth and perfectly straight, perfectly white teeth – Robert had often wondered if they were real, or if perfect teeth were the ultimate test of class distinctions – and on this night her mouth was painted bright red. There seemed to be a beauty spot on her upper lip that Robert had never noticed before; he suddenly found it quite sexy. She was very nearly as tall as he, and quite graceful, probably the result of years of forced ballet lessons. She had long limbs, even long feet, and hands with elegant fingers and dragon lady nails. Robert opened his mouth to say something, telling himself to watch it. He and Marjorie were on fairly good terms and did a lot of kidding around, but she always made him feel as though he was being observed through a one-way mirror.

"Marjorie! Don't you look lovely! Spending the evening out?" He tried to sound upbeat.

"Well, I'm spending the evening with someone special, if that's what you mean. Have a drink?"

"Tell you what, I think I'll pass. I'm meeting Herb for business, and besides, I've got a long night ahead of me."

She arched an eyebrow that looked darker than usual. "Oh! I completely forgot. Herb just called to talk to you. He's been delayed in Boston. So he'll be late. But he really wants you to wait. I guess it's important, huh?"

Robert frowned and checked his watch. Herb wouldn't be here until 7:00. He would never make it to the restaurant on time. He should call Cydney and let her know, but he really didn't want to chance getting Carmen on the phone. He decided to wait and call the restaurant to leave a message for her there.

"Change your mind about that drink, Bobbie?" Marjorie gave him a big smile, tilting her head like a child.

"Ok. You convinced me. But if you're going to call me Bobbie, then I'm going to call you Marge."

"Oh, but Bobbie is cute, and Marge is so...I don't know, so...flat," she said with just a suggestion of a glance down to her spectacular chest. It suddenly occurred to Robert that she was dressed in a manner that might be too revealing for public consumption. Where could she be going wearing a wraparound dress that was practically see-through, unless it was to a very expensive underwear convention? He looked down at the floor and examined his shoes so she couldn't see the flush rising in his face. He had been celibate for months, since leaving New York in the late winter, and that–combined with the afternoon's intense flirtation with Cydney–was beginning to drive him crazy. Marjorie held out a glass of scotch from the sidebar, which he had never before noticed set up in that room.

"So, what's the long night that you have planned?" she asked, eyes wide over the edge of her frosted glass.

"Well, to tell you the truth, it's dinner with an old friend – actually the sister of a girl I used to go with, our age, maybe you knew her. Carmen Mallone? Well, it's her sister, Cydney. Funny how these things work out."

"Hmm. Funny. It's true." Marjorie felt a thud in her stomach. She was going to have to bypass Plan A and go directly to Plan B. Marjorie had been on the pill since it had been invented. The doctor's hand literally shook when he wrote out the prescription when she went off to the first of many junior colleges. By the time she was twenty-five she had slept with at least eighteen men, mostly the sons of her father's banker friends, or varsity letter guys who raced crew and seemed to care more about their tailors and stockbrokers than their girlfriends. Other than the contractor who worked on the ever-expanding Taylord mansion, with whom she had snuck into the cab of a backhoe and wrapped her legs around his very muscular thighs – she found sex a boring but predictable method to get whatever she wanted. And what she wanted at the moment was Robert. Her father had made it clear to her that if she wanted to inherit the property, she had better find a man who could run the mill. As far as Marjorie was concerned, she had found him.

"You know, even with the air conditioning, it's awfully warm in here, don't you think?" she asked.

Robert looked around the dark wood, set off by the soft glow of polished brass fixtures. Actually he thought it was a relief after the sweatshop of the mill. Herb always said it was the coolest room in the house.

"Why don't you take off your jacket?" she continued, sensing his resistance. "Come on, you'll be much more comfortable for dinner."

"For dinner?"

"Why yes. Didn't Herb tell you? He told me that it was a dinner meeting and to start without him."

"Well, that's very kind of you, but as I just mentioned, I do have dinner plans, and I can't...you know...eat two meals. Gotta watch my weight."

But Marjorie had already pulled him to his feet and was leading him into the dining room where the twelve-foot long table was set at one end with enough crystal and silver to sink a rowboat.

"Wow!" he said, letting out a whistle, "Isn't that lovely! I was hardly expecting something this fancy." He heard her close the paneled French doors behind them and thought something dropped to the floor.

"Close your eyes," she said in a childlike singsong, reaching over and covering his eyes with her hand.

"Marge, really, I'm not wild about games."

"Oh, you'll like this one, I promise." With one hand over his eyes and the other pulling him along as though he were handcuffed, she walked him down the length of the table and sat him at the head.

"You can open your eyes now." The room was dark, with the heavy brocade curtains pulled over the paned windows that led to the terrace, and all other doors closed. Marjorie leaned over the table to light the candles and, in the puffed flame of the match, Robert could see quite clearly that she had taken off her dress.

"You like?" Marjorie asked, pivoting slowly. She was wearing a push-up bra in a soft lavender that revealed the mound of her breasts down to the nipples. It looked like something out of *Tom Jones,* one of Robert's favorite movies. Somehow she had found a matching lavender garter belt and G-string that just covered her crotch but left the smooth half-moons of her ass completely exposed. She snapped a garter at him.

"You like?" she asked again, her voice half an octave lower.

Robert realized that his mouth was wide open and he might have been drooling. He couldn't say a word. Slowly, he nodded.

"Good," she said, suddenly businesslike. "I thought you would. Be a good boy and wait here. I'll be right back." She walked all the way around the table, giving him a long view of both front and back and then disappeared into the pantry. Within seconds she was back with a tray of cold foods that she placed on the table in front of him. Robert put his brain on hold. He had no choice, really, as most of it had slid right down to his cock, which was so stiff it made it impossible for him to sit. Marjorie leaned over him every which way she could, brushing her breasts against his cheek, rubbing them against the back of his neck, while she put little morsels of food on his plate. Caviar, he noticed at one point. First time he had tasted it. But his mouth was dry and his jaws weren't working.

"My, Bobbie, you seem awfully tense." She was standing behind him, massaging his shoulders. She reached around and undid his tie. It fell into his lap, and the pressure of even that small fabric made him groan.

"How's that?" she asked. "Massage is my specialty."

He heard something snap and then the full weight of her breasts was on the back of his neck and in his hair, her nipples sharp and hard. Then, abruptly, she was gone, and Bobbie slumped forward with his head on the table, aching with lust and curiously paralyzed at the same time. Moments later he felt his thighs being stroked and his pants unzipped. He held his breath as the unseen presence under the table tongued the head of his penis in slow circles until he began thrusting himself in and out of her mouth, gasping at its depth. He tried to reach for her head to pull himself away, but she held his hand back in an amazingly strong grip and he exploded, helpless and panting. Like a dog with a bone she held onto him and he was stiff again in minutes. This time she raised herself to unsnap the G-string and sat on him, riding him with her breasts bouncing in his face, as he tried to catch her nipples with his tongue. He grabbed on to Marjorie's smooth thighs and staggered to his feet, supporting their weight while he leaned her back onto the table, sweeping away the dishes with his elbow.

She wrapped her legs around his waist and dug her long red nails into his back. He moaned something into her collarbone that was not her name and came for what seemed like an exquisitely long time.

"WHAT THE HELL IS GOING on here?" Herb Wallace's voice jolted the two of them from their half-sleep.

"Oh my God! Daddy! What are you doing here?" Marjorie was genuinely panicked. Robert turned white and grabbed for his pants.

"What am I doing here? This is my house, not a brothel!" His voice was much louder than usual.

Robert looked at his watch, glowing in the dark. He must have fallen asleep. "I...I can explain, Herb. I'm sorry. It's my fault. I...uh...we...uh." Robert was totally at a loss. Surely Herb knew what Marjorie was. He couldn't fire him for this, could he?

"Actually, Daddy, we've been meaning to tell you—it wasn't fair to keep it a secret all these months was it, Bobbie?" Marjorie looked at him with perfect calm, as though she was not standing there in front of her father with Robert's shirt half wrapped around her.

"What secret?" Herb crossed his arms, frowning. He was taller than either of them and looked older than Robert remembered.

"We're engaged! Isn't that wonderful?" Marjorie beamed, putting her arm through Robert's. He pulled back and stared at her in amazement, his mouth open. He felt as though his eyes were popping out of his head.

Herb's whole appearance changed, as though the sun suddenly rose over his face.

"Thank God!" he said, looking up to the ceiling. "I've been waiting to get her settled for years! Robert, my boy—all is forgiven! It's perfect. I'll have an heir. I can leave you two the Mill and know it's in good hands. Thank God. Thank you, God! Wait until I tell Mother." And he turned and ran up the staircase three steps at a time.

WHEN ROBERT COULD FINALLY GET dressed and scramble to find an out-of-the-way phone, he locked himself in the maid's room and called the restaurant. It was 9:30. The *maître d'* remembered a woman of Cydney's description, but she had left half an hour earlier. He dialed her home number. Carmen answered.

"Why hello, Bobbie! How nice to hear your voice."

Robert thought he would put his fist through the wall. "Hi, Carmen. How are ya? Uh...is Cydney there by any chance?"

"Why no, she went out. All dressed up. Probably picked up some guy. She does that."

"Could you leave her a message for me?"

"Shoot."

"Tell her...uh...the restaurant apologizes for the inconvenience, and they will make it up to her and that's a promise. Ok? Got that? Oh, and you can tell her that I delivered the message."

"What is this, some kinda code? You guys running drugs or something? Gee, it would be nice to see you. Maybe take in a movie..."

"Sure, Carmen, I'll call you. Thanks for getting the message to Cydney." And he hung up, sitting for a long while in the dark with his head in his hands and the phone dangling from his lap.

HE CALLED CYDNEY THREE TIMES the next day, reaching Carmen each time. Clearly, Cydney was not getting the message. He had not talked to Marjorie since leaving the house the night before, and he decided to handle it as a drunken, although fairly interesting, dream. She, on the other hand, had decided to handle it by getting the news of her engagement out as soon as possible.

So by the time Robert drove up to the Elmira B. Planter Nursing Home at the end of the day to find Cydney, he was met at the door by an elderly woman with gray hair and a cane.

She pointed at him, and said, "You're the handsome fella who's engaged to Marjorie Wallace. Good luck to you, young man, because you're going to need it. She was one of my students in school. People think she's kinda dumb, but don't you believe it. Smart as a whip, that child, and spoiled rotten."

Behind her stood Cydney, arms folded across her chest, eyes narrowed to slits of blue marble, who walked up to him and hissed, "You're a piece of dog-rolling shit, Robert Bretton. You can go take a fat flying fuck in a rolling doughnut!" She slammed the front door right in his face.

And so, in the summer of 1968, while Marjorie Wallace became Mrs. Robert Bretton in a blur of white roses and white lace, Cydney Mallone, recent high school graduate, left the old mill town of her birth and moved to the big city, where she became a waitress at The Candy Shack, Boston's premiere strip club, in a blur of red neon and hard-edged dreams.

1982. All Night Long.

"THAT'S WHY HE MARRIED HER?" asked Lillian in astonishment.

"Yup," said Cydney, switching off her machine. "If I don't feed this dog he will eat the cat."

"That's why he married her?" Lillian repeated. "And we're going to elect this guy our senator?"

"Hey, he has a soft spot for women. What are you gonna do?"

"Well, I'm not doing anything, but what about you? You could have any man on the planet. Why are you hanging around waiting for him?"

"Because he loves me and I can do no wrong. And it gives me a front row seat into marriage, which is as far as I ever want to get."

Lillian looked over at the wall where Cydney had blown up a series of black and white photo booth pictures taken of her and Robert maybe ten years ago. They looked very young and deliberately silly with mouths open, grinning madly, hands groping in a "See no evil; hear no evil; speak no evil" parody. Robert was barely recognizable. He was wearing a Boston Bruins hat pulled down to his eyes, probably why Cydney dared to keep the poster where people could see it. They looked like any other giddy goofy kids in love or lust or both. There must have been another photo at one time, as the bottom of the series had a jagged line where it had been torn off. Cydney had the originals in her wallet.

Cydney kept talking, "…And we go way back. We get each other. No strings."

"No strings? Oh my God. Those strings have strangled my inheritance!"

"Wrong choice of words. No emotional strings."

"You don't think I believe that, do you?" asked Lillian. "I'm looking over at the pictures on this wall, for example…"

"It's not as intense as you think. Besides, after he's in Washington I will hardly see him. It'll be good for both of us," Cydney said, flashing a dimpled smile.

"Uh-huh. Will you still keep his picture in your wallet? Will that be good for both of you as you're pulling out your ID to cash a check?"

The phone rang. "That's him," said Cydney brightly, dashing for the phone.

"No, not intense," said Lillian, looking at her watch. "It's only 5:00 AM. Not intense at all…"

8:20 PM. *Sunday, Nov. 5, 2006.*

LILLIAN'S THROAT WAS DRY AS chalk. It felt like she had been talking to a sleeping Cydney for hours, but her watch only read 8:20. She needed water and she needed to pee. Pacing outside the car in the curtain of falling snow, sucking on a snowball, she breathed deeply and tried not to think about her wet feet. Why didn't she have boots and gloves packed away in the trunk? Emergency snow supplies were the rule of growing up in the cruel north. What was wrong with her? She constantly harangued her adult sons about it.

On either side of the road the trees, still covered with autumn leaves, leaned in, bent nearly double with the weight of the wet snow. They formed an alleyway that could have been out of a fairytale, if it weren't for the moose in full rigor mortis, its hooves stretched out and reaching for ground it could never find, eyes huge and glassed over, neck twisted and mouth opened showing teeth in a terrified sneer.

This is exactly where she would have depended on Cydney, who in better times might have figured this out. Maybe butchered the moose and tied it up in moose steaks to deliver to clients. Or improvised a sled to drag the carcass out of the way and then jerry-rig the car to get it started.

Ok. *Be practical.* She took slow, deep breaths, creating a mental checklist to help calm her down: What to do? Take a picture of the car for insurance purposes? *No camera.* Call for help? *No phone.* Clear a path from the car to the trunk? *No shovel.* Try to figure out where they were and how far to a main road? *No detailed map.* Look for recognizable signs? *Too dark to see.* Try to remember the last place they had seen a house or person? *Too absorbed in Cydney's bizarreness.* Try to get the car to turn over? *Did that—no deal.* Remember that Robert—who is a fucking senator after all—knows we're out here.

But what about Cydney's comment that maybe he doesn't want us found? *No, you cannot go there.* She felt her heart skip a beat. *One of us has to stay sane...*

Lillian heard a sound at the car window; she cleared a patch and looked in. Cydney was awake and peering out at her. She opened the door a crack. "What's wrong with you, Lillian? Get back in the car."

Well, she sure sounded like the old Cydney.

"How are you feeling?" Lillian asked, settling in her seat and wrapping the towel around her legs.

"Where's Robert? What happened to the windshield?" Cydney sat up straight, looking around.

Lillian's heart skipped a beat. "We are stuck in my car in the woods because we hit a moose on a back road while looking for Robert's country house," she said slowly.

"Shit. I thought that was a dream."

"Well, you were sleeping pretty soundly..." Lillian said, trying to think fast. "Maybe the pills give you vivid dreams?" She had to figure out what triggers could set Cydney off and avoid them.

"So, where is he?"

"Roads must be closed. The trees are so heavy that some of them have fallen. And the wind is ferocious, coming in gusts that almost knocked me off my feet."

"Yeah, but he has an entourage, and they can clear the roads. Lillian, go check your trunk to see what tools you have. Check the kit for changing a tire. Maybe we can use it."

Well, thank God she's back to herself, thought Lillian. But Cydney was right. Where was he?

"And pull up some of the carpeting. We can wrap our feet so we don't freeze. And look for gloves."

LILLIAN WAS SO RELIEVED THAT Cydney sounded lucid that she headed back out in the snow to the car trunk. She pulled up the carpeting to reveal the spare tire and the tool kit, talking all the while. "Ok, I got the carpeting...and the tool kit. What can we do with a tire iron? No clue. And a car jack," she continued, teeth chattering. "I've never changed a tire in my life. Not gonna start now." Lillian kept up a running commentary, mostly to stay focused, as she gathered up these items and stepped back through her footprints to the door. She dropped the heavy tools on the floor and climbed in with the carpeting.

"Good idea, Cyd. We can sure use this. Who says your mind is going?" Lillian arranged herself in the seat with her share of the blanket, and handed a section of the carpet to Cydney, who sat perfectly still, looking straight ahead, hands in her lap.

"Help me out here, Cyd, c'mon." Cydney did not move.

"Cydney? Just grab this end and pull it over."

"I can't."

"Why not?"

Lillian looked over at Cydney and pulled back the blanket. Cydney sat in a lotus position with her hands wrapped tightly around the *Colt .45* that was now in her lap. She picked up the gun and turned to point it directly at Lillian.

IV

Baby Grand

1982.

BENNY FINANCE WAS FINALLY OFF Lillian's back. True to his word, Robert handed over the money to repay the goon squad and replace their loan, and Lillian went to work. Their first order of business was to knock their cost of goods down and get into the large chains. This meant high-end packaging, samples in different colors and fabrics, and a general step up in looking professional.

"And that means *acting* professional," Lillian said, as they drove in Cydney's beat-up '74 Ford Pinto over the Tobin Bridge to visit potential investors. Lillian was able to handle this dreaded bridge as long as Cydney was behind the wheel. As they sat in line for the tollbooth on top of the bridge, the car started bucking and snorting like a horse, threatening to stall out.

"Talk about acting professional—you are digging your nails into my thigh. Cut it out!" Cydney said, swatting Lillian's hand away. "I have been around you long enough to know that I will never have phobias—they are a complete waste of time."

But Lillian was too busy praying that the car would not stop dead in the middle of a cloud to respond.

"First thing I do when we make it big is buy a car that runs," Cyd continued, rooting around for fifty cents for the toll. "A new car, preferably a Porsche, but any new car as long as it's not brown." Cydney had a thing about brown—or any color in the brown family. She claimed it made her physically ill.

Thankfully, the car settled down, smoothly taking the first exit ramp down to the smokestacks, oil tankers and drawbridges that lined the Chelsea side of Boston Harbor, to arrive at the Epstein warehouse complex called Novelty Industries.

"I am not real confident that the car will go into reverse, so we'll just leave it here," Cydney said, parking at the curb. "In fact, let me get out and open your door because it won't open from the inside."

"You mean if we had plunged off the bridge I would have drowned because I couldn't open the door?" This was Lillian's worst nightmare.

"Nope, you would have been killed on impact, not because of the door."

"Why didn't you tell me this before I got in the car?"

"Because I wasn't planning on driving you off a bridge, for chrissake!" But Cydney couldn't open the passenger door from the outside either, and Lillian had to climb out through the driver's side.

"How are we going to get back in?"

"Can we worry about one thing at a time, please?"

THE MEETING WITH THE EPSTEIN brothers went well. Phil and Mitch had inherited their father's shoe manufacturing business and were trying to expand into textiles. Their eyes were glued to Cydney, who was wearing a tight wraparound white dress and electric blue eyeliner, and Lillian had to clear her throat several times to get their attention back on track. After an hour they agreed to consider piggybacking Baby Grand orders with their foam suppliers and to sublet some of their manufacturing space. Lillian figured that this could help avoid large minimum COD orders and lead to a working relationship with an established business—i.e., one with credit, *please God*.

On their way out, Lillian ran the numbers in her head, while Cydney wowed the guys with descriptions of herself hanging upside down to install a forty-foot banner in a high wind at the Boston Harbor Hotel. But, having waved good-bye to the guys watching from the front steps, Cydney couldn't open either car door.

"We should have left the fucking window down. Now neither door will open," Cyd said, shaking her head. "The only thing I can think of is the sun roof. I could rip the tarp off and crawl in."

Lillian's gaze was level with the Pinto's sunroof, a square hole covered with a rubberized tarpaulin. "We're asking these guys to do business with us and you're going to *crawl* through the roof?"

"Something wrong, ladies?" Phil called out from the front step where he and Mitch were still watching.

Cydney turned to give them a big smile as she reached up and pulled off the tarp. "It's a sunny day. We thought we'd get some air driving home!" she called gaily.

Lillian, thinking fast, headed back to the building. "I Just realized that I left a...a folder behind. Could you take me back to the conference room?" Once inside, the brothers were called to the phone and Lil raced back to the car to see Cyd slip through the sunroof and land in the driver's seat, white dress billowing up around her waist.

"How do I get in?" Lillian pounded on the window.

"Same way I did. Through the roof."

Any minute now the guys could be back. Lil clambered up the back of the car and dropped through the sunroof, as Cyd started the engine, which, thankfully, turned over.

"I don't know which is worse—my phobias or your car. Next time, I'm driving," Lillian said.

"Atta girl," said Cyd. "And you thought I didn't have a plan."

The plan worked, because the next time they drove to Chelsea, they took Lillian's car and Cydney talked her right over the bridge. Lillian felt like she had just completed a marathon. This was a red-letter day.

PROFESSIONALISM. RUNNING A START-UP BUSINESS forced Lillian to rethink everything she knew. While "dress for success" was the mantra for women in the early 1980s, she was running a factory and loading trucks, sweeping the floors and listening to her Vietnamese employees describe their escape from their ravaged country through pirate and shark infested waters. Lillian no longer bothered to clean up and wear a suit every time a banker came by to check them out. *Tough — we're running a business here,* she thought. *This is not a case study, bud; this is real.*

But it didn't take much to pierce Lillian's thickening skin. There was the time she arrived to find Cydney on the phone with the textile mill that had shipped out $15,000 worth of fabric that they had been forced to pay for up front.

"So you're telling me the truck is lost….uh-huh," said Cyd, twirling a lock of hair around a pencil. "And it's been three days. We're facing a cancel date of next week if we don't get that order out…Ok…I know you'll find the truck and when you do I'll be the first to hear about it… yeah…bye."

Cydney turned to Lillian. "Guess what? Truck's lost. Happens all the time. They'll find it." She started humming and headed to the bathroom with Lillian close behind.

"You're not serious! We paid for it upfront, not even COD, and they have the balls to tell you it's lost?" She leaned against the wall, feeling faint. "I may throw up."

"Hey!" Cydney looked over at her. "Do I have to splash cold water on you? This happens all the time. They'll find it. It's their job."

"This could be the end before it's even the beginning! Cydney! How can you be so calm?"

"Because I don't walk around worrying about stuff I can't control," Cydney said from inside the stall. "You should try it — makes it easier to get through the day."

AND SURE ENOUGH, THE TRUCK pulled in an hour later. Lillian thought about this as she watched Cydney give orders to the driver. She was a risk-taker and Lillian was beginning to admire it—even trust it. Maybe some of it would rub off on her. On the other hand, some of it she could do without. Just a few weeks ago, she had been working on package design, when Cydney's friend, Sophie, stopped by holding a pillowcase with a lump in the bottom.

"Look," Sophie said. "I got this present for Jack for his birthday and my roommate is really being a pain about it. She's out on the fire escape and won't come in until I get rid of it, so could you do me a favor and keep it for two days until Jack's birthday?"

"I guess so," said Cyd, taking the pillowcase.

"What is it?" Lillian asked, although it was none of her business.

"Oh and by the way," Sophie added, heading out the door. "It eats a live mouse once a day."

"Where do I get a live mouse?" asked Cydney. "This might really confuse the cat. Lillian, sit down, you're turning white. Do not faint on me."

"Oh my God," said Lillian, looking around. "It's a…it's a…"

"Yup," said Cyd, peeking in. "Do you have snake phobias as well as bridge and car phobias? And it's just a baby—a boa constrictor. Wow, what colors! No wonder they make them into shoes…"

Lillian pulled herself together. "Either you get rid of the snake, or you get rid of me, because I can't deal with this, and we have work to do!"

"Yeah, you're right for once. Let me find a place to put it and call Sophie, if I can find her." Cydney found an old wicker hamper, put the pillowcase inside and a can of paint on the lid to hold it down.

Lillian kept her eye on the hamper for the next hour while they went through fabric swatches and picked new colors for the interior of Carta-Babe. By then, Sophie was on her way back to collect the snake and Cydney opened the hamper to check on it. Empty.

"Holy shit! Where did it go? Sophie's gonna kill me." She dropped the lid of the hamper on the floor and stepped carefully around it. Lillian stood rigid with fear while Cydney got down on her hands and knees, trying to get a snake's eye view.

"There's gotta be an explanation. Maybe I should get a mouse. Lillian! Get the cat and the dog out of here…"

But Lillian was rooted to the spot. "Can…can they climb?" she whispered.

"You know," Cydney said, scrambling to her feet, "I've often thought about putting *Beware Of Poisonous Snake* on the door because having a dog is not enough for a woman living alone. And now I wouldn't be lying."

"You are fucking nuts," Lillian said, wondering if she really was.

The lid of the hamper moved and Cydney pounced with the paint can, tossing it on the lid, which stopped moving. "Well hey! It just crawled under the lid to hide, silly me."

When Sophie arrived with Jack, the two of them plucked the snake out of the hamper lid and put it back into the pillowcase. Lillian watched from a distance, surprisingly un-freaked out.

"Look at you," said Cydney admiringly when they left. "No tears! Hang around me for much longer and every phobia you have will disappear."

Risk-taking. Lillian thought that she had just about used up her lifetime allotment. Which was worse? Benny Finance or snakes? At least snakes didn't charge forty percent interest. They were happy with a mouse. But the risk-taking was just beginning.

ALL THROUGH 1982 ROBERT WAS on the campaign trail. In his absence Cydney threw herself into getting Baby Grand off the ground. They hired stitchers, ordered inventory, had a slew of freelancers on call—foam cutters, package designers, delivery guys—bought industrial sewing equipment, rented more space in the brewery, and the remaining 100K disappeared quickly. The jewelry was another story. Where was it? Robert claimed that the jewelry came from and was returned to Tiffany & Co.

"Marjorie swears she sent it back to New York. She showed me the delivery receipts. I talked to Tiffany's; it's part of their estate department and is on consignment."

"On consignment from whom?" asked Lillian, who had talked to Tiffany several times, getting nowhere. She knew that either Marjorie or Robert or both had to be lying. She didn't want to think about the possibility of Cydney lying.

But Cydney seemed just as intent on finding the jewelry as Lillian was. Driving through Pennsylvania to scout out additional manufacturing space, Cydney wondered out loud if Marjorie might have hidden the jewelry in the large Taylord Mills factory in East Rutherford, NJ. And so, after a late afternoon meeting at what turned out to be the very last silk loom on the East Coast, where Cydney scooped up every remnant of raw silk she could find at two-cents a yard, she announced that they would stop off at Taylord and pay them a visit.

"I think the jewels may be in the safe; the more I think about it the more I think I'm right," Cydney said.

"Well, how would we get into the safe?"

"I have the combination."

"You do?"

"Yeah. Pillow talk."

"But…" Lillian was at a loss. "They must have guards. You can't just walk in."

"They have guard dogs. But I know the dogs and to make sure they don't bark we'll buy treats. Raw meat. Do you have any Valium on you?" Lillian always carried Valium in case any bridges were on the horizon; and there was no way you could get from Massachusetts to New Jersey without crossing the Hudson.

"We'll soak the meat in valium," Cydney continued. "Works like a charm. The dogs will be out, and we have all this black silk in the back that we can wrap ourselves up in. I'll kill the lights and we're on our way."

"This is called breaking and entering and probably many other felonies. I admire your fantasy life."

"Do you want that jewelry back or not? Do you trust me?"

"Please don't ask me that, Cydney. You're the reason I don't have it back!"

"We're going. Besides, I have the gun in the car."

"What gun?"

"The one from Jamie and Carlo's break-in last year."

"You kept it?"

"Yeah. It's a piece of shit Saturday night special, but it works. I went to a firing range to check it out."

"Wait a minute," Lillian said. "I am trying to process this. You want to drape yourself in black silk, drug dogs, take the gun, disable the alarm and break into a safe? Who *are* you?"

"Hey, I am being practical! We have all of these things right here in the car. Let's take that as a sign and go for it. I'll call Bud to see who's still in the factory. Bud has been after my ass for years.

From Cydney's description of Bud Mannheim, the Taylord manager in New Jersey, as tough-guy Holocaust survivor, Lillian was suspicious. For one thing, he didn't speak Yiddish. For another, he wasn't too fond of Jews, Blacks or Latinos. Lillian had no desire to confront him.

"HEY, BUD, YOU STUD!" CYDNEY called from a phone booth while holding the phone away from her ear so Lillian could listen in.

"Cydney, my girl! You still giving it free to the boss, yah?"

"Hey, Bud—who's around? I'm thinking of coming for a visit. But like, on the QT. Not for public knowledge."

"And why would you do zat?"

"Well...maybe take you up on your offer after all this time..."

"Why? Boss letting you down?"

"The boss is on the campaign trail—haven't seen much of him."

"Heh heh. Thinking to get some on the side, huh?"

"Well put, Bud! You have a way with words. So...who's around?"

"Second shift is out on the floor." Bud's strong accent came through over the phone.

Not Polish, as Cydney had said. Definitely German. *Probably ex-Gestapo in hiding,* thought Lillian.

"But I could meet you in the back room near the loading dock," Bud added.

Lillian's heart sank as Cydney hung up and said all in a rush, "That's it – game on. We're going. Bud will be in the back waiting – thinking he's in for a quickie. We'll come in the front – after hours; no one there. Drug the dogs, kill the lights, open the safe, take the jewelry, you stand guard with the gun and we're out of there."

"Shouldn't I stay in the car as the getaway driver? That's a joke, by the way. You're nuts. Drive home."

But when Cydney made up her mind she was unshakeable. Before Lillian could stop her, Cydney had bought a pound of stew meat, soaked it in twenty milligrams of Valium, driven past the high chain-link fence marking the Taylord Mill entrance, and killed the engine. She pulled out a length of black silk from the bolt in the back seat. "Hey, look, my hands are all bloody from the meat."

Lillian couldn't believe this was happening. "Yeah, you look like Lady MacBeth, especially if you drape yourself in black. Maybe I should take a picture before you end up in a mug shot."

"Fine, just stay in the car, because you are going to screw this up."

"Look," said Lillian, taking the car keys from Cydney, "I am taking the car and driving away. I don't know you and have never seen you before. And when some interviewer asks me how we ended up in business together, I will blame it on your ass and my jewelry." Lillian could tell she had inadvertently given Cydney the go-ahead.

"What do you mean, my ass? I'll deal with that comment when my ass gets back to the car wearing your jewelry. Watch for my signal and follow me, ok?"

Lillian watched Cydney walk toward the building, trailing gossamer silk and holding a slab of bloody meat. *Boy, is she brave,* Lillian couldn't help but think. The dogs, two black Dobermans named Storm and Lutz – *I rest my case,* thought Lillian. *Bud is definitely not a survivor* – sniffed cautiously to greet Cydney, who offered the meat. Within minutes of gobbling it, they lay down for a good long nap. Cydney entered a code on the keypad, opened the door and beckoned for Lillian to follow.

AN HOUR LATER, WITH LILLIAN behind the wheel, driving at 80 mph, she crossed the George Washington Bridge without blinking an eye.

"Calm down," Cydney said. "So now we know the jewels are not in the safe."

"No. What's in the safe are bullets from your gun—traceable, I'm sure."

After pulling the breaker to kill the lights in the front office, Cydney had tried the safe combination. Twice. "That bastard changed it!"

"Let's go," said Lillian, terrified. "Any minute now…"

"We're here; we're finishing this." Cydney pulled the gun out of her belt and fired twice at the safe lock. The sound ricocheted down the hall and Lillian ducked out of instinct. Picking up a claw hammer, Cydney smashed open the damaged door. Papers. Lots of papers. A stack of $100 bills. But no jewelry.

"Storm! Lutz!" a woman's voice called from down the hall.

"Shit, that's Gertie. I had no idea she was here," Cydney whispered. Gertie was Bud's ancient wife, also with tattooed numbers on her arm, half blind, who often slept on the couch in Bud's office to keep what was left of her eye on Bud and his propensity to hit on the young, desperate Latinas who worked for him.

"She's mostly blind, so she won't see a thing," said Cydney, trying to hold Lillian back. But Lillian was already in the hall trying to see through the darkness, when the alarm went off with a throbbing shriek. Cydney flew past her and grabbed her arm, pulling her down the hall and into an alcove as Gertie stumbled past in an old housecoat brandishing a cane. They could hear heavy footsteps and voices following close behind.

"Quick, out the fire exit!" Cydney, still covered in silk, pushed open a heavy metal door, setting off another alarm, and ran around the corner past the sleeping dogs to the car. Lillian had never been so purposeful in her life as she drove up to the bridge, with Cydney giving directions and somehow trusting her not to freak out.

LILLIAN NEVER FOUND OUT IF Bud or Robert knew who had broken into the safe. Cydney claimed that Marjorie must have given Bud warning to move the jewels in case Cydney showed up. Even though the events of the evening took on the terrifying intensity of a helpless dream, so that Lillian was never sure exactly what had happened, she was sure that the jewelry would not materialize any time soon. Especially after the meeting later that year with Samuelson and Company.

AFTER ROBERT'S SENATE VICTORY IN the fall of 1982, Cydney was feeling both liberated and pissed off. She had watched his victory speech on TV – Marjorie preening alongside – while he thanked a slew of supporters. Cydney's name was not among them.

Lillian could not help but notice that Cydney, already magnificent with her tumbling hair, dark skin, tropical-sea eyes and full pouting mouth, stepped it up with outfits that were not well suited to traditional dress for success. There was the time she showed up in Manhattan for a meeting with venture capitalists wearing a black fishnet body stocking under combat fatigues. Quite a crowd of men gathered around her in their sockless Gucci loafers, flashing their large gold watches and handing out business cards. Sometimes Cydney was a prisoner of her own making; she was actually terrified of following through on most of the flirtations that she set in motion. Lillian could not compete with the raised eyebrows hanging outside the conference room as she went through her marketing plans and sales projections. As a result, Cydney ended up with everyone's business card, after hearing, "Call me the next time you're in town and have a free evening." Lillian ended up furious at Cydney and Baby Grand ended up with nothing.

In one such meeting, on the fortieth floor of the General Motors building, with a view over the southeastern corner of Central Park, misty and magical in the spring rain, Lillian arrived with Cydney wearing a white blouse unbuttoned to her waist, tuxedo pants and electric blue eyeliner. Several strings of fake pearls covered her gaping décolleté.

"What?" said Cydney. "This is very toned down."

"For you. Toned down for you. Not for these guys. All they know is cashmere sweaters and tweed suits."

"You know nothing about fabric. That's Scotland," Cydney said, rolling her eyes.

"We are asking them for one half million dollars in exchange for twenty-five percent of the company. Hello?"

"Well, we want to stand out, don't we?"

"*Oh-my-god.*" Lillian slapped her forehead so hard that it left a red mark. "Ouch! Stand out, but not get thrown out! Is this just payback for Robert being gone? Flirt with every man walking and maybe he'll get wind of it. Just do up the buttons, for heavens sake."

In the Samuelson & Co. reception area, Lillian leafed through a magazine, trying to calm down and focus on the presentation. The magazine was full of ads for designer clothes and artwork that no normal person could afford, but as she glanced through an article on the hot art market in the Persian Gulf, she stopped short at a picture of a jeweled hummingbird.

The caption: *Recent purchase by Sheik Mohammed Bin Halabi for his young British wife.*

Her heart skipped a beat. Either it was a perfect copy or it had been cut out and reset as a brooch. She looked more closely. Yes, redone in a modern setting of a stylized gold tree. Tacky and basically ruined. Before she could show it to Cydney, Samuelson's secretary beckoned them to his office. Lillian dropped the magazine and wondered how she could steal it on the way out.

Utterly distracted, Lillian was off her game, and she knew it before she even began. She tried to get Cydney's attention, fearing that a phobia attack was on its way—not that there was anything that could immediately set her off—no water, no bridges, no snakes—but Lillian knew full well that lack of appropriate triggers was no obstacle to new ones popping up fully formed. She could freak out over being on the fortieth floor, for example, or having to take the elevator down or...*stop it!*

As they rounded the corner into Samuelson's enormous office with panoramic views looking north over Central Park—fuzzy and grey in the rain, buds popping out on the trees far below—Lillian could feel the dreaded clutch of sudden vertigo. She stopped abruptly in the doorway to get her bearings and wait for the attending nausea to make up its mind. Stick around? Make a quickie appearance just to remind you who's boss? Heart pounding, she kept her eyes on Cydney greeting Samuelson as he sat with both feet encased in plaster casts propped up on a stool. Cydney leaned over to shake his hand, giving him a good view down the front of her blouse. *Good thing she hasn't buttoned it,* thought Lillian, as she grabbed on to this moment of clarity to collect herself.

"You must be Cindy," said the crippled Samuelson, laughing and clapping his hands in the air.

"That's Cydney, like a man." Cyd smiled sweetly, the ropes of pearls chinking together as she strategically tucked in her blouse.

"Well, no mistaking that! And you must be Lee Anne." He reached for Lillian's hand.

"That's Lillian," she said, getting her groove back.

AFTERWARDS, IT WAS CYDNEY'S TURN to be furious. "What was that spaceshot performance? You could barely remember your own name. Since when am I the numbers person? I had to jump in and correct you three times. I could have ripped my blouse off and the guy would still not have been interested." Cydney took one look at Lillian's face. "What is wrong with you? That was pathetic! Did you expect him to just sit down and write a check?"

"You will not believe what I saw in that magazine. The jewelry. It's been chopped up and sold off in pieces! A sheik—some guy in Bahrain or someplace. Lillian felt like she had been punched in the gut. She had to get a copy of that magazine.

"Listen." Cydney grabbed her arm. "Get back on track. We spent weeks preparing for this meeting and you blew it."

But Lillian could not let go of the hummingbird brooch. She didn't blame Cydney for being furious at her, but she couldn't help but think that her partner was hiding something. So the jewelry was really gone.

Should she tell Marc? He was ready to get the FBI to investigate Robert Bretton's role as it was, and Robert was now conveniently a ten percent stakeholder in the company. And their biggest lender. And a US senator. And, since Samuelson had passed on the deal, more important than ever.

1985. March.

NORMAL PEOPLE GO ON BUSINESS trips and worry about hotel reservations or rental cars. Lillian worried about flash floods and poisonous snakes.

"You are insane," Cydney told her repeatedly, as Lillian tended to worry out loud. She said it so often that Lillian had pushed floods and snakes to the back of her mind by the time they embarked on their trip to JC Penney headquarters in Dallas.

Lillian and Cydney arrived early at Boston's Logan Airport and headed to the Delta counter. The buttoned-down blonde behind the counter had Dallas cheerleader written all over her as she announced that the flight was delayed.

"How delayed?" Lillian was cautious here, not yet combative.

"*Ohhhh*, hard to say. Could be a while." She hoisted the bags onto the conveyer belt.

"A while like ten minutes, or a while like six hours?"

"We're having some weather in Dallas at the moment." The Delta agent was nonplussed.

"What weather?" Lillian asked.

"Oh, thunderstorms passing through."

Lillian turned to Cyd. "I knew it. Floods."

"She said thunderstorms, for crissake, not floods." Cydney rolled her eyes in exasperation. "How many times do I have to listen to this? Calm down or I'm not going with you."

Lillian considered this. Cydney was currently her hold on reality.

Two hours later, on the plane, with the seat belt sign on because of non-stop turbulence, it was pitch black outside the plane's windows – at ten in the morning – with flashes of lightning forking in every direction. The pilot did not sound particularly concerned – always a key indicator – as he announced they might land in Tulsa or Oklahoma City, because tornados were sighted everywhere between Alabama and Arizona. The stewardesses were buckled into their seats, so Lillian couldn't examine their faces for signs of terror. By then the pilot was back on the PA system informing them that he was going to "attempt" to land in the two-minute window in which they had reopened the Dallas airport.

Grown men were saying their prayers out loud as the plane appeared to change its mind several times before it touched down in what could have been a solar eclipse.

The airport looked like a movie set for a post-nuclear world. Empty and dark, except for the Avis rental booth and the perky girls in orange. The Avis agent handed Lillian a map with large sections of the city blocked out in neon yellow highlighter and apologized for the weather. Evidently it had been raining for forty days.

"And what's with these roads?" Lillian asked, waving the neon map. "Why are they in yellow?"

"Well they're a little wet; we suggest you follow the detours."

"Uh-huh. How wet exactly?"

"Very."

"You mean they're flooded."

"That's right." The agent nodded reassuringly.

Lillian turned to Cyd. "I knew it."

"But, look at it this way," Cydney said, ever the eternal optimist. "It's flat and there are no bridges."

Lillian and Cydney drove in a downpour so ferocious that the windshield wipers on the highest speed were sluggish. They could have been in a spaceship for all Lillian could see of the road. Cydney turned on the radio for local traffic reports only to hear about water moccasins turning up in back yards. Cyd killed the radio fast because she knew they had just entered Lillian's personal twilight zone.

Finally they arrived at the hotel, with a check-in line longer than waiting for a ride at Disney. Lillian kept scanning the floor for snakes that might have crawled in undetected through the air vents, carefully placing bags around her feet in protective fashion. *Can they jump?* she wondered.

But, as it turned out, they had much bigger problems (although that depends on one's phobias) because the hotel was seriously overbooked. Apparently Cyd had not picked up the hotel overbooking information because, at the registration desk, Cydney demanded a room that was not brown. "Any color other than brown is fine, although peach would be best and not too near the elevator," she said with authority.

The Pakistani clerk, frowning at the computer screen, stabbed one key repeatedly and looked up to see if this was a joke. Cydney smiled invitingly, showing both dimples and crinkling up her baby blues, while she launched into the story of her day thus far. Lillian interrupted with "brown is fine; I love brown. Anything will do."

Either the clerk took pity on them or he was charmed by Cyd, but they were lucky enough to get an inside windowless room – probably a rehabbed storage closet – and were just able to make it to their 1:30 appointment.

An hour later they were in the JC Penney waiting room – actually a windowless holding tank about twenty feet long and fifteen feet wide. There were two doors to the room; one through which they had just entered from the elevator, and one at the other end with a big sign: *Buyers Only; Do Not Enter.* Next to this forbidding door was a surveillance camera, which doubled as a receptionist, as it actually spoke to them. There was nobody else in the room, which seemed odd to Lillian. Buyers' waiting rooms were usually crawling with nicotine-deprived and very chatty sales reps toting oversized sample bags. But here, empty chairs lined the grass cloth walls, tastefully done in muted green.

The talking camera proceeded to tell Lillian and Cydney that the buyer they had traveled two thousand miles in biblical conditions to see, with whom this precious appointment had been made three months earlier, had unexpectedly been called out of town.

"That's interesting," Lillian said to the camera, reeling from this news. "Because you can hardly get into town. How exactly did she leave? By canoe? And I just talked to her yesterday; she *knew* we were on our way!"

Even Cydney, who always rolled with the punches, stood speechless, when a short balding man in a gray checked suit burst through the "Buyers Only" door, dropped his head and shoulders as though he were a running back, and sprinted to the exit. Instinctively, Lillian and Cydney sprinted out the door right behind him and managed to plant themselves between him and the elevator that he hoped would arrive fast enough to whisk him away from a well-oiled sales pitch.

"Hi," Lillian offered brightly. "We're here from The Baby Grand Company all the way from Boston to keep our 1:30 appointment with a buyer who is unexpectedly out of town."

"And we made this appointment three months ago and almost died flying in today in Noah's Ark...*ha ha,*" added Cyd with controlled cheerfulness, although Lillian could tell she was ready to tear him apart.

By now the elevator had arrived, but the women kept pressing in real close, offering business cards while he backed up to the wall, cornered. Cydney launched into a breathless twenty second spiel about *'the best baby product ever made'* while Lillian yanked the infant shopping cart carrier out of the sample bag and snapped it through its paces. *'Look! It's an infant cradle, now it's a baby support seat, and wait, it gets better; it's a toddler restraint!'*

Lillian could tell that it wasn't working. He was stuck at eye-level with a baby carrier that made him feel even shorter than the Texan big-guys he already had to deal with.

"Sorry, ladies...it's not my department—I'm diaper bags. You'll really have to talk to what's-her-name who's not in today." And he side-stepped Cydney and her flashing eyes to fling himself as far back into the elevator as he could, just as the doors closed on Lillian's thrust-out, still muddy shoe.

"And they're supposed to be so friendly in Texas," said Cyd, stuffing Carta-Babe back in the bag.

"And big," Lillian added, feeling much too big herself.

They shuffled back into the waiting room where the disembodied voice via intercom asked, in so many words, just who the hell they thought they were.

They sat back down in the suspiciously well-upholstered chairs with sample bags open and at the ready, lest any other buyers make a dive for it through the room—evidently the only way out of the inner sanctum—or as Cydney referred to it, the inner scrotum—and out to the elevators. Until this point they had been the only live humans waiting in the room, but now the elevator-side door opened and a woman in her mid-thirties, dressed in purple with brown curly hair, walked in with an air of easy resignation. She shifted her sample bag off her shoulder, let it drop to the floor, flopped down in the nearest chair and kicked off her matching purple shoes.

"Wow, purple shoes," said Cyd admiringly, never missing a beat on the fashion bodyguard watch.

"Yup, my Texas good luck shoes," purple lady said with a smile, pulling at the toes of her soaking wet pantyhose.

"Well, you will need the good luck, if our experience is anything like what you're in for," Lillian said, trying not to cry.

"Buyer didn't show, huh? Happens all the time."

"You're kidding!" Cyd and Lil said in unison.

"What time is your appointment?" Lillian asked.

"Yesterday," the woman said with a dimpled smile and introduced herself as Nicole Hoffman who owned a company called *Once were Leprechauns* in Rapid City, South Dakota. Nicole picked up her sample bag and spun it around to demonstrate the whimsical logo stitched in green and pink loops on a yellow background. Lillian examined it and the Leprechaun product catalog for a few minutes during which time Nicole and Cydney became best friends.

"Rapid City, huh?" Cyd said.

"Yeah." Nicole stifled a yawn. "It's a great place to set up shop; labor is cheap."

"Indians, I bet," offered Cyd.

"Nope, German housewives."

Now Lillian was listening.

"Yeah," Nicole continued. "There are all kinds of first and second generation immigrants who can barely speak English. It's a great setup. They work hard and I have no idea what they're saying."

"A girl after my own heart," Cyd murmured. "Hey, is Rapid City anywhere near a town called Panic?"

"Actually I live about fifteen miles from there," said Nicole. "Near the Pine Ridge Reservation."

"I spent the wildest night of my life in Panic, South Dakota," Cyd announced out of the blue, "in a place called the Buckrock Saloon."

"Yup, I know it real well," Nicole said with a chuckle. "Spent some wild nights there myself."

"Oh, one was enough for me," said Cyd, kicking off her shoes. "I was lucky to get out of there alive."

And in the middle of a non-meeting, in the middle of the afternoon, on the edge of a near-flooded city, Cydney Mallone proceeded to tell a total stranger about the wildest night of her life.

IN THE SUMMER OF 1969, Cydney was nineteen years old and a street-wise kid from the old mill town of Lawrell, Massachusetts, when she left her job as a waitress in Boston's Combat Zone to drive cross-country with her older sisters, Carmen, Mel and Risa. Mel was headed to graduate school in California, and the girls had jerry-rigged a plywood roof rack onto Carmen's 1963 blue Ford Falcon. They piled in with their girl scout camping gear, all seven boxes of Mel's record albums and camouflage duffel bags filled with linens. They figured it would take eight days to drive to San Francisco at twelve hours a day and fifty miles an hour, which was as fast as the Falcon would go.

None of the girls had ever driven farther than Cape Cod, or stepped foot out of New England, and weren't sure which state bordered what, but they figured they were tough working class girls who had left home after high school and knew all about life.

It was late August and blazing hot. They were about two days west of Chicago and planned to stop near Rapid City, South Dakota at a campground. Driving out of the Badlands at high noon, it was one hundred and five degrees and close to unbearable in the back seat where Cyd was scrunched next to Mel's ski poles, when an argument broke out between Carmen, who was driving, and Risa, who was poring over a map the size of a tablecloth plastered over the windshield.

"I told you I saw a sign saying 'Panic' back there," Carmen said.

"Panic? No way is there a place called Panic. I don't see it on the map. How could you see a sign? There's barely a road!" answered Risa.

"Panic is not a good sign. Is that a noun or a verb?" Mel called from the back.

"What's the difference?" asked Cyd, trying to free herself from the ski poles.

"A noun is a person, place or thing. Where the hell were you during English?'

"Passing notes to Regan Mulroney. And I don't see a person, place or thing, so it must be a verb; that means action, right? Panic is not the action we're looking for, so keep driving."

"It's so dusty I can't see the road," said Risa, still struggling with the map. "Stop the goddamn car, Carmen, so we can figure out where we are."

They climbed out of the car, shielding their eyes in the shimmering heat, shaking out their legs and slapping the red marks from the vinyl seats out of their bare thighs. Behind them were the twisted rock formations of the Badlands. In front of them, way in the distance, was the ridge of the Black Hills. In between was flat dusty nothing, except for a cluster of shacks up ahead.

Cydney shook out her hair like a wet towel and wandered in the direction of the nearest shack, which had a gas pump out front and a yard of junked cars in back. Getting closer she could see that it also had a placard, *The Buckrock Saloon,* hung over the front double swinging doors, with an arrow pointing to *Jail* around the back. Framing the rickety veranda was a collection of Long Horn steer skulls with Christmas lights winking on and off in the empty eye sockets, their horns jutting up off the roof like the Viking hats in a Wagnerian opera. Leaning over the veranda rail was a short ancient Indian with bowlegs and an enormous gut, grinning like mad at four white girls in short shorts and high heels, staggering around in the heat.

"Can you tell us how to get to Rapid City?" Cyd called out. He motioned them toward him and, once up on the veranda, he pointed to the swinging doors that led to a much bigger shack than first appeared. Who could resist checking out a place that was part saloon and part jail? So, they pushed through the swinging doors – just like in the movies – and walked in.

INSIDE WAS DARK AND QUIET, like the middle of the night. As their eyes adjusted, they realized they were walking through soft fresh sawdust toward tractor seat benches surrounding tree trunk tables that looked mighty inviting. Dozens of leathery cowboy hats hung from the ceiling, swaying gently in the wake of the rotating fan whose blades were made out of canoe paddles. The whole placed smelled like an expensive shoe store. A long shiny brass bar ran the length of the room and next to it the open grilled jail, as advertised – any detainee would be smack in the middle of the action. Behind the bar were racks of bracelets and rings for sale made from fool's gold dug out of the Black Hills. Another set of swinging double doors appeared to lead out back.

The girls were mesmerized; the sudden escape from heat and light caused them to drop into the tractor seats, tired and thirsty and ready for whatever might happen next. By now the owners of the saloon, white folks named Hazel and Burt Wilkinson, had introduced themselves from behind the bar and welcomed them to the 'Tuesday Special' of dollar-a-bottle Muscatel.

"You mean dollar a glass, right?" asked Carmen.

"No, ladies, dollar-a-bottle. That's the Buckrock way," said Hazel.

By any objective standard the four sisters were good-looking girls, the three eldest tall and athletic; they could have formed the nucleus of a volleyball team. But under any circumstances they would have stood out with their crack-ass short shorts, waist-length hair, and lack of brassieres–especially on dollar-a-bottle day on the edge of the Pine Ridge Sioux Reservation.

By now a couple of people had come in, with more drifting through the doors, until eight or ten guys were milling around the bar and buying drinks for the new girls in town. In a corner stood an old red Wurlitzer, the biggest jukebox Cyd had ever seen. She wandered over with an ice-tea sized glass of Muscatel and flipped through list after list of old country and cowboy songs. She was feeding dimes into the machine, floating on cheap wine and deep country tunes, when she felt someone tap her on the shoulder. She turned around to face the most handsome man she had ever seen.

His name was Rain Montay, the foreman of a lumber operation in the Black Hills, at least twenty years older than Cyd, with deeply tanned skin, black hair, dark gray eyes and–always important to Cyd–the perfect wardrobe. He must have known she was coming because on this scorching hot day he wore a sharply pressed blue and white plaid shirt with pearl buttons and gold thread, skin-tight straight-legged jeans, cowboy hat, fancy leather boots, a matching string tie and a turquoise belt buckle the size of a sewer cover.

"Pardon me, Miss, but have you ever danced with an Indian?" He introduced himself with a crinkly smile.

"No, I don't believe I have," answered Cyd in slow motion. He smelled like fresh cut lime.

"Well then, step lightly, darlin'," he said, taking her in his arms and moving out to the center of the saw-dusted floor as the twang of a lonesome guitar filled the cool, windowless space. And just like that, they were dancing.

They slow-danced for at least half an hour as more locals and Indians from the nearby reservation drifted in, some of them bringing drinks to the swaying couple. Cyd was barely aware of how much she had drunk, or the whereabouts of the other girls, or the last time she had eaten, or how many strange men were crowding the room. She was only aware of her intense physical reaction to a man who seemed much too smooth, slightly dangerous and far more in control than she was.

"Where you girls from?" he asked, eyes twinkling. Cyd had never seen eyes so piercing. She had the sense that he could look right through her.

"Eastern girls. Just outside of Boston."

"Ever been in Injun country before?"

"Nope, never been west of...oh...New York, I guess," Cyd said, thinking that she sounded like she was about twelve years old.

"Married?" he asked, his breath close to her ear. She shivered, a little too obviously.

"Huh? Me?" Now she really was twelve. "I mean, of course not. I'm having way too much fun to be married!"

"That so?" he said, raising his voice so it had both a lilt and a growl to it. "What's the most fun you've ever had?" Cyd jolted out of rhythm and landed on his foot, pulling back from the tight circle of his arms.

"What do you mean?" she asked. Even with two or three drinks this was moving a little too fast.

"Well, I mean you're a sweet young thing and that's when you're allowed to have fun. Fun doesn't figure much in the grand scheme as you get older." He lifted her a few inches off the floor and swooped her around 360°.

Cydney had spent the past year as a cocktail waitress in Boston's Combat Zone—a tough section of downtown where she was hit on night after night. She had a pretty thick skin, thicker since Robert had shown up a few months earlier, miserable after his first year of marriage and ready to split. Cydney wasn't sure where things stood with her and Robert, except that he swore he loved her because she was the wild animal he could never tame. But now here she was with a man twenty years older who looked like a wild animal himself.

But while the slow-dance was thrilling, it was starting to scare her, and Cydney began looking for an easy way to escape. Always check the exits, she reminded herself. And so, when the saloon's front double doors swung open and in clomped a large gray appaloosa horse with a young girl astride his back, Cyd chose escape. Horse and rider strutted past Cyd and Rain up to the bar where Hazel introduced her as her seven-year-old niece, Diane. Cyd chose that moment to pull away from Rain Montay and follow horse and child out of the saloon and into the late afternoon.

Back outside in the shock of heat and light, Cyd tried to regain her balance. She had no idea how much Muscatel she had drunk, and she wasn't even sure what Muscatel was, but she did know that she was seeing double. Not overlapping and blurry, but double. There were two seven-year-olds named Diane sitting up on two separate horses, for example. And Diane's pet buffalo in the junkyard had sprouted an identical twin. Maybe someone had slipped something into her glass? Better to take a break from rubbing herself against a perfect stranger and stay outside to get her bearings.

Within minutes Risa tumbled out the back door, half carried by two guys who were laughing uproariously at everything she said.

"Hey Cyd!" called Risa, trying to focus on Cydney's face. "Let's ride! They've got horses."

Yes, and we've got no bras and basically no pants and no shoes. How drunk do you think we are? Cyd wasn't sure if she thought this or said it out loud, but either way, it was a fact. Cyd and Risa had been Girl Scout riding instructors for disabled kids and Cydney knew they could handle themselves, so she didn't panic when she saw Risa hoisted up onto the back of an enormous horse. Risa's new buddies slapped its rump and the horse took off in a beeline for the hills that looked to Cydney to be about one hundred miles away. Then somehow Carmen and Mel appeared and were up on horses too, although Cyd had never known either of them to go near a horse. Then it was her turn and she was heading for those same hills, right into the sunset with the stirrup leathers scraping her bare legs, hair flying all over her face and nothing but desert and purple mountains all around.

Finally, she managed to turn the horse around and head back to the saloon, where she found Risa whooping cowboy-and-Indian war cries while barrel racing bareback. Mel – suddenly a trick circus rider – barely hung on sidesaddle to Risa's waist. A crowd of about two dozen had gathered to watch Mel fall off and all of them, including Mel, dissolved in hysterics.

Cyd had no recollection of dismounting, so someone must have taken her off and brought her back into the saloon. By now it was sunset and half the reservation had shown up to see these East Coast girls who rode bareback and drank everything in sight. Cyd edged away from Rain Montay, who was leaning over her at the bar, and found herself sitting next to a full-blood Sioux with prominent knife scars slashed up and down his left cheek.

"Hey, can I have some of your hair?" he asked in a deep slow voice, staring at her intently.

"Well, sure," she answered, not really knowing what else to say. She could see Rain looking at her with something like possessive disapproval, as the guy with the scars took out a machete and hacked off a much bigger piece of her hair than she expected, right at her shoulder. He twisted it around his enormous fingers, trying to make a ring, but her hair wasn't up to the task, which really seemed to send this guy around the bend.

"White women's hair ain't worth shit," he said, glaring at her and throwing the failed ring on the floor. Rain moved in quickly and took her arm, pulling her off the barstool and into the crook of his elbow. Cydney decided to bypass her warning signals and leaned into him.

"Thought I might be losing you there, pretty lady," he said with an edge to his voice.

"Well, if you buy me another drink, I won't be lost." *Did I really say that? What am I doing, flirting with him like this?* But Cyd reasoned that not much could happen in a crowd this size; if there was safety in numbers she was untouchable. Because by now the joint was rocking, standing room only.

"Hey," several of the guys called. "where you girls fixin' to stay the night?"

"There's a campground around here called Shepherd's Hill, right? That's what we're thinking," said Cyd.

"Shepherd's Hill!" yelled Carmen and Mel from separate corners. "Baaaa baaa Black Sheep, have you any woooooolll...?" They laughed hysterically, joined by half the saloon.

"That right?"

"Nice in the moonlight."

"Shepherd's Hill, huh?" came the responses.

"But there are sheep, right?" asked Cyd.

This was met with howls of laughter, which collided with the chorus of *Baa Baa Black Sheep*, still going strong.

Cydney, dancing again with Rain, could hear an undercurrent of *shepherd's hill...shepherd's hill...shepherd's hill...*whispered by the men.

She looked up at Rain, who didn't seem to notice the refrain, and felt someone grab her by the shoulder. It was Hazel, the proprietor, a few years older than Cydney's mother, Bianca, with skin tanned to leather and dyed blond curls. She looked like she could arm wrestle any of these guys to the ground. Hazel excused herself to Rain and pulled Cydney aside.

"It's none of my business, but you girls don't know what you're doing. You can't sleep up on Shepherd's Hill because you'll never make it out of there alive."

Cydney looked at her as though she was speaking another language. "Why? Are there wild animals?"

"Yeah, you're dancing with them."

"What? Everyone seems so nice. They've been buying us drinks all day."

"Exactly," Hazel said. "Listen to me when I tell you that you do not want to mess with these folks. Last month I tried to stop a fight over something stupid like a lost dog and almost got thrown off a cliff."

Cyd listened. Hazel continued, "I own a small cabin on the edge of town and no one knows that it's mine. Get your sisters together and meet me out back in my truck in ten minutes and I'll sneak you in there for the night. *Do not* tell anyone, and I mean anyone, where you are going."

"But I have to tell Rain; he's been so sweet."

"Are you listening? Not Rain, not anybody."

"I don't get it; he seems like such a gentlemen."

"Yeah, and I'm sure all three of his wives would agree with you. Listen, just leave your car and your stuff inside and don't touch it or you'll give us away. Believe me – get out there in ten minutes or it's going to get real serious. I live here, honey; I know what I'm talking about."

Cydney had never shifted from dead drunk to stone sober so quickly in her life. One by one she rounded up Carmen and Mel.

"Uh, we've got a little problem here, and Hazel says we have to leave now."

"Oh, don't be an asshole, Cydney," said Carmen, staggering away from her youngest sister. "You always want to ruin everything for me. I am finally free of my kids, for chrissake, and just want to have fun."

"Seriously, Hazel is waiting for us out back; we have to leave now!"

But Carmen and Mel linked arms, told her she was a jerk and walked back into the crowd. Ok, if Carmen and Mel were too drunk to listen, then she had to find Risa and get her to pay attention. Risa was a good-time girl and could hold her liquor, *thank you, Kevin,* and might even see clearly on this one. Cyd had last seen her playing cards in one of the tractor booths with a tall guy with hair down to his waist. Risa was a sucker for guys with great hair and Cyd had a sinking feeling that they had headed off to the local motel – the junked cars in the back.

Cyd shoved her way through the singing throng at the bar and almost fell out the rear doors into the purple and black night. Looking up, she couldn't tell if she was seeing real stars or was just terribly dizzy. The temperature had dropped down to nighttime in October, and her nipples stood out as if they had been rubbed with ice cubes. She started to shake and noticed how little she was wearing. *I might as well be naked,* she thought.

"Risa!" she called in a voice cracking from fear and cold. "Where are you? It's important!"

Nothing. With no sound but a million shrieking crickets in the velvet black, she held her breath and scanned the outlines of the junked cars for movement. Finally she could just make out a rusted Buick up on cinder blocks rocking slightly. Cyd stumbled over to it and pounded on what was left of the rear window.

"*Risa!* I know you're in there."

Risa's voice shot back. "*What* do you want?"

"Shut up and listen, Ok? Hazel needs us to go with her *now*. Don't argue and don't say anything. Just make some excuse and walk over to Hazel's truck. Five minutes, Ok?" And with that Cyd staggered over busted tires and old hubcaps back to the saloon to hunt down the others.

INSIDE, THE SCENE HAD REVVED up in volume and activity. At least two guitars and one harmonica played along with the jukebox, with smoke so thick it practically vibrated with the dancing crowd. Cyd spotted Carmen's head bobbing between two dance partners and frantically motioned her over to the bathroom.

"I'm outta here. Risa too. No shit. You wanna get gang-raped, that's up to you, but Risa and I are leaving with Hazel in her truck. You have exactly three minutes to find Mel and meet us out back. Hazel says there is no way we will make it out of Shepherd's Hill alive." Cydney expected an argument but, instead, Carmen burst into tears and announced that she hated men, which allowed Cyd to drag her out of the bathroom and beckon dramatically to Mel, who was dancing on a table across the room. Mel didn't take long to realize she was about to be the only woman left and hustled over to Cydney. The two of them half-carried Carmen out the back door, where they found Hazel and her truck with its lights out, engine running, Risa inside, and Rain Montay leaning on the hood.

"Going somewhere, ladies?" he asked, one eyebrow cocked.

Hazel stuck her head out the driver's side window. "Get away from my truck, Rain; what we're doing is none of your goddamn business."

Cydney paused next to Rain, squeezed his elbow with a breathy, "We'll be right back," opened the rear door, shoved Carmen inside and hopped in. The door slammed; Hazel backed up, turned the truck around and sped out of the yard.

She drove down the road for what seemed like half an hour, then killed the lights and turned around, driving back very slowly by moonlight.

Looking out the window, Cydney thought it was like being on a moon crater, much like the first moon landing that had taken place a few weeks before. Finally, the truck stopped at a small dark cabin with no noticeable neighbors. Cyd peered out the truck window, straining for a landmark. "Are we back in town?" she asked, wondering where the town actually was.

Hazel put her finger to her lips and led them inside the cabin, refusing to turn on the lights, and pulled down all the shades. It smelled like sage and mothballs. "Lock the door after I leave and under *no* circumstances do you open it for anyone." She looked at their blank faces. "Or you could all end up dead. Or worse, wish you were dead."

They nodded, locked the door after her as instructed, and then explored the three hundred square feet of living space long enough to discover that there was just enough room for the four of them if no one made any sudden movements.

"See, it's like a tent; we're camping after all," said Cydney weakly. "At least there's a toilet." Within minutes they had curled up on the Murphy bed, the couch and the floor, and had fallen into the sleep of the dead.

The next morning, Cydney woke up, not knowing where she was or how she got there. She tried to sit up, and a sledgehammer inside her brain knocked her back down. Lying there, as though underwater, she could hear Risa heaving in the bathroom, Carmen muttering about her car, and Mel announcing that she was going to California no matter what. Somehow Cydney managed to stand and pull herself together enough to open the front door. Every step hurt. The light was blinding; white hot mid-morning sun shone on a cloudless blue-sky day. Cydney stumbled out of the cabin and followed the other three down the middle of a deserted street back to the Buckrock Saloon, where, thankfully, no one was in sight.

The girls stood around the car without saying a word. Carmen found the key in the pocket of her shorts. The luggage was still in the plywood rack, no one had siphoned the gas and the engine turned over with a roar on the first try.

"Muffler," Cydney said, thinking that her head would explode.

"Yeah, we'll find a garage in Rapid City," Carmen answered. She nosed the car into the dusty street and headed west, the only way to go.

HAVING FINISHED HER STORY, CYDNEY stretched out like a cat in the plush seat of the JC Penney waiting room. "Yup," she said, yawning, "it took us until somewhere in Idaho to clear our heads. I've never had Muscatel since. Fire water. Haven't thought about that place in years."

Lillian had no idea what time it was, and the 4:00 o'clock on her watch made no sense. *When did I leave Boston? This morning?* No other human beings had entered or left their little holding tank that now seemed quite cozy with the afterglow of the desert heat of Cydney's story.

"Whatever happened to Rain?" Nicole asked.

"I have no idea. I wrote to Hazel to find out. I actually addressed the letter something like...*Hazel Wilkinson, Buckrock Saloon, Panic, SD.* It got there because she wrote me back. Apparently he moved on to some other lumber operation up in Winnipeg. Sounds like he had quite a collection of wives, girlfriends and kids all over the Wild West."

"You could have been a harem girl, right here in the good ole USA."

"Yeah, I'll add it to my resume; but don't tell Lillian," Cydney added in a stage whisper.

The Buyers' door opened abruptly and a petite woman in a bright yellow suit walked out, smiling. "Are you the ladies from Baby Grand?" she asked innocently. Cydney and Lillian nodded, mutely, as Nicole gave them a big thumbs up.

LATER THAT NIGHT LILLIAN COULDN'T help but notice that Cydney was more pensive than usual. "This is good news, Cyd. The buyer will set us up with a test order on the East Coast. We'll head down to New Jersey and work out the details."

But Cydney's head was somewhere else. "The Buckrock Saloon. Haven't thought about it in years. Carmen is still in California. She never came back."

"Sounds like you were there for a while too. What did you do? You haven't mentioned this in the three years I've been listening to you."

"I stuck around. Helped take care of her kids. She had another baby, and he was pretty sick. Still is, poor Harry." Cydney got up to brush her teeth.

"That's her son with cystic fibrosis?"

"Yeah. It's been tough for her."

Lillian didn't know what to say; this wasn't the best time to tell Cydney that she was three months pregnant. "It's hard to imagine. Don't know much about cystic fibrosis; isn't it hereditary?"

"Yeah. Very recessive. Irish, French-Canadian…who knows."

"But doesn't it run in families? Which of Carmen's many husbands is the father?"

"Another deadbeat who took off," she said through a mouthful of toothpaste.

Lillian remembered overhearing a conversation between Cydney and Robert about meeting in California. They mentioned Harry, but Lillian assumed this was a friend.

"I may have to go out and visit," Cydney said, quietly. "I think Carmen could use some help."

This usually meant that she was off to meet Robert. "Yes, I know your code. You don't have to play footsy with me."

"What code?"

"You and Robert. What was he doing while you were hanging out in California, by the way?"

"Trying to get me to marry him."

"Tough, when he's already married."

"To a witch. Who owned the gold mine."

"So everyone has their cake and eats it too, huh?"

"Yeah, it worked pretty well for awhile."

"And now? What's up? Trouble in paradise?"

"No—we're better apart. He's in DC—it's working. Marjorie is thrilled to be Mrs. Senator. But…she is still sticking it to me. I owe her a fortune, etc.," Cydney kicked off her slippers and examined her bright purple toe-nails. "She claims I own the brewery under false pretenses..."

"What?" Lillian was genuinely outraged. "Ask her how much she got for my jewelry that is now in some sheik's harem?"

No answer. Cydney turned off the light.

"Seriously, Cydney. If you don't, I will."

1986.

BY THE TIME LILLIAN'S THIRD son Adam was born in 1986, business was picking up. After five years, Baby Grand had finally secured the coveted appointment at T.Rex Toys, ruler of the juvenile industry. Lillian and Cydney prepared for this meeting as though it were an arms control negotiation.

Because she was still nursing, Lillian tried on every item in her closet to find something business-like with a top that could easily open so she could use the dreaded breast pump during the long day-trip to New Jersey. "If you pump in the lobby we'll have no trouble at all getting the buyer's attention," Cyd had suggested. She finally settled on a loose summer dress with buttons down the front to a dropped waist and a big peasant skirt with a long Isadora Duncan scarf and very high heels. This would hide the twenty pounds that she still had to lose and draw attention away from her tits. The high heels were a toss-up, but how far could they possibly have to walk? She threw sandals in her bag just in case. Cydney and Lillian talked on the phone about eight times the night before they left just to make sure they had every sample and every variation of packaging that they wanted to demonstrate.

Lillian was up at 4:30 AM for a 7:00 AM shuttle flight. She had never left Adam before and started to cry as he blissfully sucked away, sound asleep. "Get a grip," she told herself fiercely. "I am not going to Tokyo; this is a turnaround trip to New Jersey and I'll be back tonight." She kissed Marc and the sleeping boys and felt like a thief sneaking out of her own house at 5:45 AM. She wore pantyhose for the first time in a year and closed the door on a house full of abandoned males of all ages and sizes. No one called out after her.

Alone at last! she thought. *I need this.* There was something terrifying and thrilling about it. *I've been waiting for this appointment for four years. I am not wearing sweatpants, and my shoes have real leather soles.* Lillian allowed herself that moment of triumph before her usual gloom set in.

Cyd and Lillian landed in Newark to find that they'd been upgraded to the only car available – a white Cadillac with red leather interior and a hundred buttons and controls.

"We're locked in." Lillian panicked as soon as she was inside. "There's no handle to the door."

"Relax," said Cyd, fooling with a row of buttons, "this will be a blast."

"I don't believe it," Lillian said. "Either I'm in your shitbox with windows that won't open or I'm in a car worth the mortgage on my house and the windows still won't open."

"The windows won't open because the engine's not on, silly."

"What if we get into an accident and the engine cuts out? How do we open the windows?"

"We worry about it when it happens," said Cyd, handing Lillian the map.

"That's how people get trapped because they haven't thought their way out of it in advance..."

"Look, will you *shut up* and concentrate on the map."

"Why? Are we lost? We haven't even left yet!" Lillian knew she had better calm down.

"We are *not* lost; we're standing still. I'm waiting for you to find the road before you make me crazy *on* the road and then I won't be able to find the road, know what I mean?" Cydney turned the key and the windows hummed up and down.

Lillian decided that it was best to be real quiet; she didn't know why she had these car phobias. She fiddled with the window button and then hit another and all the door locks snapped shut.

"*Leave the buttons alone,*" Cyd ordered, pulling the car into the flow of traffic. "You are not allowed to touch *anything, Ok?* Your job is to pay attention to the map and any signs for the George Washington Bridge or Lincoln Tunnel. Under no circumstances do we want to go near them."

"No, we sure don't," agreed Lillian.

THE WAITING ROOM AT THE East Coast headquarters of T.Rex Toys looked like a greyhound bus terminal with huge signs saying, *Pardon Our Appearance.* Given the condition of the walls, they weren't kidding.

"Pardon our appearance while we…what?" Cyd wanted to know. "Move? Redecorate? Make more money?" There was no place to sit in the long hallway because every flimsy folding chair was occupied either by a sales rep or a stack of toys. Guys in dark suits huddled in clusters with train sets and skateboards at their feet, hauling sample cases the size of a refrigerator on wheels. The back wall was taken up by a bank of pay phones, each one occupied by a guy with creased forehead, scribbling with one hand and punching numbers into a calculator with another. Other than the receptionist, they were the only women in the room. Their appointment was for 11:00 and Lillian figured they'd be lucky if they got in there by 1:00. She had the hateful breast pump in her bag and calculated how many times she would have to get to the bathroom to pump throughout the day.

"Excuse me." Lillian approached the young woman at the front desk with hair that looked like it had been super-glued into a mass of spikey curls. She operated a phone bank of at least two dozen lines, all of which she kept on hold, while she yakked at nasal top volume to a friend on another line about a) her new bikini from Bloomingdales and b) her loser date the previous night. It was moments like this that Lillian – at the age of thirty six – realized she was no longer young. She was desperate to get this order, desperate not to have her breasts leak all over the desk, and could not imagine stuffing herself into a bathing suit of any dimensions or of going on a date.

She tapped conspicuously on the desk to get the receptionist's attention, who gave her a dirty look but stopped her conversation long enough to look up.

"Uh, how much longer do you think Mr. Rosenthal will be, because we're kind of hungry?"

"Oh, Mr. Rosenthal isn't back from his morning meeting yet and there are about four appointments ahead of you, so you have lots of time for lunch."

Lillian could feel the pulse in her throat. "You mean he might not see us until mid-afternoon?"

"Oh, at least," she said, cracking her gum. "Maybe 4:00 or 5:00."

By late afternoon, after Lillian finished two more barely successful pumpings, they were the only people left in the waiting room except for a group of Japanese businessmen. There were seven of them sitting impassively along a bench, in identical black suits, white shirts and colorless ties. They all wore glasses and carried briefcases clutched tightly on their laps with large black boxes on leashes at their feet. They did not talk, even to each other. They had been there all afternoon and looked like they would sit there for another three days, if necessary. The big buzz in the waiting room had been Nintendo—a top-secret electronic game, which neither Cyd nor Lillian had ever heard of but was rumored to be a game changer in the toy industry. But even the Nintendo sales reps were still waiting.

"If the buyer won't show up for Nintendo—whatever it is—then what hope do we have?" Lillian said, slumping in her chair just as a man wearing a lumberjack vest rushed by the front desk carrying a fishing rod. The receptionist greeted him with a fistful of pink 'while you were out' slips. "Hey, Marv," she said, still cracking the same piece of gum, "what took you so long?" and jerked her thumb in Lillian's direction.

"That's him," said Cydney. "Marvin Rosenthal. A fisherman and I know nothing about fish. We're screwed."

"At least we're moving," Lillian said, standing up as the receptionist motioned to them to follow her. She couldn't believe that a day that started with such promise was coming down to this.

BUT MARVIN ROSENTHAL WAS PREPARED to deal right away. He had set up all six of the Baby Grand products that Lil had sent and arranged them into an attractive display on his surprisingly clean desk. Surprising because his office was otherwise a mess; crammed with sample products stacked on chairs, windowsill, shelves and floor. The office was painted the bright official T.Rex orange and decorated with the friendly tyrannosaurs mascot in every combination – in soft sculpture, on painted velvet, in balloons, on quilts. It occurred to Lillian that Cydney, who detested orange, was about to comment on its revolting-ness when Marvin mercifully leaned across the desk and cleared his throat.

"So, who's responsible for sending me so many samples that they're spilling out of the cabinet so I can't even open it?" With his hat off, Lillian could see that he was about her age, mid-thirties, very New Jersey Jewish, probably had not gone to college, with lots of street smarts and gold chains. The kind of guy she would never have gone out with in high school, and she hoped he had not picked up on that.

"Well, that's our strategy," she said brightly. "We send sample after sample until we figure you've got them everywhere and then you just can't get us off your mind."

Marvin pulled a sheet of paper from a desk drawer and placed it squarely in front of him. Even upside down Lillian could see that it was a coveted vendor agreement form. Afraid to breathe, she kicked Cyd under the table. In turn, Cydney handed him their new sample package; the mock-up box they had worked on all week.

Marvin nodded and broke into a wide grin. "That's it! Now this is the box I've been waiting for. Now that you've changed your packaging, I'll give you an opening order for...he scribbled on the vendor form...fifty thousand units. Any trouble with that?"

Lillian's throat was too dry to talk. Fifty thousand units was their total production for all of last quarter. Even Cyd was speechless. Lillian must have asked for a delivery date, because Marvin said, "Let's see, how about June 1st? Good enough for a summer test until I work out Christmas orders in the fall." He stared at them. Lillian thought that maybe they looked like they'd been kicked in the stomach. "Any problem with the timing?" he asked again.

Cyd sprang to life. "No problem at all," she gushed, no longer speechless. "We knew this order was coming – my past life regression analyst told me this would happen – and we're already on it. No-sir-ee, no problem at all."

"Your past...what? Life repression?" Marvin was suddenly looking at her very carefully.

"You know, like someone who helps you understand all the lives you've lived in the past," Cyd started to explain, but Lillian cut her off.

"Most of us have enough trouble dealing with this life; but my partner is so together that she's got time to explore the deep past," Lillian said with what she hoped was a wink and not a leer at Marvin. In fact, Cydney had been working with a new-wave crackpot who had corroborated her recent dreams that she had lived through many past existences. Cydney had gone so far as to drag Lillian to the museum for a tour of the tools in the ancient Egyptian gallery that she was convinced had once belonged to her during her stint as an architect, circa 2,000 BC.

Marvin turned back to the file cabinet and began to haul out a stack of papers, while Lillian flat-out glared at Cyd. "You girls had me worried there for a minute," he said, dropping the stack on his desk and producing a checklist of all the things Baby Grand had to produce in order to get the coveted T.Rex vendor number that Lillian had lusted after for years. Once you had it, it was like your social security number – yours for life.

"Bank statements?" he asked, going down the list.

"We got 'em."

"Financials?"

"Yup."

"Insurance policies?"

"No problem."

"Product Liability Insurance? One million US coverage?"

"Yessir," Lillian said without missing a beat, although it was a lie. Cyd looked at her in amazement. Product liability had been the bane of their existence. Lillian knew that there was no way they'd get it on time, but she rolled her eyes at Cyd and grinned wildly in the two seconds that Marvin looked away.

Lillian was already doing numbers in her head. 50,000 units times yards of fabric, yards of laminating, cut pieces, four...no, five more machines and double shifts for stitchers. Better enjoy it, she thought, as Cyd kicked her under the table, knowing that she would not have even two minutes to be thrilled because worry and fear would set in immediately. How would they fund it? How would they meet payroll for the next four months until they got paid for the order?

By this time, T.Rex Toys headquarters was as quiet as a church. It was 6:45 and they still had an hour's drive to the airport. The last shuttle left at 10:00. At this rate Lillian wouldn't be in the house until midnight. God knew where her breasts would be by that point – probably on their own shuttle. But Marvin wanted to talk, and Lillian and Cydney were his willing prisoners.

"Well, ladies," he said finally, pushing himself up from his chair, "I gotta get back to kosher canyon."

Lillian assumed that this was the local lingo for the very religious neighborhood where he probably lived, but Cydney did not get the reference.

"Koocher canyon, huh?" said Cyd, standing up to pull down her very short skirt over her fishnet stockings. "There are canyons in New Jersey? News to me."

Maybe it was the skirt or maybe the stockings, but Marvin let this comment go, and they escaped with the T.Rex order into the Garden State night.

1987.

A THIRD CHILD HAD JUST about sent Lillian around the bend. Cydney had undertaken two overseas trips to find additional manufacturing in Southeast Asia and had stopped for lengthy visits in California en route, leaving Lillian managing the shop locally—not her forté. Whatever was going on between Cydney and Robert continued to spill into Lillian's lap. In order to get the T.Rex order off the ground, Lillian had been forced to get an additional $200,000 short-term loan from Robert. Even with a purchase order for half a million dollars from the industry's flagship store, the bank wouldn't lend her a dime without a lien on her house.

Lillian fumed about this to herself, because she could not reveal the source of her funds to anyone but Marc, given her deal with Robert. Just before the T.Rex shipment was due, after Lillian and Cydney had pulled several all-nighters, Lillian found Robert lingering in the downstairs hallway early one morning. Lillian did a double-take; she knew that Cyd had left the night before for New Jersey to make sure the shipment arrived in good shape. So what was he doing here?

With his back turned to her in the narrow hallway—lined with boxes ready for shipping—he seemed older, shoulders uncharacteristically sagging. And then she realized he was crying. This so disoriented her—this calm, controlled man who juggled an insane private life in the public eye—that she started to turn and sneak away. Too late. Their eyes met—his red, his face blotchy.

"Robert! Is everything ok?" Lillian hesitated to ask. Instinctively she put her hand out to touch his arm, but with the boxes in the hall, it was too narrow to walk two abreast. Trapped, he shrugged her off and pulled out a handkerchief—initialed, she noticed.

"Allergies—the dust in here is killing me. Really bad today for some reason," he said, blowing his nose.

"Can I...um...get you something—Sudafed or something?" Lillian was rarely alone with Robert, in fact had seen less and less of him at the shop over the past two years. "This is the order, by the way," she said, gesturing to the boxes. "Thank you, again, for coming through for us. T.Rex pays on time, so in thirty days we can pay you back."

He nodded, his face clearing. "Great. Good job. Good for you."

"I...uh...thought that Cydney was gone for a couple of days..." Lillian said.

"I know; there was something I needed upstairs. And I wanted to check on the new puppy."

While he had been gearing up for his second senatorial campaign, Cydney had been flaunting her fling du jour with an always younger and always inappropriate guy. The latest was a twenty-four-year-old tattooed seaman recruit who was AWOL from the navy and raised wolf pups on an island in Lake Winnipesaukee.

"I didn't know the lake was big enough for islands," Lillian had said after she ran into Mr. AWOL in the bathroom early one morning.

"This is because you are a Canuck masquerading as a New Englander."

"Or that the islands were big enough for wolves," Lillian persisted.

"Wolf pups. And I'm getting one next week. Robert is psyched."

"What does Robert have to do with it? You're seeing someone else. Someone he could have arrested, I might add." But Robert was clearly still part of Cydney's life—Lillian heard them on the phone frequently during the day. Either this was the longest break-up in history, as these muffled conversations seemed very sober, but Lillian suspected they would stay connected no matter what.

She was so surprised to see Robert in the shop when Cydney was not there that she threw caution to the wind. "Don't see much of you anymore."

He shook his head. "And you won't see much in the future, either."

"Meaning?"

"Meaning that times are changing and the gentlemen's agreement with the press about private lives being private is blown to hell, so I have to keep a low profile. Plus, after almost twenty years, I would happily divorce both of them."

This was about the most honest Robert had ever been with Lillian. She opened her eyes wide in mock or real surprise. "What did she do now?"

"Which 'she' are you referring to?"

Lillian couldn't help but laugh. "That's a pretty big secret to keep under wraps. Your guts must be in a constant knot." Neither of them acknowledged that Lillian's keeping the secret had a lot to do with it.

"We still have an agreement, correct?" Robert said, looking at her straight on with his now clear, very blue eyes.

Lillian nodded. "Reluctantly."

"Hey, I got you off the ground and kept you there."

"You sure did."

Robert now held twenty-five percent of Baby Grand, in exchange for his frequent cash infusions.

"And when we sell it, you'll do pretty well. You'll get your money back with a decent return, but will I get my jewelry back?" Lillian hadn't mentioned the jewelry in years—not since Cydney's attack on the Taylord office safe.

Robert shook his head and folded his arms across his chest. "I honest to Christ have no clue what happened to it. You know as much as I do. Lillian, we are in this together—please remember that. I am totally loyal to my friends, as I think I have proved, but…"

"But?"

"No but. We are in this together."

They looked at each other for a moment longer. Robert checked his watch. A Rolex, she couldn't help but notice. "Gotta go. See ya. How's the baby, by the way?" he asked. "Healthy?"

"Adam? Thank God, yes. Lungs like an opera singer."

"Well, congratulations. Three boys, right? That's quite an accomplishment. Along with running a business."

"Thanks," Lillian said with a sigh. "Meeting a payroll and meeting a school bus. Doesn't get more responsible than that."

Robert chuckled. "Good line; I wish I could use it."

"Well, I guess it's not too late…" the words just came out of Lillian's mouth. "None of my business, but how come you didn't have children?" *Wow. Why had she said that?*

"Never happened," he shrugged, putting his hands in his pockets, and not meeting her eyes. "Although God knows we tried."

Lillian almost fell over. Wow – more information than she bargained for. "Gee, I don't know what to say; I shouldn't have brought it up."

"It's ok. You're not the first person to ask. Sometimes things work out for the best, I guess. More time for work."

"Umm. Well…good luck with the campaign. But it doesn't look like you'll need it, running unopposed. And Massachusetts loves to be ornery and elect about the most liberal Republican in the Senate."

"Thanks for your vote, Ms. CooperSmith," he said with a wink. And for the second time he put out his hand.

"Nice watch, Bretton." *Smooth as silk, this guy.*

"Yeah, I earned it."

"With body and soul, huh?" She couldn't help but like him. Triple threat. Looks, brains and money.

"You said it." Another wink.

Lillian put out her hand and shook his. Then, for the first and only time, she gave him a hug. She watched him disappear down the long, dimly-lit hallway. *Never happened. Although God knows we tried.* Didn't Cydney once say that he'd had a vasectomy? Too much information, and none of it made sense.

Do I trust him? Lillian asked herself. *No.*

Do I have a choice? Well, maybe. Maybe it was time to think about selling the company.

1988.

After Robert won his second term as senator in 1988, Cydney's relationship with him changed. As much as Lillian admired Cydney's rock-solid sense of herself, she was getting sick of their affair spilling into her business.

"Either get rid of him or get with him. Nothing will stop his political career—he's on a roll."

"You don't get it," said Cydney. "I don't want that life."

"Look, you're going to give this guy a heart attack; he adores you. He puts up with your screwing around with guys who should be in jail."

"Oh yeah? Look who you're defending. His wife is the one who should be in jail. Besides, I am spending too much time in New York."

This had become a point of contention. The previous year, Cydney had been offered a freelance gig as designer of soft props for The New York Theatre Ballet. Since then designers had come calling, and she was gearing up to be head set designer for an off-Broadway musical, which involved lots of time and not much money. Now that T.Rex was a steady customer, decent money was coming and banks were finally lending money on their purchase orders. But Lillian was pissed—she hated to admit—not just because Cydney was increasingly absent, but because she missed her. It was one thing to be supervising the many moving pieces of their local manufacturing operation, but another to have to do it without Cydney's tough love.

They both agreed that they had one more shot at expanding their line at T.Rex, after which Lillian was secretly hoping the company would be robust enough to sell. T.Rex was now entirely in her lap, after it became clear that Marvin Rosenthal, now merchandising manager at T.Rex, hated Cydney and would only deal with Lillian.

"Hey, check this out," Lillian told Cydney. "A guy actually prefers me to you."

"Yeah, you can have him. He's gross."

"So true. And all mine. Will you come with me to New Jersey and wait outside in the car?" Lillian still hated to travel by herself.

"There are no snakes or bridges and you don't have to drive because Dushku will pick you up. What's the big deal?"

Lillian had cultivated her top-selling NY/NJ sales rep for months—a smooth-talking and super successful guy named Adonis Dushku, a.k.a. Dush, who proudly claimed to be both Albanian and Armenian.

"Cut your throat and sell you a carpet at the same time," said Cydney when she found out.

In charge of sales, it fell to Lillian to make monthly trips to the T.Rex offices in the perpetual strip malls of New Jersey. This time she was flying to LaGuardia where Dush—whom she had never met in person—would pick her up and they would drive together to T.Rex. She had spent hours on the phone with Dush—pronounced douche, as Cydney pointed out—and as with many things in this business, you could arrange to marry someone over the phone without having met them; you felt like you knew them so well.

By the time she had almost missed her plane, getting on the DC shuttle instead of the LaGuardia shuttle, and spilling coffee on her thankfully dark skirt, she was sufficiently rattled to throw herself on the mercy of Adonis Dushku, whoever he might be. And right out of central casting, slicked down black hair, pointy shoes and all, there was Dush—short, immaculately dressed in Euro-style tight-waisted suit with white hanky flopping out of his breast pocket—waiting for her. She practically kissed him.

They went over samples in the sample case that Cydney had designed to resemble a Baby Grand piano—great concept but just try to carry it around. Cydney had come up with a line of foam block furniture for a child's room, which she had created in miniature, and a kids vest with multiple pockets to hold coupons so that they could help their parents while shopping. This was their attempt to get into the educational market and the pockets had big colorful stitching that said *Pasta* and *Soups* and *Juice*. Lillian wasn't convinced, but she had to sell this sucker. They needed two more SKUs at T.Rex and this was their best shot.

"So, Dush, my man, I understand that you and Marvin are really good friends," Lillian said, trying to keep her eyes on Dush and not on the drop to the river as he drove over the George Washington Bridge. "Now that he's been promoted to merchandising manager, I am really counting on you to come through for us."

THE TROUBLE WITH BUYERS WAS that they began to think they were God. First of all, they made a lot of money. Second, they had people throwing themselves all over them offering money, products, freebies, vacations – to get an order. And the raging success of Nintendo over the past year, for which T.Rex had exclusive distribution rights, just dumped more god-like status on them. Marvin Rosenthal – head buyer and now merchandising manager, had a strong dislike of anyone who had gone to college, had an MBA, and lived in New England where he had once worked and was unable to find a decent bagel or corned beef sandwich.

After the shortest wait at T.Rex that she had ever experienced, thanks to Dush's well-known presence, they were ushered into Marvin's new corner office – a significant upgrade from his crammed cubicle during the past two years of renovations.

"Hey, Marv," she said cheerfully, "look at you. Up, up, up in the world! Mazel Tov!"

Instead of answering, Marvin leaned across his desk and stared at Lillian's neck. He grabbed hold of her gold chain and pulled it, and her, closer to his face, examining the gold coin with the names and birthdates of her three kids. Without a word, Marvin undid the top three buttons of his shirt to reveal the three gold coins around his neck, along with an Italian horn and a Mogen Dovid – the Jewish star.

"Hah. Beat you. Covering all my bases." With that he proceeded to ignore Lillian and turn his full attention to Dush. Within minutes they were exchanging jokes about condoms that didn't fit and whose cock was so big that they had to strap it to their knee, tie it to their shoelaces, use it as a cane. Somehow Dush managed to behave throughout like a perfect gentleman, even with obscenities falling trippingly from his tongue.

Lillian was used to this in the juvenile industry. Run by men. The one business that you'd think would be run by women, but no. Lillian knew better than to jump in with ribald jokes of her own. Imagine that? Women meeting with men they didn't know and telling jokes about what–slippery diaphragms? Stretch marks? Breast implants? Lillian's job was to take this merry band out to lunch in the desolate world of local strip malls.

BACK IN DUSH'S CAR, THEY cruised the identical malls–Lillian could never figure out where she was–while listening to Marvin moan about his miserable years apprenticing in Boston where the malls just didn't measure up. They ended up in a Chinese restaurant with a bright red pagoda that looked as though it had been super-glued to the sawed-off roof of a Burger King.

Marvin was not an attractive eater. Food flew out of his mouth and crumbs landed everywhere, made worse by his non-stop yakking about subjects of zero interest–a John Deere lawn mower, his next fishing trip, a collection of model airplanes. The only thing Lillian wanted him to talk about was the potential order for 250K of Baby Grand products. So she wasn't expecting much when he motioned her to lean closer as though he was about to reveal a secret and said, "So there's this guy whose girlfriend is giving him a blow job under the table, and she says to him, 'Don't come in my mouth…'"

Lillian stayed leaning in, frozen in a tilt toward the center of the table with her ear delicately raised in his direction and a contorted smile on her face. She could not look at him or at Dush.

"And…" was all she could manage.

"And he says, 'What? You think I'm crazy enough to ruin your hair and makeup in a fancy restaurant like this!'" Marvin pounded his fist on the table in a fit of laughter, causing the food to not only jump out of his mouth but bounce up and down on the place mats with pictures of dragons and signs of the zodiac.

Lillian crinkled up her mouth in a laugh simulation but made no sound. If she actually laughed, it could open the door to who knew what degenerative jokes–gang rape? Bestiality? It was a damn good thing that Cydney wasn't there. She never got jokes and might have asked Marvin to repeat it, God forbid.

But there was no stopping him now. Marvin was off and running. "Hey! How come, no pun intended–*ha ha ha!*–Jewish men come so quickly?"

Lillian chewed vigorously and raised her eyebrows in an innocuous acknowledgement of interest.

"Because they can't wait to tell their friends!" Another fist-pounding on the table.

And neither can I, thought Lillian, wondering if Marvin was stuck in junior high or if this was some kind of perverse, one-of-the-boys test. Fortunately, Dush had picked up the torch and played along, humoring Marvin in what sounded like old familiar territory between the two of them.

How do I get him back to the products? But Marvin was greeting buyers and clients from across the room, carrying on five conversations at once, gap-toothed smile flashing, sandy blonde hair curling around the nape of his very thick neck. She had to hand it to him.

Back in the office he was all business.

"Show me the furniture line. Where are the package samples? Why is the chair red, why not blue? Blue will sell better. Make it blue. *Jenny!* Get your ass in here. Where are my order forms?"

Thank you, God. Lillian held her breath. *Let him talk.*

"Coupon jacket, huh? Not sure. Can you do a test run and drop-ship to the Midwest?"

She left with a split decision and a splitting headache. Instead of the 250K she was hoping for, the two sample orders ran to 200K. Not bad. She bought Dush a martini in the LaGuardia lounge and congratulated him on his fifteen percent cut.

On the plane home she thought about that fifteen percent. $30,000 for an afternoon's work. Did she need Dush to run interference with Marvin? *Why do Jewish men come so quickly?*

Yes, she sure did.

WHEN SHE RETURNED TO THE shop, she was looking forward to regaling Cydney with her mission accomplished and its toll on her delicate psyche. But Cydney had taken off for New York and left her a note with instructions for the Vietnamese stitchers over the next few days. "Fire the Cambodians – there is civil war on the factory floor."

"Not my job," muttered Lillian. "Let them fight."

Last week someone had pitched a two hundred pound sewing machine worth $5,000 across the floor. No one was hurt, but Cydney was on a rampage. Lillian's tactic was to let the wolf loose on the floor. That would shut them right up. Plus, Cydney had left her office a mess, as usual.

Lillian was exhausted. Why she had ever thought that working for herself would be easier than just collecting a paycheck she could no longer remember. She hadn't been home since 5:00 this morning when she had set off for New Jersey.

She cleaned up her desk and shut down her computer. Cydney refused to use a computer and her desk was piled, as usual, with stacks of random notes and sketches, some of which had fallen on the concrete floor. Lillian picked them up and her eye caught a newspaper cut-out.

> Harry (Henry) Mallone D'Angelo (1970-1988)
> Passed away September 15 after a lengthy battle with cystic fibrosis.
> Beloved son of Carmen Mallone DiAngelo will be laid to eternal rest in the cemetery of Good Hope, Santa Cruz, California.

A picture was attached – taken when he was younger, probably fifteen. Strong family resemblance. He looked more like Cydney than Carmen. Funny that Cydney hardly mentioned him – such a sad story, as if Carmen's life wasn't sad enough. She had gone to California for the funeral last month and stayed for only a few days. Lillian picked up the obituary and looked closely. Actually, the child looked a little like Robert. Was that possible? Carmen and Robert? No way. Cydney would have clawed her eyes out. Lillian put it down with a sigh. *My brain cannot stretch that far; there is only so much I can take of this ever-expanding triangle.*

She checked the answering machine – the light was flashing repeatedly. It was probably suppliers anxious for upcoming orders – a little too anxious Lillian thought; always a sign that the economy might be teetering toward recession. When the current round of messages finished, she started deleting the saved messages when Marjorie's voice cut through the silence.

"Cydney, are you there? Pick up. I won't bite. Ok… Well, this is awkward. Robert's been really down. I tried. I hope you know that….Yeah. Well…I just wanted you to know that I really tried."

Lillian checked the date and time. Saved since September 15. *Robert's been really down?* And this is coming from Marjorie? *If I live to be a hundred, I will not understand them.*

1989.

By 1989, BABY GRAND HAD finally made it. Sales topped one million and the company was being courted as an acquisition target by larger juvenile products companies. *Inquiring Minds,* a new magazine touting start-up companies, was doing a story on 'Mothers of Invention' with Baby Grand as the centerpiece. Lillian had asked Cydney to be part of the interview, but she declined, saying she was too busy in New York.

"Besides, you're the mother. And the inventor," Cydney said.

"But you're the designer."

"They don't care about me. Hey, take the limelight while you have it."

"But this would be good for you, too," insisted Lillian, "now that you're hitting the big time."

"Nope. Theatre people do not give a crap about what happens outside of their own little world. They would just try to pay me less is all."

So Lillian did the interview, her annoyance at Cydney coming out in her answer to the first question:

Q. So, how did you two get your business off the ground? Neither of you had much start-up experience, right?

A. Right. We basically made it happen with her ass and my jewelry.

Q. I beg your pardon?

A. You heard me.

Q. Is this off the record?

A. No, it *is* the record.

BUT WHEN LILLIAN LOOKED OVER the final proofs she had second thoughts:

> Lillian CooperSmith, 39 years of age, a former advertising executive, is one of a new breed of entrepreneurs enjoying the benefits of necessity as the mother of invention. Plus she is a mother herself, of three sons, one of whom inspired the creation of Carta-Babe, the first shopping cart carrier to hold an infant and then a toddler safely while mom is shopping. When asked, Ms. CooperSmith referred obliquely to the early chaotic days of her partnership with fabric designer Cydney Mallone as a time when the only leverage they had was "her (Cydney's) ass and my (Lillian's) jewelry." When asked for an explanation, she reminisced about a valuable set of jewelry that she was hoping to use as collateral for their first loan, but it mysteriously disappeared and was replaced by an investment on the part of a wealthy admirer of Cydney's. When pressed, she demurred further explanation and passed off the response as an exaggeration. But this served, she pointed out, to highlight how difficult it is for women entrepreneurs to get a loan of any kind from established sources—commercial banks or factors. In fact, it's impossible, she claimed...

LILLIAN CALLED THE INTERVIEWER AND asked to have the quote removed.

"Too late. Plus it's on the record."

"But I changed my mind."

"I'm sorry, but we've gone to press. Newsstands next week."

"Heads up," Lillian called Robert in Washington – something she had never done before. He was safely five years away from his next campaign. Who could possibly care about an old fling?

"Lillian. Jesus. We had a deal." Robert was not amused.

"Your name is not mentioned. Not even an allusion." Lillian stood her ground.

"Yeah, but they'll dig."

"So, you were an investor. No big deal. You invested in an old friend that you've known since childhood," Lillian persisted. Silence. "Robert? Look, I'm sorry. They wouldn't retract it. And I was pissed at Cydney. If she had just been here it wouldn't have happened."

"She's entitled to her own life, don't you think?" Robert said, his voice low on the phone.

"Excuse me? She's having her own life because this business, now run mostly by me, is allowing her to." *What is wrong with this guy? She's cheating on him left and right!*

"You wouldn't have the business if it weren't for my money." Robert kept digging in.

"I wouldn't have needed the money if you didn't have my jewelry!"

"Ok. Calm down. You know I do not have your jewelry. I just…this is not a good time to have someone looking into my background…"

Lillian knew there was never a good time, and she was tired of this game. "Look, Robert, this is simply a courtesy call to let you know the article is coming out, so you can get your story straight if needed. Plus our deal is getting old."

"Old? How so?"

"I think it's time to sell," said Lillian. *There, I said it.*

"What will happen to Cyd?" Robert asked.

"You'll have to ask her; I barely see her anymore." Lillian hung up and looked around the room, furious. *Who the hell does he think he is?* But it wasn't Robert she was furious at. Should she call Cydney with a heads up? She couldn't get a read on whether Cydney and Robert were still together. They had both been in California last month; some Republican party pretext. Really? Digging in his background? *Screw both of them...*

THE INTERVIEW CAME OUT AFTER her third argument that week with Cydney, who was still in New York and missing in action at Baby Grand. The shop floor was in chaos—the Vietnamese stitchers refused to work with the recently hired Cambodian stitchers—and several machines were broken and in need of repair. Practically every textile related business had left the country in the last few years—with no one to replace them. The tiny ancient guy who fixed their industrial sewing machines was no longer working, and Cydney was the only person who could take a $5,000 machine apart with her teeny tiny tools and reassemble it.

"Get back here," Lillian begged her over the phone. "I'll pay you $50 an hour to fix these fuckers."

"Hilarious. Get Nga Le to fix them. She needs the money."

"She doesn't speak English. We'll end up with parts all over the floor. The order from China is two weeks late and God knows what it will look like when it finally gets here. If Walmart cancels their order we are really screwed. You know this is our ticket up and out. Once we have Walmart in the bag we have a company to sell."

"Who says I want to sell?"

"Oh my God, Cydney, make up your mind! You are not here. So I'm thinking—yeah—she wants to get out."

"Not so fast. Maybe. And maybe not."

"I am not Robert whom you can just dangle at the end of a rope!"

"Oh fuck you."

"He was here, you know. Hanging out in the hallway. And you weren't. What was that about?"

"He was? When?"

"Cydney, forget it. I am asking you to get back here and take care of business for two days. Just two days!"

THE SECOND ARGUMENT CAME AFTER Lillian had just filed tax forms
for the subcontractors who moonlighted as cutters and delivery guys
for Baby Grand. They worked near the loading docks and industrial
piers of South Boston–blasted by winds roaring in off the harbor, with
a panorama of islands and lighthouses, ships and airport–parts of the
city that Lillian rarely set foot in. Usually Cyd dealt with these guys;
Lillian did not want to know too much about them. They seemed pretty shady and made her nervous. But now she had to track down Sully
and Brian of ABC Cutting, who were being paid just enough to qualify
for a Form 1020. Lillian dreaded the call to Sully, who had fifteen-inch
biceps tattooed with pictures of the devil performing cunnilingus on
Little Bo Beep.

"Hey, Sully, how are ya?" Lillian tried to sound like she was just one
of the guys.

"Yeah. Good, good. How 'bout you?"

"Great! How's biz?"

"Sucks."

"Gee, that's too bad. *Um*...listen, I need your social security number
so I can send you the 1020 for the money you made this year." Lillian
tried to sound upbeat.

"Yeah. What for?"

"Well...for taxes, you know."

"Right, right," said Sully, chewing in her ear.

"Well, do you happen to have it?"

"Maybe."

"It's probably on your license," Lillian tried helpfully.

"Yeah, but my license is out of state. Tell ya what–I'll make a copy
and send it to you."

Do I have a choice? thought Lillian. "Ok, I guess. Then how about
Brian? Is he there?"

"Nah. Brian's not here."

"Not there, huh? Do you have his number?"

"Nope."

"Do you know where I can get it?" Lillian had a sinking feeling that this would end badly.

"Nope."

"You mean…you don't work with him anymore?"

"Nope. I don't think anybody's working with him," Sully said with a chuckle.

"*Soooo*, he's like, left the area…moved?"

"You could put it that way. Listen, if I was you, I wouldn't be asking no more questions about Brian, ok?"

"Ok, Sully. Thanks. I'll uh…be in touch if I need anything." Lillian hung up as fast as she could and felt the hair on the back of her neck stand on end. She was convinced that Brian was lying at the bottom of Boston Harbor wearing concrete shoes. She called Cydney in New York.

"What should I do? Call the police? I mean the guy is probably dead."

"Yeah, so? Are you interested in joining him?" Cydney sounded about as interested as Sully.

"But we can't just do nothing!" Lillian protested.

"First, you are letting your imagination run away with you," Cydney said. "Second, the police will think you're nuts. And third, when Sully finds out he'll come and kill both of us and chop up your kids and feed them to the fish."

Well, that shut Lillian right up.

"Believe me," Cyd said, "I grew up with guys like that. You don't see nothing. You don't know nothing.

Lillian fumed about this for days. She had no choice but to toss the Form 1020 in the garbage and pray that the IRS would never find out. Cydney's messy life trailed after her like a toddler with a blanket. It was time to let it go.

THE ARTICLE IN *Inquiring Minds* on Mothers of Invention came out in March 1989, along with a flood of requests from other entrepreneur type magazines. Lillian insisted that the 'her ass and my jewelry' comment was a joke; she had greatly exaggerated as she was known to do.

Someone looked up the 1981 Boston Globe report from the Cabot Center confrontation with Marjorie Bretton and rumors started about Cydney and Robert. Robert 'fessed up right away to being an investor in a business that was a perfect sideline to Taylord Mills and in someone he had known since childhood. What was the big deal? It died down immediately. People loved Senator Bretton; he could do no wrong. Lillian had flung her arrows – almost daggers at Cydney – and Cydney had responded in kind; she stayed in New York. And Baby Grand – finally on stable ground – threatened to founder without both women at the helm.

CYDNEY CALLED LILLIAN AFTER THE article came out.

"My ass, huh?" Cydney said.

"They wouldn't retract it."

"My mother is going to read this, you know."

"Your mother has seen worse."

"I have no idea why you would do this to me. I have done nothing but root for you." Cydney sounded genuinely upset.

"Shit – I'm sorry," said Lillian, conflicted. "Really. It was a snarky answer and I thought it might have legs. That's theatre lingo for..."

"I know what it means. I don't have an MBA but I'm not stupid."

"Ok, Cydney – I am sorry. It doesn't make me look great either. But, on the bright side – since you are the glass-half-full girl – it gives us a higher profile for selling."

"Who says I want to sell?"

"Cydney, please, can you just get up here so we can talk about it? I cannot continue to run this alone. You may not want to sell, but if not you'll have to find a replacement for you."

"And what about Robert? This is really embarrassing for him," Cydney said.

"I called him immediately," said Lillian. "His PR staff spun it perfectly. Makes him look even better. Big company CEO invests in tiny start-up to help old friend. The jewelry thing got buried – inside joke... ha ha. Plus he suggested that you didn't care all that much."

"Yeah, yeah. You're both assholes."

"That's more like it," said Lillian. "Please, Cyd, the factory floor is melting down. Could you come back so we can make a plan?"

"My show opens next week. Are you coming? I have opening night tickets."

Lillian thought that Cydney did know how to hit her weak spots. "Do you have a date? Is Robert coming?"

"Are you kidding? We haven't been seen in public since Watergate."

"And who is the guy *du jour?*"

"Too young to drink in public. If I keep getting them this young, then by the time they are old enough to have a mid-life crisis, I'll be dead."

"How young are we talking?"

"Conversation over. I'll see you after the show opens." And Cydney hung up, leaving Lillian shaking her head as she sat at Cydney's desk and surveyed her stack of unopened mail. She put down the phone and noticed that Cyd had framed the obituary with the picture of her nephew, Harry. She picked it up, thinking of her own sons, who were exuberantly and exhaustingly healthy. *Remember what's important,* she said to herself, the frame slipping out of her hands. Picking it up, she felt something on the other side and turned it over. In a tiny plastic ziplok bag, there was a lock of dark hair.

FOR IMMEDIATE RELEASE: APRIL 2, 1990.

> Cambridge, Massachusetts: The Baby Grand Company, Inc. announced today that it has been acquired by SmartStart, Inc. of Los Angeles, CA, creators of the *Oh Baby!* Catalog. Baby Grand, privately held, owns the patents and trademarks for several unique infant and toddler products, all of which will be become part of the *Oh Baby!* repertoire. According to Smart Start CEO Dan McCarthy: "We have been in discussion with the folks at Baby Grand for the past year and think our combined product lines are a perfect fit." Baby Grand President, Lillian CooperSmith

agreed. "We're looking forward to working with Dan and his team to integrate manufacturing and material sourcing so that our products have the best possible transition."

Like a dog after a trip to the groomers, Lillian shook herself free. *Free!*

She, Cydney and Robert met in Cydney's studio for the last time. Lillian hadn't been up there for a while. The place could use a good cleaning; Cyd had been spending so much time in New York that she barely lived there anymore. Dioramas of various sets covered the cutting table and Cyd's pride-of-place Juki sewing machine looked abandoned. Robert paced, uncharacteristically agitated, hands in his pockets and forehead creased.

"Sit down, Bobbie, and take a load off," Cydney said, the only person who could get away with calling him Bobbie.

"I am waiting for an important call and not thrilled about giving my chief of staff this phone number. Not sitting. So, talk, ladies." Robert checked his watch.

"You're making me nervous," said Cydney. "*Sit down.*"

Whoa, thought Lillian. *Get me out of here.*

Robert stopped pacing and glared at her. He did not sit down.

Lillian chimed in, as upbeat as possible. "Here's the deal: it's structured so that we get fifty percent up front. We work for them on salary for the next twelve months and if we make our numbers we get another twenty-five percent. The last twenty-five percent comes in over the next five years. After that it's three percent royalties on anything that is sold based on our patents. No rights to royalties on their products."

"Dollars please, not percentages," said Cydney, cutting to the chase.

"They're valuing the company today at one million. We get 500K now. Robert gets twenty-five percent of that. We split the rest. Plus I bargained hard for our key employees to stay on for a year and get a decent severance."

Robert nodded absently. "Since I'm in for 300K, and the most I'll see is 250, if that, over the next five or six years, I have no dog in this fight. It'll be a tax loss, and my original motivation is pretty eroded." He looked pointedly at Cydney. "So…whatever works for you."

Well, that was easy, thought Lillian. Robert was clearly dying to get out of there, tapping his foot and jiggling the loose coins in his pocket. They were sitting in Cydney's living room, the unmade bed visible beyond the muslin curtains.

"Not so fast," said Cydney. "Robert deserves to get his money back."

"Cydney, I don't give a crap. You take it. You'll need it."

Again, Lillian thought, *I don't want to be here!* "Ok, you guys work that out between you. Does this make sense otherwise? Robert—you ran Taylord for years—what do you think?"

Robert stopped moving, his mouth set in a hard line. Lillian had never seen him like this. "I think you should kiss the ground and not even wait until the end of this sentence. Just take it."

"Well, I guess that's from the horse's mouth," said Lillian, sounding unnaturally cheerful.

"Or the horse's ass."

Cydney! Jesus.

"Look, I need money to live in New York. It's not a cheap place to be."

"You'll end up with close to 200K upfront, plus salary for the next year," Lillian said, thinking that Cydney might actually torpedo this deal.

"Yes, but I will need this money to last for years. I have no one to depend on but myself."

It was unclear whether Cydney was talking to Lillian or to Robert, or both.

"And that's the way you want it, as you have made very clear," said Robert, adding, "I only have one caveat, and this is a side agreement between Lillian and me. In writing."

In blood, thought Lillian. She knew what was coming.

"No mention of anyone's ass or jewelry ever again."

Do I have a choice?

And for the third time, they shook hands.

In 1991, after the year of transition to Smart Start, Inc., Lillian and Cydney spent a weekend in their office cleaning out, reminiscing, a little cautious and silly. A sleepover—literally. Lillian slept over in Cydney's loft for two nights.

"These are the good old days," said Cydney.

"And don't I know it. Life goes back to working for someone else."

"Yeah, at least it will be a predictable paycheck."

Lillian looked around the loft. The poster of Cydney and Robert taken in the photo booth over her sewing machine was long gone, but pieces of the tape that had held it up were still there. In its place was a blow-up of the Baby Grand trade show booth.

"So, you're ok—with your bevy of young admirers; what's up with Robert? Last time I saw him I thought you were going to eat each other alive."

"Yeah, that was bad. We both knew things had to change and we were angry and sad. In some ways we still are," said Cydney, shaking out a bag full of old samples.

"Too late?"

"Absolutely. We are in such different places. Can you imagine me on Capitol Hill? Or him hanging out in the green room Off Off Broadway? Which doesn't mean I don't see him from time to time..."

"Yeah, I figured," said Lillian with a laugh. "Kind of glad to hear that, actually."

Lillian saw Robert one more time. And not with Cydney. He and Marjorie were having dinner—alone—at a restaurant that had just opened in the rapidly gentrifying South End. She looked like she hadn't aged a day in ten years. He was very attentive, hand on her arm, laughing at something she said. Lillian waved from across the room, which he acknowledged with a small salute, but he was clearly not in public consumption mode. She felt a tug for Cydney and wondered if she should call and report. But it was still too fresh, and she was too glad to be out of it.

9:05 PM. *Sunday, Nov. 5, 2006.*

LILLIAN SAT FROZEN IN THE back seat of her wrecked car staring at the gun in Cydney's hands.

"Where…where did you get that?" Lillian asked quietly. *Think fast,* she told herself.

"Well," said Cydney, "I shot the moose, put the gun back in my bag, gave you the bag, and somehow the gun found its way under the driver's seat. Do you think I'm stupid?"

"What are you doing, Cydney?" Lillian asked in a small voice. "Um… do you have a permit?"

Cydney started to laugh. "Seriously? You are still Miss Newton Center."

"Could you just put it down, please."

"You asked me how long I've got. Until I'm drooling."

"Well, I didn't mean…"

"Yeah, you did. And you're right." Cydney unfolded her legs and raised the gun to examine it. "Should have reloaded after I shot the moose."

Lillian let out a breath. "Well, thank God."

"No, it's loaded. I just checked. But careful maintenance of tools is the key to any successful operation – as I have often told you."

"Alright, you are scaring the shit out of me – what is going on?"

"I am not going to be drooling in an institution. Uh-uh. Not going there."

Lillian waited for Cydney to continue, her mind racing.

"I figure this is some kind of omen – us meeting up, Marjorie dead, killing the moose, Robert about to spill secrets…"

"Cydney! You have excellent doctors at the best hospitals. You have Robert who is a US senator, for heaven's sake, with contacts everywhere…"

"Nope. The doctors know nothing, which they admit. The disease is irreversible and moving faster than they expected. Last week they told me it was time to get my affairs in order."

Lillian thought that Cydney sounded as sharp as ever. She glanced at the gun. Cydney had it firmly in both hands but no longer pointed at her. No way could she wrestle it away; Cydney was deceptively strong.

"Well, that settles it." Lillian changed tactics. "Your affairs are probably a total mess and you can't get them in order, so you can't go anywhere."

Cydney actually smiled. "Nice try." Her smile disappeared. "In fact, I drew up a will and left everything to Harry."

"Harry?"

"Yes, my Harry. You remember."

Lillian had just finished telling Cydney stories about Baby Grand and must have mentioned the death of Harry, Carmen's son. *What did she mean—my Harry? He died almost twenty years ago. How could she leave him anything?* Lillian shook her head, perplexed. Cydney glared at her, breath rising in a frozen plume.

"Nice. How can you forget my Harry?" She cocked the gun and narrowed her eyes, which had gone dead cold.

Lillian could feel sweat trickling down her back, despite the freezing temperature. She was damp cold and hot flash sweaty and her foot was twitching badly. She tried not to breathe like she had just run a mile and kept her tone light. "Cydney, you've lost me. I'm impressed that you've made a will at all—that's a tough thing to do."

"Look, here's the deal." Cydney turned the gun over and stared down the barrel. "When Robert finds us tonight I need to tell him about the will. So, we need to stay awake 'til then. I need you to keep me awake. And focused. I can't get confused or agitated. The pills do that sometimes. I just need to wait. And then it will be ok."

"Ok. It'll be ok." Lillian's mind raced. "We'll stay awake. You're right, I'm sure Robert is on his way—trees are down—that's why he can't get through. He's called the state police for sure; they'll be here any minute. But, Cydney, could you please give me the gun?"

"No."

"Why not?"

"Because I'm going to use it. Later."

"No, no you're not." Lillian tried to keep her voice low and steady. "Robert will be here any minute."

Cydney sat as still as stone. Her head jerked up to stare at Lillian. "You're lying. You said something to him at the funeral, didn't you? That's why you got us lost! Jesus…you're in on something. Together. I need to get out of here!" Cydney took in big gulps of air, icy clouds forming in the car. She started to shake and gripped the gun more tightly, aiming it directly at Lillian, eyes wide and frantic.

Think fast. Paranoia, delusions…difficult to predict violent behavior…*Oh shit. Now what do I do?*

"Cydney! You cannot get out of the car. It's…it's more dangerous out there. *Maybe I should let her go?* You'll freeze to death. You just asked me – remember? – to keep you from getting agitated…so I'm pulling rank on you. You can't leave the car – it's like leaving the ship. *You* were the one who got me over my fear of everything that had to do with a ship. Water, bridges…stuck in cars."

"Yeah, and now look at us. Stuck in a car. A giant set-up. Planned by you."

"Put down the gun. Please. I'll tell you another story. Or…I'll sing!"

Cydney paused; something clicked. "Oh god, don't sing."

"Aha – you remember! I used to sing while you sewed." *That worked!*

"Yes, it made me sew faster."

Yes…! "Exactly. It was my perverse way of keeping us awake."

"Which is what you're doing now."

Oh shit… "Because you told me to."

"You used to sing on the ship – although how they paid you for that I'll never know. You were going to write an opera about you and whats-his-name…Flamingo…Fleming…"

"Memling! Good for you…" *It's working…* "An opera – you remember that, huh? I must have been on drugs."

"Uh-huh. Ignacio Memling. That's why you wouldn't cross a bridge."

"Wow. Maybe you should be the shrink. Who says your mind is going?"

"Because of the abortion."

"Well, that's a little simplistic."

"Nope. That's what it was. Guilt."

Is she trying to piss me off? Don't take the bait.

"You were smart," Cydney said, looking perfectly normal. "And lucky. That's what I should have done, after he knocked me up." She had lowered the gun, but raised it again, shaking her head sadly. "I should never have had that baby."

Huh?

V

FOUND

IN 1969, ONE LATE NIGHT two months after Marjorie and Robert's honeymoon, Robert showed up at Cydney's door in Chinatown and refused to leave. For two months she had hung up every time he called and had sent back his letters with 'Return to Sender; Addressee Unknown' scrawled in her handwriting.

But that October night, after her waitress shift at the Candy Shack, she found him asleep on the stoop in the shadows – a well-dressed man in a trench coat, huddled in a dark corner in the middle of Chinatown. She took her billy club studded with nails out of her knapsack, ready to wield it against the usual suspects – drunks, horny old men out from the strip clubs, pimps, and creeps – but stopped cold when she realized who it was.

Should I walk away? But in the two minutes that she took to step back and watch the curve of his neck on the doorpost, hair curled around his collar, she went from rage to sadness to longing, until she saw the glint of gold on his left hand and went right back to rage.

She nudged his toe. "What are you doing here?"

There was an all-night diner on Tremont Street where they sat and she listened while he talked.

Ok – so Marjorie seduced him – he's a guy after all – but so what? You get laid and you get married? Who does that?

"I was so stuck," Bobbie said. "She just sprung it on her father. He's my boss! I went to him the next day, ready to quit – told him this had been a big mistake. He offered me the company; he'd been trying to get out for years. The company! But it came with his daughter. I just caved. And…and the draft! A marriage deferment could keep me out. My mother begged me not to do it. But, what about my father? What about all the men who died for that damn mill."

"Oh, so you did it for your country, huh? Or for your father? You are falling even lower in my estimation," Cydney said. "Why are you telling me this?"

"You are wise way beyond your years."

"Fat lot of good that does me."

"I'm telling you this so you will know what happened. So you will think that—yes, I'm a piece of shit, but here's why. And I can't stop thinking about you."

Cydney narrowed her eyes. "Tough. I haven't thought about you at all."

"Bullshit."

"*Who* do you think you are, Robert Bretton? Barging into my life *twice* in six months with bullshit intentions." She stood up, but he grabbed her by the wrists to pull her down.

"Hey, calm down!"

"Don't fucking touch me," she said, folding her arms. "I am exhaust-ed. I've been dealing with sleazebags all night trying to cop a feel while I serve them jugs of warm beer. I stink, in case you haven't noticed. Why are you here—seriously? You've got everything you wanted—the house, the business, the maids, the limo, the hot girl…"

"No—it's a deal from hell and I knew it. It was a mistake. I'm ready to walk away."

"And do what?"

"I have a Harvard MBA—I'm not nobody. I've run a business. And hey—I've proved that I can learn from my mistakes; that's the American way, right?"

"And what about Marjorie? She will track you down and skin you alive."

"Well, that's the biggest problem," he said, burying his face in his hands. "Oh, Cydney. I told her I was leaving and she told me she's preg-nant." His shoulders started to shake.

"Well, duh. What did you think she was going to do? Is it yours?"

Robert started to laugh, in spite of himself. "See, I told you—wise beyond your years. She says she went off the pill right after she set her sights on me."

"There's a vote of confidence…are you sure she even has a uterus? Perhaps she's only half human."

"Ok—she is my wife…and possibly the mother of my child."

Cydney stood up, pushing back her chair so quickly that it hit the ground. She put her hands in the air. "Going now. Don't touch me."

"You can't go alone—it's dangerous out there."

"Yeah? Look around. This is where I live. On the $20 tips I make every night. On rent that is so cheap that I can save $100 a week. That's more than my father made sometimes in a whole month, when he wasn't falling down drunk, or maybe you don't remember that. Go back to your wife; you've left this behind. Poor me. Poor you."

Robert followed her home. She slammed the door in his face and raced up the three flights of stairs to her cold water studio painted Pepto-Bismal pink, shaking. In the morning he was still there, on the doorstep, fast asleep.

BOBBIE WOULDN'T QUIT. HE SENT Cydney flowers. She threw them in the trash. He sent letters. She ripped them up. He showed up at odd hours. Finally, he came to the Candy Shack, where she found him sitting at the bar in the middle of a rainy May afternoon reading the *Wall Street Journal*.

"Why don't you just wear a sandwich board that says FBI?"

"Why won't you answer my calls, damn it?" Bobbie put down the paper and grabbed Cydney's wrist.

"Damn it?" Cydney shook her arm free. "Aren't you an expecting father?" Cydney knew that Marjorie had miscarried and was pregnant again.

"Where'd you hear that?"

"Carmen. She's moving out to the West Coast."

"Good for her. Get as far away from here as possible."

"Agreed. I'm going with her."

"You are? Oh, Cydney, no!"

"Why? This is my life."

"Because…you hate Carmen. And you can't leave me."

"Get over yourself, buddy. I have a boyfriend."

"Bluff. You do not."

Joe, the bartender, reached over and stuck his face two inches from Bobbie's. "Everything ok here, Miss Cydney? This guy getting a little too close?"

"He's fine, Joe," Cydney said. "Local boy makes good. Old friend… I'm taking a break for ten minutes, Ok?" Cydney pulled Robert into a back room and closed the door. "This has to stop. I'm leaving. Don't you get it? You have done everything you can to apologize, but what's the point? Go ahead and live your life."

"I'm not sure I'll be able to live with myself if you leave."

Cydney sighed. "You are expecting a baby! What am I supposed to do?"

"I love you," Robert said, looking as though he was about to cry. "I've never said that before. To anyone."

"You don't even know me."

"I do," Robert said quietly. "This whole year you've completely out-classed me. Doing whatever needed to be done. Staying true to yourself. It would have been so easy for you just to let me in, give you money, take you away. Try to convince me to leave Marjorie. But you didn't. I don't think I have ever known anyone with that kind of backbone."

"So why are you trying to break it?"

"Because I am a selfish son of a bitch; you're right about that. And I need that strength. Maybe when we're together it will rub off on me."

"I'm leaving no matter what. No matter what happens between us. Is that clear?" Cydney said.

"I'll take my chances."

"You are very sure of yourself."

"I have a pretty good track record," Bobbie said, grinning sheepishly.

"You have a pretty shitty track record." Cydney studied him. She was leaving. She had wanted him for years. And maybe now she had the upper hand.

Cydney left her shift early, to the glares of Joe the bartender and big Mike the bouncer, and Robert signed them into the Ritz as Mr. and Mrs. R. Brown.

IN THE HOTEL ROOM—Cydney refused to stay in the honeymoon suite—she and Robert stood staring at each other, fully clothed, across the enormous bed.

"Take your clothes off," Cydney said.

Robert did not need any encouragement. He pulled his shirt over his head and stepped out of his jeans.

Just as beautiful as Cydney had imagined. Soft curling hair on his chest. Smooth stomach. Long legs. Dark patch of pubic hair with a thickening penis. He did not ask her to take off her clothes.

Fully clothed, Cydney crossed the room and walked around him, slowly, showing no emotion, hands to herself. Standing behind him she traced the line of his spine from top to bottom with her fingernails, leaving spidery white marks on his skin. Robert shivered, but let her set the pace.

Instead, Cydney took up her position on the other side of the bed and folded her arms across her chest. "What should do we do now?" she asked.

"Awkward. *Ummm*. There's room service—are you hungry?"

"I thought you were taking me out for a romantic dinner."

"Don't you think this is romantic?"

She shook her head.

"You're right," he sighed, starting to get dressed and waiting for her to stop him. She didn't. "Maybe you're always right and I should just get used to it."

"Don't get used to anything, buddy."

"I know! How about the car?"

"The car? Can we eat in the corvette?"

"Well, I broke that rule the moment I saw you, so why not?"

They ordered very expensive burgers and took off in Robert's corvette out to the Charles River recreation area in Waltham. They ate in silence with the lights off and the last of the sunset reflecting over the ribbon of water as it escaped the bounds of the city into the rural suburbs. Sitting with their hands in their laps, Cydney looked around for a napkin. Robert pulled her hand gently to his mouth and held it there, kissing her palm softly.

Cydney tried to pull her hand away but it weighed ten pounds, cradled in Robert's. She couldn't move – swimming in slow motion through heavy water, looking for air that was not to be found.

Robert pulled her onto his lap; it was a tight fit in the bucket seat. "Look how tiny you are." He buried his face in her hair. "Now I just want to take care of you." Somehow he knew this was the wrong thing to say.

"Let's go back," Cydney said. "I've never been in a hotel room before. That was the largest room I've ever seen."

"Ahh. So it's the room, huh?"

"One thing at a time. First, let me check out the room."

"Because you've already checked me out. And...?"

"And...?" Cydney raised her eyebrows in mock astonishment, grinning.

"Well, are you buying?"

"Are you for sale?"

"See?" He shook his head. "You are way too smart for me."

"Not buying. Maybe renting. Short-term lease. No matter what happens I am outta here in one week, Bretton. Next Sunday. Carmen is leaving – my parents are taking care of her kids while we're gone. Risa and Mel, too. All of us. The four Mallone bad girls on the road."

"Can I come?"

"No. You are married and responsible. And going to be a father."

"Please stop saying that. My erection has been like a pogo stick. Up, down, up, down. What are you doing to me?"

"It's about time, Bretton, that someone gave you a hard time."

He started the car. She put her hand between his legs. "I'd say, up. Keep it that way."

"Yes, boss lady. I will do my best." He roared out of the parking lot and almost flew onto the Mass Pike, taking the access ramp on two wheels.

In the fall of 1969, when Cydney arrived in California with her sisters after their hell-raising cross country trip, she realized that she had missed her period. She had been vaguely nauseous since the scene at the Buckrock Saloon, but she chalked this up to alcohol poisoning. When she finally looked at a calendar and counted the weeks, almost two months had passed since Bobbie showed up at the bar and they'd had their intense fling, spending every night in a different hotel, ordering room service at 2:00 AM, laughing hysterically, never getting dressed. Robert had told Marjorie he was away on business and Cydney had him all to herself. It was weirdly not sexual, but deeply intense, almost as though they had melted into each other. She hadn't realized this until the explosion of her high octane attraction to Rain Montay, which, by contrast, was pure animal attraction. So, while she couldn't figure out this powerful thing with Bobbie, she wasn't at all sure that she wanted to start it up again. Jesus—he was married; no matter what he was willing to promise. And way more Catholic than she, or even he, had realized.

"You believe that stuff?" Cydney had asked, curled across his naked chest in the enormous bed at the Ritz.

"Yeah...is that so strange? Millions of people believe it. It got my mother through some hard times after my father died, raising me alone with no money."

"But, that's like believing in magic."

"It's a leap. Like believing in anything you can't see. Like love."

"My father thought the church was a pile of horseshit," Cydney said, raising herself on one elbow. "Wouldn't step into one. Wouldn't say why. My mother dragged us to Mass every Sunday and he refused to go. I used to bust out the bathroom window and stand outside freezing in my

Sunday nylons, knees turning blue." She crawled on top of Robert, sitting up, hands on his chest. "Catholics don't get divorced. Or use birth control, I've noticed. Good thing I have my diaphragm."

"Good thing I have sharp teeth and can put holes in it."

"*Get out* of here!" She pushed him away, playfully. "That is a *stupid* thing to say and really creepy to even think about."

"Well, it does taste disgusting, in case you ever want to check it out for yourself."

SHE HAD CALLED HIM TWICE from a payphone in Oakland where Carmen had found a dilapidated two bedroom duplex and a job as a waitress. Cydney offered to stick around and look after her nieces when they got home from school in the afternoon, while she looked at art schools.

"Cydney!" Robert said, voice fuzzy over the phone. "When, when, when are you coming back?"

"Miss me?"

"I am desperate to see you!"

"Why? All I do is give you a hard time."

"Yeah, I love it."

"Not so fast. I am checking out the world. You will not believe how different this place is—drugged out hippies everywhere. I'm going to learn how to tie-dye and batik.

"I'm giving you another two weeks and then I'm coming to get you."

"Yeah, yeah. You are a respectable married man, running a business with a pregnant wife."

At that they were both silent. Cydney had a momentary flash of terror. *Shit, that could be me.*

"Seriously, Cyd, I really miss you. Please come home."

A PREGNANCY TEST CAME BACK positive. The doctor at the Oakland clinic looked at her sternly when she asked about getting rid of it. "What about your husband?"

"No husband," she said, wondering why she was suddenly whispering. "I'm only nineteen – I'm too young to be a mother."

"Well, you should have thought of that a few months ago."

Cydney opened her mouth to say, *you asshole,* but nothing came out.

"As you know, abortion is not legal in California."

"Well…what if I was a…Hollywood starlet? Would it be legal then?"

"Are you?" he asked, suddenly interested.

An even bigger asshole, thought Cydney. "Yeah…I am." *What the hell – she might as well try it.* "Making a movie with…Clint Eastwood! Starts shooting in two months. So you see…I couldn't be pregnant."

"Uh-huh. Well, I could give you the address of a clinic in LA, very expensive. But maybe you could have dinner with me first." He winked at her.

Cydney stared at him. "Why don't you give me the address now and I'll have dinner with you later, when I'm not going to throw up on your plate."

Asshole! What an asshole! Cydney fumed while walking back to Carmen's and trying not to panic. What could she do? She had to get to LA and find that clinic in Beverly Hills. It would cost a fortune. It didn't even occur to her to tell Robert; he might actually leave Marjorie, and she was beginning to realize that she didn't want him to. She didn't want any of it – not marriage, not motherhood, not the respectability that would surely come with being Mrs. Robert Bretton. Not the rage of rejected Marjorie. Nope. She would have to scrape the money together and get herself to Hawaii where abortion was legal.

But when she walked into Carmen's kitchen, exhausted and nauseous, there was Robert sitting at the table with Carmen's youngest daughter on his lap. Just like old times.

"How did you find me?" Cydney dropped her packages on the floor and thought about flinging herself into his arms. She didn't. Carmen's eyes went from one to the other.

"What's up with you two?"

"How did I find you?" Robert asked, sounding annoyed. "I called your mother. Then I called Carmen and told her I'd be here on business. Didn't she tell you?"

"No, because Carmen is still mooning after you. How's your wife, by the way?" Cydney turned to pick up the cereal boxes spilled on the floor so Robert couldn't see her face. *What do I do now?*

"Cydney, let's go for a walk." Outside, in the bright California sun and the rundown streets of Oakland, Robert tried to take her hand. She pulled it away.

"Not again. I can't keep seducing you. It's too much work. It's making me crazy! I've been calling every few days..."

"Well, no one gave me the message."

"And the phones work in both directions. Why haven't I heard from you?"

"I have no money. I'm flat broke."

"So come back. I'll help you find something. Cydney, I have missed you so much..." He took her in his arms, picking her up so she couldn't escape. She gave up and buried her face in his neck. He smelled great – lime and musk. For the first time in weeks she wasn't nauseous.

"Carmen said that Marjorie had another miscarriage."

Robert put her down. He got quiet and his face stilled. "Yeah. At four months. Pretty awful. Third time."

Cydney stopped walking and covered her face with her hands.

"What's wrong? Cydney, what is it?"

"Bobbie, this is crazy terrible. We're talking about Marjorie miscarrying and I'm...I'm pregnant," she said in a voice so low he had to lean in. "I'm pregnant."

Robert looked like someone had punched him. "Cydney...I don't know...I mean...how long?"

"Almost three months."

"That would be...us? Right?"

She nodded.

"Ok. Ok. I'll make this right. I'll file for divorce right now. I'll call her tonight. We'll, we'll..."

"Robert, stop it. No, you won't. She just had a miscarriage! I hate her but I'm not that vicious. It won't work. I'm getting an abortion. I have to get to Hawaii. It's legal there."

"Cydney–no! It's a baby. Didn't the church teach you anything?

"Didn't the church teach you about adultery?"

"I'll divorce her; I'll get an annulment."

"I don't want to marry you! And I don't care about the church."

"You can't just be an unwed mother with a...a bastard!"

Cydney pulled away from him. "*Why* would I marry someone who says something so stupid?"

"I didn't mean it–it's just that you are driving me crazy! You're pregnant. I love you. This is a perfect reason to get divorced."

"Yeah, but it's a stupid reason to get married! Look, I am *not* having a baby. I am nineteen years old, and I will not end up stuck like my mother and Carmen in a dead-end life." Cydney had spent enough of her adolescence baby-sitting the hyperactive children of alcoholic girls barely out of their teens in smoke-filled trailers with cigarette burns on the Salvation Army furniture.

RELUCTANTLY, ROBERT GAVE HER $1,000, no strings attached. She went back to the doctor in the Oakland clinic who told her that she was fourteen weeks pregnant and would have to go to a hospital for a D&C.

Cydney threatened to take an overdose of pills.

"Look, I can give you the name of someone in Hawaii," the doctor said, still put out that Cydney had no interest in 'having dinner' with him, "but it will cost more than what you've got."

She called Robert from a phone booth with the Bell operator requesting "another six quarters for the next two minutes" over and over again.

"Robert! I cannot do this. I will jump out a window or take a drug overdose. *Please!* I am leaving for Hawaii in the morning."

"No, Cydney, please don't. It's been almost four months. It's a...a baby!"

No it's not! No it's not! "Listen. You cannot talk me into this. You are a married man. You want me to tell your father-in-law? He'd be happy to give me the money."

"Tell him. Then I'll get divorced and marry you."

"I do *not* want to get married. Don't you get it?" Cydney was close to tears. "I can't do this. Please, just send me another $1,000 so I can figure it out." She hated asking anyone for money, had never done it in her life, having worked since she could practically walk on her own. "I feel like an alien is taking over my body!"

Robert agreed to wire her the money on condition that she would call him when she received it and they would talk calmly before she did anything. But that night, taking a bath, Cydney looked at her nipples, growing darker and larger and felt something like a butterfly fluttering in her belly. This was really happening. Robert arrived the next day. They walked for hours.

"February. The baby is due in February," he said, counting on his fingers. "I'll be here – set up an account for you and Carmen. After she adopts the baby, I'll start an account for him. Or her, of course." He squeezed Cydney as hard as he dared. "You don't know how happy I am," he said, kissing her on the top of her head.

Cydney stayed silent, thinking about the near alcohol poisoning from the Buckrock Saloon.

"You know, I got really, really drunk a few months back; maybe that's not the best thing to start off with."

"Hey, Irish and French Canadian – the kid will come by it honestly."

"Not sure it works that way."

Bobbie was thrilled, but Cydney felt like she was walking in slow motion through heavy water.

9:50 PM. Sunday, Nov. 5, 2006.

"THERE IS SOMETHING OUTSIDE THE car. I knew it." Cydney sat up straight and grabbed the gun. "Look. Three of them." Lillian couldn't see a thing. It was snowing much too hard. Cydney started to whisper. "Listen, I think I can sneak out and surprise them. Maybe I won't have to use the gun."

Jesus, it was working so far, what went wrong?

"Cydney, look at me," Lillian said. "There is *nothing* outside. If there were we would hear it." But Cydney's eyes had clouded over, and she had a vague and slightly panicked look on her face. "*No!* I know they're out there. The rest of the moose. They've come for him and...for me. Well, I shot him."

"What other moose? I...I doubt it." *How many moose can live around here?* "Look, I'm clearing a patch in the window," Lillian said, leaning over Cydney and trying to ignore the gun in her ribs. "And there's nothing, see?" Tree branches hung at improbable angles, encased in ice, their tops almost touching the ground. Even in the pitch black the snow gave off a thin blue light.

Cydney shook her head, talking earnestly to whatever she thought was outside the window. "He was suffering. I had no choice. It was quick—really. It looks terrible, I know, but I couldn't clean him up before you got here." Cydney stared into the middle distance, talking to someone other than Lillian. "Please try to understand. No, don't come any closer. Stay there." She raised the gun and pointed it at the window, arms out straight. Her voice started to rise, and her shoulders shook, but she tightened her grip on the gun. "*No*, stay where you are! It wasn't my fault, don't you get that?"

Lillian shrank back in her seat. There was nothing outside the car, but Cydney certainly believed there was. This was no act. Hallucinations? That was one of the Lewy Body symptoms. Maybe Lillian should play along.

"What's out there, Cyd?"

"Three of them. Huge. Full-grown moose. Fabulous antlers."

"What are they doing?"

"Staring at me. Sad. And angry. Could go either way. *Shhh!* I'm trying to listen." She gripped the gun and pointed it at the window.

"The moose are talking?" Lillian gently put her hand on Cydney's arm to lower the gun. Cydney shrugged her off.

Lillian reached over to peer out the window. "Yes, I see them," she said, playing along. "Wow! Huge, like you said."

Cydney held her face to the patch cleared in the glass. "They're going," she whispered. "Back into the woods. Look how beautiful they are." She let out a long sigh and shook her head. "They're gone. I'm a terrible person."

But Cydney would not take her eyes off the window, shoulders tensed and ready to pounce. She turned to Lillian. "Something's still out there," Cydney whispered.

Lillian froze, listening, but all she could hear was the pounding of her heart. "Cyd, we've been through this. You sent the moose away."

"They're back. Look."

Just then Lillian did hear something—one step, two steps and something like a moan. Her spine shimmied as though someone had poured ice cubes down her back. *Jesus Christ.*

"I told you," said Cydney.

"Wh...what could that be?"

In a flash Cydney opened her door, stepped out with the gun in firing position and disappeared into the driving snow. No sound. No shot.

Lillian followed her.

NEXT TO THE DEAD MOOSE stood a small moose, maybe a yearling, with no antlers. It sniffed at the carcass and pawed the ground. Behind it in a shadowy cluster was the rest of the herd. Lillian was terrified and fascinated at the same time. She didn't dare call Cydney's name. Where was she? The yearling must have caught sight of Cydney on the other side of the car. It took a step forward. And another. The ghostly chorus behind it followed.

"Cydney! Get back in the car."

No answer.

Lillian had a sudden urge to bolt away from the car and run in the other direction, but years ago it had been drilled into her to never leave the ship, and the car was as close to a ship as she could be. She knew nothing about moose, but doubted that they would charge the car.

"Cydney! Please. Get back in the car!"

But Cydney was nowhere to be seen.

Do not panic do not panic do not panic, Lillian told herself between chattering teeth, not knowing whether to be relieved or terrified that Cydney was out there in the storm. Over the roar of the wind she thought she heard something. A shift in the direction of the moose family? Moving toward her or away? *Is this what it's like to be blind?* She was stuck in the woods, half-frozen, with a herd of moose and an unrecognizable person with a gun. How long could she hold out without doing something stupid—like leave the car? *Never leave the ship.*

LILLIAN TRIED TO LISTEN, BUT the wind was actually howling, whipping up her trench coat and ballooning it into an inside-out umbrella. Ice pellets stung her forehead. She stamped her feet, now wrapped together in the towel. *I will never leave the house again without an emergency kit of blankets, water, food, flares…Flares?* Hold on, Cydney smoked! She had a lighter in her purse. *Why hadn't she thought of that?* Go get it.

Back inside the car, her frozen fingers struggled with Cydney's pocketbook, emptying the contents on the floor. She groped around for a lighter, finding the pack of cigarettes and the empty flask. Struggling with the wallet, stuffed to bursting, she opened the clasp and random items spilled out. Finally, the lighter! She tried once, twice, three times to flick it on, blowing on her hands. *Oh my God, light! Now what do I do?* In the pool of light she looked at the mess on the floor and pulled out the envelope with Cydney's medical information. If they ever got out of here, she'd need this for the EMTs.

On the floor she saw the worn strip of black and white photo booth pictures taken of Cydney and Robert years ago, which must have fallen out of her wallet. Folded and greyed out. The same photos that were blown up and hung as a poster in Cydney's studio. She started to stuff the loose items back in the bag and pulled up another photo. One she'd never seen before, and apparently the missing fourth picture ripped from the bottom of the original strip. It was in much better shape – must have been covered by a credit card. No faces, shot from the shoulders down, but in the same clothes. Just a hugely pregnant belly and four hands splayed across it. Two hands were Cydney's – pearly nails and all. And one hand was Robert's, protectively placed over Cydney's protruding stomach. She knew that hand. She had shaken it many times. *Do I trust him? Do I have a choice?* She turned it over. Scrawled in Cydney's handwriting: "C&R, Jan 31, '70. 8 mos. and counting."

Lillian stared at the photo. The trips to California. Robert crying in the hallway. The lock of hair in the back of Harry's obituary. Who does that other than a mother? What had Cydney just said? *"That's what I should have done after he knocked me up."*

Harry. Not Carmen's son. Cydney's and Robert's son. *God, I'm stupid. Right in front of my face.* But, wow – they hid it well.

"YOU'LL RETURN THE FAVOR SOMEDAY," Cydney had once said to her – perhaps even the night that they broke into the Taylord safe and Lillian had driven effortlessly over the George Washington Bridge.

"What favor?" Lillian had asked.

"Saving me from myself, although I have been around you long enough to know that I will never have phobias. They are a complete waste of time."

Lillian couldn't agree more. Neither could her therapist, who had been trying to work her through the shrinking boundaries of her life since – probably since her wedding. It was soon after that, when Marc and Lillian had collected their respective law and business degrees, that Lillian had been offered a job with the upstart BYO Agency, working on the Cunard Cruise line account. She was hired specifically because she had worked on one of their premiere ships for over a year. En route to meet the Cunard representatives in Newport, Rhode Island, she drove over the Pell Bridge, longest suspension bridge in New England, and into a moment of vertigo. The span of the bridge tilted sideways and Lillian jolted her body to the right to compensate. The car veered precariously into the oncoming lane, where no cars advanced, and then the moment passed. Just a moment. One second, two seconds...but it shook her up badly. *What the hell was that?* She was pretty rattled during the meeting but hoped it didn't show. During the lunch with Cunard executives, leafing through glossy photos of gorgeous ships, interior ballrooms, intimate lounges, the bar, the library, the map room, she excused herself and stood at the mirror in the Ladies room, white as porcelain. Was she coming down with something? Great timing; her first big account. The vertigo came back in a heated flash and she dove to the stall to retch. Now she was shaking; her knees actually knocked together as she clung to the sink, rinsing out her mouth. By the time she collected herself to finish the meeting, calling on every acting stage-fright experience she had ever known, and was hightailing it home – it happened again. Vertigo on the bridge.

This time she hit the brakes, and the car behind slammed to a stop rear-ending her at 30 mph. Her head was swirling and perfectly clear at the same split second. *I did that. How did I do that? Why did I do that? What is wrong with me? Am I having a stroke?* She told Marc that something had run right in front of the car while she was crossing the bridge and she instinctively hit the brakes, but their one decent car was now in the shop and their insurance rates would hit the roof.

BIT BY BIT LILLIAN'S WORLD shrank. First it was big bridges over open bodies of water, then secondary bridges over rivers, then drawbridges, then roads that turned into a small arch covering a stream. She bought every map she could find and pored over them with highlighters. When she got pregnant with David a year later, she hoped desperately that maternal protectiveness would kick in and she would stop obsessing over this nonsense. It didn't.

After David was born, she saw a shrink who wanted to put her on anti-anxiety medication that seemed to be an alternative to electroshock therapy. Instead, she got pregnant again. Maybe this would do the trick. And then she met Cydney. It was Cydney who hauled her ass over bridges berating (*your phobias are a waste of time; I will never let myself get phobic*), belittling (*do you know how lucky you are Miss-Newton-Center who did not have an alcoholic father*), encouraging (*that's my girl, I knew there was a reason I chose you*), and finally getting her so exasperated and let's face it–admiring–that Lillian just had to give in. By the time she was able to drive effortlessly over the Tobin and the Triboro and the George Washington bridges, she would have trusted Cydney with her life. There was no way she could let her go now. There was a time when she would have never believed that she could have saved or helped anyone as tough as Cydney. But that time had come.

BACK OUT IN THE SNOW, the lighter was useless–it was coming down in sheets, and the wind must have whipped up to 40 mph. Then, in a lull in the wind she felt, more than heard, a sensation of movement again. She kept her eyes glued to where she thought the moose family had been, ears pricked up like a dog. Nothing. Nothing except one purple high-heeled shoe.

The car looked like a lopsided igloo, its front sagging heavily from the impact with the moose–now buried in a white shroud with protruding hooves. Trees came right up to the passenger doors, their lower limbs threatening to collapse on the roof. There was no way Cydney could have walked into the woods with one shoe–even though the shoes were useless. Lillian bent over to pick up the one left behind. Cydney had tiny feet–maybe size six. Lillian's size eight feet had added a half size with each pregnancy and now clocked in at nine and a half. She struggled through the snow bank several feet into the woods, bent over double, branches slapping her face, looking for footprints. Nothing.

"*Cydney!*"

She doubled back—*never leave the ship*—against the wind, which pushed Lillian into the car door as she struggled to open it, knocking the breath out of her. In that sharp moment of trying to catch her breath, she thought she heard a chain saw. Listen. Wind. Listen. Chainsaw. The car door was ajar—had she left it open? She climbed in and reached over for the blanket, her hand finding instead the steel cold butt of the gun, and next to it, Cydney—passed out. Lillian was shaking so hard her foot knocked against the back of the seat. She almost cried with relief. *Cydney. Thank God you're back.*

Lillian touched her cheek. Freezing. *Should I shake her?* "Cydney, you have to wake up! I hear chain saws. They're going to get us out of here. We can get you to a hospital."

"*No.* No hospital." Cydney struggled to sit up, flinging her arms wildly and looking around for the gun. But Lillian had it and was holding on tight. Cydney looked at her with perfectly clear eyes.

"What time is it? Where are my pills?"

"We don't have any water. They're going to be here soon, so don't take anything until we can get some food and water and get warm. You've been really out of it."

"Bullshit. Where's my other shoe? I dyed them myself."

A good sign! "Whatever it is, it's getting closer." Lillian could hear the whine of something mechanical—sounds of civilization, something other than howling wind.

"I don't like it." Cydney sat up and put on her soaking wet shoe.

"Well, you don't have much choice. We've been waiting for hours. Heat. Dry clothes. Food."

"Nope. Something's not right."

Now that rescue was on its way, Lillian was feeling more in control. *Please hurry up.* "Tough. We are sitting right here and not moving."

"Maybe they won't see us. Maybe the moose will scare them off."

"Not if they hear the chainsaws."

"I hate chainsaws."

"Right now chainsaws are our friends. But I hate them too," Lillian acknowledged. "You know, I would have gone to your mother's funeral if I had known. Why didn't you tell me?"

Cydney stared straight ahead. "Because I was too overwhelmed. Everyone was there. Carmen, her kids, Robert. We hadn't all been together since Harry died. And I think I was already sick. Carmen was furious. She claimed I made quite a scene."

Harry. "Cydney, you have never talked about this. Not in all the years we worked together. Was he really...Carmen's son?"

Cydney nodded.

"Who was his father?"

"Robert."

"Cydney, look at me." Lillian took her gently by the shoulder. "Robert and Carmen...really?" Should she keep probing or leave it alone? She took a breath and closed her eyes.

"Cydney, I have to ask: who was his mother?"

"Me."

"Wow. So that's it. You and Robert all those years, protecting Harry, raised by Carmen. How could I not have figured that out? Did anyone else know?"

"Carmen, obviously; Robert supported her and Harry for years. And Marjorie."

"She did?"

Cydney nodded. "Robert told her when he first ran for Senator, in case it came out. She completely flipped out. She threatened to have me killed."

"And why...so many questions. Why didn't you just get married? It sounds like he wanted to."

"I didn't want a baby. I made that clear to Robert. Marjorie had had three miscarriages and he treated me like I was the original Madonna. And I didn't want to marry him. Sometimes you don't know what you don't want until it's under your nose. I was nineteen, for crissakes. I wanted a life of my own. And I thought...no, I knew...that the alcohol poisoning at the Buckrock was a bad start. It really worried me. And then he was born with all these complications – couldn't breathe, couldn't digest anything. It was a nightmare. We were in our own circle of hell: Carmen a single mother – broke with two kids. Me – nineteen and clueless. Robert – twenty-six and married to the boss's daughter. He was trying to do the right thing for everybody; get divorced or stay married, don't have an abortion, support the baby, give money to Carmen, stick it out with me. I told you. I should have had an abortion."

Lillian winced.

Cydney looked at her – totally lucid. "Sounds terrible, huh? Once it's a person with a name you're supposed to melt. But it doesn't work like that – at least not for me. The poor kid had a miserable life, and made everyone around him miserable. Robert wouldn't agree; he was totally devoted. You know how people are always telling you that ruined children are a gift? They're full of shit. Giving life to someone who drains life and will suffer a terrible death is a crime. You wouldn't know that because you have healthy children. And then, we found out it was cystic fibrosis, no cure. Hereditary. So, on top of everything – it was our fault! But how did we know we were carriers? No one else in either family had it. I thought alcoholism was about the worse thing that ran in the family. Wrong."

Lillian sat stunned. Was this the Cydney she had known for years? The Cydney who had boundless love for abandoned puppies and puny cats?

"Just telling it like it is. Why lie? It's the truth. The poor child ruined everyone's life – mine, Carmen's, Robert's. My father had a heart attack and died after he found out. Fifty-five years old, imagine that. My mother was a widow for the last thirty years of her life."

Lillian closed her eyes. "I don't know what to say. I am so sorry that you were going through this all those years and I never knew. Couldn't be supportive, or anything. And my kids hanging out in the shop…"

"That's why he had a vasectomy. Because he was a cystic fibrosis carrier. And that's probably why Marjorie kept having miscarriages. Lucky her."

"Doesn't it take two carriers to have a child with the disease?" Lillian asked.

"We just couldn't figure it out. A family curse somewhere."

It wasn't until 1962 that Bianca told her daughters about the dead baby Celeste, on the night before Carmen's wedding. By then Kevin was a heavy and constant drinker, and although he was only forty-five at the time, he looked a good fifteen years older.

It was after the rehearsal dinner while the three generations of women, Pauline, Bianca and her daughters, sat at the long table after the others had gone. They were wondering how to pay the bill. Kevin had left home to pick up his tuxedo at 4:00 o'clock that afternoon and not been seen since. The money for the dinner was safely stashed in a manila envelope whose whereabouts were known only to him.

Bianca kicked off her beige fake silk pumps and massaged her toes, trying not to jostle Pauline, who had fallen asleep in the chair beside her. Carmen had been very brave walking down the aisle, and not only because her future brother-in-law was filling in for her father: Her high school boyfriend and love of her life, Robert Bretton had dumped her now that he was a big Harvard success. On the rebound, she had taken up with a local kid who was headed for Vietnam, got knocked-up, and here they were.

By now Kevin's absence was almost the rule, so no one had made a big deal about it. Carmen hadn't eaten a thing and looked like she was going to throw up again. Bianca wasn't feeling too terrific herself. How are you supposed to feel when you see your kids doing exactly what you did when you've preached at them for years to do the opposite?

"That son of a bitch," Bianca suddenly blurted out. "It's been the same since Celeste. I should have left him then and there."

She stopped herself. Many things she had said about Kevin over the years, but leaving him had not been among them. Maybe she'd had a little too much herself. She lifted her wine glass and sloshed the rest of the pale pink liquid around. Carmen wanted rosé. Bianca thought it looked like cool-aid and tasted not much better. If you were going to drink, you might as well drink.

"Who's Celeste, Mom?"

Bianca looked up at Cydney's question. Was she the only one who didn't know? Celeste's baby picture had stood on her night table in its tarnished silver frame with the others all these years. She looked around at their puzzled faces and sighed. Of course not. None of them could have known.

"Celeste was the baby in between Risa and Cydney, a baby we lost."

Silence. Risa lit a cigarette.

Cydney spoke up. "Lost? What do you mean, lost? Like you left her someplace?"

"No, stupid," said Mel. "God, is she dumb."

"Girls, girls," said Bianca absently, shaking her head. "Don't fight, please. It's true; we lost her. Your father and I. There was an accident, a car accident."

"Oh my God!" said Carmen, waving Risa's smoke away. "You mean she died in a car accident? You told us she drowned! What accident? Was Daddy driving? Was he...was he drunk?"

"Well, I don't know. He swears he wasn't. But it was hard to tell in those days. You'd never have recognized him – the sweetest, kindest man. Oh well, he's tried, poor soul. That much I know. But I never forgave him. And he'll never forgive himself."

Her voice trailed off and her daughters leaned forward to catch the last words. They waited for about thirty seconds and then Mel and Risa attacked while Carmen and Cydney leaped to their father's defense. Bianca sat among them looking shrunken in her chair, with her stocking feet barely touching the ground, unnoticed in the unleashed power of her outraged children.

She knew there was a reason she had never told them. Every little piece of herself was pulled out, picked clean, laid bare, and claimed by one of them as their own. They contradicted her own memories so often that she was no longer sure whose memories they were. Surely it would have been easier to have sons.

Kevin walked into the restaurant five minutes later. They heard him singing to the waitresses before they saw him turn the corner with three-dozen long stemmed red roses in a single giant bouquet. He waltzed over to the table holding the bunch of flowers like a dancing partner, and during the course of several dips and turns plucked half the bouquet apart and gave it to Bianca. The other half he gave to Carmen. He finished with a flourish and a deep bow, which he managed gracefully – in spite of an extra twenty or so pounds – and held his hands out to his wife for a dance.

They all stared at him. His outstretched hands, pricked from rose thorns, looked like the statues of saints suffering ecstatically on someone else's behalf.

"Not a smile from my girls?" Kevin's voice had lost none of its lilt and hope, although it was a little gravelly at that moment. "Took much longer to get these than I thought. Had to drive all the way down to Haverhill and back, but I'm here and tomorrow is set to be a beautiful day."

Each time Bianca forgave him a little less, until she had no more than a puny reservoir of forgiveness left in her heart. And the heart should be a full cup, running over. No matter what you put in, love brims up to the top. Isn't that what the nuns taught her? She put her shoes back on. Well, at least he showed up. She was afraid to ask if he had brought the money, but he was already pulling the envelope out of his jacket pocket.

"Someone put a dime in that Juke Box! I'm dancing with your mother, dancing girl of my dreams."

"Oh, Daddy, cut it out!" said Mel, under his spell.

"Watch out, 'cause any one of you is next. You, Carmen, before you go off with your Don Juan, get ready to dance. And you, Cydney, before you grow up. Good God! Look at her!"

One by one, they each rose to take a turn on the empty dance floor, Carmen holding a fake bouquet of ribbons and bows collected from her bridal shower the week before; Cydney wearing Mel's hand-me-down junior prom dress. Bianca knew that he would melt her children's anger away as they twirled and dipped on the dance floor. All of them were under his spell.

Kevin adored his girls – all of them. His daughters, his wife…he just wanted to give them all the things he never had. Even Robert's mother Claire. Oh yes, he still felt an obligation to Claire.

Growing up with this strictly Catholic adoptive mother, who made him so terrified of the demons in his own penis that he was afraid to take off his underwear, he believed the priests who told him and all the other scrawny, knock-kneed ten year old boys from dirt poor families, that a special circle in hell was reserved for masturbators and fornicators. When he was chosen by Father Levesque as an altar boy his mother cried tears of happiness. So, after Father Levesque showed him the evils of masturbation, which the good priest insisted on demonstrating weekly in order to imprint its awfulness on young Kevin, the normally rambunctious child changed overnight. Much to his mother's delight. No longer disruptive in school, flinging apple cores into the ceiling fans or pieces of chalk at the rear ends of bespectacled teachers, the church seemed to have calmed him down.

Far from it. Kevin turned to his neighbor Claire Mallory, who sat behind him alphabetically, and confided that he hated Father Levesque.

"You, too? Does he give you wine?" Claire asked.

"Yeah. After."

"I tried to tell my mother. She walloped me."

"Maybe we should run away together," Kevin suggested.

"Yeah. Maybe we should."

Kevin Mallone grew six inches in one year and Father Levesque told Kevin's mother that he had outgrown the angelic look Father preferred for his altar boys. Kevin went back to flinging apple cores, discovered beer, joined the football team, and noticed that Claire had grown breasts.

"Remember when you said that we should run away together?" Claire asked him one day as they walked home from school.

"Yeah." Silence. "Is he still…?"

"Giving me wine?"

"Yeah, I guess."

"Well, I'm running away."

"We could get married." The thought just came to Kevin like a gift.

"We're fourteen – how could we get married?"

"Well, would you? If you could?"

"I would do pretty much anything to never step foot in that church again," said Claire.

"So, stop going to CDC. I have. Mom is furious. Tough titties."

KEVIN WENT TO CDC CLASS with Claire the next afternoon, and sat next to her through the class, leaning back in the too-small chair, his long legs obstructing the aisle, arms folded, glaring at Father Levesque. *Touch her again, you fucker, and I'll kill you.*

Claire went across town to the other parish, where the priest was kind, and old, and just what he was supposed to be. She convinced Kevin to come with her and meet her new friend Bianca.

KEVIN AND CLAIRE DATED OFF and on through high school. They were tight, in the way that people threatened with terror make bargains: *if we ever get out of this I will dedicate my life to you.* But Kevin was hard-pressed to dedicate his life to anything; his fondness for wine and beer was dragging him down. He dropped out of school and joined the army. When he was discharged after D Day, still in one piece, he came home to find Claire married to Henri Bretton, who had broken his back working on the shop floor of Taylord Mills, the largest employer in town. Kevin's hatred of Taylord Mills was right up there with his disdain for the church. Bianca, Claire's friend, was spending a lot of time helping out at the Bretton's while Henri attempted to recover, and Kevin pitched in. He had dried out in the war – but now that he was home, with nightmares of body parts flying through the grey dawn and bleeding out on the beach – liquor was quick and easy. Claire noticed right away. One night when he was visiting and Henri had finally collapsed in sleep, exhausted from pain, she ran her hands through Kevin's hair and started to cry.

"What's happened to us, Kevin? I'm not even twenty-two and married to an invalid. We'll never have kids."

It was in Kevin's nature to give everyone what they wanted, as best he could. "You know I'm interested in Bianca, right?"

"Yeah, she's perfect for you. She'll kick your ass 'til Kingdom Come."

"I'm gonna ask her to marry me."

"Do it. Maybe you'll have better luck," Claire said, sitting in his lap.

"But I haven't asked her yet," Kevin said, thinking this over.

"Until then," said Claire, standing up and pulling him over to the couch, "I'm going to pretend that you're still mine."

Kevin added this sin into the pile for which he would never ask, or receive, forgiveness.

Maybe Bobbie was his son, and maybe he wasn't. He never asked, and after he married Bianca a few months later, it became less important. Carmen came along, looking nothing like Bobbie, and soon after, Camelia, Clarisa and Celeste – all of them red-heads with freckles; different as day and night from Bobbie's dark looks. And they were on the road, traveling with the fair. Lawrell faded into the background. But then Cydney arrived, after the awfulness with Celeste. Claire came to visit with seven-year-old Bobbie one day when Cydney – looking like a hot-house flower who had been kidnapped from gypsies – was in her high chair. Kevin saw it right away. He had been on the wagon since Celeste, but with this new weight he went out and bought a bottle, filling his hip flask and keeping it with him always.

11:05 PM. Sunday, Nov. 5, 2006.

Dogs barking. Chain saws. Usually the soundtrack to a horror movie, but Lillian could have kissed them all. "Cydney! Snap out of it. They're almost here."

Tears ran down Cydney's face. "He's going to put me somewhere. Please don't let him."

"Robert adores you—you know that."

"No, he doesn't. He's hoping I will disappear."

"No chance. Now that Marjorie's gone. I mean—not to be speaking ill of the dead—but you know… Cydney, you sound totally normal; you'll be fine. And we'll get you to the best doctors."

"I'm not fine. I had a gun pointed at you for the past three hours."

"Nope, nope. You put it down. See, I have it."

"You don't even know how to use it."

"I had no intention of using it," said Lillian. "My hands are too stiff to use anything."

Lillian could hear shouts beyond the trees as an arc of light pierced the veil of snow. She opened the door to yell, "Here! We're here! Over here!" Her voice was cracking. "You too," she said to Cydney. "I don't know how much they can hear over the wind. Open your door and shout."

"I'm not sure I want to be found," Cydney said, picking up the gun that Lillian had dropped.

In May 1972 Kevin was recuperating from his third heart attack. He had been stone cold sober since Cydney left home. With the girls gone, he moped around the house, watching TV and smoking. Claire dropped by one afternoon when Bianca was out. They sat across the room, quietly.

"How's the heart?"

"Broken."

Claire knew that Carmen's son had been diagnosed with cystic fibrosis. He had been born six months after she married some loser in California.

"That poor child. Cystic fibrosis. Where did it come from? Carmen's husband?"

Kevin closed his eyes and let out a stream of smoke.

"Harry? That's his nickname. His real name is Henry. Claire, you are smarter than that."

"You think Robert…and Carmen? Oh God. It can't be. That ended years ago. I held my breath until it was over…"

"Worse. I think it's Cydney's. She stayed out in California for a year."

Claire was silent. "Robert and Cydney. So, that's why he keeps going to California on business. If Marjorie finds out she will kill him."

"So, we're carriers. Isn't that what they call it? Why? We didn't hurt anybody. Henry was dying; I wasn't married yet." Kevin closed his eyes.

"Well, we have hurt someone. Maybe Father Levesque was right."

"Don't mention that bastard ever again. He should roast on a spit."

Claire's eyes filled with tears. "I don't regret it. How could I regret having Bobbie? He's been my life. I thank God for him every day."

"Come sit next to me."

She did, holding his large hand in hers, tracing the lines in his palm. "It's been a long time since I've touched a man."

Later that night, Kevin had his fourth heart attack from which he did not recover.

11:30 PM. *Sunday, Nov. 5, 2006.*

"Who are you?" Cydney raised the gun. "Where's Lillian?"

Lillian looked around to be sure she wasn't dreaming. "Cydney, it's me."

"You're lying." Cydney's eyes had gone dead cold.

"This is no time to joke; they're almost here." Lillian knew that she had to stay calm; rescue was on the way.

"*What* did you do with her?" Cydney's voice rose to an unfamiliar pitch.

Lillian put her hands up in surrender like in the movies. "Cydney! This *is* me. Obviously."

"Prove it."

"I've been telling you stories about us for hours!" Lillian was close to tears but forced herself to think through the symptoms of Lewy Body Dementia–paranoia, delusions, hallucinations, Imposter Syndrome. *Did Cydney think she was an imposter?* Vaguely she remembered something about not being able to recognize visual cues–auditory, yes, but not visual. Patients could recognize someone's voice but not their physical self. Perhaps when Cydney's eyes were closed she recognized Lillian, but not when they were open?

"Cydney! Close your eyes and listen to me. Just listen. Remember how we met? Your brewery? Marjorie and the necklace? T.Rex Toys… feeding valium to Storm and Lutz? Please close your eyes; I know it's hard but you've got to trust me. That's it." *Should I try to take the gun? No!*

Lillian continued to talk while Cydney ranted that Robert worked for the CIA and was coming to get her. She stayed calm even when Cydney forced her to take off her clothes to prove that she wasn't an imposter and checked her arm for track marks. In the background Lillian could hear the chain saws getting closer. *Hurry up hurry up.*

"Listen to me. I don't care about the jewelry. It *is* history. I care about you. Do you remember my phobias and how you got me over them? I will always be grateful to you because you saved my life. Remember our all-nighters and telling stories about how young and stupid and hopeful we were? We are joined at the hip whether we like it or not. We are our memories, and I won't let you lose them; I promise."

A SHOUT IN THE DISTANCE: *over here!* The arc of a flashlight rippling over the car. Cydney shielded her eyes and crouched down. Then the sky was lit up with a flare and a voice hollered, "Cydney!"

Lillian jumped out of the car and tried to yell back, but found that she had no voice.

The next day. Monday, Nov. 6, 2006.

AFTER LILLIAN AND ROBERT LEFT Cydney's room at the Pittsfield hospital, she called Marc to give him the headlines, checked in to the local Holiday Inn and lay in a hot bath for an hour with all the gin and vodka she could find in the minibar. Probably not the best plan when you're dehydrated, but anything to settle her hands that were still shaking. The following morning she would be back at the hospital to meet Robert, and she needed to get her thoughts straight.

She gave the doctors all the medical information found in Cydney's pocketbook, and the diagnosis of the perplexing Lewy Body Dementia was enough to order her medevac'd to Mass General Hospital the next day.

She and Robert sat in a booth in the back of a local coffee shop. Dressed in a sweatshirt and jeans with a Bruins hockey hat, no one recognized him.

Lillian knew there was no easy way to start this conversation so she just jumped in. "Cydney told me she hadn't seen you in years. True? Not true?"

"Lillian," Robert took a big breath and set his elbows on the table, "there has never been a time in thirty-five years when I haven't been in touch with Cydney."

"This is none of my business, Robert, so don't think I'm prying, but last night was terrifying. I need to understand what happened. Why did you ask me over to your house to begin with?"

"How long do you have?"

"As long as it takes." And Lillian wrapped her hands around the heat of her coffee cup and wondered if she would ever be warm again.

ROBERT WAS SILENT FOR A full minute and then he began. "Harry was born in the spring of 1970. Cydney stayed in California with Carmen, who adopted the baby. Cyd refused to marry me, so Marjorie and I stuck it out. Marjorie had suffered three miscarriages, and I knew she would go crazy if she found out that Cydney was pregnant, so we kept it a secret. After a few months we got the diagnosis of cystic fibrosis, which was devastating. Maybe I was a carrier and that's why the miscarriages? So, there we were in this nasty triangle – quadrangle, really – of me, Marjorie and Cydney, and now Carmen. The mill was doing well, and I set up an account for Harry and Carmen. I flew out every few months to see him; Cydney was – I don't know – in denial, furious at me, angry at herself, miserable that she had put Carmen in this position. We were all at a nasty standstill held together by the thread of Harry's precarious life.

So, ten years went by. Articles appeared about me in the national economic press; how Taylord Mills was a blueprint for keeping manufacturing in America. But I was leveraged up the wazoo. I had borrowed a fortune to keep the business afloat, keep Marjorie's lifestyle intact, buy the brewery for Cydney, support Harry and Carmen. Really, I felt like I had three wives, and it served me right. It was like a lifelong penance for fucking up everyone's life. Then the chance came up to run for the Senate and I grabbed it. It was before the days of Gary Hart when the press left your private life alone, and maybe there was a part of me that hoped I'd be exposed as the fake bastard I am.

But no, astonishingly not; I sailed through. But I had to tell Marjorie about Harry in case the press dug it up. And she flipped out. At the same time Cydney had started the business with you, and a promising but very expensive treatment had opened up for Harry. It cost $10,000 monthly and insurance wouldn't cover it. When Marjorie found out that I had a son she was ready to kidnap him and adopt him herself. You can imagine how well that went over. So, evidently, she took out her anger by harassing Cydney with threats to repay the loans and then – bam! Cydney showed up with the damn jewelry and Marjorie stupidly took it. Well, I figured for sure that would do me in. But, although I did not know this at the time, the morning after you saw her at the Cabot Center she gave it to a broker who broke it up and sold it as redesigned pieces. I didn't realize it then, but that must have been the source of the funds that Marjorie used to support Harry's medical treatments until he died, after another eight miserable years. By the way, the money was all hers—the mill, the profits, the house, the investments. If I had left her I would have been broke. All my personal money had gone to Cydney and Harry. And then to you and Baby Grand."

Lillian thought her head would burst. How many emotions can you cram in your brain at once? "You mean you lied to me. For years. Straight-faced?"

Robert shook his head. "Technically, no."

"And this was going on the entire time that Cyd and I worked together? And I didn't have a clue? Jesus." Lillian didn't know what to make of this. It was as if someone told her that a pet dog was actually a coyote. Or that her husband was a Soviet spy. "Did Cyd know about the jewelry?"

Robert shook his head more emphatically. "I knew that would end it between the two of you. Plus, I didn't really know what happened to it myself. I suspected once money appeared for Henry's treatments, but I kept out of it."

"Wow. Are you the male version of a happy homewrecker?"

Robert gave a little shrug. "That's fair. In our defense, we were trying to protect a dying child. Cydney had her tubes tied; I had a vasectomy; after that, all three of us were barren. We were all with Harry when he died in 1988."

"Jesus. That was just when we got the T.Rex Toys account. We were so happy. Adam, my third son, was a newborn. Cydney adored him; she adored all my kids. Oh my God," she said under her breath, "and all that time her own son was dying. What a heartless bitch I must have been—obsessed with my own stupid phobias."

"We were all locked in our own private misery or delight. That's the human condition, I guess. I threw myself into work. So I got good at my job—easy—those were the Reagan years and everyone rode his coattails."

"And Cydney? When did this Lewy Body awfulness start?"

Robert rubbed his temples and shook his head. "So, about three years ago, Cydney started being more forgetful than usual. She was always behind in paperwork—as you know—and that chaotic charm wears thin."

"Yeah, tell me about it," Lillian interrupted, remembering.

"But this was different. She got angry and accusing—something she had never ever been, and jealous—also not her. And clingy—I was too annoyed to think about it—and just bruised, frankly. So I kept her at arm's length. Every once in a while she'd take up with someone totally inappropriate..."

"Like a married senator?"

"Ok—I deserve that...someone much younger; an apprentice—an itinerant musician, usually a hunk who was tough, tattooed and increasingly young enough to be her son."

Yeah, thought Lillian, *she loved young men. Even with Robert she always had a wandering eye.*

"And Marjorie had moved on," Robert continued. "She went back and forth between DC and Lawrell, and after we bought the place in the Berkshires, she decided she was an architect and an interior designer, and started studying Krav Magah—the Israeli Defense Force self-defense method in hand-to-hand combat. Jesus, she was tough. She could flatten me in about two seconds. Once she almost broke my nose."

"These women were out for blood, eh?"

"Yeah. I kept as far away from both of them as I could, which wasn't very far as it turns out. Cydney showed up on Capitol Hill one day; she had never done that in the twenty years I'd been there. She was a voice on the phone that my admins knew really well. They thought she was family. She came in looking like a million bucks, sat down and told me that we had to make decisions about Harry. He was getting ready for college. Because she hadn't gone to college she needed to get him into a good school. My jaw dropped. I thought this was a sick joke; he'd been dead for years. But she was so serious that I sat up and took notice. I took her to the National Institute of Health and they ran a bunch of tests. I told them she was a close relative; that's the only way I could get her an appointment. So, after months of tests back and forth, they came back with this horrible diagnosis of Lewy Body Dementia. I was just reeling. I thought I would have a heart attack."

Lillian was silent.

"Really—I went to get checked out by my doctor who knew about Cydney's diagnosis and he asked me—out of the blue—what I was going to do about my sister."

"But you don't have a sister," Lillian said, perplexed. "Do you...?"

Robert turned to her, his clear blue eyes the same color as Cydney's, filling with tears.

"You've lost me. I have no idea what you're saying." Lillian felt that chill coming back.

"My doctor thought it was interesting that we were both cystic fibrosis carriers. He wanted to run tests to see if we were, impossibly, siblings."

"And...?" Lillian held her breath. She couldn't believe she was hearing this.

"I wouldn't let him. What was the point? So I could beat myself up even more? Besides, there was no one to ask. My mother died about ten years ago. I kept a suitcase of her personal things, old letters, cards—mementos that I had never gone through. I knew that she and Kevin and Bianca all went way back. She and Kevin dated in high school before he went into the army. And I knew that Kevin had been very helpful after my father's accident around the time my mother had introduced him to Bianca. So one night I got quite drunk and dug out the suitcase."

In 1972 KEVIN WAS BURIED in the Blood of the Lamb Cemetery next to the baby Celeste. Cydney stared at the open grave, surrounded by women in black—her stoic mother, her sisters, and Claire Bretton—looking ashen. Bobbie was in the background, unaccompanied by Marjorie; Cydney was sure they had had a big fight about it earlier that day. It was the first time that Carmen had been back to the East Coast, and Robert had paid for her to fly out with her daughters and Harry, who was almost two and having enough of a good stretch of health to chance having him on a plane. Cydney just wanted to get through this—Carmen, Robert, Harry, herself—all in the same room. If her mother figured it out, she'd have a heart attack and they'd both be gone. She put her head in her hands and felt Robert stiffen somewhere behind her – she knew he wanted to wrap his arms around her.

Cydney knew that another yawning grave was waiting for her son – he might have a few years at most. Robert appeared at her side, holding his mother's arm. Claire seemed unusually upset. Cydney didn't think that she and Bianca had been that close. Something seemed to be off between them – maybe all those years of Bianca having a husband while Claire did not.

Later, back at the house, after people had left, Claire offered to help clean up. Harry's high chair was in the kitchen – Carmen had been very protective and hustled him off to bed. In the few moments that Claire had seen him she thought her heart would burst. Carrying a stack of dirty dishes to the kitchen sink she passed Bianca standing at the stove, staring into space. They turned at the same time, bumping gently.

Their eyes met and held for a moment – Bianca's dry; Claire's filling with tears.

"I know," she said.

Lillian was quiet. She noticed that her hand was trembling. The Lillian of two days ago would have gone on a phobic Parkinson's alert. She felt like she had aged ten years. "I have no idea what to say." *You really never know a god damn thing about anyone.* She cleared her throat. "Ok. I feel like I've just heard a deathbed confession. Does anyone know?"

"No one. Actually, I don't even know for sure. There was nothing specific in my mother's papers. But she and Kevin were close, that was clear. And she was beside herself when I was going out with Carmen in high school. She couldn't wait to get me out of town and was furious when I came back. It's possible that Kevin is my biological…I can't even say it… but I won't go there. So, I'm going to leave it that way."

"Does Cydney know?"

"God, no. How many ways can you send someone around the bend?"

Lillian remembered Cydney's fear of Robert 'finding' her, 'spilling the beans,' 'putting her away,' 'he's the only one who knows'. Should she tell him? Maybe it was just the disease talking. "So, does Carmen know?" she asked Robert. "Did Marjorie?"

"No one." He shook his head. "And I know that you won't…"

"Yes, sir. Our standing agreement." *Who would have believed it? It just goes on…*

Lillian ordered more coffee, desperate to change the subject. "And I've forgotten that you're in mourning. Shit, I'm sorry, Robert. How are you doing in the middle of all this?"

"Thanks. I'm probably in shock, more than anything. But to be practical, here's what I've discovered from Marjorie's will. She left a lot of money and invested wisely. She made a fortune before the dot-com bust, got out in time and somehow didn't lose it after 9/11. Kind of witchy, actually. I was relieved to know that she left money specifically to buy back the pieces of your jewelry, and there is quite a chain of correspondence with various Russian oligarchs and Gulf Sheiks, so some of it has been set in motion. I'm sure I'll have to deal with the political consequences, but that's my problem. Bottom line: I'll get it all back, and I have contacted Cartier to see if they can restore it."

"So, Marjorie ends up as the good guy, huh?"

"Well, yeah, or I wouldn't have stayed married to her all these years."

Again, Lillian's head was reeling. "What happened to her? How did she really die?"

"It was a freak accident. She fell and hit her head. She got up and seemed to be fine; she refused to go to a doctor and then collapsed. By the time she got to a hospital she was in an irreversible coma. The guy she was with–her personal trainer–was sobbing so hard I could barely understand him. You'd think he was the husband, not me."

If there were a prize for the worst week ever, Robert would get it. It was amazing that he was still functioning. "What will Cydney live on? What will happen to her?" Lillian asked. Marc had done well as a law partner. Lillian was making good money as an ad executive. They had put three kids through college and graduate school, and could finally lighten up. The jewelry was a distant memory.

Robert cleared his throat. "I'll take care of her with the help of Marjorie's money. How's that for irony? And Carmen is moving back to help. I'll finish out this term and announce that I am not running again. The jewelry is yours. There's not much that's right about any of this, but this is right. I've struggled with the question of whether I did the right thing by strong-arming Cydney into having the baby. There is no right answer. It wasn't right for Cydney, although I couldn't swear to that, and it was hell for me, but I thought it was the right thing at the time. Harry was a person, and I learned a lot about compassion and holding on."

"Interesting – Cydney said the opposite last night when she was lucid."

"What exactly?"

"Well, something about when people talk about a damaged child being a gift, they're just trying to say something uplifting about a terrible situation."

"That's true, too. It's all true and not that clear-cut."

"So, you're still a Catholic?"

"Not practicing. I think all life has value. And I know life is messy. And I am not God. So take the jewelry."

"It feels weird, since it's been such a long time," said Lillian. "I'd like to contribute something to a cystic fibrosis fund. And Lewy Body research."

"Cystic fibrosis is finally a good news story. Genetic testing has almost eliminated it. Carriers can abort very early on if the fetus has the disease. So much for Catholic doctrine. Plus with new drugs, people live into their thirties and forties. As for Lewy Body...contribute all you want. But not the jewelry. Cydney would kill me; it's the least I can do for her."

Afterward

2016. April.

"Marc! Call Uber—we need to get a move on." Lillian checked her reflection in the hall mirror. She had just had her hair cut and streaked back to its natural blond. Not bad. "David! Get the kids into the car. We'll meet Jonny and Adam at the museum."

Lillian had spent the day organizing a dinner party to be held at the Museum of Fine Arts in Boston after the opening of the new rare jewelry gallery, which featured, as part of its opening exhibit, the suite of Art Nouveau jewels belonging to the late Lady Alice Kuper, designed by Cartier in 1919 and painstakingly restored over the past several years. The necklace was on permanent loan to the museum and Lillian had splurged on a party in its honor—or rather in honor of all the unlikely participants in its disappearance and reappearance.

The dinner was set up in one of the small galleries, which was roped off to the general public. She checked the tables one last time. In addition to her family—David, his wife and her granddaughters; Jonny and his gay partner; Adam and his girlfriend—she had invited Robert and his new wife, Adele. At seventy-one, Robert was still almost Italian-movie star handsome, with all his hair, grey—but hair, regal bearing, and beaming with happiness. His youngish wife—at thirty-nine—was seven months pregnant. Lillian laughed out loud when he told her over the phone.

"What about the vasectomy?"

"Sperm donor."

"You and Abraham, huh? I hope you will live long enough to tear your hair out over his or her teenage years."

Lillian checked the list. She had arranged a table setting for each guest. So, Robert and Adele, Carmen and her grandson Harry, various business associates, and next to Robert a setting that would remain empty.

Lillian took pictures of the empty place setting, all in pink, with her brand new iPhone. On the pink rosebud china she put a piece of black silk, a polaroid of Cydney wearing a Carta-Babe on her head, Boris' dog tag, Kevin's whiskey flask, and a tiny Ziplok bag with a curl of dark hair. And even though she knew that Cydney would not recognize or understand any of it, she checked the picture and clicked "send."

And added, *With love, L.*

Acknowledgements

I am much indebted to Margot Sage-EL and Watchung Booksellers, Montclair, NJ for early advice to go for it and for later advice to get an editor. For early readers and encouragement, heartfelt thanks to Jessica and Naiff Bethoney, Barrie Peltz and Judith Lubershane. To my psychologist friends Amy Gerson, Ph.D and Erica Kaplan, Ph.D, thanks for key insights into Dementia with Lewy Bodies; for friendship, advice and support, thanks to Judy Katz, Shelley Brown, Nancy Atkind, Bonnie Hellman and Susan Aberman. The gestation of this novel took place under the wing of the long ago members of the Harvard Fiction Workshop and the Arlington Writers Workshop. Finally, to Beth Bruno, editor extraordinaire, and to Marcus Alonso and Leap Year Press, a deep curtsy for waving a magic wand over the manuscript and turning it into a book.

And to my own "Great Kids" Sasha and Max — still my best creations. To Detlev — thanks for being lifelong partner in all things. With special thanks to Debbie Silke for stories and equilibrium, and to everyone who ever came in contact with The Great Kid Company.

E.B. LANDE is a writer, entrepreneur, former high tech executive and teacher who lives in the Boston area with her husband. She is the author of *The Every Mother is a Working Mother Daybook* (Lansdowne Press). Founder of The Great Kid Company, her essays have appeared in *The Boston Globe* and in regional publications.

For more, visit www.eblande.com.